More Than I Can Say

More Than I Can Say

Kris Francoeur

For Paul, who I love more than I can say.
As always, for Sam, who believed

Prologue

Dressed in shorts and a t-shirt, Jackson started up the 5.8-mile trail to the summit. He was looking forward to training outdoors for the Spartan Race, instead of in the city gyms.

Almost a mile in, he paused to adjust his pack before beginning to run again, happy that no one else seemed to be out this early on a Sunday morning. As he picked up his pace, he heard a noise behind him. Glancing over his shoulder and saw a small blonde woman rapidly approaching. As she caught up, she shouted. "Stay left!"

"Huh?"

She pointed to the greenery on the right without breaking stride. "Nettles. You're in shorts, you'll get stung."

He swerved left. "Thanks."

As she ran past him, Jack got a view of her very shapely backside framed in running tights, her fitted tank top highlighting her curves, and a very distinctive tattoo of a star on her left shoulder.

In less than a minute, she was out of sight. Intrigued, he picked up his pace, in an effort to catch up.

As Jackson reached the wooden steps that he had read were just below the summit, he heard her voice again. "Careful. Last step is cracked."

He adjusted his stride as his foot was about to come down, then slowed even further as he came into the clearing at the top of the mountain. There she was, standing on a large flat rock, water bottle in her hand.

Seeing her face fully for the first time, he smiled. Bright green eyes were framed by blonde hair pulled back in a severe ponytail. She looked at him in curiosity. Jackson felt a surge of physical awareness as he realized how beautiful this stranger was. "Thanks for the warnings."

Georgiana took a sip of water, feeling herself react in a way that hadn't happened with any man in a very, very long time. Dark brown hair swept back from his face, contrasting with the blue-gray of his eyes. Even from a distance, it was clear that he would tower over her, but then again, most people did. The well-defined muscles in his arms and legs made it clear that he trained regularly. She wondered who he was, as she knew almost everyone who ran trails in the area. "You're welcome."

Jackson snagged water from his pack. "Great trail." He looked at his watch to gauge his time. "Do you run it often?"

"Yes."

Her brief answer sparked his curiosity, and it suddenly became a challenge to get her to say more. "Is it always this quiet?"

She nodded. "It's closed for several months in the spring and early summer because the peregrines nest here. But even when it reopens, it's usually pretty quiet because it's steep and long. Not everyone's up for the challenge."

"True."

She stood up and tucked the water back in her trail pack. "When you go down, stay to the inside on the steps. They wobble."

"Wait. Are you training for something in particular?"

She grinned. "Yes." She waved to him as she started toward the trail. "Have a great trip down."

Chapter One

Jackson Ryder stood by the windows trying to imagine what the space would look like when the office became his. He had to admit, it was a fantastic room. The two walls of windows, one looking toward downtown, the other toward the mountains, provided great natural light, something that had been sorely missing in his office in D.C. His favorite occupational books would fill the built-in shelves, but that desk needed to go right away. *What a monstrosity,* he thought.

Charles Bannon, the outgoing Superintendent of Schools, swung back and forth in his large executive chair. "Sorry George is so late."

Jackson shrugged. "No worries. Is he late a lot?"

Somewhat distracted, Charlie replied. "Huh? Oh... Not really." He picked up his mug and took a sip. "Sure you don't want coffee?"

"I'm sure."

"I still don't get why you didn't meet George when you interviewed. I mean, you met all the other principals."

At that moment, Priscilla, the superintendent's office assistant, came into the room with a file. "Dr. Ryder didn't meet George then because of the Haiti trip, remember? It was right after April break, and you approved an extra two days leave."

Jackson felt himself grow irritated. This George was not only late for their meeting today, but had asked for an extended vacation. This was exactly the sort of sloppy administrative oversight some of the board members had hinted at when they'd offered him the job.

Charles stood up. "I'm going to go see if Royce knows where she is. Back in a minute."

She?

Alone in the office, Jackson wandered around looking at pictures. In two of what seemed to be family photos, Charles Bannon was accompanied by two stunning blondes who he assumed were his daughters. In shock, he realized one of the women was the same woman he'd met on the trail the other day. *Could she be Charlie's daughter?* For a moment, he wondered if she was single, then shook his head, admonishing himself for thinking about dating when he'd arrived in town only a few days prior. He needed to get his living situation and job settled, then he could think about a social life.

Charles came back into the office. "Found George downstairs dealing with an accident report from summer school." He shouted out toward the outer office. "George, get in here!"

As Jackson turned to the open office door, one of the beautiful blondes from the picture…the one he'd found himself thinking about almost non-stop since Sunday…walked into the room. Dressed in a simple light blue short-sleeve dress and sandals, her hair was up in a simple twist. She looked better suited for going to the horse races at Saratoga than running a school. She smiled at the stunned man, a flicker of recognition in her eyes. "Dr. Ryder, I'm Georgiana Hewitt, Principal of Deerlane Community School. I apologize for being late."

Having trouble seeing her as an employee, Jackson strove for a completely professional tone. "Ms. Hewitt, nice to meet you."

Charles cleared his throat. "Actually, it's *Dr.* Hewitt."

She smiled fondly at the older man. "Charlie, I only use the *doctor* when I need to impress someone. Dr. Ryder is welcome to call me George like everyone else."

Jackson's voice stayed calm. "*Dr.* Hewitt. Sorry we didn't meet in April."

Charles scratched his nose. "George was volunteering down in Haiti." He tipped his head, looking at Jackson. "I'm sure you know of her mother's work."

"Her mother?"

"Dr. Katherine Hewitt."

Jackson was stunned. He'd read everything Katherine Hewitt had ever published, and even followed her Twitter and blog. "Katherine Hewitt is your mother? And you work *here?*"

Clearly comfortable with people asking her about her mother and her own career choices, she smiled. "This is where my family's from and I like working with kids, not doing constant statistical analysis and dealing with NGOs."

Jackson was rarely at a loss for words, but he found himself feeling completely off-kilter. "Really?"

Charlie gestured to the chairs facing his desk. "Please, the two of you, sit down."

Georgiana gave her new boss a perfunctory smile, as she processed that this was the man she'd found so attractive on the trail; the one she'd chastised herself for two days after for not getting his name. Now she was going to be working for him? *Shit.* She struggled to get her wits together, and as was her habit when nervous, she rubbed the inside of her right arm. "Are you settling into town? When are you officially here full-time?"

His tone continued to be excruciatingly formal. "The moving truck arrives later today, then I'll take one more run back to D.C. I expect I'll be here full-time as of Monday." He shifted in his seat, feeling the need to maintain his status as her supervisor in the conversation. "Why don't we plan an official meeting on Wednesday at your school? You can give me a tour and I can get an overview of your budget and staffing plan for the next fiscal year."

Before Georgiana could respond, Charlie shook his head. "That won't work, Jack. George is presenting at NAESP next week." He looked at George. "You're leaving Tuesday, right?"

Jackson had forgotten the conference was next week, not planning on attending the national conference for public school principals this year. What the hell was a Vermont principal from the middle of nowhere doing presenting at the largest principals' conference in the country? "Presenting? On your mother's research?"

Without thinking about what she was doing, George rolled her eyes. "No, she presents on her own work, not me. I'm presenting on community-based, full-service public schools."

"Oh." In his head, Jack wondered how she'd been selected to present at such a prestigious conference. *Had she used her mother's connections to get the invitation?* "Then we'll need to schedule for when you get back."

"Sounds like a plan."

Just then, Priscilla walked through the partially open door. "Sir," she said looking at Charlie, then at Jack, "Sir…" She then looked at George. "George has a call.-They have an issue at the summer program."

Georgiana stood up and Jackson found himself noticing her legs as she strode across the room. "Charlie, can I use your phone?"

"Of course." He hit a button to connect the call. "Here you go. On speaker?"

"Sure." Georgiana leaned back against the desk and Jack had to remind himself not to stare at her curves or the way the sun made her hair shine.

"Hey Dot, it's George."

"Thank God!"

"What's up? By the way, you're on speaker."

"It's the situation with Peter."

"I just talked through the insurance form with Royce. We're all set."

"No, that's not it. His dad called here screaming about you. He says we didn't have the right to send him to the emergency room."

Georgiana's voice was soothing. "We had every right, but I'll call him. His number is 555-1999, right? I'll call him right now."

"You got it. Thanks."

"See you in a bit." George walked around behind the desk and quickly dialed the number.

After three rings, the phone was answered. "Hello?"

Her voice was calm. "Jim, it's Georgiana Hewitt."

The male voice yelled. "You bitch! You had no right to send Peter to the emergency room. No right. I'll get you, you bitch. I'm going to the board, to the superintendent, to the governor if I need to!"

"Jim, you're on speaker and I have both Charles Bannon, the current superintendent, and Jackson Ryder, the incoming superintendent, here with me. So, after you and I talk about Peter, you're welcome to talk to them about any concerns you have about my professional behavior, okay?"

Jackson had to hide a smile.

She continued. "Jim, Peter fell today when he was on the top of the jungle gym and I'm pretty sure, as is Nurse Tatiana, that his arm's broken. When he fell, we called you and left three messages. As it says in the handbook, if we can't reach you, and your child needs emergency medical attention, we'll take the student to the ER."

"You should've waited for *me* to decide if he needed to go!"

"Jim, we've talked about this before. We have no emergency contacts other than you. We waited, with him in pain, for almost an hour to hear from you. When it had been more than an hour, our nurse took him to the ER, and they're there now. Do you want me to pick you up and give you a ride to the ER?"

Jackson's mouth tightened in frown at the idea of her giving a ride to a man who had just threatened her. *We're going to talk about personal safety and professional boundaries,* he thought.

His voice sounded sulky, but he wasn't yelling anymore. "No. I'll drive over. You *still* shouldn't have sent him to the ER."

"Jim, I did what I needed to do to take care of Peter. Now I'll step out of the room if you want to talk to the superintendents about me."

"No. Fine, I don't need to talk to them. I'll go over to the hospital."

"Okay. Will you let me know what they find?"

"Yeah."

The men in the room could hear him hang up and Georgiana double checked that the speaker was off as well. Charlie looked at her pensively. "He knows that they'll see other bruises if they're there, right?"

She nodded as she came back around to sit down. "Yes. I mean, I've personally reported on him six times since January. One of these times they'll actually *do* something."

Jack realized the implication of her words. "You suspect abuse?"

"We don't *suspect* anything. We know it, but we can't prove it enough to get DCF to do anything."

"DCF is child protective services in Vermont?"

"Yes, Department of Children and Families." She twisted the circle of silver and gold around the ring finger of her right hand, and Jackson realized she wasn't wearing a wedding ring. *What kind of single woman her age wanted to be a school principal? What kind of school hired a single woman for such a role?* Jack forced himself to focus on the conversation at hand as she continued. "Peter's in seventh grade and his dad killed his mom in a domestic dispute when Peter was about six months old. The boy's grandmother got custody while his dad was in prison, and kept it even after he was released, but she died last year. Custody defaulted to the boy's father, despite his criminal record. Since he's been living with his dad, there have been multiple times when Peter had bruises or marks. So, when Peter fell today, we knew he'd have to go to the ER, but we know they'll probably also see other marks or notice healed fractures when they examine him. His dad knows it too."

As much as he didn't want to be impressed by her, Jack had to admit that her handling of the situation was professional and appropriate, much more so than he'd often seen in other districts. "Sounds like you've handled it well."

"Thank you."

Charlie looked at his watch. "Not trying to give you the rush, kiddo, but we have a meeting with the executive committee of the board in a few minutes."

Georgiana stood back up. "That's fine. I should get back to my building anyway."

Jackson rose and held out his hand. "Dr. Hewitt, it was nice to finally meet you. I'll have Priscilla schedule that meeting for after your conference."

She looked at him curiously as she shook his hand. "Dr. Ryder, you don't need to have Priscilla set up a meeting. I'll be back in my office the Monday after and I'm there every day. My leave schedule is visible on your calendar here and you're welcome to come whenever. I'm always prepared to talk budget or staffing."

"You don't want prior notice?" He tried to keep the surprise out of his voice.

Her eyes sparkled with humor. "Well, Tuesday mornings I normally sacrifice a few kindergartners on the back field, so prior notice then would be appreciated, but otherwise just stop in whenever."

Charlie chuckled. "Enough, George. He doesn't know your warped sense of humor yet."

"Fine." She smiled. "It was nice meeting you. I look forward to working with you."

"Likewise."

After she left the room, carefully shutting the door behind her, Jackson sat back down and looked at Charlie thoughtfully. "What's her story?"

Charlie leaned back in his chair and put his feet up on the desk, thinking through his answer after having seen how Jackson reacted when she'd walked through the door. "You mean, why the hell is a woman who looks like that still single, living in the middle of bumblefuck, leading a school? Is *that* what you mean?"

Jackson chuckled at the bluntness. "Yes, that's what I mean. And what's the story of your connection to her? She's in some of your pictures like a member of the family."

"She is family, so to speak."

"What do you mean?"

"My wife Anna grew up here. Georgiana's mom and her family are from here. Katherine and Anna have been best friends basically since birth. When Katherine got pregnant, she was unmarried and decided to have the baby. Except it was twins and when they were born here, Katherine stayed around for a while. But her work meant more to her than her family. Eventually, her parents took guardianship of Georgiana and her brother. We just started including them in most of our family events. They're exactly two weeks younger than my daughter Jill, and Jill and George have been buddies since they could walk and talk."

"They didn't live with their mom full-time?"

"They did for years. They were dragged wherever the UN sent Katherine, living in tents in refugee camps, staying in hotels when she presented at conferences, things like that. She home schooled them and had them attend whatever school she was working in at the time. When they got to late middle school, her brother Payton pitched a fit about wanting to live in one place for a while. That's when they went to live with their grandparents."

"And her brother?"

"He's a Navy SEAL, stationed in Virginia." A huge smile spread across his face as he picked up his phone and swiped the screen to get to his photos. "This is Payton, known as PJ, and George last month at the pre-wedding barbecue for my daughter, Ellie." He turned the phone and Jack could see Georgiana in a sundress, with a huge man standing next to her, an arm wrapped around her. "Those are the twins. He's as huge as she is tiny but when you see their eyes and hair, you know they're from the same gene pool. Close as two siblings could be. Fiercely loyal to each other, competitive about everything, obsessively independent, frighteningly smart, and strong as hell."

"And her doctorate?"

"Educational leadership with an emphasis on the psychology side."

"And she's a principal here? She just stayed in Vermont after high school and college?"

"Hell, no." Charlie knew the details by heart. "She graduated from college at twenty. Got her masters by twenty-two. Taught in Harlem for several years while she started her doctoral program. Got promoted to principal of that school, PS 193, by twenty-five, Ph.D. Two years later, around the time her marriage fell apart, she left Harlem to do research for a bit. The following January, the principal of Deerlane had a heart attack. When we opened the search, no one applied. *No one.* Deerlane was listed as the worst school in Vermont. Not proud of that. I knew George was beginning to feel homesick. Her grandparents had moved out of the family home into assisted living, where they are now, and she and PJ took over the land and house."

"Not her mom?"

"No, it didn't mean anything to her, so her kids got it. Anyway, here I was without a principal, or even an applicant. It was the middle of January, so I called her up and asked if she'd think of taking it as an interim position. She said yes and in June, the board unanimously voted to keep her. She's been here ever since. Under her, the school has gone from 'most failing' to not even on the watch list."

"How long ago was that?"

"Eight years." He raised an eyebrow. "She's thirty-four. Divorced, no children. Lives on the family farm out on Crystal Pond. She has alpacas, chickens, a couple sheep, a goat, a steer, and a huge vegetable garden. When she's not running the school, working with her mom, farming, or speaking nationally, she also weaves, hikes, kayaks, and runs. She's fluent in French and Spanish, conversational in probably ten more languages. She bakes the best damn chocolate chip cookies in the county, runs the Spartan Race each year, swears like a sailor when she's mad, and throws an amazing Thanksgiving dinner for anyone and everyone." He gestured toward the phone. "And she knows every one of her students better than any educator I've ever known. She knows the parents *and* the grandparents. She has the memory of an elephant, never loses her cool, and is frightfully organized. I could go on..."

Jack tried to keep his mind on the conversation, but he got distracted by the idea of her in the Spartan. "Doesn't the community worry about a single woman leading a school?"

"She's divorced. She's a known commodity here, so the community never minded her marital status. Everyone knows she married right out of college, and I think it would've worked just fine, except he had an affair with her best friend."

"Ouch."

"Yeah. The funny thing is that they all came through it okay. Her ex and his second wife, the best friend, come to Thanksgiving most years." Charlie thought it was interesting that Jack had asked about her divorce but not about where she'd gone to school. "And you?"

"And me what?"

"Divorced?"

Jackson nodded. "Three years ago. That's part of why I wanted to make such a drastic change by coming here." He pushed his hand through his hair. "And she's presenting at the conference?"

"Uh huh."

"Did you approve the presentation?"

"Are you kidding? I trust her implicitly."

"Are you going to see it?"

Charlie shook his head. "No. I've seen her present on it before. Besides, by then, I'll be retired. I'm going to be sitting on my boat, fishing."

"Maybe I should go."

Charlie tried to hide his smile, thinking that maybe there was more to Jackson's suggestion than just seeing her present. "I think that would be a great idea."

Chapter Two

Georgiana was at her desk the next morning when her direct line rang.

"Hey George, it's Priscilla."

"Hey. What's up?"

"I thought you should know that I'm booking a flight for Dr. Ryder to go to Seattle. The way it worked out, he's on your flights and staying in the same hotel."

"He's going?"

"Uh-huh."

"Why?"

"Charlie says he wants to see your presentation."

"Interesting."

Two hours later, an email arrived in her inbox. It was brief: *Dr. Hewitt, I will be going to the conference in Seattle. I suggest we carpool to the airport. JR*

Georgiana sat, twirling her spinner ring around her finger. It made perfect sense to carpool the hour and a half to the airport. It did, really. But she had to admit that spending that much time with him sounded stressful. The man was painfully attractive and the last thing she needed was to start having thoughts about him. It wasn't that she didn't date, but, well, she didn't date much and certainly didn't date at all around Newburgh. And the man was her boss. She needed to make sure she didn't let even the smallest thoughts about his appearance enter her mind. But if she was going to be working for him, she might as well get to know more about him while clearly setting the professional boundaries.

She typed: *Dr. Ryder, Carpooling sounds great. Why don't I pick you up at 6 a.m. on Tuesday? G.*

Five minutes later: *Good. Do you know where I live? 586 Hillpond Road. JR*

Chapter Three

Tuesday morning Georgiana came downstairs to the kitchen just as Shroom knocked on the screen door. She waved him in, happy as always to see her surrogate father figure. "Hey."

The older man grinned at her, his gray hair pulled back in a ponytail, his almost-white beard neatly trimmed. "Hey, yourself. You ready to go? What do I need to know?"

She poured him a cup of black coffee and handed it to him before she took one herself, adding a splash of cream but not stirring it. "Normal routine. Just the animals, and water the garden if we don't get rain tomorrow. I'll be back late Saturday night, so I won't see you until Sunday."

"Sounds good." He leaned back, looking at her fondly. "So, the gossip is that the new superintendent's a hottie. Your thoughts?"

She laughed, used to his gentle interrogations about her social life, or lack thereof. "Shroom, he's my *boss*. I'm not thinking about his looks. I just want him to leave me alone to run my school, that's all."

He nodded, noticing she didn't answer his question directly. "Meaning you do think he's attractive."

She blew out a sigh. "He is. Not that it matters, but he is."

"Why's he going to the conference?"

"From a positive viewpoint, maybe to see my presentation and be supportive. From a more cynical viewpoint, to make sure I'm not screwing around on the company dime."

"Which do you think it is?"

She looked at her coffee for a second, pondering. "I don't know, so I'm trying not to overthink it."

"It'd be good for you to start dating again." Before she could reply, he held up his hand. "Don't say it. I know, you had that thing with Boone. But that wasn't a real relationship. You need a man in your life again, for real."

She stood up and kissed the top of his head, inordinately thankful to have him as part of her life. "Don't start, old man. I'm good. You know how I feel about dating someone around here, with my role."

"So, because you have a public role, you don't get to have a private life?"

"Enough. I need to be on the road in ten minutes."

Chapter Four

A half hour later, Georgiana turned into the long gravel driveway and pulled up to the front of the light green house with the deep front porch. As she turned the car off, she saw Jackson come out the front door, stopping to lock it behind him. No matter how much she didn't want to notice his looks, she couldn't deny that the dark blue short-sleeved shirt fit him perfectly, as did the dark gray pants. *Damn!* She needed to stop noticing things like that.

As she came around the car, Jack swallowed hard, admiring her simple black leggings, ballet flats, quietly elegant ivory tunic with a deep neckline, and an amethyst pendant hanging just low enough to make his eyes drop more than they should. "Georgiana, good morning."

"Good morning." She popped open the back hatch of the Jeep and he put his travel bag in the cargo bay. "Ready to go?"

"I am. You sure you don't mind driving?"

She laughed as she buckled her seatbelt. "Dr. Ryder, you live in Vermont now. You have to drive at least ten minutes to get milk, so you get used to it. It's just part of the day."

"Jackson, or Jack."

"What?"

"Please, call me Jack or Jackson. If we're going to be working together, the 'Doctors' will get old fast."

"All right, Jackson." She backed down the driveway and headed south toward Burlington. "I guess we should have introduced ourselves on Sunday."

"Seems that way." He tried to make his words sound nonchalant. "Charlie says you run the Spartan."

"I do." She glanced at him quickly. "You planning on it too?"

"Yeah." For the next few minutes, they chatted about the races.

As they continued down the highway she asked, "So what do you know about the area?"

"Not much more than what's on the Chamber of Commerce site and what the realtor told me as she was convincing me to rent the house."

Over the next half-hour Georgiana told Jackson about each town as they passed through. He was fascinated by her memory and her attention to detail. As they came onto the interstate, her phone rang. Looking at the display on the dashboard, she tapped the screen. "Hey, I'm in the car. You're on speaker. My new boss is here. PJ, Jackson. Jackson Ryder, my brother PJ."

The voice on the speaker was deep. "Jackson, nice to virtually meet you."

"You too."

Georgiana passed a slow-moving sedan. "What's up? I'm about six miles from Stanton's Gulf, and since they still haven't put in the cell tower there, I'll lose service soon."

"Just calling to tell you to have a good trip. When do you actually present?"

"Thursday afternoon."

"Seriously, Thursday. Big day for you! Ready for it?" He snorted. "Dumb question."

"Of course, I'm ready. Where are you?"

"Home. Hopefully, for a bit. If nothing comes up, we have leave. Not this weekend, but next. Want company for Grandpa's birthday?"

"That would be wonderful!"

"Hey, going back to your trip. Is ass-wipe going to be there?"

"Peej! My boss is sitting here. Shut up. And yes. Leave it alone. I'm over it. Why can't you be?"

"Because it was wrong, that's why."

Georgiana shook her head, not wanting to get into yet another argument with her brother over her failed marriage. "PJ, I need to go. It's rude of me to be talking with someone else here. I'll call you Thursday. Otherwise, do you want me to pick you up at the airport?"

"I'll rent a car. Love you. Talk to you Thursday. Jackson, have a great trip."

Jackson was surprised he'd remembered his name. "Thanks."

"Bye, baby sister."

"Bye, old fart."

After disconnecting Georgiana asked, "Did you know I'm a twin?"

"Charlie told me. And your brother's a SEAL?"

"He is. He's stationed in Virginia now but comes home when he can."

"It's nice you're so close."

She snorted. "I think probably all twins are close, but with our upbringing, being close was how we survived."

The word "survived" made him remember something, "I meant to ask you, what happened with the student you sent to the ER?"

Her voice showed her frustration, "His arm was broken. They set it, noted other bruises and healed fractures, and put him into conditional custody."

"Which means?"

"Sorry, I forgot you're coming from D.C., so the terminology is different. It means that a DCF caseworker has been assigned, and technically has custody, but he's at home with his dad. The social worker will check in with us, and with Peter, but I can promise you Peter won't say a word against his father."

"Damn, that's too bad."

Over the rest of the drive, they made small talk, chatting about Burlington and the upcoming lake festival in Newburgh, and about the upcoming conference. At the airport, she pulled into the garage and they each grabbed their bags. After checking in and going through security, they found seats in the lounge. Georgiana put down her bags and stretched her back. "I'm going to get coffee. Do you want some?"

"That would be great." He reached for his wallet. "Here, let me give you some money."

She waved him off. "I got it. You can buy me a drink when we get to Seattle."

"Deal. Cream and sugar, please."

She came back with the coffees and handed him his. "Will you be horribly offended if I work on a report while we wait?"

He laughed. "Not as long as you aren't offended if I sit here and read *The New York Times*."

When the flight was called, her row was first. "I'll see you in Seattle."
"See you there."

Five minutes later, Jackson's row was called. As he boarded the plane, he noticed that she was in her window seat with a very attractive older man sitting next to her, clearly already trying to get her attention. Georgiana looked like she was working hard to ignore him. As he passed her row, he stopped and turned toward her, leaning in and raising a brow. "See you in Seattle?"

She smiled, realizing he was trying to help her with the unwanted attention. "See you in Seattle. Remember, you're buying drinks."

His smile was warm as his voice dropped conspiratorially. "How could I forget?"

Chapter Five

Six hours later, as he walked toward the baggage carousel, Jack could see Georgiana staring resolutely ahead as the same man was standing next to her, still talking. As he approached, she sent him an imploring look. Without stopping to think, he winked at her and grinned, then came in close to put his arm around her and kiss her hair. "How was your flight, babe? Sorry we couldn't sit together."

The man stammered, "Oh, shit. Oh, sorry. Sorry," and hurried away.

Jackson's arm dropped off her shoulder. "Problem solved."

She looked up at him and started to laugh. "Holy shit! I can't believe you just did that but thank you."

His look was thoughtful. "The way you look, you must have to deal with that a lot."

"What do you mean?"

"You're a gorgeous woman who doesn't wear a wedding ring. You must get hit on a lot." He looked uncomfortable. "I'm sorry, I shouldn't have said that. I am so sorry."

Georgiana slipped her hand through the crook of his arm and gave a gentle squeeze. "Jackson, I really appreciate what you did. And as for your comment, I'll take it as a compliment. And no, I don't get hit on. I live alone in the middle of the Northeast Kingdom, and I work obsessively. Everyone knows that."

"Really?"

"Really." The baggage started to snake by. "C'mon, let's get our bags and a cab."

The two of them checked in at the hotel and realized that they were staying on separate floors. As they walked toward the elevators, Jack slowed his pace. "Do you want to get an early dinner?" He paused. "Please understand, I know you didn't plan on coming here with me."

Her tone showed her amusement. "I'd love to have dinner with you. No one I know is here yet, so I'd be eating alone otherwise."

He felt irrationally pleased by her words. "Okay then. How about we meet in the bar for the drink I owe you, then we can go find dinner?"

"Perfect. See you in an hour?"

In her room, Georgiana quickly unpacked and took a shower, the warm water cascading over her. As she rinsed her hair, she thought about the strange interaction at the airport. No matter how much she wanted to fight it, the reality was that Jackson Ryder was easily the most attractive man she'd encountered in a long time. With a sigh, she stepped out of the shower and pulled on a robe, wrapping her hair in a towel before stepping back into her bedroom and picking up her cell phone. She hit speed dial and smiled at the voice on the other end. "Senator McLaine's cell phone."

"Hi Judy, it's George. Is Molly available?"

"Hi, George. One minute, she just stepped into the other room."

Thirty seconds later, her best friend's voice came through the phone, "Hey Gigi, what's up?"

"I have a big-ass problem."

"You do? What's wrong?"

"I have the hots for a guy."

"Who?"

"The new superintendent. I'm in Seattle with him for the conference and I *really* need to get thoughts about him out of my head."

"Why? Is he married?"

"Divorced."

"So, what's the problem?"

"I can't have a relationship with him. I need to stop thinking about the fact that I'd love to see the man naked, and I'd give anything to see if he tastes as good as he smells."

"Jesus, you've got it bad!"

"No shit. That's what I'm trying to tell you!"

There was a pause, and she could hear Molly speaking with someone, presumably Judy, before she came back on the line. "Hey, I need to be on the floor in about five minutes, so I've gotta go. But here are my thoughts, for what they're worth. I don't see anything wrong with you dating him as long as you both understand the rules and roles. Otherwise, you have two options: a lot of cold showers and keeping your distance, or jump him there to get it out of your system."

Georgiana laughed. "Leave it to you to break it down that simply. Okay. I can do this, whatever *this* is. Go make the world safe for democracy. Love you."

"Love you too, Gi. Talk to you soon."

Chapter Six

Minutes later, Georgiana stood in front of her closet debating over what to wear. Her choices for this trip seemed to have a more "notice me" message than normal. Subconsciously, she must have been trying to get his attention. *So why not really try?* She pulled a short black skirt from the hanger, topping it with a deep rose Asian-inspired short-sleeve blouse, knowing that the mandarin collar flattered her. The next question: heels or flats? Heels looked sexier, but flats were more aloof. How obvious was she willing to be? Finally, she pulled black flats out and slid them on, then took a final look at her hair and makeup before heading out the door.

As she entered the hotel lounge, she could see Jackson leaning on the bar, his back to the room. Taking a long moment to look him over without him knowing it, she admired his broad shoulders, his straight dark hair brushing against his collar, and she couldn't help but wonder what his hair would feel like if she was to run her fingers through it. When he turned to face her, she realized that the deep blue of his shirt was almost the exact shade of his eyes, and the open neck of his shirt showed off his tan. *Stop!* Her professional mind clamored for her to stop thinking of him in that way; no matter how attractive he was, a relationship, even if he was interested, was a bad, bad, *bad* idea.

She suddenly realized he was surveying her just as intently as she had looked at him, and for a split second, she recognized raw desire in his eyes. She tried to calm her breathing as she walked toward him. "Hi."

"Hi." He smiled and the ultra-serious expression left his face. He looked young and relaxed, and she found him even sexier. "You look great."

She was pleased but tried not to show how much his compliment meant to her. "Thanks." She grinned wickedly. "You clean up nice too."

He gestured toward the bar. "What would you like? And do you want to sit here?"

"Whatever they have on tap from Old Stove Brewery. And sure, here is fine."

He tipped his head, looking at her with even more interest. "You've been to Seattle before?"

She slid onto a stool. "Several times. When my brother was stationed at Coronado, I flew out pretty regularly. We used to fly up here to feel more like we were in New England. As far as I can tell, Seattle is a big Burlington. And you?"

He sat next to her. "My sister went to college here, so I came out a couple times." The bartender came over and Jack ordered two beers. When they arrived, he raised his glass. "Cheers."

They sat companionably, sipping their drinks, discussing the conference. When their glasses were nearly drained, Jack asked, "Dinner? What are you in the mood for?"

Her answer was quick. "Seafood. Vermont isn't exactly a seafood hub."

He laughed. "True." He waved the bartender over and asked for a recommendation. A few minutes later they were strolling down the street. At the restaurant, they ordered quickly and settled back, each with a glass of wine.

Georgiana looked at him intently. "Okay, so knowing Charlie, he's told you everything about me except my blood type, and he may have thrown that in for good measure. That puts me at a distinct disadvantage here. Who are you, Dr. Jackson Ryder, and why are you now a superintendent in the Northeast Kingdom of Vermont?"

He took a sip. "How do you know Charlie told me anything about you?"

"Because Charlie has no boundaries when it comes to me." She chuckled.

Jack nodded. "Good assessment. So, what do you want to know?"

"Schooling, background, training, and why Vermont?"

Her question struck him as odd. "You didn't read my vitae? It was all public record."

She shook her head. "I believe heavily in the idea of accepting what I cannot change. I chose not to be on the hiring committee, so in the end, reading your paperwork would've either frustrated me because I thought they'd made a bad choice, or intimidated me, which isn't one of my favorite things."

Deep down, he was bothered that she hadn't been interested enough to read it after they'd first met. "I can't imagine you ever being intimidated."

"It doesn't happen often, but when it does, it makes me really cranky." She took a sip of wine and thanked the waiter as he put her seafood puttanesca in front of her. "Answer the question, please."

"Dartmouth undergrad, Georgetown for my master's, Columbia for my doctoral. I taught middle school, was a principal in Atlanta, worked policy in D.C. for a while, then went back to being in a school and became an assistant superintendent in D.C. I decided I needed to get out of the city and make some changes in my life after the dust settled from my divorce, and I opted for a more rural area. I narrowed my search to areas within an hour of skiing, with major cities within four hours, then looked for districts with a clear mindset for growth."

Over the rest of their meal, they talked quietly about their views on various topics in education. On the walk back to the hotel, Jackson realized it was the most enjoyable evening he'd had in a long time. On the elevator, he looked down at Georgiana. "What's the schedule for tomorrow?"

"I have to be at the convention center at nine to make sure it's all set for my presentation. Then, no plans."

"I think we get a harbor cruise in our package. Want to go in the afternoon?"

"Sounds great. I'll call you when I get back?"

"Do you have my cell number?"

She grinned. "Not yet."

He pulled his phone from his pocket. "What's your number? I'll call you right now and then you'll have it."

"555-2669." A moment later, she felt the phone buzz in her pocket.

When the elevator stopped at her floor, she turned to him. "Thanks for dinner."

"Thanks for joining me."

Chapter Seven

At the convention center the next morning, Georgiana quickly went through her technology needs and visited her presentation room.

On her way back to the hotel, she stopped at a craft store and bought several skeins of fingering weight yarn, not having a specific project in mind, but loving the color and texture of the yarn. She felt momentarily annoyed with herself when she realized the blue-gray in the self-striping skein was the exact color of Jack's eyes.

As she came out of the store, her phone buzzed with a text. She smiled as she saw Molly's message. *"Hey, so what happened?"*

She typed. *"Drinks, dinner."*

"And?"

Georgiana stopped and sat down on the stone bench in front of a bookstore. *"And nothing. Well, not nothing. We are going on a harbor cruise this afternoon."*

The response was almost instantaneous. *"Wear jeans, you look great in jeans."*

She'd already been thinking about what to wear, and knew Molly was right. *"I will."*

"Good. Gotta run – let me know how it goes!"

Back at the hotel, she changed into jeans and sneakers but had to slow down to think about a top. *Super casual t-shirt or a more feminine blouse? Blouse. One or two buttons undone? Two.* She looked in the mirror and as critical as she was of her own looks, she knew the outfit worked. She pulled a headband on to hold her hair off her face, put on a bit more eyeliner, and finally pulled out her phone.

He answered on the second ring. "Hi."

"Still up for the harbor?"

"Sounds great. I'll meet you in the lobby in ten minutes."

On the walk to the harbor, Jackson tried hard not to act like this was a date, and tried to not think about how the snug faded denim jeans emphasized her curves. He made a point to ask about her morning, trying to keep the conversation on school matters. Waiting for the gangway to be opened, he tried not to notice how the neckline of her blouse revealed the hint of a shadow between her breasts.

On the boat, they climbed to the top deck. Georgiana pulled sunglasses from her bag and slipped them on. Without meaning to, he grinned at her wholeheartedly. Her eyes narrowed suspiciously as she looked at him over the rims. "What?"

"You look about sixteen years old. How the hell do you scare anyone enough to run a school?"

She laughed. "You haven't seen my glare yet. It can silence a room immediately."

"Really? That, I have to see."

Walking back to the hotel, Jack asked as casually as he could, "Dinner? Or do you have plans?"

She tried to keep her voice nonchalant, not wanting him to know how pleased she was with the invitation. "No plans. Dinner sounds great."

"Do you want to change, or go right now?"

"Depends where you want to eat. I'm not going to someplace swanky in jeans, but burgers, we can do now."

"Which do you prefer?"

She pondered for a moment. "Let's go change and then find someplace relatively quiet. The conference will be noisy tomorrow."

"Perfect."

Chapter Eight

An hour later Jackson had to control his very physical reaction as Georgiana walked toward him in a sleeveless black dress and heels. The amethyst necklace was back enhancing her beautiful neck. As she looked at him in his dark gray suit, he was pleased to see her eyes flicker with awareness too. He tried to keep his voice steady. "Hi. Ready?"

"I am."

At the restaurant, they ordered quickly. Their conversation gradually shifted from the educational conference and theories, to sharing their own interests and experiences. As they ate, the conversation stayed personal, never moving back to professional topics.

Walking back to the hotel after dinner, he realized she was rubbing her arms. "Cold?"

"A bit." Instantly, he pulled off his blazer and put it over her shoulders. The smell of his cologne surrounded her and again she marveled at how attracted she was to this man. *Damn, she needed to control her reaction to him!* "Thanks."

"You're welcome." At the hotel, he held the door for her. He stopped in the lobby. "Would you like a nightcap?"

She knew she should stop this now. Before the logical part of her brain could intercept her words, she nodded. "That would be great."

In the hotel bar, she handed his jacket back and they sat in a corner booth, the table softly lit by candlelight. They each ordered a glass of wine and as they sipped, the conversation turned even more personal, now including their families and hobbies. Their divorces seemed to be the only topic not touched upon. At one point, she made a smart comment that made him laugh, and without thinking about it, he reached out and squeezed her hand. With that touch, they both jumped and then sat staring at each other in silence, still holding hands. Suddenly a large group of young men came into the bar, shouting at each other. The intimate moment ruined; she pulled her hand back. She smiled wistfully. "There goes the ambiance."

"I know." He looked at her across the table. "So?"

His voice was so intense that she immediately felt his magnetism. "Yes?"

"I'm not ready for this conversation to end," he motioned toward the boisterous group gathered near the bar, "but this isn't working for me."

Her eyes were dark as she looked at him. "Me either." She clarified. "Both. This isn't working now *and* I'm not ready for the evening to end."

"Then what's the plan?"

Georgiana realized he was letting her call the shots at this point. For a split second, she hesitated, knowing she was going to be angry with herself if she slept with him. But that part of her was quickly silenced by the recognition of how very much she wanted to be alone with this man, even if it was for nothing more than an extended conversation.

She licked her lips and Jack felt a lightning bolt of desire jolt through him. She smiled slowly and slid her hand closer to his on the table so just their fingertips were touching. "Why don't we order a bottle of wine and take it upstairs?"

He found that light touch unbearably arousing. His eyes never wavered as he held her gaze. "Your room or mine?"

"Yours. You're on a higher floor, and I bet the view is better."

Moments later, they walked toward the elevator just as a group of people were coming through the lobby. Jack put his hand on her lower back protectively. On the elevator, she stood in front of him and smiled as his hand moved around to her waist, pulling her in to him.

In his suite, she walked over to the huge plate glass windows, the city glowing before them. When the room service waiter delivered the wine, Jack tipped him and carried the open bottle and glasses to the small table between two armchairs facing the view. He came up behind her and stood quietly, close enough that she could feel the heat radiating from his body.

Her voice was soft. "The view is breathtaking."

"So are you."

She turned and her sudden grin was devilish. "You, too."

"Me too, what?"

"Breathtaking."

He shook his head. "Nah. I just know how to clean up. I think that's what you said."

She stepped forward and gently placed her hand on the lapel of his jacket. "Well, you do clean up quite nicely."

He placed his hand over hers. "Thank you."

With her hand still on his chest, she smiled up at him. "C'mon, you promised me a glass of wine."

They sipped their drinks sitting side by side. Several minutes after they settled into the armchairs, Georgiana reached down to slide off her heels, putting her feet up on the ottoman. A few minutes later, his feet rested next to hers. The bottle was almost empty when she stood up and stretched, her eyes trained on the lit Space Needle in the distance. She didn't hear him come up behind her but felt the warmth of his body and she leaned back against him, not saying a word.

His arms came around her, pulling her close, and her hands came up to stroke his arms. With her touch, he realized just how urgently he wanted her.

Still wrapped in his arms, Georgiana turned around and looked up at him, her eyes glowing in the soft light. For a moment, her rational brain begged her to stop before things became even more intimate. That inner voice was silenced as she smiled at him, then lifted her arms to go around his neck, pulling him down to her. Her kiss was gentle and quick, but both of them felt a distinct jolt when their lips touched.

He looked down at her and gently brushed a strand of hair away from her eyes. He sighed, his desire for her warring with his conscience. "Georgiana."

"Jackson."

"Should we talk about this?"

Her look was serious, but she didn't pull away. A slight smile curved her lips. "What? Should we talk about how this probably isn't a good idea? We both know that. But right now, here, I don't care."

He smiled and leaned down to rest his forehead against hers. "Me neither."

She pulled back enough that she could look him in the eye. "Well, we're single, we seem to find each other attractive, and no one's pressuring anyone into anything."

Her wording amused him, and he pulled her closer so he could lean down, his lips barely touching hers. "You *seem* to find me attractive? As I remember it, you just kissed me first."

"That's because you were taking too long to do it."

He laughed. "Then I better remedy that."

He kissed her. It started softly but quickly deepened. With a growl low in his throat, he swept her up into his arms and carried her to his chair, lowering them both, never breaking the kiss.

Her hands moved up to tangle themselves through his hair, then her breathing changed as he slid his hands slowly up from her hips to her waist. As his hands continued to slide upward, one of hers slid down to start unbuttoning the neck of his shirt. He broke the kiss reluctantly. "Are you sure?"

Her gaze didn't waver. "I'm sure."

He reached behind her to find the zipper of her dress, gently sliding it partway down her back. "I have a clean bill of health."

"Me too."

"Protection?"

"I'm on birth control."

Jackson took her hand. "Then c'mon. Let's get more comfortable."

In the bedroom, one small light glowed on the corner of the bureau. Standing by the end of the bed, she reached up to continue unbuttoning his shirt before tugging it free from his waistband. She ran her fingertips down his chest and smiled when he hissed. "Stop, I'm barely restraining myself as it is. Touching me like that isn't helping."

He gently turned her around, unzipping her dress the rest of the way, nudging the straps off her shoulders. The dress pooled at her feet. He gently unhooked her necklace. "As much as I love this on you, I think it's going to be in the way." Holding her firmly by the waist, he began to kiss his way down her back, stopping just long enough to stroke his fingertips across the tattoo on her shoulder. "That is absolutely beautiful." He kissed just below it. "I noticed it when you raced by me that day."

As his kisses reached the bottom of her spine, he reverently traced the line of lace edging the top of her panties before unhooking her bra. That too, soon dropped to the floor, leaving her clad only in a tiny wisp of silk.

She was amused. "So, are you planning on getting undressed too?"

"At some point." He turned her around and she felt her own arousal grow as she watched him looking at her breasts. "Right now, I like this arrangement."

She looked at him; his shirt unbuttoned and open, still wearing his pants. She reached out and unbuckled his belt, pulling it free. Her hands were sure as she reached to unzip his pants, pushing them down over his hips so they could join the growing pile of clothes on the floor. Pushing his shirt off his shoulders, she made a move to drop her panties as well. "I like this one better."

Still wearing his boxers, Jack's eyes burned with desire as he finally saw her luscious breasts fully, which he'd wanted to do ever since their first encounter on the running trail. "Lie down. On your stomach."

Georgiana did as he asked and smiled when she felt his weight on the bed. His touch was feather-light on her shoulders, long strokes down her back, over her ribcage, then eventually down over her backside and legs. She began to move restlessly, feeling him beginning to kiss everywhere he had touched, keeping in control until she felt the tip of his tongue stroke the back of her right knee. She couldn't stand it anymore and turned over quickly. "Now, Jack."

He stopped, clearly pleased with himself. "Now what, Georgiana?"

"No more playing. Now."

He slid up next to her, his hands possessively on her breasts just before he leaned closer to suck on first one, then the other nipple, then tracing her tan lines with the tip of his tongue. "Aren't you impatient?"

She arched her back, allowing him easier access to her breasts. "Yes, I am. Next time, we can take it slower, but I want you inside me *now*."

Jack rolled over so he was above her, braced on his forearms. "You're sure?"

"I'm sure."

With a graceful movement, he peeled off his boxers and tossed them aside. He then slid into her warmth, amazed at how ready she was for him. He felt himself swell even more as he entered her. For a moment, he tried to slow his pace but the need to possess her overtook him. "I'm sorry, I can't wait. I need you too much."

She reached down to grasp his hips, urging him deeper inside her. "I don't want you to go slow. I want you now."

With that, he let go of his last vestige of control and surged into her repeatedly, finding himself pulled closer and closer to his release each time he entered her. Her breathing quickened with each thrust of his fullness. He felt her hands reach down to grasp his backside, holding him back from pulling out too far between each plunge. "No, please. I need you inside me."

With that, Jack buried himself in her, kissing her deeply and feeling her body tighten around him as she reached her release, and the sounds of her pleasure pushed him over the edge too.

As their breathing started returning to normal, he started to roll off of her, but she held him close. "Don't. Stay where you are."

For a moment, he realized that he'd just made love to a relative stranger and instead of feeling awkward, all he wanted to do was to start all over again.

Still braced on his elbow, he looked down at her and kissed her reddened lips. "I've got to be crushing you."

"Breathing is overrated. Right now, I don't need to breathe."

He slid one arm under her to roll them both over. She was now resting on top of him, their bodies still intimately connected. "Now you can breathe." He started slowly running his hands down her back, suddenly needing to touch every inch of her again. "And I can touch you."

Without pulling away from him, Georgiana slowly moved to brace herself on her arms, her hair falling over them like a veil. She moved so she could slowly trace the muscles of his chest, smiling as she felt his body respond, still buried so deeply inside her. She stopped his hand from its travel toward her breast. "Uh uh. You got to play, now it's my turn."

"Why can't we both play?" He stretched his arm, trying to pull away from her hand, and he smiled as she stretched with him, keeping his hand away but brushing her breasts against his chest in the process. "That works too."

She leaned down to kiss the base of his neck. "Did you let me play before?"

"Fair enough." He put his hands up over his head. "You're in charge."

Georgiana slid up his body smugly, finally breaking their intimate connection. As she moved to kneel beside him, he shook his head. "Damn, I liked it better just a moment ago."

"Patience."

He rolled onto his side and reached up to pull her lips to his. "I have absolutely no patience whatsoever where you are concerned. I haven't since the very beginning."

She nibbled his lower lip. "Me neither." She gently pushed his shoulder, forcing him back down. "Now behave and let me have my way with you."

In the light, he caught sight of her inner right arm and reached out to stroke the raised skin. "What's that?"

She stopped stroking his chest and moved her arm so he could see the intricate design more clearly. "A souvenir from Ethiopia, from many years ago."

"Oh." He had so many questions he wanted to ask, but they were lost as she started to touch him again.

Chapter Nine

The next morning, Georgiana grimaced at herself in her bathroom mirror. Stale makeup was not her best look. Shaking her head, she dropped her rumpled clothes in the laundry bag and muttered, "I'm too fucking old for the walk of shame."

She leaned against the wall of the shower, letting the scalding water pelt her skin. Considering the amount of wine she'd had the night before, her head should have been pounding. Instead, other than the surprise that her moral compass *didn't* feel out of whack, she felt great. She suddenly grinned and told herself, *So what? You slept with the hottest man around. The sex was fabulous. Get over yourself.*

Stepping out of the shower, she heard her phone buzz. There was no surprise in seeing a text from Molly. "*So? No call or text last night, does that mean you were busy? Happy B-day by the way!*"

Georgiana grinned and tapped a smiley face and fireworks in response.

Ten seconds later, the response arrived. "*Good for you! Have a great day – love you.*"

An hour later, Georgiana walked into the lobby. She tried to tell herself she was dressed for her presentation, but the truth was that she'd dressed to impress Jackson. She knew the white blouse fit her beautifully, the black skirt showed her curves, and the black heels made *everything* look good. As she stepped from the elevator, she saw him waiting for her, and for a split second, that raw desire was clear in his eyes again. Internally, she grinned with glee. Seemingly four rounds of lovemaking hadn't been enough for him either. She smiled and walked toward him. "Good morning."

"Good morning." His voice lowered to almost a whisper and she could feel the now-familiar rush of heat. "Again."

They walked to the convention center in companionable silence, not touching, but painfully aware of each other. In the dining room, they sat at a corner table and ordered breakfast. The conversation stayed lightly flirtatious, and Georgiana enjoyed every minute of it.

Abruptly, Jack morphed from the young sexy flirt to the formal snot from their first meeting. His voice became painfully formal. "The Deputy Secretary of Education is coming this way. *Please* don't express your opinion on the newest version of the ESSA to him."

She immediately felt her temper flare. "Excuse me?"

"Richard Henshaw. We're old friends and colleagues. Please don't give him your opinion this morning." He missed seeing her eyes narrow as he turned to smile at the man walking toward them.

Georgiana looked over her shoulder at the familiar figure and crossed her eyes.

The tall blond man, impeccably dressed in a light gray suit with a rich dark purple tie gave her a confused look as he stopped by the side of their table, standing between the two of them. "Jesus, Gigi, I haven't even said hello yet, and you're already making faces at me?"

Jackson watched in shock as she said, "My new boss just told me to behave around you, thus ruining my plans for the morning."

The blond man leaned over and kissed the top of her head, much like a parent would a child. "Gigi, you've never behaved around me, even when things between us were good." With that, he turned to Jackson. "Jack! So good to see you. I heard you were going to be here but didn't imagine you'd be here with Gigi."

Jackson was stunned. "Gigi?"

"Gigi." He gestured toward Georgiana. "Georgie, George, Georgiana? The pain in the ass sitting here, otherwise known as my ex-wife."

Georgiana gave his arm a shove. "Hey, I'm not a pain in your ass anymore."

"No, just his if he has to put up with you every day."

She looked at Jackson's face and realized he hadn't fully put it all together, and she pushed her anger at his earlier comment aside for the moment. "Jack, Richard is my ex-husband. I should've realized when you said you did policy work in D.C. that you two had met. Rick, Jack is my new superintendent."

"Charlie finally retired?"

"Yeah."

Rick shook his head, clearly amused. "Damn, Jack. If I'd known, I would've sent you a case of the best scotch. You'll need it, working with her."

She smiled at him, her eyes showing her humor. "Fuck off, you ass," she said lightly.

"Love you too, Gigi." He squeezed her hand. "Happy birthday, too."

Jackson was shocked. "It's your birthday?"

"Uh-huh."

He looked at her intently, thinking back to the hours of intimacy and how she'd never mentioned today was her special day. "You didn't tell me that."

She shrugged. "Until I was around fourteen, I never celebrated a birthday like most Americans."

"Her mother doesn't believe in such celebrations," Rick said dryly.

She ignored the comment. "So, PJ and I don't do much about our birthday."

Before Jack could say anything, Rick pulled an envelope from his suitcoat. "Knowing you, you already know what this is, but happy birthday from Molly and me. She said you'd already been texting each other this morning."

She grinned delightedly. "I hope it's what I think it is."

"It is." He smiled. "And if Jack isn't sick of being around you, there's an extra ticket in there. I can't believe it worked out that the Red Sox are in town when you are. And Mom and Dad said they're paying for beers and hot dogs."

With childlike excitement, she pulled out three tickets for the Seattle Mariners for that very night. She leaned over and hugged him. "Thank you!"

"You're welcome. Let me know where you're staying, and I'll pick you up for the game."

Chapter Ten

Twenty minutes of small talk later, Georgiana stood up. "I'm going to the keynote."

Rick looked at his watch. "You have fifteen minutes and it's right upstairs."

Her voice was sure. "And I want a good seat."

He shook his head, the years of putting up with her need to be early for everything clear in his mind. "Fine, then go. We'll get there at a normal time like *sane* people."

She looked at him with sparkling eyes but before she could do anything Rick said, "Don't flip me off in front of your new boss."

She rolled her eyes and stalked away, not saying anything to Jack as she left.

Rick looked at Jack, who still looked vaguely shell-shocked. "She has to be at things early. Used to make me crazy."

Jack's brain was still spinning. "Oh."

Rick took a sip of his coffee. "Sorry, Jack. When I heard you were headed to New England, I didn't stop to think Vermont. And I sure as shit didn't think you'd be in her district. I would've let you know the connection if I had."

"So, she's your ex-wife?" He shook his head. "The one who once threatened to kill you?"

"Uh huh." Rick looked down at his hands, suddenly very serious. "My ex-wife, the first woman I promised to love and cherish for the rest of my life, and frankly, I wasn't good at that. We got married too young; I didn't know what I wanted and by the time I figured out I wanted to spend the rest of my life with Molly, I'd pretty well broken Gigi's heart in two. Not only did I fuck around, but it was with her best friend."

Jack's brain was racing from all of the revelations of the last few minutes. "But you're good now?"

"Better than good. It took a couple years and a few huge fights, but eventually, the three of us figured it out. They're still the best of friends. Gi and I still talk education, and once or twice a year the girls go away for a weekend together. And it just so happens that twice a year, Gi and I go see the Sox because Molly hates baseball." He shrugged. "Only because of her truly fucked-up upbringing could she have made peace with all of it in her mind, but it works."

"What do you mean?"

"You know who her mom is, right?"

"Of course."

"Well, Katherine felt that Gigi and PJ should go wherever she went, so they did, until they were fourteen. For all those years, her needs, *their* needs, were thought of long after the needs of whatever group Katherine was working with at the time. She felt that birthdays were a luxury they didn't need. They didn't go to regular school because they'd get pulled up and moved whenever Katherine wanted. The good part is that they can roll with the punches better than most people. The other part of that sort of crazy early life means that both of them compartmentalize better than anyone I know. Once she'd vented her anger with me, with both Molly and me, she put it behind her. PJ? Now he can compartmentalize in his own life, hence being a top-notch SEAL, but he's still not forgiven us. He will never fully forgive me—er, us. He loves her too much and I hurt her very badly. When we see each other, we're civil, not much more."

"*When* you see each other?"

"At Thanksgiving." He grinned. "Oh, you have to come to her Thanksgiving dinner. We come up, half the town is there, and it's the biggest event around." He looked at his watch. "We should go."

When they reached the convention hall, the room was packed, so they stood in the back to listen. After the keynote, Jack looked around for Georgiana, and Rick realized what he was doing. "She's already headed to her presentation room."

Jack looked at his watch. "But she has twenty minutes, why would she rush?"

"That's her. Want to go watch? That'll make her batshit crazy, which is always fun."

"Sure."

When they arrived, the room was almost full. At exactly the start time, Georgiana turned on her mic and smiled at the group. "Good afternoon. If everyone can get settled, we're ready to begin. For those of you I haven't met, I'm Dr. Georgiana Hewitt, Principal of the Deerlane Community School in Newburgh, Vermont. We are a full-service community school."

Over the next three hours, Jackson watched with awe as Georgiana gave a fast-paced, informative, interactive presentation. At the first break, he turned to Rick. "Wow."

Rick nodded, knowing what he meant. "Best damn teacher I ever had the pleasure of watching anywhere. When she started teaching in Harlem, she'd have classes of forty kids and her energy level and expectations were just as high." He looked pensive for a moment. "Frankly, there was a part of me that was sad when she said she was leaving the classroom for administration because I saw her reach kid after kid who'd been labeled 'unreachable.'"

At the end of her talk, Jack and Rick waited as a large group of attendees vied for Georgiana's attention. Finally, the room cleared, and as she organized her notes and materials in her bag, she said in a snarky tone, "Couldn't the two of you go bother someone else for a while? You needed to stay for the entire thing?"

Rick came forward and squeezed her hand. "You've still got it. I didn't plan on staying, but I was too engaged to leave."

For a millisecond, Jack saw a flash of insecurity cross her face. Her voice was quiet. "Thanks. I mean it."

"I know." His voice was cheerful. "Okay, so now can we go to the game?"

She laughed and Jack saw the happiness in her eyes as she looked at her ex. "Hell, yeah. I want to run back to the hotel and change, then I'm ready."

As the three of them walked back to the hotel, Jack realized that Georgiana was saying very little overall, and nothing to him personally. At the hotel, Rick excused himself to go meet someone briefly, stating he would meet them in the lobby in an hour.

Jack and Georgiana were finally alone in the elevator. He cleared his throat, wanting to start a conversation with her. *How could we go from making love early this morning to not even speaking on the walk back?* "You were amazing."

"Thanks." Her voice was clipped.

"It was a great overview for me of your school, and it was a fabulous presentation."

Her tone stayed cold. "I'm good at what I do."

"You are, clearly."

She didn't respond. At her floor, she stepped off the elevator. "See you in the lobby."

"Georgiana?" He held the sliding door open.

"Jack, I'll see you in the lobby." She walked away, not looking back.

In his room, he suddenly realized why she might have been so cold to him, and picked up his phone to text her. *"Are you mad at me?"*

"Why would I be mad at you?"

"Are you asking because you aren't mad or because you want to know if I'm smart enough to figure out what I did wrong?"

"Ding, ding, ding -- we have a winner."

She could be sarcastic, even in a text. Jack was amused, even as he was frustrated that she'd held on to being mad at him all day. *"I shouldn't have made the comments I did this morning about how to act."*

"You think? Think about how you treated a fellow professional."

"In my defense, I didn't know the connection between the two of you."

"That's not an apology."

"I'm sorry."

"What are you sorry for?"

"For telling you how to act."

She didn't answer for several minutes, and Jack sat looking at the phone, waiting for her answer. Finally, he typed, *"I'm sorry, I was an idiot. Forgive me?"*

Still no answer. He felt himself getting angry back. *What does she want from me?* Just as he was about to send another message, there was a soft knock.

He opened the door to find Georgiana standing there dressed in jeans and a t-shirt. She smiled and he could see she wasn't angry anymore. "I didn't answer because I was on my way here."

He felt the draw of her smile. "And why were you coming here?"

"To tell you in person that you were an ass this morning."

Without thinking about what he was doing or why, he reached out his hand and stroked the side of her face. "I was an ass this morning."

"Okay, as long as we both agree."

He took her hand and pulled her into the room. "I'm sorry."

"You're forgiven." She put her hand on his chest, and through the cloth of his shirt, she could feel his heart beating. "I was going to make you hang there a bit longer, but I took pity on you."

He grinned. "Thank you. I was about to make an idiot of myself and send another text begging your forgiveness." He covered her hand with his. "I should've apologized this morning. I should have, even just by text."

"True."

"I was having too much fun eating breakfast with you, completely forgetting the whole conference thing really, and when Rick came our way, I snapped."

"I know." She grimaced. "I probably should've told you that we might run into him here. Sorry about that."

"It's okay."

She pulled him over to the window. "We need to talk before we go to this game."

He looked down at her, seeing the beginning of a blush on her cheeks. "Okay."

She took a deep breath, so deep it was almost a sigh, then said hurriedly, "Here's the thing. I know, *we* know, that this is a really bad idea, and that this has to stay in Seattle. We can't keep this going when we get back to Vermont. But while we're here, I want to do this." She stretched up on her tiptoes and kissed him.

Desire slammed him like a tidal wave. His arms closed around her tightly, pulling her into him for full body contact. Within seconds, they were both breathless from the embrace. Georgiana pulled back reluctantly but smiled as she looked up at him. "So, I take it that I'm not the only one who feels that way?"

Taking a deep breath, trying to control the near-overwhelming urge to pick her up and carry her to the bed, he stroked her bottom lip with his thumb. "No, you're not the only one."

"Then we need to get the rules straight." She gestured to the chairs by the window, her tone bossy. "Sit down. I can't have this conversation with you touching me."

Her tone amused him. "Yes, ma'am."

She sat on the ottoman looking at him. He tried not to notice how her nipples were pressing against the thin cloth, and finally dragged his eyes back to her face. She raised an eyebrow. "I want you; you want me. Just three days ago you started a new job. There is no way that this will play well when we get home, so as I see it, we have two choices. The first choice is that we say last night was incredible, but we need to stop now, and we keep our hands off each other. We don't talk about this again. The second is that while we're here, we are with each other here at night, then when we get on the plane to go home, it's done. What happens in Seattle, stays in Seattle."

"Do you really think the board would have that much of an issue?"

"In your first week, yes. Besides that, you and I have to work together, and when we really get to that, this isn't going to work. Look how quickly you managed to piss me off this morning."

In his heart, he knew she was right. "What about a third option?"

"What's that?"

He reached out to take her hands. "Tonight we're together, tomorrow we bag the conference just to be together alone, then we have tomorrow night. Then we go to the airport and leave what happened here, here."

Deep down, she felt the beginning of a worry that so much time together might be too much, that it would be too hard to walk away from him, but that concern evaporated as his thumbs began to stroke the inside of her wrists. "Damn."

"Damn what?"

She stood up and stepped toward him. His hands rested possessively on her hips, pulling her close. "You do that, and I go stupid. I like option three."

"Me too."

She leaned down to kiss him, then pulled back. "Okay, so we understand the rules?"

"We do."

"Then I'm running back upstairs to grab my wallet and a jacket. I'll see you downstairs in ten minutes?"

"What are you telling Rick?"

"The truth. He's probably figured it out already anyway."

Five minutes later, Georgiana stepped into the lobby and saw Rick sitting on a couch, checking emails on his phone. She sat down next to him and smiled when he didn't even look up. "Hey, ready to go?"

"Yeah, Jack will be right down."

He kept swiping through emails on his phone. "Did you sleep with him in Vermont too, or just here?"

She started to laugh. "I told him you'd have figured it out. Just here. Too much good wine last night."

"There's more than wine there, Gi. Good for you."

She snorted in a most unladylike manner. "It's a case of what happens in Seattle, stays in Seattle. We can't keep going once we get home. He just started the job; you know how school boards react to things like this. Besides, as you know better than most, I'm a pain in the ass to employ. We'll probably want to kill each other professionally before the month is out."

He shook his head. "Not arguing with any of that. I'm just saying that I think it's going to be hard to put this genie back in the bottle."

Just then, Jack stepped off the elevator. Georgiana and Rick stood up, and the three headed to the game.

Chapter Eleven

Over the next three hours, Jack had to admit he couldn't remember the last time he'd had so much fun. The three of them sat on the first-base line, cheered loudly, drank beer and ate junk food. He watched in amusement as Rick and Georgiana had a spirited discussion about bunting, then switched to argue about the ESSA before transitioning back to a conversation about the relative merits of knuckleballs.

After the game, the three went back to the hotel. In the lobby, Rick looked fondly at Georgiana. "As always, thanks for letting me share in your birthday baseball event."

She hugged him. "My pleasure. Thanks for the tickets. And I'll call your mom and dad this weekend to thank them for feeding me."

He smiled. "They'd like that. They still miss you." He looked at them both. "Will I see you guys tomorrow?"

Georgiana picked up Jack's hand and squeezed it. "No. We're bagging tomorrow to spend some time alone before we go home."

As they got on the elevator, Jack wrapped his arm around her, pulling her close. "So, how about you get your stuff and just stay in my room for the next two nights?"

Fifteen minutes later, Jack heard her at the door. Opening it, he felt a visceral pull at the sight of her standing there, bags over her shoulder. She grinned. "Have any room for me?"

"Hell, yes." He took the bags from her. "Come in."

As she walked into the room, an ice bucket with a bottle of sparkling wine, a plate of cheese and crackers and fruit next to it, and a small chocolate cupcake, were carefully arranged on the small side table. "You've been busy."

"I actually took care of all of this before the game." He gestured toward the table. "Happy birthday."

She grinned delightedly. "You can be very sweet. Thank you."

"You mean when I'm not pissing you off?"

"Exactly." Stepping forward, she ran one finger from his mouth to the spot at the base of his throat where she could see the flutter of his pulse. "Do you mind if I take a shower? I love ballparks but now I'm grimy."

"Of course, I don't mind."

"You going to join me?"

Heat spread through him at her invitation. "Happily." He pulled two hotel bathrobes from the closet. "After you."

He turned on the shower before pulling over a chair and putting towels on it. As she undressed, Jack watched, his hands almost twitching with the urge to touch her again. He even found the messy bun that she pulled her hair into unbearably sexy. She smiled at him. "You going to stand there and just watch, or are you showering too?"

"Can't I do both?"

In the shower, she stood under the warm spray then reached for the soap, lathering her hands before she turned toward him. "Turn around."

Over the next long minutes, the two of them took turns soaping each other, the sexual tension growing. When she reached to stroke his manhood, he stopped her. "Nope. I have plans for you after this shower."

"Really?"

"Uh huh."

"And what if my plans involve right now and right here?"

"Patience. You'll like my plans, I promise."

Georgiana could feel her body responding to his words and his touch. Even in the wet warmth of the shower, she could feel her own heat and the need for him to give her the sexual release she'd craved all day was almost more than she could bear. She sulked. "Fine."

Stepping out of the shower, he quickly wrapped a towel around his waist, then chose a fresh one to dry her body with slow caresses. He held a bathrobe while she slipped into it, then put the other one on himself. "Come with me." He pulled her by the hand to the two chairs by the window, tugging the ottoman over, then sitting down on the chair, his feet propped up. "Come sit on my lap."

Georgiana did as he directed, her face showing her hesitancy. "Okay."

Once she was seated, he nibbled the side of her neck. "Do you trust me?"

The touch of his lips made thinking difficult, as did his very apparent arousal pressing against her as she sat on his lap, but her voice was sure. "Yes."

"Then lean back and relax." He reached down to untie her robe, pushing it open before he gently urged her thighs apart. "I need to touch you when I can't be inside you."

"What do you mean?"

"Every time I've touched you in the last twenty-four hours, it's been with the goal of making love to you, being inside you." As he talked, he rested his hands just above her knees, still dropping kisses on her neck and shoulder. "I spent every moment today, even before we agreed to do this tonight, thinking about how much I want you." His hands began to slide up her legs. "So, I need to show you how much I want you, and make you as crazy with desire as I am."

"You know how much I want you. You don't need to show me anything."

"I do." He kissed the hollow of her collarbone. "I need to send you over the edge, just like this, just touching you." He blew gently on her earlobe and watched as her nipples immediately tightened. "Will you let me? Trust me."

For a split second, she felt uncertain. She'd never had a man ask something like this of her. But her need for him was too great. "Of course."

Slowly, he used both hands to stroke the inside of her legs, hearing her breathing change as his hands warmed her flesh. He continued to caress her inner thighs with one hand as his other reached up to gently pinch first one, then the other nipple. His hands slipped higher, moving closer to the apex of her thighs and as she began to squirm, he held her still. "No. Right now this is just about your pleasure, not mine." With one finger, he gently stroked the line between her legs, hearing her whimper in pleasure. "I need to do this." Whispering in her ear, he kept stroking her, finally, slipping his fingers into her wet warmth. "Jesus, you're the sexiest woman I've ever known. Just touching you makes me insane."

"Jack, please."

"Please, what?"

"I need you inside me." Her tone was pleading, even as she began to move with his insistent fingers.

"I'm inside you, baby. Stop fighting it and let yourself enjoy this."

While his fingers continued to slide in and out of her in a timeless rhythm, her breathing turned to gasping and he could feel her muscles begin to tighten around him before she gave in. He felt her spasm around him, her entire body shaking like a leaf.

Still feeling her body tighten and release in the most powerful orgasm of her life, Georgiana sat forward, shedding her robe altogether as she stood before untying his, then moving to straddle him. "Now, Jack. Now!"

He reached up to grasp her hips tightly, feeling her body still throbbing as he went as deeply into her as he could over and over again. He felt her body clasp him tightly as she came again and with a shout, he poured into her.

Long minutes later he stirred, still holding her tightly in his arms. *Jesus, what the hell is this woman doing to me?* He'd never wanted to make love to a woman like that before, just so he could please her. He'd never come so close to orgasm just knowing he was giving pleasure. He kissed her temple, stroking her bare back. "You're going to be the death of me, lady."

She pulled back, a satisfied smile on her face. "Thank you." She reached up to cup his face with her hands, then leaned forward to kiss him. "That was amazing."

"Happy birthday."

She started to laugh. "I may get to like birthdays."

"How about a snack now?"

Over the next hour, they sat and chatted, drinking the bottle of Prosecco and nibbling on the cheese and fruit plate before sharing the cupcake. When the picnic was done, Georgiana went to brush her teeth, then came back to gaze at him. "Bed?"

In bed, both naked, her head resting on his shoulder, his voice rumbled in her ear. "What do you want to do tomorrow?"

"Wander around, go to Pike's Market, maybe the Space Needle..."

"Sounds like a plan."

They had been sleeping for a few hours when she awoke. Without making a sound, she rolled over and started stroking his chest. She knew the instant he woke, feeling the energy in the room change. His voice was deep, still sleepy. "You know, I was trying to be a gentleman and let you sleep a bit tonight, since I certainly didn't let you sleep last night."

"I can sleep when I get home. I can't do this then..." She continued stroking his chest, each time moving lower and lower, feeling his muscles tighten with her touch.

He rolled on his side to look at her, the only light coming from a slit between the curtains. "Then don't let me stop you."

They made love slowly, without talking, their bodies entwining with a familiarity that would have seemed impossible just a day before. Georgiana was cradled against his chest. He stroked her back, not in the way he had earlier, but now just needing to touch her. He tried to keep his voice light. "Ready to sleep again for a bit?"

"Not really." Her voice sounded sad. "I don't really want to sleep when we have so little time together."

He kissed her temple. "I know."

Chapter Twelve

The next day they made love in the shower before getting dressed. Walking through the sunshine toward Pike's Market, they held hands like a couple of teenagers, ducking into a bakery to linger over pastries and coffee. Afterwards, they wandered through the market and surrounding neighborhood, Georgiana buying a gift for her grandfather's birthday, then picking out a pair of new earrings. Jack watched in amusement as she kept going back to look at a particular bracelet: hammered silver with an inlay of gold Celtic knots. He tried to think of a way to distract her so he could buy it as a belated birthday gift, but couldn't come up with a way that wouldn't seem suspicious. He knew it was silly, but he really wanted to give her a tangible sign of their time together. Suddenly, she stopped and handed him her shopping bags. "I'm going to run to the ladies' room. I'll be right back."

While she was gone, he quickly walked back to the little kiosk, handed the clerk cash, asking her to wrap the gift. She had just put it in a bag when Georgiana reappeared. "Hey."

He smiled. "Hey, yourself."

"What did you get?"

"An early birthday gift for my niece."

That afternoon, they visited the Space Needle before heading to a pub for an early dinner. After dinner, he pulled her to a stop outside the restaurant. "Ready to head back to the hotel now?" He stroked her cheek, smiling as she stepped closer to slide her arm around him. "I want to be alone with you."

"Me too."

Back in his room, she looked at him, her eyes dark in the soft lighting. She led him over to the windows, looking out at the city as it began to glow below. He wrapped his arms around her and smiled as she leaned back against him, whispering in her ear. "This is how it started. You leaned back against me and when we touched each other without an audience, I knew I was sunk."

"The sinking was a hell of a lot of fun, wasn't it?"

"It was. It *is*." He tightened his embrace. "I'm not ready for it to end."

"Me either."

He nuzzled her neck. "Tell me again why we would be an issue?"

She ran her fingers down his left arm, loving the way his skin felt, already feeling her body craving his touch again. "Jackson, for the last few days, we've been able to forget that I work for you. We get home tomorrow and that's our reality. We already saw how quickly we managed to piss each other off about Rick. Just wait until it's something I really care about, like lunch menus or the bus schedule. The board will have an issue from a supervisory standpoint. Who, other than us, would really know if this was a consensual arrangement, or me being coerced by a superior?"

He kissed her cheek. "How could anyone think you could be coerced about anything? You're not exactly a shrinking violet."

He felt her take a deep breath, and she moved, her left hand coming up to rub the raised design on her right arm. "Jack, when I started at Deerlane, I was sexually harassed by someone who used to work for the district. It got pretty ugly. It was bad enough that I almost left, and all of it was *very* public. If people found out that something happened this quickly between us, it would cause a whole lot of gossip. Neither one of us needs that."

For a moment he felt rage flow through him at the thought of any man intimidating her, and he wanted to ask a million questions, but with her simple explanation, he knew she was right. "Dammit, why the hell did the stars have to align this way?"

She turned in his arms and grinned wickedly. "Look at it the other way. Aren't we lucky that we got these few days together?"

He growled and swept her up in his arms. "Fine, Pollyanna." He strode toward the bedroom. "Then at least we have tonight."

They barely slept that evening. In the end, they made love four more times, but it was more like one long romantic interlude. As dawn broke, he looked down at her and brushed a curl back from her eyes. "Damn, lady. I am going to miss sharing a bed with you."

"Likewise."

They showered and dressed in near silence, then finished packing before heading down to the hotel restaurant for breakfast. At the airport, they sat next to each other, not touching or talking. Finally, their flight was called, and again, Georgiana's row was called before Jack's. She stood and picked up her carry-on before leaning down to kiss him briefly. "Thanks for a helluva trip." She took a deep breath, and he saw her pull her professional persona over herself like a cloak. "I'll see you in Vermont, Dr. Ryder."

When his section boarded a few minutes later, he looked for her as he came down the aisle, but her eyes were firmly glued to the window.

Back in Vermont, they gathered their luggage. At the car, Jack looked at her. "Want me to drive?"

"I've got it."

On the ride home they listened to music, barely talking, both of them trying to re-acclimate. At his house, Georgiana walked to the hatchback and helped him retrieve his bags. "See you soon."

"See you soon."

That evening, Georgiana opened her suitcase and was startled to find a small, wrapped package among her things. She pulled the gift tag from under the ribbon and read it with surprise. *Belatedly, happy birthday. Wear it and think of me. Jack*

She carefully opened the small box and stared in awe at the bracelet she had so admired in Seattle. She slipped it on her wrist and smiled. Picking up her cell phone, she texted him. *"Thank you, it's beautiful. No matter what, I will think of you, of us, whenever I wear it."*

A couple hours later, she smiled as her phone buzzed and she saw the new text from Molly. *"In a meeting but wanted to see how the trip home went. What's the plan with J?"*

"No plan. The trip was fine. It felt weird to go from 0 to 60 to 0 again."

"Gi! Stop being stupid. If you like this guy, don't give up on him!"

Georgiana sat looking at the phone, then slowly typed, *"The thing is, I don't really know if, even if it was possible, if he'd be interested. And, it would be sooooooooooo complicated. Better just holding onto the memories. Love you, gotta go."* And she turned off her phone.

Chapter Thirteen

On Wednesday, she was at her desk when Dot buzzed through. "Hey, what's up?"

"Our new boss is about to come through the front door. Were you expecting him?"

"No, but I told him to stop by whenever. Send him in."

Georgiana stayed seated at her desk as Jackson walked through the door. His smile was coolly professional. "Georgiana. Good morning. I trust today is okay for a visit?"

She matched her tone to his. "Like I said, any day is fine."

Over the next hour, she took him on a tour of every inch of the school, introducing him to students, teachers, and staff. She then took him back to her office and showed him the schedule and staffing plan for the upcoming school year.

As the meeting progressed, Jackson felt himself relax, realizing that the two of them were having a perfectly normal professional conversation. Maybe she'd been right, they could keep what had happened in the past.

Over the next month, Jackson realized that Rick's comment that Georgiana's ability to compartmentalize was impressive was absolutely the truth. He didn't see or sense so much as a hint that she remembered their time together. The only sign that anything had happened was the bracelet that was always on her wrist.

The last week of August, Jack's assistant superintendent, Tony, strolled into his office. "So, what're you doing this weekend?"

Jack shrugged as he leaned back in his chair. "Don't know yet, I'm still getting to know the options around here."

"Then I have a suggestion for you. This weekend is the refugee festival in Bolton, and it's really cool."

"*Refugee* festival?"

"Yeah, I know it sounds weird but it's an annual event with all the groups who have come to Vermont over the years. The Bosnians, the Lost Boys, Syrians, Bantus, families from Bhutan, Mexicans, and El Salvadorans, and a couple other groups are all there. They provide the food and music and there are craft booths. It's all for a free-will donation to support resettlement efforts here. It's awesome. Georgiana helps organize it."

That caught his attention. "What?"

"George, she's on the resettlement board, so she helps put this all together."

"Really?"

"And if you're going, bring a tent and sleeping bag. You can camp there for free, and the music goes most of the night."

"Sounds like fun."

"You're welcome to follow us over."

"That would be great."

Saturday morning, Jack pulled into Tony's driveway, smiling as Tony's eldest daughter Allie, whom he'd met only a month before, came running out of the house and launched herself at him, squeezing him in a huge hug. "Jack, Daddy says you're going to the festival too!"

He had to admit how much it pleased him that she sounded so happy. "I am."

"Do you want me to ride with you, so you won't be lonely?"

Jack looked down at the seven-year-old and grinned. "Allie, I'd love to have you ride with me, if that's okay with your mom and dad."

An hour later, after Allie had explained everything about the festival to him, Jack pulled into a parking space. "Okay, Allie, now you need to show me what to do."

Her look was incredulous. "We look for George, silly."

Walking along with their family, Jack basked in their energy and love.

Suddenly, Allie started jumping up and down, her voice jubilant. "There she is!"

Angela looked at her oldest fondly. "She's headed our way, Pumpkin. Patience. She'll be here in a few minutes."

Jack watched as Georgiana walked across the field toward them. She was almost to them when Allie took off like a shot. Georgiana knelt down and braced herself for the little girl's hug. The two of them walked back toward the group, holding hands and chatting away. Jack tried to redirect his thinking as he realized how good Georgiana looked in a brightly patterned sundress and a straw hat with a soft gauzy scarf draped around her neck. She looked like she should be on an exotic beach, not in a dusty field in Vermont.

When they reached the group, Georgiana hugged Angela tightly. "Hey Angie, so glad you're here!"

"Me, too, Gigi. Seems like forever since we've done something just for fun."

Georgiana kissed Zaccheus on the forehead as he grinned toothlessly at her. "Hey, little dude." She then leaned down to hug Madi. "My favorite littlest princess!"

Straightening, she kissed Tony's cheek. "Thanks for coming."

"Wouldn't miss it."

Georgiana turned toward Jack, trying to keep her voice normal. "Jack. I didn't know you were coming."

Jack couldn't tell from her voice if she was pleased or not. "I didn't either. Tony invited me last night."

"Great."

Just then Allie yanked at Georgiana's skirt. "Is he here? Is he?"

Georgiana stroked her hair. "Not yet, kiddo. But he texted me about an hour ago that he'd just crossed the border, so he should be here any time."

Allie's face got serious. "Is he going to call you when he gets here, or should I listen for him?"

Georgiana chuckled. "What do you think?"

"Listen for him."

"That would be my suggestion." Georgiana looked at the adults, trying not to notice that Jack looked delectable in his soft gray linen shirt and jeans. "Hey, are you guys staying tonight?"

Tony nodded. "We are, and I think Jack is." He looked over at his friend. "Jack?"

Jack felt heat spread through him at the idea of staying here overnight in possible close proximity to Georgiana. "I'm staying."

Georgiana felt a wave of nerves hit her. How was she going to stay away from him here? Away from work, his magnetic pull was almost more than she could bear to think about. "Well, I'm up on the hill like always; you're welcome to go set up camp up there."

Angela smiled. "Sounds great."

Throughout the day, Jackson never stopped moving. After containing his shock as he met a group of Lost Boys of the Sudan, who clearly were old friends of Georgiana's, he found himself meeting so many new people he couldn't keep track. He ate incredible foods from around the world, picked out bracelets to buy for his nieces and sisters, then got coerced into a brutal soccer game with Tony and some others. The yelling in the game was multi-lingual, except for the cursing, which somehow seemed to flow into English pretty well.

As he came off the soccer field at the half, he smiled at Georgiana as she brought him a bottle of water. He twisted the top off. "Thanks."

She shook her head ruefully trying not to stare at the legs his shorts exposed, and really tried not to look at his bare chest. *Damn, why did he have to be on the skins team?* "Good to see you can be as much of a competitive idiot as the rest of them. You know, if you're going to play soccer in the full sun for over an hour, you should at least have a sip of water once in a while."

"From what I hear, you calling me competitive is a bit like the pot calling the kettle black." He grinned and playfully slid the cold bottle down her arm, not missing when her eyes darkened with awareness. "Are you taking care of me?"

She rolled her eyes. "As one of the organizers, and the only one whose native language is English, if you collapse of heat exhaustion, I'll be stuck with the damn insurance paperwork."

"Yeah, yeah." Jack heard his name being called. "I think I have to go be a competitive idiot again."

"You do."

His smile was full-out flirtatious. "Going to stay and watch? I'll buy you a beer after."

For a moment, he saw the hesitation in her eyes. "Jackson..."

He held up his hands in a gesture of surrender. "As friends, just friends and colleagues."

"Fine, *a* beer."

After the game ended, Jack walked off the field, laughing with the other players, and agreed to join their men's league. It'd been a long time since he'd played that hard and he'd had a blast. He walked toward Georgiana, who was lying on her back, propped up on her elbows on the hillside. She had watched the game, but he hoped she'd really stayed to watch *him*. Her sun hat was tipped forward so her eyes were shaded, and Jack let himself enjoy the view, carefully noticing how the neckline of her sundress dipped just low enough to expose the shadow between her breasts. She'd tucked the skirt under her, so her legs were bare to just above the knees. For a moment, he imagined sitting beside her and sliding his hand up her leg, feeling her sun-kissed skin warm with his touch.

Jack stopped at the bottom of the hill and met her eyes for a moment before pulling his t-shirt over his head. He slowly climbed the hill and flopped down beside her, rolling on his side so he could see her face without turning his head. "Hey."

"Hey." She sat up and he tried not to stare as her breasts pushed against the thin fabric of the dress as she moved. "Drink water, dummy." She handed him another bottle.

"Thanks."

"You're welcome."

The two of them laid on the grass, Georgiana explaining to him where the other players had come from originally and Jack drinking the water. When he was done, he stood up, and held out his hand. "C'mon, I need to change, and I promised you a beer."

Taking his hand, Georgiana let him pull her to her feet, then brushed off her dress. "You go change, I'll go check on the various stations. See if you can find Tony and everyone for dinner."

He grinned smugly. "You're trying hard not to be alone with me."

Her tone held a warning. "Jack..."

He stepped closer. "What?"

She swatted his arm. "Get over yourself, Dr. Ryder."

"Ouch, reverting to the 'Doctor' defense."

She laughed in spite of herself. "Yeah, yeah."

An hour later, Jack came up behind Georgiana as she talked with a group of women wearing hijabs, all of them, including Georgiana, speaking quickly in Arabic. Jack placed his hand on her lower back, telling himself he didn't want to interrupt the conversation. In reality, he just wanted to touch her again.

She recognized his touch immediately and felt the familiar surge wanting nothing more than to turn into his arms, which she knew she shouldn't do. Looking over her shoulder quickly, she raised one eyebrow at him, then stepped forward, breaking the contact. She kissed the oldest woman on the cheek, quickly saying something in a language he didn't recognize, then gestured toward the beer tent. The other women looked at Jack, several giggled, and one said something to Georgiana that brought gales of laughter from all of them.

Georgiana grinned at him. "A beer, Dr. Ryder?"

"Lead the way." Once they stepped away from the other women, he asked, "So what was the giggling about and why do I think I was the brunt of it?"

She laughed outright. "You were. I told them you were buying me a beer hoping that I'd finally agree to dance with you tonight. They had lots of comments about your looks." She looked up at him. "All complimentary. But their suggestions went a lot further than dancing."

His tone was dry. "So let me get this straight. You're standing there speaking fluent Arabic, gossiping about what a hottie I am with a group of Muslim women."

She corrected him, trying not to laugh. "I'm not fluent in Arabic, just functional, but…" For a moment, she let herself look at him flirtatiously. "Yup."

That night, the festival shifted to a huge bonfire and music. The ethnic music varied throughout the hours, and as the stars started to glow in the sky, many people started to dance.

Jack watched in wonder as Georgiana danced with the large group of Africans in a choreographed tribal dance, moving so intently that he couldn't look away. As others joined the dance, she came over to Jack, and leaned in to speak in his ear. He felt his body respond to the heat of her breath. "Come dance with me."

She stood back up and held out her hand. He took it and followed her into the swirling crowd, wondering, *What the hell changed so she's touching me again?*

They danced for hours before the music softened and slowed. As the moon rose high in the black sky, Georgiana finally stopped dancing. Without speaking, they moved to the side of the group, almost hidden by the shadows. "It's time to call it a night," she said. She looked down at her bare feet, and even in the semi-darkness, he could see her blush. "Thanks for dancing with me."

He knew Tony and Angie had taken the children back to the tents to sleep long ago, so he gave in to temptation and reached out to stroke her cheek. "My pleasure."

She reached up to cover his hand with hers. "Jack…"

He leaned down and kissed her softly. Her sharp intake of breath showed how surprised she was, and Jack felt her pull back, just before melting into him, her arms going up around his neck as she returned his kiss.

Long moments passed as they stood in the shadows, kissing as if they'd been apart forever. His hands slipped down her back, pulling her closer, needing to feel her body against his.

Suddenly she stepped back so the cool night air rushed between them. "We can't do this."

He tried to pull her toward him again. "We can."

She looked around, seeing people closer to them than she wanted. "Let's take a walk."

They walked hand in hand away from the fire, heading up the hill toward their tents. She stopped and motioned to the ground. "Can we sit and talk for a bit?"

"Of course."

Seated, still holding his hand, she looked down at her feet. "We can't do this, Jack. We can't."

"Damn it, Georgiana, we can." He picked up her hand and brought it to his mouth, pressing a kiss to the back of her hand. "Do you want to?"

"Do I want to what? Make love? You know I do." She looked uncomfortable. "Or at least I *think* you know that."

He grinned. "Well… Let's say you do give mixed messages sometimes."

She ignored him. "Do I want to go out with you? Yes, I do. But we can't. We can't."

"Go out with me." Jack moved closer, one hand stroking her upper arm. "I don't mean sleep with me tonight, no matter how much I want you to, just say you'll go out with me. To dinner, to a movie, to a concert, whatever."

Georgiana let go of his hand to wrap her arms around her bent knees. "I can't, *we* can't. We both have public roles, and this would be bad. We can't do this."

"The board would have an issue with me, not you. If I'm willing to take that chance, why can't you?"

"Jack, I can't. This, my world here, my job here, it's all too important to me. I can't risk it."

"That's bullshit and you know it."

Pain crossed her face. "We can't risk this." She suddenly leaned forward to kiss him lingeringly. "I wish it were different, Jack." And she almost ran up the hill to her tent.

The next morning, Jack awoke to the sound of a zipper, which he recognized after a moment as a tent door opening. Still in his sleeping bag, he sat up and rubbed his eyes, listening for any conversation but hearing none. He laid back down but gave up the idea of sleeping after a few minutes. He quietly pulled on jeans and a t-shirt, not bothering with shoes.

From where she sat on the ground, leaning against an old maple tree, Georgiana watched as he opened the door of his tent, slowly stepped out and stood to stretch, unaware that she was watching him. For a moment, she gave in to the temptation and boldly looked at him, taking in every detail: his mussed hair, the jeans resting low on his hips, the t-shirt hanging perfectly on him, even his bare feet, which for some reason seemed so sexy to her.

His expression went from open and relaxed to guarded when he realized her eyes were on him. "Good morning."

Damn! The morning huskiness of his voice resonated deep within her. "Morning. Coffee?"

How could she sound so normal after the night before? He tried to sound casual. "You just happen to have a Keurig in your tent?"

She shook her head and reached behind her. "No, but I happen to have a Thermos of coffee that I just went down to get." She handed him an enamel mug without rising. "Here, there's sugar in it for you. The coffee has cream already in it."

He felt a rush of pleasure. Even if she wouldn't go out with him now, she not only remembered how he liked his coffee, but had gone out of her way to prepare it for him. "You did this for me?" He sat down beside her before filling his mug with coffee. "Thank you."

"You're welcome."

As Georgiana threw a load of laundry into the washer later that day, she gazed out the back window toward the pond, thinking back over the events of the weekend. Her phone buzzed and she noticed that two different texts had come in simultaneously.

The first was from Jackson. *"Thanks for a great weekend."*

The second was from Molly. *"How was the festival?"*

She messaged Jack. *"You're welcome. Have a good week."* Then she hit speed dial for Molly.

Molly answered on the second ring. "Wow, it had to be quite a festival if you're calling me instead of just texting."

"Nah. Just putting in laundry." She pulled a seltzer from the fridge. "Mol, I have an issue."

"Your boss?"

"Why do you say that?"

"Oh, don't get pissy on me, Gi. You and I talked when you were in Seattle, Rick said he'd never seen you look at a guy like you look at Jack, and besides, all other issues you handle on your own."

"Hold on." Georgiana sat down on the couch, swinging herself around so her feet hung over the back and her head hung down toward the floor. "Okay, I'm in thinking position. Help me figure this out."

"Figure what out? What happened?"

"He came to the festival, I gave him mixed messages, then I asked him to dance with me, he kissed me, we kissed for a while, then I told him we can't do this."

"Do what?"

"Be a couple. We can't be a couple."

"Why?"

"Why?!?" Georgiana's voice grew louder and incredulous. "He's my boss. That's why! Jesus, Mol, you should understand this better than most."

"Okay, here's the thing. The only one who could possibly get in trouble here is him, not you. And unless there is a no-dating-employees clause in his contract, I don't think even he could get in trouble. I get that the board might not like it, and maybe they could be hyper-vigilant about other matters that they can control, but if that's okay with him, then date the man!"

This was not the answer Georgiana wanted to hear. "You just don't get it."

"I get it. I get that you were burned gossip-wise with Tyler. But this is different. This isn't a creep hitting on you. Shit, you went to bed with him, and as I remember your account, you kissed him first."

Georgiana sighed. "I guess..."

"What's there to think about? Do you like him? I mean, beyond the physical attraction, do you like him? What about him appeals to you other than how much you want to jump his bones?"

"I do like him." Georgiana wiggled on the couch, finding a more comfortable spot. "If I step aside from the physical, if we didn't work together, I'd be doing everything to make something happen with him. He smart, funny, sexy as hell, he likes baseball, loves the same outdoor stuff I do, and shit, he even likes *The Goonies*."

"Well, that's the clincher. We all know that if a guy likes that movie, you're hooked." Molly's voice softened. "Look bestie, here's the thing. There are still things that are awkward for us to talk about, but I get that the last time you fell in love with someone, it didn't work out. I know that what you had with Boone was love, but you weren't *in* love. It seems like you really like this new guy, and yet you're not letting it happen. Maybe you need to think about whether you're putting up roadblocks here because you're afraid this might be a serious thing. Maybe claiming it's a job-related thing is easier than dealing with the emotions?"

Still upside down, Georgiana rubbed her forehead. *Was Molly right?* "I'll think about it, I promise."

"Good, that's all I ask."

"I'm gonna go get ready for the week, okay?"

"Sounds good. Love you."

Chapter Fourteen

Jackson found himself thinking of Georgiana more and more. He'd be running and suddenly think of how much fun he'd had at the baseball game with her. One night, he even looked up the availability of Sox tickets, wondering if she'd be interested in going to Boston for an afternoon game on a weekend. He felt like a teenager with a crush.

The second week of September he had a brainstorm. She'd refused to go out with him, but what about asking her to share a ride to the Spartan Race? Time together without an audience, no strings attached.

On Friday afternoon, as the administrators' meeting ended, he moved to stand near the door. As the principals left the room, he put out a hand to stop Georgiana, gently touching her arm. "Could you stay a moment? I need to speak to you about something."

"Of course." She stepped back to the side of the entry and watched while the others left.

As another principal stopped in front of Jackson, he started asking a detailed question regarding free and reduced lunch eligibility. Jackson tried his best to answer in a concise manner, but couldn't help seeing Georgiana glance at her watch. Jack finally blew out a frustrated breath. "Georgiana, no need to stay. I can catch up with you over the next few days."

"Are you sure?"

"Go ahead. I'm going to be here a while."

"Okay, call me if you want."

"I will."

That night, Jack sat holding his phone, debating whether to call her. He had really wanted to ask her in person so he could see her reaction. But if he was just asking her to share a ride, it would seem less pointed to just call or text her. Texting seemed the best approach. With a sigh he typed. *"Hi, I wanted to talk to you today to see if you wanted to ride together to The Spartan."*

A minute later, his phone rang. Georgiana's voice showed her disbelief. "You are completely unbelievable. We just had a long conversation about not dating, and now you ask me out again?"

He laughed, despite realizing that would probably make her even madder. "I wasn't asking you out." He explained. "We're both racing next weekend, it's a five hour round trip drive, and it seems stupid for us to take two cars when we could ride together."

"Really?" She asked, her voice loaded with suspicion. "This isn't an end run to change my mind?"

He decided to stick with humor. "Wow, Georgiana, wow. Pretty sure of your appeal, aren't you?"

He could hear the smile in her voice as she capitulated. "Fine. Yes, a ride would be great. Thank you."

"Then next Saturday, you come on over to my house at five. I'll drive."

"Sounds good."

Five minutes later, his phone buzzed with a text. *"Thanks for the suggestion. See you then if not before."*

A few days later, Jackson stopped for gas on his way to Deerlane. While waiting to pay, he heard someone call his name. "Hey, you're Dr. Ryder, aren't you?"

Jack turned to see a small, paunchy, bespectacled man approaching him. "I am."

"Tim Mattison." He stuck out his hand. "I'm a sub in the district. I was going to call you, but figured I would just go ahead and introduce myself when I saw you here."

Jackson shook the offered hand. "Nice to meet you, Mr. Mattison. What can I do for you?"

"Well, I'm not getting called much lately, and I just wanted to see if there was an issue."

"I'm not aware of any problems. It's the beginning of the school year, so hopefully we don't have a need for a lot of subs yet."

"Hmm, well, I thought I'd ask. Most years I've been called more by now."

"I'm sure you'll be called when there is a need."

"Suppose you're right. Sorry to have bothered you, and welcome to the area."

Jackson was buzzed through the front door at Deerlane Community School. "Good morning, Dot."

"Good morning, Dr. Ryder."

"Is Georgiana around?"

She nodded. "She's teaching PE down in the gym."

Jack walked down the hallway, wondering why she was teaching PE when Tim Mattison was complaining about not being utilized.

As he stood in the doorway to the gym, he watched Georgiana doing yoga with a group of high schoolers and tiny children, who he presumed were the pre-school students. For a split second, he had to work to repress his very physical reaction to seeing her leading the group in a downward dog pose. As soon as she realized he was standing in the door, she stood up and said, "Chase and Ben, you're up. Elders, remember to help your little partners with the poses." Georgiana watched while the young men moved to the front of the group and seamlessly began instructing them in the next pose. She came to the doorway of the gym. "Dr. Ryder."

He got right to the point. "Why are you teaching PE? Get a sub."

"We couldn't find one, then Janie had to go home sick, so the little ones joined PE for the afternoon."

"I just saw a Tim Mattison at the gas station, and he said he isn't being called in. Why didn't Dot call him?"

Her voice kept perfectly calm. "Because I won't have him in my building."

"He's a vetted sub in this district. Call him."

She shook her head. "I won't. He makes children uncomfortable, and the female staff find him creepy. I trust them."

Jack's tone became colder. "Garbage. The district vetted him."

Georgiana moved so she could see the students more clearly. "I won't hire him."

"You're disobeying a directive? Without a legitimate complaint or any evidence of wrong-doing?"

She nodded, her eyes still on the students. "I am."

His voice became dangerously quiet. "You *will* start calling him to sub. Do I make myself clear?"

"You do." She looked at him for a split second, her eyes cold. "If we're done, I need to get back to my class."

The next day, Jackson finished his last morning meeting right before lunch. He stretched and called out to his assistant. "Priscilla, I'm going to go do drop-ins at the schools. I'll be back in plenty of time for my meeting with Tyler Abrams at three."

"Sounds good."

Jack visited two schools rather briefly, before he admitted to himself that he was really just filling time before he dropped in at Deerlane to see if Georgiana had followed his directive. How was he ever going to get her to go out with him if they were battling professionally? Pulling into the parking lot, he pushed the buzzer and waited for the response. No answer. He pushed the buzzer again. No answer. The third time he pushed the buzzer a man's voice came through the speaker. "Yes?"

"It's Dr. Ryder."

"Hold on, I need to figure out what button to push."

Once the door clicked, Jackson walked down the hall to the main office and almost fell over when he found Tim Mattison at the front desk where Dot normally sat. "Tim! What're you doing here?"

The man shrugged. "I got the call they needed someone today. When I got here, Dr. Hewitt said I'd be subbing for Dot because she was needed elsewhere."

A flash of anger filled Jackson. He tried to keep his voice level. "Where's Dr. Hewitt?"

"She's teaching French down in Room 116."

Jack stalked down to Room 116, trying to tamp down his temper. He opened the door to the classroom. "Bonjour!"

The class chorused. "Bonjour."

"Dr. Hewitt, may I have a word?"

"Sure." Georgiana gave instructions in French, then walked toward Jack, stepping into the hallway so she could keep an eye on the class through the sidelights. As much as he tried not to notice how she looked, for just a moment he felt himself react to seeing her in high-heeled sandals, a fitted black skirt and a white blouse, the ever-present bracelet around her wrist. "Yes?"

"You know what I'm going to say." He took a deep breath. "I specifically told you to hire Tim for subbing and I find him sitting in the office, and you in a classroom again. You were given a directive."

As with the day before, she didn't look at him, but kept her eyes on the students. "And I followed the directive. I told you I would not have him work with children, but you said to hire him anyway. I did. I hired him to sit at the front desk and answer the phone and unlock the door. I moved Dot to pre-school. I did what you said."

His voice rose. "You did not, and you know it. I told you to hire him to teach, not answer the door."

"I told you that I wouldn't have him work with children."

"You were given a directive."

"I know. And I chose to follow it in a way that was both following your order and honoring my professional beliefs."

"Then I have no choice but to say that you'll be in my office at 4:00 today to formally discuss your behavior." He tried to soften his tone. "Of course, you can, and should, bring representation from the union with you."

She rolled her eyes. "I don't need representation. I'll see you at 4:00."

At five minutes of four, Georgiana arrived at Jackson's outer office. As she entered, his office door opened and he walked out, still chatting with a man she couldn't see. Her stomach clenched violently when Tyler Abrams came into view. She felt like she'd been kicked in the stomach. Her face went paper-white instantly.

Jackson clearly missed her reaction. "Georgiana, I don't know if you know Chittenden Orange Superintendent Tyler Abrams?"

Before she could respond, Tyler cut in. "Oh, we know each other." Something in his tone made Jack uncomfortable as Tyler continued. "Hi, Georgiana, good to see you, as always."

"Tyler."

"How are things with you?"

"Fine."

Just then Tony, the assistant superintendent, popped out of Jackson's office. "Georgiana, I need to see you for a moment before your meeting. Can you pop into the conference room with me, please?" He looked at Tyler. "Sorry to interrupt, you know how these things go."

"Of course." Tyler's voice dropped lower. "Again, good to see you. Hope we can catch up soon."

Georgiana stood, desperate to get out of the room. "Where did you want to meet, Tony?"

"Conference room."

Now in private, Tony looked at her in horror. "Shit, George. I didn't realize you were going to be out there. Jack had me sit in on his meeting with

Tyler, then told me I needed to stay for a personnel issue. If I'd known you were out there, I would've had you moved so you didn't run into him."

Georgiana tried to focus on the man in front of her, trying to repress her revulsion at having seen Tyler in the other room. "It's okay. I appreciate that you would have had you known."

"You okay?"

"Yes." She looked at her friend as the shocked expression started to leave her eyes. "No, but I will be." She stood up straight, took in a huge breath, her facial expression showing her inner determination. "I will be fine."

Jackson poked his head into the conference room, his voice terse. "Tony, may I see you for a moment?"

In his office, Jack looked at Tony in confusion and irritation. "What the hell just happened?"

"Are you reprimanding Georgiana?" Tony demanded.

"Yes. No, not formally. This is just a conversation about a choice she made about substitute teachers. But what does that have to do with what I just saw in the outer office?"

"Okay." Tony tried to soften his tone a bit. "Did you pull her file to read it?"

Jack felt irritated that a subordinate was questioning his professional practice, as well as avoiding his question. "No, the matter is pretty simple. Why?"

"Because that ass Tyler Abrams sexually harassed her when he was here. And somewhere in her file is a formal letter from this district saying that there would never again be a situation where she was put in the same room with him without prior notice."

"What?" Jack tried to follow what Tony was telling him.

Tony nodded. "That was the agreement settled upon to protect her, as well as protect the district from getting its ass sued for putting her in a hostile work environment." Tony shook his head, still perturbed by the situation. "When I heard her voice, I knew I had to get her out of there. Saying I needed to meet with her was the best excuse I could think of at the moment."

Jack felt stupid for not having read her file sooner. "What happened?" He clarified. "I mean, what happened between them?"

Tony tried to keep his disgust out of his voice. "The first Christmas she worked here, she went to the admin holiday party alone."

"And?"

"And Tyler had too much to drink and kept pestering her. When she left, he followed her out to the car, put his hands on her and tried to kiss her. I'm sure she could've handled it by herself, but Mike, the principal of Centerville, and his wife were also leaving, saw the whole thing, and intervened. Tyler got his hand slapped but continued to hit on her on the sly. He just wouldn't stop. Charlie stomped on him pretty hard. George just wanted the matter dropped. She didn't want to be on anyone's radar for any reason. At the next holiday party..."

Jack's voice was full of cynical disbelief. "Let me guess. It happened again."

"Yeah. It was pretty much an on-going thing the whole time she'd been here. Anyway, at that party, Tyler had been drinking and being overly obnoxious. George has started sorta dating a guy who's in her brother's unit, and she brought him to the party. However, when she was in the kitchen by herself, Tyler attacked her. My understanding is that he cornered her in the back part of the kitchen, had her pinned against the counter, and had his hands all over her before she was able to yell loud enough for her date to intervene. To this day, I'm surprised he didn't kill Tyler. So Charlie loaned Tyler out to Lyndon State for the rest of the school year, and he was told to apply for jobs elsewhere. The district drafted a letter, so it would be in writing, that George wouldn't be put in a situation where she was around him without prior notice."

"Shit." Jack tried to think, both angry about how she'd been treated and furious at himself for not knowing and therefore putting her in that situation.

"Uh huh."

Jack stood up. "Okay, I need to get her in here." He went to the door. "Priscilla, could you get Georgiana?"

"Of course."

George walked into the room and Jack gestured to the empty chair in front of his desk next to Tony. "Please, have a seat."

She sat down silently, not looking at him, but Jack could see how deathly pale she was.

He sat down at his desk and tried to keep his voice completely professional. "You know why you're here, but first, I need to bring up what just happened in the outer office."

She kept her eyes averted, her voice icy. "No, you don't."

"Yes, I do." He said firmly, but not unkindly.

Her voice was sharp, and a flush of color returned to her cheeks as she looked at him with palpable anger. "Let me be clear, *Dr.* Ryder. I have an agreement with this district regarding Tyler Abrams and the district just chose to not follow that agreement. I will not speak with you any further about this without my lawyer present." She sat up straighter in her chair and took a deep breath. "I respectfully request that you say whatever you need regarding what happened with Tim Mattison and let me go back to work."

Jackson chose his words carefully. "I'm sorry about what just happened. I didn't know your history with Abrams. That's not an excuse, as I should have read the file. I sincerely apologize."

Georgiana tried to relax her grip on her right arm, but she was still fuming. "Do you not know enough about sexual harassment to understand that continuing to bring it up continues the harassment? I will not have that conversation with you." Her voice was cold as steel.

Jack tried to focus on the original reason for their meeting. "Georgiana, we're meeting today because I specifically told you to hire Tim Mattison as a substitute teacher, and you refused. When I told you a second time, you hired him, but not in the position designated."

She shrugged. "I'm not disputing that I refused to follow your directive as you intended it. In addition, I don't plan on rebutting anything here. I'm anxious to get back to my school so I can get ready for my community dinner."

"Do you understand that this sort of behavior in regard to a directive can't continue? That any further such refusal would be seen as insubordination?"

Suddenly her eyes showed a flash of irritation. "Of course, I do."

Jack realized he was reacting emotionally to the situation, wanting to apologize again for what had happened with Abrams, trying to hold onto his professionalism regarding the reprimand.

"I'm asking for a truthful answer. Will this behavior continue?"

She leaned back in the chair, looking at him, her eyes openly hostile. "No."

"Then we're done here today?"

"We are."

A few hours later, Jack pulled into the Deerlane parking lot for the second time that day, ready to attend the community dinner. No matter how wrong her behavior had been regarding Tim Mattison, he still felt crappy about the whole issue with Abrams. He didn't like feeling stupid, and he had to admit that he'd blown it by not pulling the whole file.

Over the next couple of hours, Jack was thoroughly impressed. Georgiana had beautifully orchestrated the entire event, and it was warm and enjoyable from start to finish. As the evening began to wind down a little before nine. Jack helped the senior students pick up the cafeteria and enjoyed talking with them about school and their hopes for the future. At nine o'clock, Georgiana made an announcement thanking everyone for coming, thus ending the event.

Georgiana stood in the school doorway, saying goodnight to people as they left the building. Once everyone was gone, she walked back to her office to get her things. Her phone rang and she smiled as she saw it was Boone. Thank God that their friendship had survived their doomed romance! She hit the speaker icon. "Hey."

"Hey, beautiful. You okay?"

Georgiana pulled her chair out to sit down, glad to be off her feet. "Ahh, you just got my pissy texts."

"I did."

From where she was sitting, she couldn't see that Jack had come into the outer office, where he could hear the conversation. She continued. "Yeah, I'm okay. The day *sucked*. I got my hand slapped at work, I have a screaming headache, and I had to see Tyler Abrams today. But I'm okay now. Please don't tell PJ."

Boone's voice was so loud, Jack could hear him clearly. "What the fuck are you talking about, you had to see Abrams?"

Her voice was wry. "Did you miss the part where I said I have a screaming headache?"

Boone's voice dropped. "Sorry. What happened with Abrams?"

"I had to go meet with the superintendent about refusing to follow an order and Tyler was there meeting with him before me. I didn't know about it, and we ran into each other as he came out of the office."

"And?"

Her voice lowered and Jack could hear the tension. "And… he came out, saw me, looked me up and down like I was a pole dancer, then made a comment about how good it was to see me or something like that. Told me he hoped we could catch up soon. Then Tony came to my rescue, saying he needing to meet with me in the conference room."

"What kind of a fucking idiot is your boss to let this happen? Besides the obvious fact that it's wrong, I'd think just from a liability standpoint he wouldn't be that stupid. You could easily sue their asses off for this one."

Georgiana was quick to defend Jack. "He didn't know. He hadn't read the file. I know he wouldn't have put me in that situation if he had."

There was a pause. "Still not acceptable." His voice softened. "You okay?"

"Yeah." She paused. "No. No, I'm not okay. I mean, I *will* be, but it knocked the wind outta me."

"I'm so sorry."

"You have nothing to be sorry about. It just threw me for a loop, and I needed to vent. Lucky you, you're the one who gets my messages when I'm upset and can't tell PJ."

"You can always message me anytime, about anything. You know that, right?"

"I do."

"Gigi, I was teaching a class today, otherwise I would've called earlier. I'm sorry you had to wait hours for a response."

"It's okay. I made it through the day, and I'll be fine."

"Tell me about the headache."

"I have a headache. No big deal."

"How long have you had it?"

"A couple days."

"And you'll go to the doctor if it isn't better in a day or so?"

"Yes, Mother."

"Smart ass." He chuckled. "Why don't you come down for the weekend? Sun, no stress, good food and company…"

"Boonie, thanks for the offer, but I'm good. I've got the race this weekend, which will help clear my head more than anything else."

"Fine. You know the offer always stands."

"I know." She stood up, picked up her bag, and turned off the speaker, putting the phone to her ear. "Hey, I'm packing up and going home now. I'll call you tomorrow?"

"You're still at work? It's after nine."

Her tone became cranky. "Yes, and I've been here since five-thirty this morning, so I'm going home now. Talk to you tomorrow."

"Sorry for snapping at you. Love you."

"Love you, too. Thanks for calling." Stepping into the outer office, Georgiana jumped when she noticed Jack leaning up against Dot's desk. She tried to relax, but her defenses were up, and her voice came out cold. "Unless you have something you need to say to me formally, I'm going home."

"Who were you talking to?"

"That's none of your business."

Jack cleared his throat, not wanting to think about his visceral reaction to her talking to another man; someone who clearly was involved in her life enough to know about Abrams; someone who felt a bond so strong he'd invite her down for the weekend; someone who would profess his love for her, which was clearly reciprocated. "We need to talk about today."

The flash of anger in her eyes was quick but clear. Her tone was cutting. "We've already discussed Tim Mattison. As for Tyler Abrams, I'm not going to discuss that with you."

"Damn it, Georgiana. Stop and let me explain."

"Explain what?"

"About Abrams."

"Let me recap this for you. He stepped over the line. I did what I was supposed to do. I told him to stop, verbally and in writing, then it became a safety issue. That's all in my file. I did nothing wrong, that's what the formal findings said. The fact that I was put into this situation today? That's not okay. I understand you didn't know but I'm *done* talking about it."

"Georgiana, I'm sorry about what happened, I wouldn't have put you in that situation if I had known."

"Fine. Are we done?"

"I'm trying to apologize here!"

"Apology accepted." She shook her car keys. "I'm going home."

"Wait, we need to finish this conversation."

Her hands on her hips, she looked at him, and for a moment, he could see how tired she was. "With all due respect, it's after nine."

"I know. I'll be quick."

"No, Jack, I'm not having any further conversation with you about this right now, or frankly, about *anything* at all right now." She rubbed her forehead. "I got up this morning with a screaming headache that I can't seem to shake. I've been here since five-thirty this morning, taught all day, got chewed out, ran a community event, and on top of all of that, was violated *again* by having to be in a room with Tyler Abrams. Then, you came to the event tonight with no idea that it might be stressful for me to have you here considering what happened today. I think I've handled all of this pretty well today, insubordination aside, but now I'm going home. Period."

Jack stepped back. "You're right. Go home."

Chapter Fifteen

Three days later, Jack walked into the admin meeting with trepidation, not knowing how Georgiana would react. They hadn't seen each other since their disastrous last conversation.

As he walked into the room, he realized that Georgiana and Tony were already in the room, laptops open, laughing. "Good afternoon, Tony. Georgiana."

Both chorused, "Afternoon," not showing any signs of discomfort at his presence.

After the meeting, Jack was thankful for the total quiet of the empty room. Picking up his phone, he was surprised to see that a text had come in part way through the meeting. The message was brief. *Do you still want to ride to the race together?*

He stood looking at the phone. Georgiana had made it clear that she wouldn't go out with him, so was this a gesture to show she wasn't holding a grudge about the Tyler Abrams issue? Or was it more? He put the phone in his pocket, not sure how to answer.

As he backed out of his parking space, he speed-dialed his little sister. Lyndsay answered on the second ring. "Talk fast, big brother. Your nephew will be awake in a few minutes, and the little prince demands to nurse as soon as he gets up."

"Hey, Lynds."

"What's up? You don't usually call on a weekday."

"I know, but I think I need some advice."

"Wow! What about?"

"A woman." Checking his speed, he slowed down. "I need to understand."

"Okay, tell me the whole thing."

Jack told his sister everything, from the first meeting to the strange text message earlier that afternoon. When he was done, there was silence on the other end of the line until he said, "Lynds, you still there?"

"I'm here." She paused. "Have you ever had a one-nighter before her? Or, in this case, a couple-nighter, with nothing after it?"

"No." He chuckled. "I wanted to once, but her roommate was there, so I left."

"So, this woman changed your pattern of behavior right from the beginning?"

He thought about it. "Yes."

"Then here's my take. It doesn't sound like she fools around. I mean, if the outgoing superintendent didn't tell you any rumors about her, it's a safe bet she's kept her nose clean. So, it was a change of behavior for her too. Knowing you, she has to be someone pretty special for that to happen."

Jack pulled into his garage and turned off the ignition. "She is."

"And then you went to this festival, got physical again, at least a bit, but more than that, you seemed to act like you were together?"

"Yes."

"And asked her out again, and she turned you down..."

"Uh-huh."

"Which isn't something you've ever really experienced before…"

"Not since Mary Anne MacGregor turned me down for the eighth-grade winter ball."

"Still hurts your ego, doesn't it? Mary Anne is a bitter old cow now, so let it go."

He laughed. "Hello! Advice?"

Her voice got more serious. "Maybe there's something there, more than just her divorce, more than this harassment thing. Something has her scared of a relationship, whether with you or someone else, and she's using the professional thing as a defense mechanism."

"What do you mean?"

"I mean, something in her past has her throwing up roadblocks like crazy here. It sounds like she was interested enough to have the time with you in Seattle but is too scared now to move ahead when it could possibly turn into a real relationship."

"So, what do I do?"

"You like her?"

Jack swallowed. "I do."

"Then give it time. Drive her to the race and just treat her like a colleague or friend. Don't ask her out, don't hit on her, don't touch her unless she touches you first. Give her time to reach a point where she feels safe enough to give it a try." In the background, Jack could hear the recognizable sounds of his nephew beginning to fuss, and Lynds groaned. "His highness is awake, but if you want to talk more, give me a call back in like an hour."

"Sounds good. Thanks, Lynds."

Jack looked at Georgiana's text, then slowly typed his message. "*Yes, meet me at five at my house.*"

"*See you then.*"

Saturday morning, Jack was loading his gear into his car, when he heard Georgiana's car turn into his driveway. She parked at the side of his garage, and got out. "Good morning."

Jack tried not to react to the sight of her in running tights, every inch of her lower body clearly outlined. "Good morning."

She pulled her bag off the front seat. "Ready to go? Sure you don't want me to drive?"

"All set."

At the racecourse, they each got their numbers, then checked the board for their start times. Georgiana would start in the second heat, Jack in the fourth. She laughed as she looked at the assignments. "Damn, I thought I would get to show you up in the same heat, now I'll just have to rely on the final time."

"I'll beat you." He grinned, "After all, my legs are a bit longer than yours, so I cover more ground with each step."

Her eyes sparkled, "We'll see. Want to bet on the outcome? I say that my time will be better than yours, with me doing the full obstacles even though I could do the women's version."

"You're on. Loser buys dinner."

"Deal."

Hours later, Jack sprinted toward the finish line, glad to have the grueling course behind him. The final obstacles on the fourteen-mile course had pushed him almost to his physical limit, but he had to admit he'd enjoyed passing other competitors several years younger than him. As he passed under the final banner, he looked up, checking his race time on the overhead clock. While it wasn't the best time he'd ever had, it was pretty good considering this was his first time on this course.

As he walked around to cool himself down, he spotted Georgiana off to the side of the crowd, watching the racers finish. *Was she looking for him?* He walked toward her, seeing the telltale mud from the course streaking her legs. Her smile was warm. "Hi, how'd it go?"

Jack fought the urge to pick her up and kiss her. "Good. You?"

"Really well."

Over the next hour, they waited for their final times. As the results posted, Georgiana grimaced. "Damn it, you won."

Jack checked the list again, shocked by how close their times were, "By six minutes over a fourteen-mile course, when I also have a full foot of height on you. Jesus, Georgiana, you had to be blazing through that course to be that close to my time!" He shook his head. "I can't even gloat, I clearly should hang my head right now." She started to laugh, seeing him start to grin at her. "But, yes, I'll gloat. I won. You owe me dinner."

"I do."

Over the next half hour, they got cleaned up, and headed to the parking lot. At the car, Georgiana stopped with her hand on the door handle. "Want me to drive?"

He smiled. "I've got it. You pick someplace for us to eat on the way home."

"Sounds good."

They pulled back onto the highway after stopping for dinner. Jack kept his eyes on the road. "How long have you been racing?"

She shifted in her seat so she could look at him. "Eight years, I guess. You?"

He shrugged. "I ran cross country in high school and college, but it wasn't until about six years ago that I started cross-training instead of just running."

"What changed?"

"What do you mean?"

"If you were *just* a runner, what changed to make you want to do this sort of race?"

He thought about it. "Truthfully, my marriage was failing, even if I didn't want to admit it. Training filled a void."

"Oh."

He continued. "We'd moved back to Atlanta, but my wife was still working in D.C., so we had a commuter marriage. I'd always run, but suddenly I had the work weeks when I was alone, so I started training more."

"You know, we never talked about our marriages." She chuckled. "Well, actually my marriage and divorce actually walked up to the breakfast table. We didn't talk about yours."

"Do you want to now?"

She looked out the window, wanting to know more about him but not wanting to sound too interested. "Sure."

He struggled to explain it all. "We met at Dartmouth, got married soon after, went to grad school, then moved to D.C."

"What does she do?"

"She's a lobbyist."

"For?"

"Then, for insurance companies, now for pharmaceuticals."

"Okay. Go on."

"We moved to D.C. I worked policy, that's how I met Rick. Then I realized that I really wanted to go back to working in schools, so I took a job in Atlanta. We did the long-distance thing for a couple of years, then I took a job back in D.C., thinking that we were at the point of being a full-time couple again, not just on weekends."

"And?"

"And…we realized we wanted completely different things. I wanted a house in the suburbs, or at least a place with a little yard for a garden. She wanted a townhouse, no lawn to mow, someone to take care of everything. I wanted to start talking about a family; she felt that our nieces and nephews should be enough. I wanted to buy a vacation home in Maine on a lake away from everything; she wanted a condo in South Carolina in a resort area. It seemed like every time one of us had an idea, the other wanted the complete opposite." He blew out a deep breath. "It's not that we split in a fiery manner, our marriage just died a slow, lingering death."

"I'm sorry."

He continued, almost as if he hadn't heard her. "Then one day she announced she was going away for the weekend with friends, and I realized how happy I was that she was going to be gone for those few days. That's when I filed for divorce." He paused. "So, that's how I started training for races like this. What about you?"

Georgiana thought for a moment. *Why not tell him the truth*? "After my divorce, I had a really, really hard time. I mean, up until the second I walked into the room and found Molly and Rick, I thought my marriage was fine. I was head over heels in love with him and thought we had it all. When I realized it was a complete lie, I crumbled. Training became part of how I healed."

As she turned her gaze out the front window, she could see flashing blue lights ahead. Her voice shifted as she realized she was gripping her upper right arm tightly. Forcing herself to unclench her hand, she said. "Okay, time to let you focus on the road."

Later that night, after watching the Sox on TV, Jack stretched and headed to his bedroom. It had been a great day. The race had been a complete blast; he'd spent the entire day with Georgiana without it disintegrating into an argument or pushing the boundaries, and he had learned a lot more about her. Maybe, just maybe, she'd begin to trust him enough to give them a try.

The next morning, he awoke early and laid in bed watching the sun beginning to peek around the edges of his curtains. With a sigh, he got up knowing there was no way he was going to fall back asleep again.

Coming down the stairs, he realized that his phone was sitting on the table instead of plugged in upstairs as usual. He picked it up and was surprised to see a text message waiting for him from Georgiana, that had been sent at almost eleven the night before. *"We need to talk, tonight if possible."*

He picked up his phone, suddenly worried as he texted back. *"Hi, just got your message. My phone wasn't with me last night. Do you want me to call you?"*

A few minutes later, as he was making coffee, it buzzed again. *"Yes."*

He dialed her number immediately. "Hi."

Her voice sounded strained. "Hi."

"You okay?"

"No. Yes."

He tried to lighten the mood. "That was a clear response. I'm really sorry I didn't get your text last night."

"It's okay. I can't really expect you to be sitting around day and night waiting for a text from me." He could hear her say something to someone, then she said, "I'm fine, or I will be. I need to tell you something but I'm standing at Jones' right now and I can't talk here."

"Come here." As the words came out of his mouth, he hoped she would take the invitation the right way.

"What?"

"You said we need to talk, so come on over."

"Are you sure?"

"Sure. Do you want coffee?"

"Please. I'm getting donuts. What do you want?"

"Glazed or chocolate."

"See you in about fifteen minutes." She paused. "Thanks, Jack."

Exactly fifteen minutes later, her car pulled into his driveway. He walked to the front door and opened it just as she raised her fist to knock. "Hi."

Georgiana looked at him, trying to stop her immediate physical reaction to seeing him standing there in faded jeans, barefoot, wearing a faded Columbia t-shirt, slight stubble on his chin. She held out the bakery box. "Here, have some donuts, since I'm probably going to stress you out."

He took the box. "Donuts always make up for any stress. Come on in. Let's sit in the kitchen."

He put the box on the kitchen table, which was already set with napkins and plates. As he turned back around, he tried not to notice how well the yoga pants fit her, or how the thermal shirt, which should have seemed frumpy, made him want nothing more than to scoop her up and take her to bed. "Coffee?"

"Please."

"Still just cream?"

"Still just cream." He handed her a mug and she gave him a perfunctory smile. "Thanks."

He pulled out a chair across from her, sat down, and took a donut before sipping his coffee. He leaned back in his chair and looked at her seriously. "Okay. Talk to me."

She picked up a spoon and turned it over and over in her hand, her eyes glued to it. "I really, really don't want to talk with you about this."

All the progress he'd felt they'd made the day before seemed to evaporate. "Okay, but you were the one who said we need to talk."

She took a deep breath, feeling the anxiety fill her again, and Jack watched in concern as her face grew pale. "When I got home last night, there was an envelope on my front door and a bouquet of flowers."

Jack felt a swell of jealousy but then realized that with her reaction, there had to be more to the story. He tried to keep his voice neutral. "And?"

Her voice got very small. "They were from Tyler Abrams."

Shock and disbelief made his voice louder than he intended. "What?"

"The note said that he was just stopping by, that he'd stopped by the school first, hoping to see me to talk through everything and to take me out to dinner."

He tried to hold onto his professional persona but failed miserably. "Seriously?" he asked, his voice still a bit on the high side from being dumbfounded.

She tried to smile, then shrugged and took a bite of her donut. "Seriously."

"And?"

She swallowed, then sighed. "And… I made sure he was gone, locked all the doors, and tried to figure out what to do."

"Why didn't you call me?"

"Because I keep telling you that we need to keep our relationship strictly professional, and this is a personal thing." She took a sip. "I called Frank Jamison and asked him to come over."

Jack knew the name. "The sheriff?"

"And one of my brother's closest friends. He knows about what happened years ago. He looked at the note, we talked, and he paid Abrams a visit. Then Frank came back to fill me in on the conversation." She took another sip. "He said he told Abrams to stay away from me, completely and totally, and…"

"And what?"

Her next words came out in a rush. "And he said that Tyler said that he'd assumed that when we were both there at the office, it meant that I was over it and he could contact me again."

Jack put down his cup of coffee as her words hit his brain. "Fuck. So, *my* not knowing about the situation, which is completely my own fault, put *you* in danger?"

Georgiana looked at him, and for a moment, she let herself bask in the concern and grief in his eyes. "Jack, this is Tyler Abrams' issue, not yours. How he could misconstrue the encounter the way he did is completely delusional on his part."

"Thank you, but you know as well as I do that I put you in that situation." Self-loathing filled him and he tried to keep his voice calm, wanting to do nothing more than find Abrams and beat him up.

"Let it go." She broke off a piece of her donut, taking a bite. "So, here's why I needed to talk to you about this..."

His hurt was clear. "You wouldn't have told me otherwise?"

"Don't go there." Her eyes were serious, and he suddenly realized that there were deep shadows under her eyes; she was clearly exhausted. "The thing is, if he tries to make contact again, I'm going to get a Relief from Stalking Order and then the whole thing will be public, including the encounter in the office." Just then her phone rang, and she looked at it before answering. "Hey Frank, what's up?"

The voice was so clear, Jack could hear it across the table. "Hey, Gigi, can I stop by for a minute? I need to talk to you about Abrams."

She looked at Jack, who quickly said, "Have him come here, if you don't mind."

She nodded before answering Frank. "I'm at Jack Ryder's, the old Petersen place. I was just telling him all of it. Can you come here?"

"Sure, we'll be there in five minutes."

"We?"

"Rose is coming too."

After hanging up, Georgiana stood up and looked out the window, her arms wrapped tightly around her. Jack stood up, holding his mug. "More coffee?"

"Please."

He refilled the mugs, set them on the table, and came to stand behind her. Her voice was brittle. "Don't even think about it."

"What?"

"You're thinking about putting your hands on me right now, trying to help, thinking I need comfort. Don't do it."

Feeling rightfully chastised, Jackson took a step back to give her space.

A moment later, they heard a car pulling into the driveway. Jack was pleased that he'd already met the sheriff and the county's State's Attorney, Rose (Patten), so at least he knew with whom he was dealing.

After greeting them at the door, Jack let them to the kitchen, where Georgiana was standing at the window. She turned. "Hey, Rose."

"Georgie." The tall brunette turned to smile at Jack. No matter how hard she fought the feeling, George couldn't squash the flash of jealousy that arose seeing another woman look at Jackson so warmly; especially one who was divorced and known to be on the prowl. "Jack. Good to see you again."

"You too, Rose."

Jack poured them coffee, and the group sat at the table. Rose looked at Georgiana. "So, here's the thing. After Frank filled me in this morning on what happened yesterday, I want you to file a no-stalking order."

"Why?"

"Because I'm concerned that if he's feeling this bold, he'll keep pushing it. If the order is there, we can step in immediately."

Jack nodded. "I agree. I think it's a good idea."

Georgiana sat in silence, then shook her head. "No."

Frank was the first to speak. "*No*? You've got to be kidding."

"No." Her voice became sharper. "I'm not doing it. If I go on face value, I can understand how he misconstrued what happened. Now he's been warned and if he does anything, I will immediately get an order. But I'm not putting this out in the public eye otherwise."

Rose put her mug down with a thunk. "George, be reasonable here. You know what he's capable of and you know that it's likely it's going to be an issue. Stop it now."

"If it's going to be an issue, it's going to be, regardless of a worthless piece of paper." Her voice became more relaxed. "I'm perfectly confident in my ability to defend myself. I understand the system. I'm not stupid and I'm not doing the order. Period."

Frank tried to lighten the mood. "Gigi, I think I'm the only one here who you've ever hit, and I still remember the shiner you gave me, but I really think getting the order is wise."

"I know you do. And I appreciate the thought; the care you're putting into this, but I'm still not doing it."

Rose looked at Frank in confusion. "Shiner?"

He laughed and nudged Georgiana's hand. "Yeah, I tried to kiss her when we were about eleven and they were visiting for the summer. She hauled off and decked me. Then PJ found out and beat the crap outta me." He suddenly looked more serious. "How's he taking this news?"

Georgiana's eyes widened in horror. "He doesn't know and *won't* know. Promise!"

"You didn't tell him? What about Boone?"

"Neither one knows anything about last night, and you won't tell them!"

Frank looked at her in concern. "You tell them *everything*. Why not this?"

"I told Boone about running into him and he didn't take it well, but he promised to not tell PJ. I tell them about last night, and one, or both of them, will go off. It'll get ugly fast." She looked at Frank seriously. "You know I'm right about that."

"Fine." He grimaced. "I don't like it, but I won't tell them."

"Thank you."

Jack had kept quiet for as long as he could. "Georgiana, I'd like you to file the order."

"I know you would. I know you *all* would, and I'm still not doing it."

Jack tried to keep his tone professional. "I'm asking you to do it."

"And I'm refusing. This is my own personal business, and you don't have the power to order me to do anything that has to do with my personal life."

Jack pushed his hand through his hair, wanting nothing more than to throw something. Suddenly he looked at Frank and Rose with a light in his eyes. "I want to file a no-trespass on school properties."

Georgiana looked at him with fury. "Knock it off, Jack."

He ignored her. "Frank, if I sign a no-trespass on school property, that's a public record. You would have the record as to why in your files, but Georgiana doesn't have to go to the courthouse to file it."

Frank nodded, a smile spreading across his face. "Yes. And then if the asshole shows up anywhere around school property, which is where everyone knows Gigi normally is, we can nail him."

Georgiana looked at the three of them sitting at the table and struggled to keep her composure. "Frank, Rose, please excuse us, but I need to speak to Jack in the other room for a moment, please."

In the living room, Jack started to speak but Georgiana cut him off. "Let me be clear, Jack. If you do the no-trespass order, I will resign effective immediately. I will use vacation time for the two weeks necessitated by contract, and I will be gone."

Her words stung. "You can't be serious?"

"I'm completely serious."

"Georgiana, be reasonable. I'm just trying to protect you. You won't do the no-stalking order, so I'm trying to find a way to start a paper trail that will keep you safe."

"The paper trail won't do a damn thing. You know that. If he is going to push it, he's going to push it." Her tone was level as she looked directly at him. "So let me lay it out again. You need to make a decision here and now. You sign the order, I resign today." She turned on her heel, heading back to the kitchen, a befuddled Jack following her.

Frank and Rose looked at Georgiana and Jack expectantly. Jack took a deep breath, then swallowed. "I support Georgiana's desire not to file an order at this time."

Frank looked at Georgiana. "You're being an idiot. Stop it. You know what PJ would say."

She snorted. "He wouldn't say anything. He'd get in the car, be here in a scary short amount of time, kill Tyler while making it look like an accident, then smile and say that it's taken care of."

Frank tried to hide a smile. "True."

Rose grimaced. "I don't want to hear these things. Please, George, be reasonable."

"I am. It's my life, my decision, and I understand the risks."

Frank sighed. "Do you really?"

"Jesus, Frank, yes, I do. I'm the one he attacked, remember? I want him as far away from me as possible."

"Then file the damn order."

Her facial expression showed her response before she spoke. "Enough people talked about it all back then, I don't want that to happen again. I just want this to go away, and I think this will do it."

Frank shook his head. "Then we're done here.". As Frank hugged her before leaving, he smiled. "Stubborn P.I.T.A."

She tried to smile, although she was still so angry. "No one has called me Pita in years."

"To your face, Gigi, to your face. I'm sure people still call you that, just probably not to your face."

Rose was confused. "Pita?"

Frank chuckled. "Pain-in-the-ass, which half the town frequently called her when we were in high school."

After they left, Georgiana rose to clean up the dishes, rinsing them carefully, then saying quietly, "Thank you."

Jack knew how hard that had to be for her. "You're welcome."

At the front door, she slid on her coat hurriedly, not wanting Jack to help her with it, knowing if he touched her, she wouldn't leave. Her hand on the doorknob, she asked, "Did you ask her out?"

His voice showed his confusion. "Who?"

"Rose."

"What are you talking about?"

Georgiana turned just enough to see his face, "Did you ask her out?"

"No."

"Why not?"

"Because I'm not interested in her."

Something in the earlier interaction made that hard for Georgiana to believe, as clearly Rose had been interested in *him*. George waited for him to continue.

He shifted uncomfortably, "Fine. She asked *me* out."

For a split second, Georgiana felt jealousy fill her, and she needed to ask. "Did you say yes?"

"No."

"Why not?" She's gorgeous, smart, and interested. Why didn't you say yes?"

"I'll tell you the same thing I told her, I'm involved with someone."

Her shock was clear, and Jack thought he saw a flash of hurt on her face. "You are?"

"Yes."

"Since when?"

He reached out to touch her cheek, "Since Seattle."

"What?"

A slight smile started. "I'm not going out with Rose because I still am interested in *you*."

Georgiana shook her head in disgust, "You are an idiot."

Two days later, Georgiana pulled a pile of mail from the box at the end of her road, and distractedly flipped through the envelopes, tossing several catalogues onto the passenger seat so she could automatically drop them into recycling. Three of the envelopes remaining were expected, but she noted with some interest that one envelope had her address written by hand and had no return address.

She got back into the car, automatically locking the car doors. Slitting open the mystery envelope, she pulled the folded paper out.

The note was brief.

Georgiana,

Again, I seem to have offended you in some way, and I think if we could only get together for a drink or dinner, I'm sure we could work this out. I know that Frank had told me to stay away from you, but I know you well enough to know that you would never have been at Central Office that day if you weren't interested in seeing what we could have together.

I look forward to hearing from you –

Tyler

Georgiana tried to take a deep breath, but her throat was so tight with fear that she couldn't really do it. Setting the note on top of the catalogs with her shaking hands, she sped toward the house.

Pulling into the garage, she made sure the heavy door was closed before she got out of the car. Envelope and note in hand, she headed into the house, picked up her cell phone, and hit one of the speed dial buttons.

Two hours later, she texted Jack. "*T. sent me a letter today, I felt it went too far, I have filed a temporary relief from stalking order, which is being delivered to him today.*"

A minute later, her phone rang. Jack's voice was clipped with anger, "What the hell happened?"

Georgiana leaned back on the couch. "When I picked up the mail today, there was a note from him."

"And?"

"And it said that he was sure if we just got together for a drink, we could work things out."

"Are you fucking kidding me?"

The residual adrenaline from the nerves made her quick to sarcasm, "Yes, Jack, I'm kidding you. I just thought I'd fucking mess with you, since I had nothing else going on today."

"No need for sarcasm, Georgiana!"

"Yes, there was. There absolutely was a need for sarcasm. You asked a stupid question." She took a breath and tried to control her emotions, "Yes, he sent me a note."

"Why didn't you call me immediately?"

"Because I called the *police* immediately."

"Oh." He took a deep breath, "I'm glad you did."

"Frank came over, did a temporary order, and he delivered it about twenty minutes ago."

"And?"

"And Frank just called me and said that Tyler didn't like it, but he doesn't think he'll be a problem anymore. Although Frank admitted that he'd thought that after their last conversation too."

"And you're okay with this going to court, being public?"

"No, but I'm ready for it if needed." She rubbed her head, the low-grade headache that had started at the mailbox was beginning to grow. "The order is a temporary one. If he stays away from me for the next two weeks, I plan to not file the one in court, but I will if needed."

"Okay." He tried to show down his emotional reaction to the situation, "You okay? Would it help if I picked up a pizza and brought it over?"

"Thanks, Jack. I mean it. But…no, I'm stressed and tired, and all I want to do is get into warm clothes, have a cup of tea, and go to bed."

"Okay." He paused, "If you change your mind, I'm here."

"Thanks."

Chapter Sixteen

Later that week, Tony walked through Jack's office carrying a folded newspaper. "Have you seen this?"

"No, why?"

His assistant superintendent opened the paper and handed it to Jack.

Jack's eyes flew open in amazement as he saw the headline: *Tim Mattison, local teacher, arrested for indecent exposure.* "Shit!"

"Uh huh."

Jack rubbed his forehead. "Well, that's going to make my next conversation with Georgiana rather interesting…"

After Tony left, Jack sighed, and looked at the phone on his desk. He needed to man up, call her and admit she'd been right all along. He buzzed his assistant, "Priscilla, could you get Georgiana on the line?"

Less than a minute later, Priscilla sent through the call to Jack. Georgiana sounded amused. "Either I'm in really big trouble, or you've broken your dialing finger. Since when do you have Priscilla make your calls?"

He started to laugh, glad to hear the humor in her voice. "Since I was sitting here feeling like an idiot, and I needed a couple more minutes to gain the moral high ground."

"I take it that you read the paper this morning."

"Yes. And while I will still contend that you went about it the wrong way, I owe you an apology. I should have trusted your judgment more."

"While I would tell the kids that sort of justification doesn't make for a real apology, I'll take it."

"Thank you."

Several days later, Jack walked into the main office at Deerlane as Georgiana came out of her private office. He noted with interest that she was dressed in a severe dark gray dress and heels, much more subdued than normal, basically covered from head to toe. She smiled, although it seemed forced. "Dr. Ryder. I didn't know that you were stopping by today."

"Dr. Hewitt. May I have a word?"

She stepped back into her office. "Of course." Once inside, he could see her purse already on the desk, with her car keys next to it. He didn't bother with small talk. "Do you want me to go with you?"

Her nerves were humming with the anxiety of the day, but she shook her head. "No, thank you. I can do this."

"I know you can do this. What I'm asking is if it would help to have company."

For a moment, Georgiana let herself think about the courthouse meeting less than a half-hour away. She would have given almost anything to avoid having to go. "Thanks, Jack, but I can do this, and if you go with me, it will make it all even more public."

"But I'm the one who put you in this situation."

"No, Tyler Abrams did. Not you." She shrugged. "I tried to keep it from going this far, but that last email just made it so I have to do this. It has to be a full-out order."

Jack pushed down his rage as he thought back to the email she'd received just two days before, in which Tyler had asked her if she was going to attend an upcoming professional development statewide event and commented that he was sure if they could just talk there, they could smooth the whole thing out... Jack shook his head. "Are you going alone?"

"No. Frank and Rose will be there, my lawyer, and the judge is an old family friend." She stood up straighter, and looked him in the eye, "Thanks for your concern, Jack, but I've got this."

"Okay." He gestured toward her purse and keys. "Ready to go? I'll walk you out."

"Sounds good."

In the parking lot, he held the car door for her. "Georgiana, will you promise me something?"

She tried to smile. "Maybe. Depends on what it is."

"Will you let me know how it goes?"

"Of course."

That evening, his phone buzzed. *"It's done. It was fine. Thanks for your support."*

He stood looking at his phone, then slowly typed, *"Are you okay to talk about it? Can I call you?"*

"Sure."

She answered on the second ring. "Hi, Jack."

"Hi."

"Do you want the long or the short version?"

"Whichever you want to give me."

She sighed. "I got there and met Frank and Rose in the sheriff's parking lot. Rose went ahead and made sure Tyler was in another room. We met with the judge, he met with the judge, all of it in the closed courtroom, no public allowed, then the judge signed the order, which is sealed due to the public nature of what we do professionally."

"What does the order say?"

"For the next year, he can't contact me in any way. If he does, he will be arrested."

"Did you see him?"

She nodded, then realized he couldn't see her. "Yeah. As we walked out of the courthouse. Frank was with me, so I just kept my head down, walked to the car, and drove away."

"You okay?"

"Yeah. I am. Tired, sad it got to this, embarrassed that I couldn't fix it without the law being involved, but okay." She tried to relax her tight muscles. "Jack, forgive me for ending this conversation, but I really need to go for a run."

The idea of her going for a run after just getting a protective order startled him, and his voice was louder than he intended. "You aren't going for a run now! Not after just going to court!"

Her voice was calm. "I need to vent the nervous energy out of my system. I'm just going over to the school track to run. It's well-lit, public, and I'll be fine."

"Will you let me go with you?"

"Jack, I don't need a guard."

"Please." He needed to make her agree. "I know you think you'll be fine, but humor me, okay. I just don't think it's wise to be out alone right after doing that order, but I get the need to do it, so I'm offering to run with you."

"Oh." She thought about his offer, "I'd love some company. Are you home? I could pick you up in ten minutes."

"Sounds good."

Exactly ten minutes later, Jack heard her car pull into the driveway. He locked the door behind him and walked toward the car.

Georgiana sat behind the wheel, and even though the evening was still fairly warm, she was wearing a heavy sweatshirt, and he could see she was wearing full leggings. He smiled. "Hi."

"Hi."

As they pulled out of the driveway, the display on the dashboard lit up showing an incoming call from her brother. Georgiana shook her head as she pushed the decline button. "I'll talk to him later."

Suddenly, the screen filled with a text message, "*ANSWER THE PHONE NOW!*"

She blew out a sharp breath, "Fuck." She turned briefly toward Jack. "Sorry. I don't think I can avoid this call right now. Do you mind?"

"Not at all."

She hit speed dial, and within seconds a loud voice shouted, "And you didn't think I should know this!"

Jack watched in fascination as Georgiana gripped the steering wheel tightly. "Stop tracking me, you asshole!"

"This is why I need to!"

She tried to soften her voice. "PJ, I know you're mad, but I'm driving right now, and Jackson is with me, so let me go do my run, then when I get home, I'll call you back and you can yell then."

"Jackson is with you? Good! He was my next call."

She hissed, "Knock it off, PJ."

Her brother ignored her. "Jackson, you there?"

"I'm here."

"What the fuck were you thinking putting her in a room with Abrams? I mean, I know better than anyone how irritating she is, and how fast she can piss you off, but seriously, you didn't read her file before slapping her hand? You put her at risk! You want to put *yourself* at risk, fine, but you won't put my sister in harm's way!"

Jack was surprised that he didn't feel any anger at the attack. "I know. And I have apologized for my stupidity. I would never have knowingly put her at risk. *Never.*"

PJ's voice shifted. "And you, little sister, what the hell were you thinking, telling Boone but not telling me? And you made Frank keep it a secret too? That's bullshit, Gi." He paused. "I knew something was up, I've been coming out of my skin for weeks now, but it wasn't until I got a copy of the court docket a little bit ago that I figured out why. What were you thinking?"

Georgiana was used to weathering her brother's temper. "I was thinking that if you knew, you'd blow a gasket, just like you are! I could handle it, I *did* handle it, so back off, PJ."

"I'm not backing off. You're my baby sister and I love you. And where are you right now? And if you aren't home, why the hell is the alarm off at the house?"

Her temper flared again. "How many times have I told you to stop hacking my system? Just because you have the skills doesn't mean that it's right for you to do it. The house is locked, and I'm going for a run." She grimaced as she looked over at Jack. "And after Jack heard I was running, he yelled about me going alone, so he's going for a run with me. So, the house is locked, I'm safe, and don't get yourself in a tizzy."

Suddenly they could hear PJ chuckle. "Well, even though you were stupid enough to get her into this, Jack, I give you some credit for not letting her run alone."

Georgiana yelled, "He's not *letting* me do anything! I agreed to have him go running with me, period." She put on the blinker to turn into the school parking lot. "We are at the school, and I am going for a run now."

"Remember the alarm is on when you get home. Don't scare the crap out of me by setting it off."

"Yeah, yeah. Love you."

"Love you, too, baby sister. Jack, thanks for running with her tonight."

"My pleasure."

Almost ninety minutes later, Georgiana pulled back into his driveway. "Thanks for going with me." She stopped the car, and looked at him, her cheeks getting redder. "I really appreciated the company."

"You're welcome." He smiled, "Anytime you want company for a run, let me know."

"I will."

That night, Jack stood at the window in his home office, looking out over the back field, the moonlight making for some interesting shadows. As he watched the leaves moving in the breeze, he thought back to his recent conversations with Georgiana. The relief he felt at her finally having the formal protection order conflicted with his own anger at having been the root cause of everything that had happened. Then he thought back to the odd conversation with her about Rose. Why had she asked him if he'd asked Rose out? Why did she care? Did her asking mean that it would have bothered her if it had happened? The look on her face when he'd said he was involved with someone so clearly showed her hurt, maybe there still was some hope for them after all…

A few days later, Jack stood in front of the administrators at their bi-monthly meeting and gestured to the slide on the screen. "And I will be proposing to the consolidated board that we move toward all pre-school students, district-wide, receiving their in-school services at Deerlane over the next two years. This will mean an approximate increase of forty students in their program, which can be handled by increasing the program from one to two classrooms. Deerlane has the room and staffing to do such." As Georgiana sat in total shock, she watched as Jack gestured toward two other principals sitting to his left. "I've already met with Mike and Jan about the idea and they're very supportive. Of course, it will involve all of us looking at the logistics to make sure we've planned every detail, but it seems like the best move for our students."

Georgiana clenched her fists under the table, digging her nails into her palms as she tried to keep her face from showing her disbelief. He'd just announced a major change to her school, which he had clearly discussed with others, without her having any knowledge of the proposal at all. Mustering her best professional persona, over the next hour she answered questions when prompted in the general group discussion and made damn sure that she didn't make any eye contact with Jack.

The meeting ended just before three, and Georgiana packed up her bag in frigid silence before heading toward the door. As her hand touched the knob, Jack's voice carried from across the room. "Georgiana, I need a word with you."

She made a show of looking at her watch before saying calmly and sweetly, "Dr. Ryder, I have a parent meeting back at school in five minutes. Could I give you a call after that?"

He was taken aback. "Most admin go home for the weekend after these meetings. You have another meeting?"

She spared him a dismissive glance. "Yes, sir."

The "sir" caught his attention. "Fine, then go to the meeting and please call me after."

She didn't respond as she closed the door behind her.

When almost an hour and a half had passed without hearing from her, Jack considered that she might be blowing him off. Packing up his things, he called out to his assistant. "Priscilla, I'm heading over to Deerlane. Have a great weekend!"

Ten minutes later, he pushed the doorbell at the school. Dot's voice rang cheerfully through the speaker. "C'mon in, Dr. Ryder."

When he opened the door to the front office, Dot looked up at him, a sparkle in her eyes. "Hi."

"Hi. Is Georgiana in, and free?"

"She is." She held out a large manila envelope. "This is for you. You should open it before you go in there."

"What is it?"

She tried to suppress her grin. "Charlie left it for you. Use it wisely."

Stepping to the side of the desk, Jack unwound the tie on the envelope, then pulled a piece of paper and a small package of mini peanut butter cups from the package.

Jack,

If you're reading this, it's because something you've done has truly pissed G off. Some words of advice: hand her the chocolate first, let her talk, <u>don't</u> interrupt. Once she has it out of her system, she'll be fine. For future reference, Reese's work best when she's mad, but don't EVER get the ones with the wrappers, they just make her madder.

-Good luck! Charlie

Jack looked over at Dot in amazement. "Seriously?"

"Seriously. It's a tried-and-true method."

Jack couldn't believe what he'd just read. "And you put up with this sort of garbage? You need to pacify her with chocolate?"

Dot's eyes widened. "God, no, Dr. Ryder. Georgiana never loses her cool with any of us. It's you guys, her bosses. You're the only ones who make her that mad."

"Fine." He tucked the note in his pocket and took the bag of candy. He knocked on the door twice, then turned the doorknob as he heard her voice usher him in.

Standing behind her desk looking down at her laptop, her astonishment was clear. "*You*? What are *you* doing here?"

He kept his voice calm, trying not to react to the scathing tone. "I asked you to call me after your meeting and you didn't, so I figured I'd stop by." He held out the bag of chocolates. "I was told to give you these."

Her eyes narrowed. "Damn, Charlie. He instructed you as to how to handle me?"

He tried not to smile. "No." He looked down so she wouldn't see his smile. "Yes. He left a note of warning for me and the chocolates for you."

She took a deep breath, then reached out for the bag. Opening it, she dumped a few on her desk then handed the bag back to him. "Fine. Help yourself."

He gestured toward the small table. "So, may I sit?"

"You're the boss. That's up to you."

"Georgiana…"

"Yes! Sit down." Just then there was a knock. The door opened and a hand holding two seltzers appeared. Georgiana walked over, took them, and poked her head around the door to roll her eyes at Dot. "I'll get you for being Charlie's accomplice."

"Yeah, yeah, scared out of my wits. I won't sleep tonight; I'm so scared of you."

Georgiana chuckled. "Good, keep it that way."

"I will." Dot grinned at her. "I'm going home now."

"Sounds good." Georgiana smile was genuine now. "Thanks, Dot. Have a good weekend."

"You too. Night, Dr. Ryder."

"Night, Dot."

Georgiana stalked back to her desk, putting a can of seltzer next to him on the table, then opening one herself. She perched on her desk and took a sip without saying a word.

Jack looked at her, trying to figure out how to open the conversation. Finally, he leaned back in his chair. "So, I asked to speak to you after the meeting because I wanted to talk to you about my proposal."

She continued to examine the top of the seltzer can. "Okay."

"But you couldn't stay."

"True."

"So, let's talk now."

"Little late for that now, isn't it?"

He felt his temper flare at the sarcastic tone but tried to hold onto Charlie's recommendations. "Okay, fair point. Say what you need to say, Georgiana."

She stood up, still looking at the can. Turning to set it down, she walked around her desk to look out at the students still playing on the school fields. Although her body language betrayed her tightly controlled anger as she leaned against the windowsill, her voice was deceptively calm. "You announced a proposal to make a major change to my building as if it's a done deal, without ever talking to me about it."

"Uh-huh."

"You never asked what I thought, or if I had any long-term plans here that might be impacted."

"Uh-huh."

She turned and shook her head. "Jack, you completely ambushed me in a public meeting. You made an announcement that I knew nothing of and now you are acting like I'm the unreasonable one for being upset."

"I'm not acting like you're being unreasonable."

Her voice grew louder. "Yes, you are! If you thought you'd done something wrong, you should've started with an apology."

His temper flared and his voice rose. "I don't owe you an apology. It's my prerogative to make program decisions for this district, period. Just because you've been allowed to run your own show in the past doesn't mean that you get to do so now!"

"I don't expect to run my own show. I expect to be part of a functioning *team*, which clearly, I'm not right now!" She sighed. "Truly, I have no issue with the expansion of our pre-school program. And I absolutely know, *get*, and accept that you have the right to make these decisions. The reason I'm mad is because you didn't talk to me about it, but you spoke to Mike and Jan. I know there will be times when I will be surprised by things, but what got me was that you took the time to talk to others, but not to *me*... especially when it's going to impact *my* school the most. That's what got me mad."

"I…" He stopped, remembering Charlie's words. "Continue, please."

Her voice sounded almost sad. "Sitting in a meeting where things that impact me and my school directly were discussed, and I wasn't part of the conversation, that's an issue for me." She looked uncomfortable. "You don't talk to me about much of anything. I know, I talk to the other administrators. You're in their schools all the time, you call them, you text them. Good lord, most of them you text to tell them to have a good weekend, but not me. If that's the way you want to do things, I'll live with it, but you can't expect me to jump up and down with joy when I'm kept out of the loop."

"You're the one who keeps putting up the roadblocks, not me."

Her look was tired. "Jack, I meant keeping the physical or emotional distance between us, so we don't repeat past personal mistakes." She paused to face him, and he was struck by the vulnerability she couldn't hide.

She looked down at her bracelet and rubbed it almost reverently. "Not mistakes. I refuse to think of it as a mistake. *Choices*, our past *choices*. But that's completely different from having a professional relationship. I mean, we *work* together, or supposedly do."

She kept looking at the bracelet and her voice got lower. "How do we get to the point where you communicate with me like you do with the others? What needs to change so you treat me like I'm part of your professional *team*?"

He let out a frustrated sigh. "I hadn't realized I was, but…deep down, I've probably not been contacting you as much as the others so you would see that I wasn't trying to push you into being a couple. I didn't want you to think I was trying to hit on you."

"I get that. But it seems like we may have gone too far in the other direction…"

"True." He rubbed his temple. "Can we talk openly here? Now?"

"Of course."

"To be painfully honest, you're the only employee I've ever had any sort of personal…" He searched for the right word. "Relationship, whatever, with. Normally, I'd say I'm pretty good at communicating, but I have no idea what the hell to do with you."

She nodded in understanding. "It's weird for me too."

"So, what do we do?"

"In terms of our working together, I'm just asking you to try to communicate with me the same way as you do with the other principals. I'm asking you to treat me like my supervisor, and share information with me accordingly. Can we try that?"

He held up his hand as if taking an oath. "On my honor, I will try to communicate with you as I do with the other principals."

She laughed. "Thank you." She stood up. "C'mon. It's time to call it a week."

"Wait, don't you want to talk more about the proposal?"

"No. Not right now at least. I want to go home for the weekend while we're not pissed at each other."

He started to laugh. "Good point. Let's go home."

The next afternoon Jack picked up his phone and typed. *"I owe you an apology for what happened at the meeting yesterday. You were right to be mad and I'll try to be better about communicating with you."*

A few seconds later he grinned in delight as a smiley-face emoji with fireworks going off behind it appeared on his screen, with the message, *"Hallelujah!"*

Another message followed that one. *"Thanks for the apology."*

He thought for a moment and then typed. *"You're welcome. See you Monday, if not sooner."*

"See you then."

Chapter Seventeen

Halfway through October, Georgiana realized that she hadn't felt well for weeks. She was constantly exhausted with a persistent low-grade headache.

One Friday afternoon as she was sitting in the district administrators' meeting trying to pretend she was paying attention, she was nearly overcome with nausea. In an effort to not throw up all over everyone, she tried holding her breath, but it didn't help. She tried a tiny sip of water before she then suddenly realized she had to leave, or she would humiliate herself completely.

She bolted from the room, making it to the ladies' room barely in time. Leaning against the cold blue-green masonry wall, she tried to remember when she'd last had a stomach flu. It had to be at least fifteen years; one of the benefits of living in hell holes all over the globe was that she had developed an iron stomach. But this? She felt like crap. Grimacing, she rinsed her mouth out at the sink.

When she left the bathroom, she was shocked to see Jackson leaning against the opposite wall, a stern look on his face. His voice was urgent. "Are you okay?"

Her face burned with embarrassment. "Fine. Just a stomach bug. Sorry for running out of the room. I'm okay now."

"No, you aren't. I'm taking you home right now. Tony can finish the meeting." She realized that her bags were on the floor at his feet. "Let's go."

"I don't need a ride home. I can go back to the meeting, and then I'll go straight home, I promise."

"You're going home *now*. That's an order. I'll give you a ride and if you need to pick up your car tomorrow, I'll come get you."

She wanted to argue, bristling at his authoritarian attitude, but the world was beginning to spin again, and she knew she needed to sit down before she fainted. "Fine," she said shortly.

At his car, he opened the door, and she slid in silently. As they pulled out of the lot, she asked, "Do you know how to get to my house?"

"No."

"Take route 2 for three miles south of town, turn left onto Granger Street, then left onto Hewitt Lane. It's the big farm on that road."

"I'll find it." His voice was gentler now. "Close your eyes, it should help the nausea."

They were just out of town when she realized she was going to be sick again. "Jack, stop the car!"

"What?"

"Now!"

The car was still rolling when she leaped out and bent over, vomiting again. Jack quickly got out and went to her side, silently holding her hair back from her face. When she was done, she stood up, her color a ghastly green. "Thanks."

"You're welcome."

"So, you were right that I shouldn't drive."

"Uh-huh." He opened her door. "C'mon, let's get you home."

She was silent for the rest of the drive. When they pulled into her driveway, her hand was on the door latch before the car fully stopped. "Thanks for the ride."

"Wait, I'll carry your stuff in for you."

"I can do it."

His voice was bossy again. "I didn't say you couldn't do it, I'm saying I'll do it. Stop being so stinking stubborn and just let me help."

"Fine."

Her hands were shaking as she unlocked the front door and disarmed the alarm. Stepping inside, all she could think about was lying down. "Thanks, Jack, really. I'll be fine now. I'm going to change my clothes, then lie on the couch."

His voice was calm. "Then go change. Once I see you settled on the couch, I'll leave. I promise."

Ten minutes later, she came down the stairs from what he assumed was her bedroom, wearing leggings and a hoodie, even though the day was warm. "Happy? I'm going to the couch. You can leave now."

His tone was dry. "When you're *on* the couch, lying down, then I'll leave."

She came around the edge of the sofa and realized that while she'd been upstairs, he had made it into a bed for her, a glass of water waiting on the coffee table next to a plate of saltines. She turned to look at him in confusion.

"You look like you're barely able to stand up right now, let alone make sure you stay hydrated. I figured sheets and stuff would be in the chest. I was right. Get on the couch or I'm not leaving."

Sullenly, she laid down, but the sigh of contentment as her head hit the pillow gave her away. She rolled her eyes at him as he tried to hide his smile. "Fine. Happy now?"

"Yes." He tucked the blanket in around her. "Stay here and rest. If I find out you don't take care of yourself, I'm coming back up here. Do I make myself clear?"

"You don't have to do this."

"Do what?"

"Take care of me. I would've been fine."

"You were sick, I could help. Don't overcomplicate this." He put her phone on the table by the glass of water. "I have no plans tonight, so if you need something, just call or text me, okay?"

"Okay."

Georgiana fell asleep just as soon as the door closed behind him.

The next morning, she woke up feeling fine; energetic and raring to go. After breakfast, she called Shroom, her neighbor and father figure, to give her a ride to get her car. That settled, her phone buzzed with a text from Jack. *"How are you today?"*

"Fine—all better, thanks."

"Good. Do you need a ride to get your car?"

"No, headed there right now. Thanks again."

It was almost three o'clock that afternoon when she realized that her nausea was returning. How could she have felt so good in the morning, but have it rebound on her now? Maybe she'd pushed too hard in the garden in the midday sun, but it had felt so good to be out in the dirt.

She and Shroom were leaning against the fence watching the alpacas play with the steer when she swallowed so loudly that Shroom noticed. "You okay?"

"Damn stomach bug still has a hold of me."

The farmer stood back and looked at her, seeing the greenish tinge to her skin. "How long have you been sick?"

"On and off for about a week or so, I guess. I just can't beat it."

"Kiddo, when you went to Seattle, did anything happen between you and your boss?"

"What are you talking about?"

"Well, I figured that since you didn't talk to me at all about anything in Seattle, other than the presentation and the Red Sox, that ...."

Embarrassment burned her cheeks. "Shroom, this isn't the time to talk about this, but yes, we did. Leave it alone, okay?"

His voice was patient but clear. "You're pregnant, Georgie. You're *pregnant*. You got pregnant in Seattle, and you don't have a stomach bug—you have morning sickness. Or in your case, afternoon sickness."

As she absorbed his words, she realized that he could be right. She'd never had regular periods, so she hadn't thought about not having one in the last two months. And they'd used protection, so pregnancy had never crossed her mind. "Shroom, holy fuck. You're right."

"Uh huh. Of course, I am."

Her eyes filled with tears. "Oh my God. Shroom. Oh my God."

He hugged her and felt her tears wet through his t-shirt. "We can figure this out. First, you're going inside and getting something healthy to drink. I'll drive over to Newport to get a test, so no one knows who it's for. Then, if I'm right, we are going to sit down and make a plan."

"We don't have to drive to Newport for the test. We have them at school. I just need to go to school to get one from the supply closet."

"Okay, then I'll drive you down. Grab your keys."

An hour later, Georgiana came out of the bathroom, tears of absolute joy running down her face. "I'm going to be a mom, Shroom. Me, a mom!" She swiped at a tear. "I never thought it would happen, and now it is."

"Congratulations, Georgie. You'll be a helluva mom, too."

That night, the two of them sat at the table, a pizza between them. Shroom drank a beer while Georgiana sipped seltzer. There was a lined pad of paper in front of her and as they talked, she jotted notes. Shroom took a sip. "You need to go to the doctor first thing this week. Get the tests you need, go on vitamins, whatever you need."

"Check."

"You need to call PJ and Boone."

"Check."

"You need to tell him."

"You mean Jackson."

"Yes. He needs to know."

"I know." Her look was pensive.

"What's the deal with him?"

"It's complicated…" Georgiana searched for words. "We did, well, you know, in Seattle. He would have liked to continue once we got back home. I said we couldn't, after all, he's my boss."

"So?"

"So, I don't want anyone saying that I get special treatment because we're together. Because I don't like people gossiping about me. I don't know, there are at least fifty reasons why it would be a crappy idea."

"It seems like that ship may have sailed now, sweetie. Now you're going to be parents. I think the gossip may not matter anymore."

"True."

"How do you think he'll take the news?"

"I don't know. I mean, we didn't have any life conversations, so I don't know if he'll freak, be excited, or just be okay about it. Should I wait until I go to the doctor so I'm certain and have more details?"

"Probably a good idea."

"What if he's upset?"

"Wait and see. Don't borrow that trouble yet." He reached out for her hand. "Do you like him? I mean enough to want to have a child together?"

Her eyes shone. "Yeah, I do." She rested a hand on her abdomen. "I do like him, and it was never that I didn't want to be with him. I thought I *shouldn't* be with him, now, well, it's completely different."

That night Georgiana called her brother, smiling when he answered. "What? It's my 'me time.'"

She grinned knowing that his "me time" was when he would binge-watch "The Walking Dead" while his girlfriend Julia was working a night shift as an ER nurse. "I know, I know. But this is important."

His voice changed immediately. "You're pregnant."

"How the hell do you know that?"

"I had a dream last night that you told me."

"Shit, PJ. Yes. I mean, I just took a test, but it was positive."

"Excited?"

Her voice broke. "So excited I can't stand it. I mean, the funny thing is that when I was in Seattle, I bought this yarn. Baby-weight yarn, which I never buy. So tonight, I'm going to start a blanket."

"So, are you going to tell me who the father is?"

Her voice was quieter. "My boss. I mean, my new boss."

"Jackson?"

"Yeah."

"And does he know?"

"Not yet. Not until I confirm it with the doctor."

"Are you guys dating?"

"No!" She paused. "It was supposed to just be a fling. He asked me out last month, and I turned him down again, because, well, it seemed like it would be a big public issue, especially after Tyler."

"And now? Won't this be a big public deal?"

She chuckled. "Yeah, it will be a whopping big deal."

"How do you feel about him?"

"I like him. I mean, I think I could really like him."

The two siblings talked for almost an hour, planning, laughing, talking about the future. At the end of the conversation, PJ said, "Hey, Georgie, Boone just got home. I can see his lights. You need to call him."

"I know. He's next on my list."

Georgiana dialed Boone's number with shaking fingers. He answered on the second ring. "Hey, my day is improving by the second, just hearing your voice."

"Hi."

"What's the matter?"

"Nothing's the matter, but I need to tell you something."

"Okay. What?"

"I'm pregnant."

There was a pause and she squirmed uncomfortably, then heard him chuckle. Relief flowed through her at the sound. "Well since I know I haven't been in your bed for almost a year, it's safe to assume that I'm not the father."

"I went to a conference in August."

He interrupted. "The one you were presenting at?"

"Uh-huh."

"And who is he?"

"My new superintendent. It was a fling. We agreed that needed to be the end of it and came back to Vermont."

"Why did that need to be the end of it?"

"Boone, he's my boss, for God's sake. That's a bad idea all around. Good God, why does no one get that?"

"I'll disagree with you. If you liked him enough to go to bed with him, which isn't like you, there was something more there. It's stupid to forget about it on a fucking technicality."

"Stop. We aren't talking about that right now. We're talking about the fact that I'm pregnant with his child."

"Fine. How did he react?"

"Jesus, you sound like my brother. He doesn't know yet. I'm waiting until I go to the doctor, then I'll tell him."

There was a pause and she waited, knowing that he needed to process this in his own way. Finally, he cleared his throat. "Here are my thoughts, for what they're worth. Life would've been way simpler for both of us if we could've fallen in love with each other. You know that I love you, and will *always* love you. But I'm not in love with you, just like you aren't in love with me. Now, that little sprout growing in you? I love that kid already. So, when you tell this guy that you're pregnant, hopefully he'll do the right thing and want to be part of your life, and I can be just Uncle Boone."

"That would be amazing."

He continued. "But if he doesn't, then I'm going to be at your doorstep, and you're going to marry me, like it or not. That little sprout isn't growing up without a dad, not like we did."

Georgiana started to cry. Leave it to Boone to get to the root of her darkest unadmitted fears. Her voice trembled. "Thank you, Boonie."

"But, Georgie, you need to tell him *now*. I mean, if I was the dad and I found out you told other people first, I'd be rip-shit."

"I'm going to the doctor on Monday. I think I should wait until after the appointment to make sure everything is all right. Then I'll tell him, I promise."

There was another long silence, "I think he should know now, but I do understand your point."

After hanging up, she sat back on the couch. Placing her hand on her stomach, she smiled. "Okay, little sprout," she chuckled, "or sprouts. Maybe Mommy should start a blanket for you." A sudden rush of emotion choked her up. "I guess there was a reason for getting that yarn after all..."

Late in the afternoon on Monday, Georgiana sat nervously on the exam table. Dr. Liz smiled. "So, you know what I'm going to say. You're pregnant. Based upon your information, you're about eleven weeks along, so you're due at the beginning of May. All your test results look good, although your iron level is low, as is your potassium. I'm going to give you a prescription for prenatal vitamins and something for the nausea. You need to eat more, a *lot* more right now. You've lost eleven pounds since your last appointment. Keep in mind you're eating for two now." She looked at the chart. "Next month we'll know for certain if we're talking one baby or two, since obviously you have twins in your family. Otherwise, you can go about life as you normally would." She paused. "Does the father know?"

"Not yet. I'm going to tell him later today or tomorrow. I wanted to see you first."

"Are you dating him?"

"No..." Her voice trailed off, unsure of how to explain the situation.

Liz laughed. "Well then, my friend, I think you need to think about what you want from him. Are you just looking for him to know and have a basic role, or are you hoping for a relationship?"

"I don't know."

On the ride home, she pondered Liz's question. Was this the universe's way of pushing them together? For a millisecond, she let herself feel the joy at the idea of being with him again. Would he be as excited as she was? He said he'd wanted to start a family with his ex-wife, so would he see this as joyful news? What if he wanted nothing to do with her or the baby?

By now, she'd arrived home, and after putting her things away in the house, she walked out to sit on the dock, staring at the still water of the pond. Well, if *he wanted to* be part of his child's life, they were going to have to deal with the public reaction. If he didn't want to… She shook her head. *No, not going down that path right now*. It was time to just wait and see. When should she tell him? Tomorrow after work would be best. She could call first thing in the morning and ask him to stop by the house so they could talk about something. If he wanted to know what, well, she could tell him she wanted to wait until they were face-to-face. If the conversation went well, great. If it didn't, she stopped herself. She'd deal with that then if it was the case.

The next morning, she nervously called Priscilla. "Hey, it's George."

"George! I haven't talked to you in ages."

After a few minutes of small talk, she got to the point of her call. "Could I speak to Jack, please?"

"Not possible, George. He just left the office, headed to the airport. He's going to D.C. today and won't be back until late Thursday night. Then he's in Montpelier on Friday."

Disappointment clogged her throat. "Oh. Okay. I'll text him directly, then."

"Sounds good."

Her hands shaking, she texted. *"Jack, I was wondering if you could stop by my house on Friday, when you're back from Montpelier."*

"Is something wrong?"

"No, I just want to talk about an idea with you."

"Sure, I can be there by five."

"See you then."

The anti-nausea medication worked so well that Wednesday evening Georgiana went for a short run, her first in almost two weeks.

That night, a commotion erupted in the barn. Awakened from a deep sleep, she ran out of the house in her pajamas, sliding barn boots on as she crossed the driveway to the barn. The animals inside were all agitated, kicking at the walls and running in their pens. She moved into the sheep pen first to see what had upset them, but before she realized the danger, her ram charged her and knocked her hard into the wall. Disoriented, she stood up, the breath and sense knocked out of her. Seeing the ram pulling back to run at her again, she scrambled over the side of the pen just in time.

When she got out of bed the next morning, her head was pounding, but she didn't think to worry until she went into the bathroom and realized she was beginning to spot. Calling her doctor, Liz's voice was soothing. "I'm sure it's fine, but why don't you come over as soon as you can, just so I can check you? But I don't want you to drive, get a ride."

She knew that Shroom would take her in a heartbeat. "I'll be right over."

An hour later, she was getting dressed in the exam room when Liz said, "You have a concussion, a pretty good one, and you have a cracked rib. Beyond that, in terms of the pregnancy and why you're spotting, it's too soon to tell. I want you to go home and go to bed, stay off your feet tonight and tomorrow, at least. If all is well, you'll get some rest at the very least."

By the next morning, Georgiana knew the truth as the bleeding and cramps worsened by the hour. On her way to the doctor's office, she texted Jack's number and left a message canceling their meeting.

At the end of the appointment, the doctor looked at her sadly. "I'm so sorry. You need to rest and see if your body can pass the fetus naturally, otherwise we'll need to do the procedure on Monday. I recommend that you stay home for at least the first few days next week to let your concussion and ribs heal."

Georgiana's voice was forceful. "Are you saying I *have* to?" The idea of sitting alone in her house for another moment was more than she could bear.

"No. I'm saying I recommend it. If you pass it this weekend and you insist on working Monday, I can't stop you, but I'm telling you it'd be better for you to take some time to heal."

After her appointment, Georgiana got into the car with Shroom and as he pulled out of the parking lot, she put on her sunglasses and started to cry silently.

At home, Shroom walked her to the door, unlocking it without a word. In the house, he put down her bag and held out his arms. She went to him and started to cry in earnest. "It's my fault, Shroom. I should've called you to come help me with the barn. I shouldn't have gone out there alone. If I hadn't been hit, it wouldn't be over."

He hugged her tightly. "George, it just wasn't your time, sweetie. The right time will come."

"No, it won't, and I need to accept it." Her voice was hopeless. "I just need to accept it. This is my fault *again*."

He was patient. "Little girl, enough. You're tired, emotionally overwrought, and concussed. You are going to lie down, like she said, and you are going to rest. Your body needs to do what it needs to do now, and you need to let yourself rest and grieve." He kissed her forehead. "Give me the paperwork on the concussion so I can read it."

"Shroom…"

"No way. Give it to me and let me look at it."

She handed over the page in silence. His voice was stern. "It says right here. No going up and down stairs alone. You read that, right?"

She wiped her nose on her sleeve. "I'm going to lie down on the couch, like she said. I won't go up and down stairs without you." Her voice suddenly sounded very young. "Could you come back tonight and eat with me?"

"You got it. I'll bring dinner, okay?"

"Okay."

As he stood in the doorway, he looked at her kindly. "You going to tell him you were pregnant?"

She sat down on the couch, wincing. "No, Shroom. He was supposed to come over tonight so I could tell him then, but I cancelled that this morning. There's no reason to tell him anything now." Just then an abdominal cramp hit, and she waited for it to pass. "I mean, if I was pregnant, I'd tell him. But now that I'm not, there's no sense in stirring all that up."

By mid-day, Georgiana had sent both Boone and PJ a text. *"I miscarried overnight. Not up to talking right now, love you."*

Chapter Eighteen

When she heard a vehicle pull into the driveway that afternoon, she was sure it was Shroom. Hearing a knock on the front door, she stayed on the couch, curled on her good side and yelled, "Come in."

She heard the screen doorknob rattle, then heard a voice she instantly recognized. "I can't, the door is locked."

Shit! What's Jackson doing here? She'd messaged him first thing that morning to cancel the meeting. Standing up, a cramp gripped her so hard it took her breath away. "Be right there."

She shuffled to the door, suddenly realizing how awful she probably looked. How fast could she get rid of him? What would happen if a cramp hit while he was here? What the fuck was she going to do now?

She opened the front door, keeping the screen latched between them. "Jackson."

"Georgiana." He was clearly confused, seeing how she was dressed. "Don't we have a meeting?"

She blanched as she realized that she needed to let him into the house because anything else would look really weird, and she unlatched the screen, pushing it open. "Shit, I'm so sorry. I messaged you first thing this morning that I needed to cancel. I apologize for getting you out here for no reason. I was sure you'd gotten my text."

At that moment, the phone in his pocket buzzed. He shook his head ruefully as he looked at the screen. "Ahh." He turned the phone so she could see the screen as it populated with text after text. "I was in Montpelier all day. It seemed funny that I didn't get a text or a call all day. I must not have had service."

"Sorry about that. I should've just called you directly."

"That's okay." Still standing outside the screen door, the knob in his hand, his look was searching. "Why did you cancel?"

She looked down at her feet. "I'm sick, and originally, I wanted to talk to you about an idea, but after more reflection, realized we really didn't need to talk about it."

"You were sick again? What's going on?" He opened the door more. "I'm here now, are you going to let me in?"

Shit! What was she going to do if the pain hit while he was in the house? How the hell was she going to keep him from knowing more? She swallowed nervously. "Of course."

He followed her into the house, realizing that she was dressed in black leggings and a faded long-sleeve Navy t-shirt that hung almost to her knees. He noted with interest that she clearly wasn't wearing a bra.

She walked into the kitchen and as she turned toward him, he caught sight of the angry bruise on her left temple. Without thinking about what he was doing, he put a firm hand on her shoulder, taking her face in his other hand as he turned her head so he could see the bruise, noticing that she avoided his eyes. He struggled to control his concern. "What the hell happened to you?" Coupling her evasiveness with the bruise, he felt his anger start to rise. "Why were you out sick today, and where the fuck did that bruise come from? Was it Abrams?!?"

She pulled away from his touch and for a moment she could feel tears prickle in her eyes. *Damn it!* All she needed right now was to cry in front of him. She took a deep breath, wincing as her ribs stabbed her with pain. *At least it wasn't a cramp!* Her voice came out almost as if a sigh. "This has nothing to do with anyone, certainly not him. My *ram* took offense at me being in the barn the other night and hit me hard." She turned to pick up the teapot. "It happened Wednesday night. I thought I was okay, but on Thursday morning I didn't feel right so I went to the doctor. She diagnosed a concussion and a cracked rib. She told me I need to rest for a couple of days." In her heart, she knew that while all of that was true, she was leaving the most important part out. "Do you want tea?"

"Sit down."

"What?"

"Go sit down. I'll make the tea."

All of her sadness suddenly blossomed into anger, and being ordered around was more than she could bear. She barked, "My house. I'll make the goddamn tea."

"Georgiana, so help me God, if you don't sit down right now and let me make the tea, I'll pick you up and *put* you on the couch."

"You wouldn't dare!" She turned toward the faucet to fill the teapot and her body swayed with dizziness. Jack moved with lightning speed and before she knew what was happening, he had cradled her in his arms, carrying her over to the couch. She tried to wiggle out of his arms but the pain from her ribs stopped her. "Put me down! Damn it, Jackson, put me down!"

He put her on the couch, ducking as she took a swing at him, a ghost of a smile crossing his face as she almost connected with his cheek. "Sit there. I'll put the tea water on and get the mugs ready. Then I'm coming back over here and you're going to explain all of this to me, start to finish."

She sat on the couch, fury filling her. She grabbed a Kleenex, wiping her eyes as tears started to brim. She didn't realize that he could see her from the kitchen and as he saw her blot her eyes, his face tightened with worry.

A few minutes later, he came back into the living room and sat down in one of the armchairs across from her.

Her voice was hostile. "Not acceptable, Jackson. Not at all."

His voice was calm and reasonable, which made her even angrier. "You basically told me that you're supposed to be resting. You were going to make me tea and clearly you were dizzy. Stop being so irrationally stubborn. I told you to sit down, you didn't. I warned you, you ignored me, so I followed through on what I said I'd do."

Long past remembering that this man could fire her, she almost shouted. "Bullshit. You crossed the line, and you know it."

The tea kettle whistled, and he stood up. "Where's the tea?"

"Cupboard to the left." She grumbled.

"Do you want anything in it?"

Her tone was sullen. "No."

A few minutes later, he came back with two mugs. Placing one in front of her, he sat down next to her and slowly reached out his hand toward her, watching for her reaction. When she didn't swing at him, he gently pulled her chin toward him and carefully lifted her hair off her temple. He felt sickened as he saw the extent of the bruising for the first time. "Forgive me for being a stupid city boy, but how did a *sheep* do this to you?"

She pulled away, knowing that she had to keep space between them. Her emotions were way too close to the surface, and it would be so easy to fall into his arms. "There was a commotion in the barn, so I went out there. Something was going on in the sheep pen, so I climbed in, and the ram hit me from behind. I remember hitting my head, but I also clearly hit my side and cracked a rib."

"You went in the barn alone at night? What the hell were you thinking?"

The second comment pushed her anger level up again. "I have a *farm*. I'm in the barn day and night, and a lot of the time, I'm alone."

"That's ridiculous. I bet that damn ram probably had fifty pounds on you. You could've been killed."

"I'm fine. I took a blow, that's all."

He tried to control his frustration and his overwhelming sense of worry about her, feeling that there was more to the story than what she was telling him. He tried to keep the emotion out of his voice. "And the doctor said you have a concussion and the cracked rib? That's it? You were checked carefully?"

In her heart, she knew she should tell him, but she couldn't do it. "Yes, I was checked carefully."

"And you're supposed to be resting, right? And you're doing that?"

"Yes. I've sat on this stupid couch for two days. Okay?"

He smiled, knowing how mad she was at him already, and enjoying the petulant look on her face. "And how pissed are you going to be when I tell you that I need a doctor's note saying you're cleared for work?"

Shock and anger made her turn faster than she should have. The pain in her ribs announced itself first, followed closely by a cramp worse than any before. Her sharp intake of breath told Jack how much pain she was in, but she jumped off the couch and swayed, grabbing the couch for stability. "Not fair. If you'd gotten my message today, you wouldn't be here, and we wouldn't be having this conversation. It's Friday night. I can't get a doctor's appointment until Monday morning at the earliest. Now, because of you, I wouldn't be able to be back at work before mid-day Monday." Her voice cracked. "That's unfair."

His voice was calm, but insistent. "I think we've already established that I'll physically move you if I need to. So right now, sit down. We can have this conversation, but not while you look like you're going to pass out."

She sat down on the couch and clasped her hands in her lap. Her tone was pleading. "Please, I've never missed two days of school in a row for a medical reason before, and I need to get back there on Monday. Please."

"Drink your tea."

"What?"

"Drink your tea. At least a sip. You look like you're probably dehydrated too."

She picked up the mug but put it down again as her hands were shaking too badly to hold it without spilling. The grief, the physical pain, and the emotional turmoil of having him sitting on her couch were too much. Swallowing hard, she tried to take a deep breath. She picked up the mug in both hands and took a sip. "Happy now?"

"Happier."

She put the cup down. "Jack, please. I'm doing exactly what the doctor said. I plan to rest all weekend. Why do I need to get cleared before I go back to work? Please. If you hadn't come up here today, you wouldn't have known any of this. I shouldn't be punished because you didn't have cell service."

He sat back, his gaze never leaving her face. "Would you have told Charlie?"

"What are you talking about?"

"If Charlie was still the superintendent, would you have told him you were injured?"

She looked down at her hands, knowing that she would have told him all about the injury, just not about the miscarriage. She whispered. "Probably."

"Then why didn't you tell me?"

Georgiana felt her abdominal muscles tense and realized that another cramp was going to hit. She closed her eyes and waited to speak until the pain passed, unaware that he was watching her with great concern. Trying to control her breathing, she finally opened her eyes to look at him. "Partially because you were away for the last few days, but really because it's not as simple with you."

"Why?"

She slammed her hand down on the arm of the couch in fury as she shouted, "Because we slept together and then made a decision about the boundaries. I don't want to talk to you about my body. It was bad enough that I had to talk about Tyler Abrams with you. It got worse when I threw up in front of you. I don't want to talk to you about how much it hurts to breathe right now or how much my head hurts. I just want you to get the fuck out of my space and leave me alone."

His voice showed a hint of humor. "Probably doesn't help to yell either. Does it?"

She saw his amusement and blew out a sigh. "No, it didn't help to yell, either. My head hurts more now, thanks."

Just then, her phone buzzed with a text. She looked on in horror as Jackson glanced at the screen and saw a message from Boone. "*G, what the hell happened? Call me NOW!*"

The phone buzzed again. *"Love you now and forever."* And again. *"Do you want me to come up there tonight? I can get emergency leave."*

Jack's felt like a knife had been stabbed into his hear. "Your boyfriend?"

"Did you just use the word *'boyfriend'*? What are we, thirteen?"

"Yeah...Well...Is he?"

She closed her eyes again, sighing with exasperation. "No, he's not my boyfriend."

He needed to argue with her about this. "He seems to think he is. He just sent you several messages clearly knowing something happened to you."

Georgiana opened her eyes and pushed her hair back in a frustrated movement. Again, Jack saw the angry bruise. "He's not my boyfriend, he's my friend. His name is Boone."

"Is he your lover?" Jack was taken aback by how much her answer mattered to him.

She shook her head. "No. He's in my brother's unit, and I've known him since I was eighteen. Several years after my divorce, we became lovers, but that ended about a year ago. But we aren't in love with each other. Never have been, never will be. It's not that kind of a relationship. Now we're just friends, nothing more."

"Is he the guy that came to the second party when Tyler Abrams got out of hand?"

Georgiana was startled that he knew about that. "Yes."

"So, he's pretty important to you."

"He is. He's my good friend. Period." She looked at him seriously. "Jack, whatever you think of me right now, I can promise you that if I was seeing someone, I wouldn't have been with you in Seattle."

Jack really wanted to believe her, but his tone betrayed his doubt. "Okay."

"And yes, I did text him that I got hurt, but they were out on a training mission, so I guess he just got the message."

He tried to keep the judgment out of his voice. "He's important enough to you that you told him you got hurt?"

"Yes, I told Boone. He's my friend, one of my best friends. I was feeling whiny and sorry for myself, so I texted a friend. I texted my brother too. Boone's getting back to me, nothing more. I love him, he loves me. But again, not that I should have to explain this to you, we aren't in love with each other. I was feeling down and reached out to someone who makes me feel safe."

Tears filled her eyes as in her mind, she thought, *because subconsciously I needed to know that someone would love me and my child if you rejected us.* Then she sniffed forcefully. "Jack, I whacked my head. My thinking isn't necessarily as clear as I would like."

Just then the back door opened, and she heard boots on the tiles in the entryway. Relief flooded her as she heard Shroom's voice. "Georgie, where are you?"

"In the living room..."

Shroom was clearly surprised when he came into the room and saw Jackson. "Hey kiddo, didn't know you had company. Want me to come back later?"

She shook her head. "You're fine. Michael Mumley, the new superintendent, Jackson Ryder. Jack, my friend Michael Mumley, commonly known as Shroom."

Jackson stood up and held out his hand. "The Michael Mumley who grows mushrooms?"

"One and the same."

"I bought your book for my dad. He grows shiitakes."

Over the next few minutes, Georgiana only half-listened as the two men discussed mushroom cultivation, trying to relax her body to keep the cramps at bay. She was not really paying attention to the conversation when she heard Shroom say, "So, Jackson, I made chicken and dumplings for dinner tonight to make sure she eats something. Would you like to join us?"

Jackson smiled. "That sounds great."

Georgiana stifled a groan. "That would be wonderful, just wonderful..."

Over the next two hours, Georgiana tried to find her bearings while the two men chatted. She sat silently while they discussed Shroom's role on her farm and talked about their views on organic farming. It was a completely different side of Jack than she'd ever seen and with a start, she realized she'd begun to fantasize about what it would be like to have him truly be part of her personal life. Just as she realized how her mind was wandering, a cramp hit her so hard it made her drop the fork she'd been using to push food around on her plate. The clatter startled both men and they looked at her in concern. Jackson's voice was insistent. "Are you okay?"

She tried to control her breathing, trying to ride out the pain even as the grief filled her again. "Just breathed wrong."

Jack pushed his chair back. "C'mon, you're going to lie down again."

She shook her head, fighting the urge to cry. "I'm fine. Just sit down."

He held out his hand. "I'm not asking, I'm *telling* you. You're going to lie down."

"Jack! Stop ordering me to do things."

Shroom broke in before Jack could respond. "He's right. You've been sitting up for a while. It's time for you to go lie down. Stop being contrary."

Georgiana looked at Shroom and he could see the hurt in her eyes that he'd sided with Jack. She didn't say a word, just shoved her chair back so hard it almost tipped over as she walked out of the kitchen. She started toward the stairs, and Shroom grinned broadly at Jack as he said loudly, "You're not supposed to go up and down the stairs without company right now, remember?"

"Fuck off, Shroom!" She stopped at the bottom of the stairs; her voice suddenly much quieter but her anger was still clear as she said, "Will one of you walk me up the stairs?"

Shroom stood up. "Jack will. I'll do the dishes."

Jack walked over to the stairs and tried to hide a smile as he saw her standing at the bottom holding onto the railing, not looking at him. When he was standing next to her, she started up without a word. At the top she muttered. "I'm going to brush my teeth and use the bathroom."

While she was in the bathroom, he looked around the upstairs. Her bedroom was warm and comfortable. For a moment, he let himself wonder what it would be like to sleep here beside her, waking to look at the sun glinting off the pond below, looking to the mountains beyond. Sliding glass doors opened to a large balcony. Down the hall, two bedrooms shared another full bath. In the far corner of the house was a room filled with neat shelves of yarn and fibers, with a spinning wheel and a loom in the middle of the room.

Jack was looking at the blanket on the loom when she walked in behind him. Her voice was calmer. "This is my fiber studio."

He touched the blanket. "It's beautiful." He suddenly saw the photo on the beam of the loom. "That's the pattern you're weaving?"

She stepped closer to pull the photo down to hand it to him. "It was a blanket I saw two years ago when I was in Syria working with my mom. I wanted to see if I could replicate the pattern."

He looked around the room. "Did you spin the yarn yourself?"

"No. I have fiber milled each year. I spin some for my own weaving and knitting. But for a project like this, I wanted the challenge to be the design, not the materials."

He handed the photo back to her. "It's beautiful. How long have you been working on it?"

She shrugged. "I started designing it last spring but didn't really start putting in time on it until late summer." She put the photo back then ran her hand over the blanket. "I'm sorry I yelled at you."

He gestured to the bench of the loom. "Sit down. Please?"

She sat, and he squeezed in next to her, turning to look at her. "If you're apologizing, so am I. I'm not trying to piss you off. I'm just worried."

"And you think I'm stubborn and not taking care of myself?"

He smiled. "Yes, I think you're stubborn as hell. I just want to make sure you're okay."

"I'm doing what the doctor said."

"Really? If Shroom hadn't said something, would you have walked up the stairs alone just because you were mad at me?"

Immediately, her tone was defensive, "Other than that, I've been careful."

"Okay." Taking a chance on her reaction, he reached over and squeezed her hand. "I just want you to be careful. In one week, I've seen you get sick, then get hurt, and it worries me."

It came home to her then how much she cared about what this man thought of her. "I'm okay. Just a little beat up right now." She stood up, needing to put physical space between them. "Can you walk me back downstairs?"

"My pleasure."

Shroom was just hanging up a dish towel, the kitchen gleaming. He turned as he heard their footsteps. "Hey, I forgot to get ice cream today. I'll pick some up tomorrow. You sleeping down here again tonight, kiddo?"

"Don't worry about the ice cream, I don't need it. Yeah, I'll stay down here again tonight."

Jack glanced over at the living room. "Where? On the couch?"

She shook her head. "No, there's a guest room."

"Where?"

"Come with me." Georgiana walked him through the downstairs. The formal dining room at one end of the house had a beautiful Queen Anne table and hutch, another set of French doors opening out to the porch overlooking the pond. On the other side of the house was a small guest room and bathroom next to what was clearly an office.

He looked at her in interest. "Your office?"

"Yes."

"Why so far from your studio?"

She shrugged. "Because they're two very distinct parts of my life. I don't want them to mingle."

Shroom called from the living room. "Georgie, we need to plan out tomorrow."

Jack looked at her. "What's tomorrow?"

"Shroom has to go to Burlington to a food festival, so we need to figure out what's going on here." A look of exhaustion crossed her face. "Be right there."

In the living room, she sat gingerly on the couch. Jack took the armchair across from her, next to Shroom, who stroked his beard. "So, I need to be on the road at six tomorrow morning. I'll come by, take you upstairs and down, then get you settled. I'll call Mark…" He saw the look of confusion on Jack's face, "He helps on my farm, a friend. Anyway, I'll call him when I get home tonight to have him come do chores. There are leftovers in the fridge. Then when I get back, I'll check on you. I'll even pick up some Cherry Garcia on the way home."

She shook her head. "I should be fine tomorrow. I can take care of stuff here. I'll be okay."

Filled with the need to protect and care for her, Jack interrupted. "Shroom, I've got tomorrow. I can come up and check on her. I can do chores too." He smiled at her, seeing her eyes widen. "She can walk with me out to the barn and tell me what to do."

She snorted, then winced. "Like you'd do anything I said…" Her voice got more serious. "You don't have to. I'm fine without a babysitter."

His gaze was intense. "You're not fine right now, and you know I'm going to do it anyway. You might as well not argue."

After Jack had left, Shroom leaned down to kiss Georgiana's hair. "Little girl, I like him. I like him a lot." He saw the tears building in her eyes. "I'll be back in the morning to walk you upstairs and down, then he'll come over. Maybe this is what is meant to be."

Chapter Nineteen

At four in the morning Georgiana woke to an agonizing cramp and knew that it was done. Minutes later, her cell phone buzzed with a text from her brother. *"Love you."* And she knew that he'd felt it too.

When Shroom came in at five-thirty, he saw the exhaustion and bone-deep sadness on her face. "When?"

"About an hour ago."

He sat down at the table and squeezed her hand where it lay next to her cold cup of tea. "Sorry, sweetie. I wish it'd been different."

"Me too." Her voice broke. "Shroom, I don't want Jack here all day. I can't keep myself together around him. All I want to do is lie down and cry."

"Then lie down and cry. And if you won't tell him, which I think you should, then just say it's because of the blow to your head that you're emotional." He smiled. "How about I get a little sapling at the festival today and we'll plant it for the little one? Just us."

The tears ran down her cheeks at his thoughtfulness. "I'd love that."

It was somewhere around ten in the morning when Georgiana heard tires on the driveway, and she struggled to sit up on the couch. *Why is he here so early?* What was she going to do with him around all day? At least the cramps were easing.

His knock was accompanied by the doorknob being turned. As he looked into the living room, he was concerned. "Why isn't the door locked? You're here by yourself. Anyone could come in."

Her voice was wry. "*Anyone* just did. I had Shroom leave it unlocked in case I was asleep when you got here. I figured I probably wouldn't see you until mid-afternoon."

As much as it worried him that the door had been unlocked with what had been going on with Tyler Abrams, he still had to smile, glad her sarcasm was returning. "I figured maybe you'd like to go outside for a bit while the weather's nice." He headed toward the kitchen. "Let me put this stuff away, then you tell me what you want to do."

She swayed when she stood up, and Jack said sharply, "Sit down."

"I'm not sitting down. I need to stand up some." She walked toward the kitchen. "What are you putting away?"

He was already unpacking bags of groceries. "Food."

Her tone was indignant. "I don't need you to get me food!"

"You seem to *think* you don't need food, but you do." He opened the freezer and put some Ben and Jerry's in the door. "When was the last time you got groceries?"

She leaned against the counter. "A couple weeks ago."

"Well, it looks like you haven't eaten much in a while, so I brought food. I even got the ice cream."

She bristled. "What do you mean by that?"

"By what?"

"By saying that it looks like I haven't eaten much."

His tone was kind. "Georgiana, when we made our rules in Seattle, one of my own rules was to consciously *not* look at your body, because frankly, my attraction to you is no less now than it was then. But when I got here yesterday, it dawned on me that you've lost a lot of weight."

For a moment, she felt a reflexive warmth spread through her at the thought that he still found her attractive. She sat down at the table, pushing that feeling aside. "I'm fine. Just got busy, then had the stomach thing and eating didn't seem appealing. I'll bounce back, no worries."

"You'll bounce back a lot faster with food in the house. Tonight, I'm making dinner and I'm going to nag you until you eat more than you did last night."

She gave him a sour look. "You're such a pain in the ass."

"True." He leaned against the kitchen sink and for just a moment, she let herself admire how good he looked in his faded jeans and dark gray t-shirt. "Did you eat anything this morning?"

The blush on her cheeks gave him the answer but he repeated himself. "What did you have to eat this morning?"

She whispered. "I had some tea a little bit before Shroom came over."

"And he was here at what, five? It's ten now and you haven't had anything to eat or drink since then?"

He could almost see her swallow her guilt before demanding, "Stop the inquisition!"

"It's not an inquisition. You're hurt and your body and head will heal faster if you stay hydrated and nourished."

She looked down at the table and didn't say a word. Several long seconds passed before Jack said softly, "Georgiana?"

She shook her head, still not looking up as she tried to pull herself together.

He came over to the table and squatted down so he could see her face in profile and could see the glisten of tears. "Look at me," he said with great tenderness.

She shook her head again and he put a finger under her chin, turning her head to face him. She still didn't make eye contact. Tears were running down her cheeks and he wiped one away with his thumb.

He could see her trying to hold back sobs, but that gentle touch was her undoing. Taking her hands, he stood, pulling her up with him so he could wrap his arms around her. One of her hands grabbed a handful of his shirt, much like a child would hold a security blanket. As her body shook with silent sobs and he just held her, stroking her back and not saying a word. His shirt became wet and still he just stood and held her, not speaking. Cradling her, he realized how physically fragile she'd become in the last months; he could feel the bones of her spine under his hands. When she finally stopped shaking, he could feel her trying to take a deep breath. Her voice was meek as she softly said, "Thank you."

He kissed the top of her head, his arms still wrapped protectively around her. "For what? Making you cry?"

He could feel her shake her head, but she didn't look up or pull away. "You didn't make me cry. Not really."

"Then tell me what did."

She leaned back, finally looking up at him. He was amazed by how painfully beautiful she was, even with red and swollen eyes. She shifted her focus to his shirt, and said, "I got snot on you."

He looked down at the shirt. "It'll wash out. What made you cry?"

"You being so nice. I don't know what to do with you. You're bossy and controlling, and you keep telling me what to do and I hate that. My head hurts like hell and I can't take a deep breath. I'm light-headed and I absolutely, totally, and completely *hate* needing anyone to take care of me."

His arms were still around her as he continued to stroke her back. "What do you mean? Why do you need to figure out what to do with me?"

"You boss me around, you picked me up and carried me yesterday, you won't let me make a decision for myself. But you're also being so sweet and considerate, and it's confusing. My brain is too scrambled to know what to do with it all. I get so mad at you, then you make sense, and I'm mad because I feel like an idiot."

"You know that right now you need to heal…right? You know that you need rest, food, all of that, but…right now, you can't do it on your own. And that's okay. Everyone needs someone sometimes."

"No, they don't." She said with defiance, her voice becoming rather indignant. "I don't. I hate this. I hate needing someone to remind me to fucking eat something. I hate that I can't go out and take care of my own animals. I hate that I need someone to walk me upstairs to change my clothes. I hate knowing you're right that I'm not ready to go back to work on Monday, and I hate that I'm going to sit here, unable to do anything because I got hurt." She turned her head sharply as her eyes filled with tears again. As she moved, he felt her body sag against him. "And I hate that I'm fucking dizzy! I can't clear my head and my emotions are all over the place." She was practically shouting by now. "I hate, hate, *hate* that."

His voice was soothing as he finally understood what was going through her mind. "Sit down." He quickly added, "Please?" before she could protest.

She sat in her chair, rubbing her eyes with shaking hands. He sat down next to her and pulled her hands toward him, so he was holding both of them in his. "Let me recap. If I've got this wrong, tell me. You're overtired with a concussion, coming off the stomach flu, and you have a broken rib. All of that would be a lot. Just from what Charlie's told me of your upbringing, it's probably safe to say that at least until you moved back to Vermont, you had a fairly strong need to be in control of your world, your body, your mind. My guess is that your mom wasn't big on the warm fuzzies."

A ghost of a smile crossed her face. "That's an understatement."

"So, needing help isn't something you're comfortable with—"

"True."

"And then, it being me helping you is making it worse."

She looked down at their hands, letting her silence answer.

"Why is my helping you an issue?"

Georgiana looked at him without speaking, debating how much to tell him, finally deciding to be honest. "Because I don't know how to feel about you. If Seattle hadn't happened, and we just worked together, I'd think it was weird that you're being this helpful. There's no way you would've picked me up yesterday, made a comment about me losing weight, or held me while I cried."

"Probably true."

"And my thinking is so muddled. I don't know whether to pitch a fit so you leave or ask you to hold my hand and keep me company. I don't know if

I'm reading too much into things, or not enough. I don't know whether to throw something at you or kiss you." She rubbed her temple and smiled. "You're confusing the fuck out of someone with an already-addled brain."

He squeezed her hand. "It's just as confusing for me. You were pretty clear at the festival that being a couple was out of the question. Some mixed messages aside, you've been pretty clear that you didn't see us as a possibility. Then you ran out of that room last Friday and scared the shit outta me. When I came yesterday and saw that bruise on your face, I was ready to kill whoever hurt you." He looked at her, tipping his head and smiling gently. "I was so mad that you were hurt and hadn't told me. The fact that you called Boone instead of me? I was ready to punch something."

She tried to lighten the mood, "Have you thought about talking to someone about your anger issues?"

"Yeah, yeah. I know this is weird, I get it. I'm confused as hell too. You're stubborn, painfully opinionated, and without question, the *most* competent, *least* needy woman I've ever met. You absolutely frustrate me." He rubbed his thumb over her knuckles, "And even having said that, I *still* want to be around you, and I feel a need to protect you, even if it's from yourself."

She chuckled and for the first time in the two days, Jack saw her face relax. "I probably do need to be saved from myself right now."

"I'll say."

She swatted at his hands, smiling as he grabbed her hand. "Insufferable ass."

"True." His eyes twinkled. "So now will you please eat something?"

"Fine, if it'll make you stop nagging."

"What do you want?"

"I don't know. Nothing really, but I know you're right." She looked around the room, seeing the package on the counter by the toaster. "Half an English muffin?"

He remembered her choices in Seattle. "With peanut butter?"

"With peanut butter."

Five minutes later, he put the plate in front of her with a cup of hot tea. She smiled at him tiredly. "Thank you."

He sat down across from her watching as she took a small bite. "Tell me about your childhood."

"Huh?"

"Your childhood. Tell me about it."

"Why?"

He grinned. "So, I can understand why you're so stubborn and independent."

She took a sip of tea, then another. "My mom got pregnant when she was twenty-five, a doctoral student working her internship through a collaboration between the Peace Corps and the UN. She never told us who our dad was, so I don't know how they met, or where."

He interrupted. "You don't know who your dad is? Like, not at all?"

"Not at all. Not even a clue. Anyway, she got pregnant. She came home here, finished her program through distance-learning, and had us. As I understand it, we were just under a year old when she left here and took us to a UN refugee camp in Laos so she could work."

"Seriously?"

"Yeah. By the time we were five, we'd lived in UN encampments in Laos, India, and the Gaza Strip. By the time we were ten, Bosnia, Somalia, Syria, Yemen, Bangladesh, and several other lovely war zones. Everywhere she was sent, she took us with her."

"And you lived in the camps?" Jack tried hard to keep the judgement out of his voice. How could a parent willingly put her children in such hell holes?

She nodded, trying to assess his tone. "Uh huh. She took it very seriously, still does, the idea that she shouldn't live better than the populations she works with, so we lived in the camps like everyone there. I guess we had a more stable food supply, but not much else. We went to the camp schools, but at night, she also home-schooled us. *That,* she was really good at. When we came back to Vermont, both of us could've graduated high school at fifteen because we were so far ahead."

"How did you have any sense of security living like that?"

She took another bite of muffin. "We had each other, PJ and I. *We* were the security. Mom loves us, but her love pales in comparison to her dedication to her work. We relied on each other for love, security, safety. You know how resiliency theory says that every child needs an adult who makes them feel like they are the center of the universe?" Jack nodded. "My mom never made us feel that way. Our grandparents and Shroom did, we did for each other, but not Mom."

"Hence why you are so close to Shroom…" It was a statement, not a question.

"Absolutely. He was always here when we came home to Vermont, and when we moved back full-time, he was the most parent-aged adult we had in our lives. He was the bridge between us and our grandparents." She took a sip of her tea, then looked into the mug, lost in memories. "Once in a while, Mom would let us come back here to see our grandparents. We could navigate any airport in the world on our own by the time we were ten, so she'd drop us off and we'd get back here. I remember always feeling weird with kids here because they had rooms of their own, closets full of stuff, choices for meals. We each had basically two small bags of stuff and a shared a trunk of books and supplies, always shared a living space, and we ate whatever was available." She snorted. "I can remember hearing Ellie talk about her lunch box, and the lunches her mom made for her to take to school. We were maybe ten at the time, and I couldn't imagine having little bags of chips in your lunch. Often, we had flatbreads, rice, and beans, sometimes that was it for weeks at a time." She shrugged. "Different realities but helped us to understand how others were living."

"And you lived like that until you were what, fourteen?"

"Almost fifteen." Her voice became even quieter, and Jack found himself straining to hear her. "We rebelled, my grandparents rebelled, my grandfather threatened to take Mom to family court for custody, and finally she let us stay here permanently."

"And your grandparents, what are they like?"

A true smile crossed her face. "They're a hoot. My grandfather—"

He interrupted. "The farmer. He had the farm before you, right?"

"My grandfather, the federal court judge *and* farmer."

His voice rose. "What?"

"He was Vermont's federal judge by day, farmer by nights and weekends." She looked at Jack with the first light in her eyes he'd seen in days. "And my grandmother was the first sex therapist in Vermont. They're quite a pair."

"Where are they now?"

"They live in an assisted living place near Montpelier."

"And Shroom?"

"My grandparents had two children—my mom and my uncle Jason. Twins, like us. Jason was killed in Vietnam before we were born. Shroom was his best friend. They went to law school together. Shroom clerked for Grandpa, then he and Uncle Jason opened a firm together in Burlington. Both of them went to Vietnam. Uncle Jason was drafted and didn't fight it, Shroom enlisted. Jason was killed and after Shroom came back from his tour, he started showing up here to help around the farm. He and my grandfather built his house up in the woods and when they gave PJ and me the land here, they deeded ten acres to him."

Jack's mind tried to reconcile the idea of the mushroom man being an attorney. "Is he still a lawyer?"

"Yes, but only pro bono cases. He makes enough off the mushrooms and his writing to do what he wants. He helps me around the farm and has sort of assumed a father role for us over the years."

"And your mom?"

"She comes back to Vermont once every five years or so for a few days, then leaves again. I go see her a couple of times a year, wherever she's stationed. PJ sees her less often."

He realized that she'd eaten almost all of her English muffin while they'd been talking. "Finish your breakfast." She rolled her eyes at him but ate the last bite. He stood up and picked up the dishes, rinsing them and putting them in the dishwasher. "Do you want to take a rest, or go outside?"

"Outside sounds good." She looked very young and shy. "Do you want to see the property?"

"I'd love to."

Over the next hour, they slowly walked from the house to the pond, then along a neat path to a second house, PJ's, hidden from view on a cove of the pond. They then walked back to the vegetable garden. Jack realized her steps were slowing. "Okay, it's time for you to rest. Do you want to sit on the porch or go inside?"

"The porch."

"I'm going to get you settled, then go inside and get you something to drink." He looked at her hopefully. "Any chance you'd eat something, too?"

Remembering that the doctor said her potassium level was low, she said, "A banana?"

"You got it."

When they were both seated in the Adirondack chairs, Georgiana gave Jack a long look, although her eyes were hidden behind sunglasses. "So, now that you know why I'm so fucked up, tell me about *your* childhood."

He leaned back in his chair. "Well, I guess it's fair to say that my childhood was the exact opposite of yours."

"Lucky you."

He nodded. "Yeah, I was lucky. I *am* lucky. My mom and dad met on their first day of college, fell in love, and got married the day after they graduated. Dad went to law school, Mom to med school. When they'd both graduated, they had the three of us. They're still head over heels in love with each other, live in a small house with a white picket fence, and we had every possible sense of security growing up."

"And your siblings? I know you said you have a sister who went to art school, but I don't remember if you said anything about any others."

"My older sister, Jenn, is an employment lawyer, part of Dad's firm. She's married, has four kids and her husband is a high school physics teacher. My younger sister, Lyndsay, is an artist in New York. She's married to a wonderful woman, and they just had their first child, a son, in May."

Over the next hour, as they sat and talked quietly, it dawned on Jack that it was the first time they'd talked without tension, without that painfully strong sexual awareness of each other, and without the imposed genteel veneer of their professionalism. He looked over at Georgiana and realized that her nose was getting pink. "Time to go inside for a bit. You're getting sunburned."

She sat up, wincing. "Probably a good idea."

In the house, she took off her sunglasses and Jack could read the exhaustion on her face. He gently rubbed her back. "How irritated will you be if I say you should lie down for a bit?"

She smiled but didn't pull away. "I'd argue just on principle, but still know you're right."

"Ahh, progress. How about you just admit I'm right about everything?"

She laughed and he realized how much he'd missed hearing that sound lately. "In your dreams." She suddenly felt light-headed and reached out to steady herself by holding onto his arm. "What are you going to do?"

"I brought a book. You sleep, I'll read, and in a while, I'll make a late lunch, early dinner."

"Okay." She sat down and Jack lifted her legs onto the couch. He smoothed the blanket over her. She shifted to find a comfortable spot and she looked up at him. "Thanks for hanging out with me today."

He squeezed her hand. "My pleasure."

"You can wander around and look at whatever you want, watch TV, whatever."

"I can amuse myself. Just sleep."

Georgiana saw him settle in the chair across from her, his feet up on the coffee table, and she snuggled into the pillow. Within a minute, her soft breathing told Jack she'd fallen asleep.

Almost two hours later, he stretched and stood up quietly, trying not to wake her. He put his book on the table and wandered upstairs, browsing through the family photos throughout the rooms. In picture after picture, he could see Georgiana and her brother growing up. He noticed that in some, as Georgiana got older, she was wearing the traditional dress of Muslim women and wondered how an independent woman like her handled being in such restrictive environments. *How could she be as normal as she was with such a strange upbringing?*

He heard a noise downstairs and went to the landing to check, assuming she was just turning over. Suddenly her voice cut through the air with a note of panic. "Jack!"

Later, he would wonder how he got down the stairs so fast. As he came into the living room at a full run, he could see absolute terror on her face as she struggled upright on the couch. He went to her, crouching down to pull her into his arms. "It's okay, I'm here."

Her voice sounded almost childlike as she clutched his shirt. "You weren't here. I dreamt that you got hurt, and I woke up and you weren't here. I didn't know what to do."

He rubbed her back soothingly, knowing that her concussion had clearly caused the nightmare. She was shaking with residual fear. "It's okay. I just went upstairs to look at the photos, that's it. I was right here until just a few minutes ago and I'm not hurt. I'm fine."

She pulled back to look up at him and put a trembling hand on the side of his face. "It was so real." Her eyes filled with tears. "And my brain is so fucking muddled right now."

"Hey, it's okay. It was a bad dream, that's all. Your brain is trying to get synapses going again and some of them are going to be a bit wacky right now."

She took a huge breath in, then hissed as the pain hit. "Fuck! I am so sick of not being able to breathe!" She tried to smile. "Sorry for scaring you."

He chuckled, pushing a damp curl back off her forehead. "We'll call it my cardio for the day."

She breathed in slowly, and he could practically see her reassemble her thoughts. "You were looking at photos?"

"Uh huh."

She stood up, trying to calm her heart rate. "C'mon. I'll walk you through them. I may even be able to remember where they were taken."

They wandered through the house, and at each photo, she told him where it was taken and something about her experiences. When they were back in the living room, he was pleased to see her color was much closer to normal. Suddenly, she smiled. "You know you have to do chores soon, right?"

"I do. Are you up to going to the barn now?"

"I believe I am."

Jackson was stunned at how pristine the barn seemed. Georgiana motioned to a row of boots by the door. "You'll need those."

He pulled off his sneakers and pulled on a pair of barn boots. "Sit down. You can boss me around just as well while you're seated, so I don't have to worry that you're going to fall over."

"Fine." She sat on a bench by the large pen as the group of alpacas came into the barn, attracted by the sound of her voice. She stood up and leaned against the fence, rubbing their necks. She looked over and saw Jack giving her a pointed look. "Oh, fine." She sat down with a huff, then winced as the pain hit.

"Serves you right," he laughed.

Just then there was a loud noise from the other side of the barn and Jack stared in amazement as the largest cow he'd ever seen came in from the pasture making a plaintive sound. "Holy fuck, what is that thing?"

Georgiana stood up carefully and walked toward Jack. Without thinking about what she was doing, she took his hand and pulled him forward to the fence as the animal came over. "This is Bully." The creature made the same sad sound again and put his head over the fence, stretching toward them. "Hi Bully." She rubbed his nose. "I know, I've missed you too." She took Jack's hand and put it on Bully's nose. Jack tentatively stroked the huge animal. "He's my pet steer. He weighs close to two thousand pounds but he's the most docile, well-behaved animal on the farm."

"You have a bull?"

"No, he's a *steer* now. He was in transport to the meat auction, the truck was in an accident, and the animals got loose. He came over to the school and was playing on the playground with the kids. I bought him from the farmer, had him castrated so he won't ever get aggressive, and he's lived here with me for," she paused, thinking back, "for almost five years." She rubbed his nose again. "He gets sad if he doesn't see me every day and I haven't been out to the barn since Wednesday. He just needs to know I'm still here."

Jack leaned forward to rub the big guy's neck. He started to laugh. "You have a fucking steer."

Just then the sheep trooped in and started bleating in their pen. Georgiana sat back down on the bench and smiled at Jack. "Now *I* get to tell *you* what to do."

Over the next hour, she talked him through feeding and watering the alpacas, the sheep, Bully, the chickens, and the goat. She taught him how to gather eggs, clean the pens, and how to make sure all the latches on all the gates were closed.

When he was done, he sat down next to her on the bench, a satisfied smile on his face. "That was the most fun I've had in a long, long time." He looked behind him at the happily munching animals. "What an amazing group of creatures."

"Ah, the city boy is hooked." She nodded. "They are amazing. They're all so different but all of them make me happy."

He suddenly remembered something. "Where's the sheep that hurt you?"

She shrugged. "Gone. Shroom took him to the neighbor's farm until we can figure out if it was just a bad night or if he's getting aggressive. If it was just a one-time thing, he'll be back in a few weeks. Otherwise, we have an agreement with Bully's home farm to take him for their lambing program."

Jackson stood up and held his hand out to her. "Okay, how about I get cleaned up, then food?"

For the first time in days, Georgiana realized she almost felt hungry. "Sounds good."

Chapter Twenty

In the kitchen, Jack pulled out a chair. "Sit down and keep me company."

"I can help."

"You can *watch*." He looked around the kitchen, clearly in search of something. "Where's the concussion protocol from the doctor?"

"How do you know there is one?"

His grin was confident. "My mom's an ER doctor and when I called her last night trying to figure out how much of a controlling ass I needed to be with you, she said they would have given you a list of instructions."

Georgiana was glad she'd shredded the pregnancy handouts. "It's on the windowsill."

He found it and scanned it quickly. Putting it back on the windowsill, he turned. "Okay, I'm getting you some seltzer now, but it says you can have a small glass of wine with dinner if that sounds good."

That sounded better than good! "That would be great."

Georgiana's phone rang from the kitchen table. She looked at the screen and grimaced before connecting the call. "Hi Mom, you're on speaker phone and I'm here with my friend Jackson."

The connection was poor, as if to make it clear that it came from very far away. "Hello, Jackson. Georgiana, how are you?"

"I took a knock this week and have a concussion, but otherwise I'm okay."

"Well. Then heal quickly, Georgie. Sweetie, I can't talk for long, I have a camp directors' meeting in five minutes. I just wanted to say that there's a change for December."

Jackson watched with interest as Georgiana's face became pinched, and he was frustrated on her behalf that her mother didn't ask for more details about her health. His own mom had asked a million questions about her when he'd called her last night. Georgiana's voice was controlled. "What's the change? I already have my travel booked. I sent you the info, remember?"

"I know you did, Georgie, but in two weeks I'm heading to Chad. I expect I'll be there until spring at least. So, you'll need to change your plans to come to Chad instead."

Georgiana leaned forward, her head resting on one hand while the other started kneading the side of her neck. "Seriously, Mom? Chad?"

"Georgiana! You know we go…"

Georgiana's voice was sharp. "I know. We go where we are needed. *I know.*"

"So, call the travel office and make the change."

"Mom, again, I have a concussion. I'll call, but it's going to be mid-week at least. I need to make sure my brain is clear. I still have the same block of time available. I remember how hard it was to get land transfers the last time we were in Chad, so I may not be there as long as you'd like."

"Ask your boss for some extra time."

Georgiana couldn't look at Jack, knowing he was watching this conversation with great interest. "I took extra time in April. I can't do it again now."

"I disagree, but fine. All right, Georgie. Love you, gotta go."

"Love you too, Mom."

After disconnecting, Georgiana sat in silence, rubbing her neck. Without saying a word, Jack walked over, gently moved her hand aside, and began to massage her shoulders. At first her muscles were taut and unyielding, but within seconds they began to loosen. With a sigh, she leaned back against him and closed her eyes. "Thank you."

"That help?"

"A lot." The phone rang again, and she opened her eyes, checked the number, and chuckled. "Should've known." She connected the call. "Hey PJ. You're on speaker."

"I know. Hey, Jackson."

How did he know I was here? Jack thought.

Georgiana saw his confusion and squeezed his hand where it rested on her neck. "I told him you were going to be here today."

"Oh. Hi, PJ."

Her brother's voice was amused. "I've had a headache since you got your bell rung, I've gotten used to it, but a few minutes ago it went nuclear. Mom called?"

Georgiana laughed. "Yeah. Sorry about that. She almost gave me an aneurysm."

"What did she want?"

Jack debated sitting down or continuing to massage her neck. Feeling her muscles tense again, he decided to stay where he was as she said, "She's headed to Chad in two weeks."

PJ's voice became strangely quiet with controlled anger. "So, she wants you to go to Chad." He paused. "Tell me you said no."

"I told her I'd go to Damascus. Now she's moving, I'll go to Chad."

"What the fuck, Georgie? *Brilliant* idea. White woman going to Boko Haram territory?"

"PJ, don't start. If you think it's a problem, go with me." She groused. "I hate Chad, but I told her I'd go. Besides it's not like I haven't been there before."

"Seriously, stop trying to please her. *Nothing* is going to please her, and you know it. Unless you're willing to leave your job and join her full-time. Otherwise, you're a failure to her too, just like me. The difference between us is that I accept it and you keep trying to change it."

"PJ, stop. I know you don't agree with me on this but it's *my* life."

"Think about it. Normal mothers don't tell their children to prove their love by spending their vacations in refugee camps. They don't. Even batshit crazy parents don't suggest that their daughters go places where the locals would love nothing better than to kidnap said daughter."

"Then go with me or shut up!"

A loud sigh came through the speaker. "I'm not going with you but let me see who's there so at least I know who can come in and save your pathetic ass if needed."

Georgiana thought for a second. "What about Chas Paul?"

"He was there a couple months ago. Let me message him and find out. If he's there, I'd feel a helluva lot better."

"You'll let me know?"

"Of course."

"Hey, knowing my brain is addled, are you at the computer?"

"Yeah, I am. I just messaged him."

"Please pull my vaccination record? Is my yellow fever vaccination still good?"

There was a pause in the conversation, but in the background, Jack could hear tapping on a keyboard. PJ came back on the line. "Your yellow fever is fine, but you'll need a cholera booster."

"Okay."

"Hey, just got a message from Chas. He's there until March first. He says once you have your itinerary, send it to him and he'll send you a welcome committee."

"Thanks."

"Hey Jackson, you still there?"

Jack was surprised that PJ still remembered his presence. "Yeah, I'm here."

"Does my sister look as tired and beat up as she sounds?"

Keeping one hand on her tense neck muscles, Jack moved to the side to look at her. He smiled as he stroked her cheek. "She looks pretty tired and the bruise on her head is pretty nasty, but her color is way better today."

"Thanks for being there. Will you text me your number so I can reach you if Ms. Stubborn won't answer my calls, or if I want to know how she really is?"

Jack's eyes sparkled with amusement as he looked at her. "No problem."

"Great, thanks again. Gigi, love you, miss you." PJ laughed. "Now that I've given you shit about December, we still on for February?"

A broad grin lit her face. "Of course, we are! Your turn to book."

"I'm on it."

When she hung up the phone, Jackson put out his hand. "Give it to me."

Even as she handed it to him, she asked, "Why?"

"Those two phone calls just put your tension level from 'pretty relaxed' to 'about to lose it.' It's time to put the phone away."

After using her phone to text PJ his own number, Jack silenced her phone and put it in the living room.

He came back into the kitchen and found Georgiana turning the seltzer glass around and around slowly. He sat down next to her and took one of her hands. Tangling his fingers through hers, he tried to keep his voice neutral. "Okay, explain to me what just happened."

She squeezed his hand. "Welcome to my crazy family." She shifted uncomfortably, knowing how strange this would sound to him. "If I have time, I go to wherever my mom is during the December break. I go and teach so the regular teachers get some time off."

"You go work for the UN?"

She looked down at their hands. "I *always* work for the UN, regardless of what my mom is doing. I do consultation and research for them, write for them, and when I can, I go work in the camps with my mom."

Even to his own ears, his voice sounded incredulous. "*You work for the UN?*"

"Yes."

"And Charlie knew this?"

"It's in my contract. I negotiated it when I accepted the job here." She stood up slowly, still holding his hand. "Come with me."

In her office, she gestured for him to shut the huge pocket door behind them. When the door was closed, Jackson could see a world map framed on the inside of the door with a large "Welcome Home!" at the top. The map was covered with multi-colored pegs.

Jack was confused. "What's this?"

Her tone was wry. "Why Dr. Ryder, use your tools. Check the key."

Jack bent down to see the handwritten key in the bottom right corner, then looked up at the forest of pegs and suddenly realized what they signified. "This shows where you've lived!"

"Lived, visited, traveled, whatever. Grandma made it for us when we were kids and updated it whenever we came home so we always remembered that *this* is home. We keep it up now more out of tradition than anything else." She laughed. "Of course, some of PJ's work is classified, so those locations aren't included."

"Holy shit."

"Indeed. Most of the white pegs are camps where we lived as kids, most of the red are camps I've gone to work in since college."

"Wow."

She pulled him to the side of the door, and he realized there were bunches of lanyards hanging there. She pulled one forward and turned it over so he could see her picture on a United Nations I.D. He turned to look at her and without thinking of what he was doing, he reached up and put a hand on the side of her face. "Jesus, Georgiana, every time I think I may be figuring you out, you surprise me again."

"Sorry about that." She looked down, suddenly shy. "I don't really talk about it because it sounds weird to most people, and I get tired of trying to explain it in a way that makes sense."

"Enough revelations, my brain is spinning." He smiled. "Come back to the kitchen and keep me company while I make dinner."

In the kitchen, Georgiana sat down, then smiled as he pulled out a chair and said, "Put your feet up."

She complied, then took a sip of seltzer, watching him wash his hands at the sink. With his back to her, he said, "I thought salmon, pasta, and vegetables. That sound okay?"

"Yeah." She paused. "That actually sounds really good. I think I may be getting hungry."

"Good."

The kitchen was quiet as he started gathering ingredients. She finally broke the companionable silence. "So, aren't you going to ask if my brother is right about my mother?"

"No." He turned from the sink where he'd been cleaning vegetables. "As I said, I keep trying to figure you out. Every time I ask you a question, as far as I can tell, you give me a true answer. But even as dense as I can be and as controlling as I can be, I know there are some things that may be too much for me to ask." He smiled at her, his eyes filled with warmth and acceptance. "Yet. Too much for me to ask about *yet*."

"You can ask." Suddenly it mattered to her that he know the truth about her relationship with her mother.

"Then I don't need to ask, just tell me."

She thought for a moment. "When we moved back here with our grandparents, Mom saw it as a betrayal. PJ went to the Naval Academy, which she hated. Then I got married at twenty, which she didn't support. Since my divorce, she's been trying to convince me to leave public schools and go to work with her. So yes, PJ is right that she sees us as failures. And he's right that I still try to please her when he routinely tells her to go fuck herself."

"What do you mean she didn't support you getting married? Because you were so young?"

"No, because it was *marriage*. She told me over and over that she hadn't raised me to need a man in my life, and that I was not a true feminist if I wanted to get married." She looked so sad for a moment that Jack fought the urge to comfort her. "She didn't come to my wedding, my college graduation, PJ's graduations, when I got my doctorate, or anything like that. We're disappointments to her."

"Jesus, I'm sorry." He tried to find the right words. "I can't imagine anyone saying that either of you is a disappointment."

Georgiana tried to smile but sadness lingered in her eyes. "Thanks. It's just the way it is. But PJ's right. I keep banging my head on the wall and trying to make her happy by going to the camps." Before he could interrupt, she said, "Wait, before you say something that'll piss me off, you need to know that I actually *do* love going. Not to Chad, but I do usually love the trips. They give me a good kick in the ass, shake the dust off my brain and survival skills, and when Mom and I can talk strictly education, we do pretty well."

"Okay." He walked over to refill her glass. "Promise me that when your head is clearer, we can talk about this Chad trip?"

"Why?"

He searched for the right words. "Well, your brother, who doesn't seem to be an alarmist, seems really freaked that you're going. That makes me jumpy."

Georgiana looked at him for so long that he wondered if she'd really heard his question. Finally, she spoke. "I think before we have that conversation, we need to figure out why we are, or aren't, in a situation where I would be talking with you about what I'll be doing on my vacation days."

"What do you mean?"

She smiled and he could see humor returning to her eyes. "Jack, if we're going to start having conversations about my travel plans, that means it's because whatever *this*," she made a motion with one hand that went back and forth between them, "is between us is more than just you helping me out when I've whacked my head."

He walked over to the table and stroked her cheek. "I think we both know this is more than that."

She smiled and reached up to squeeze his hand where it rested on her cheek. "I think we do, but we probably need to figure out what that means." She shrugged. "That being said, I recognize my brain is still pretty mushy, so I need to beg your patience until I'm ready to have that talk."

"Deal."

Over the next half hour, they talked about completely innocuous things while Jack made dinner. When the meal was ready, he poured them each a small glass of red wine and put a plate in front of her before getting his own. "Eat." He paused and smiled. "Please."

A half hour later, Georgiana pushed a mostly empty plate away. "Okay, that's more than I've eaten in the last three days put together." She smiled. "That was really good, thank you."

"My pleasure." He stood up and quietly began to clear the dishes. When she started to stand up to help him, he raised one eyebrow at her, and she sat down in a bit of a huff. He grinned. "Ah, progress. I didn't have to threaten you this time."

She rolled her eyes. "It's not worth it to hear you bitch about it."

"Whatever your motivation, it works for me."

Once the kitchen was gleaming, Jack hung the dish towel up and went over to her. He held out his hand and smiled when she silently put her hand into his. He tugged gently, pulling her to her feet, looking concerned as he saw her wince as she moved. "I really would like to see you more comfortable, you know."

"Me too."

"Now that I have you on your feet, what do you want to do?"

She thought for a moment. "Do you mind walking down to the pond with me?" She looked out the window, seeing the deepening colors of the beginning of the sunset. "We could go sit out there for a bit before it gets dark." Suddenly, her face darkened with a blush. "I'm sorry. I was assuming that you were staying for a while. You don't have to. I'll be fine."

"Seriously?" With his free hand, he stroked her arm. "I'm not going anywhere."

"You gave up your entire day for me."

"It was my choice." He grinned. "And I've had a great day here with you."

She looked very young and unsure of herself. "Really?"

"Really." He squeezed her hand. "Now, if you want to go to the pond, we'll go to the pond."

They walked in silence down to the water and sat on a wooden bench. Jack rubbed his thumb across the back of her hand. "Are you going to get mad if I put my arm around you?"

She smiled and shook her head. "No. I should probably do the moral thing and say that we need to figure this out before we let it go any further, but" — she looked at him seriously — "I want you to." He put his arm around her and smiled as she moved closer, tipping her head so it was resting on his shoulder. He took her hand in his and they sat watching the sunlight glisten off the still water of the pond.

Almost a half-hour later, Georgiana stirred and pulled back to look up at him. "Where are we?"

He turned so he could look at her more directly. "Where are we, or where do I want us to be?"

Her brow furrowed in concentration. "Both, I guess."

His eyes never left hers. "Where I'm at, is that I don't want to do the keep-away game that we agreed on in Seattle. I admit that jumping into sleeping together that fast probably wasn't the wisest idea, but it was never about just finding you attractive." He saw a momentary look of confusion cross her face. "Georgiana, hear me clearly. I'm more physically attracted to you than I've ever been to anyone in my life. *Anyone.* Even right now, when I know you feel rotten, and have a pretty ugly bruise on your face, you still make me crazy with how much I want you. And I find it both exciting and terrifying. But I wouldn't have gone to bed with you just on physical attraction alone. I like you. I love talking with you, seeing how your brain works. I love that you understood the pitch count at the ballgame. I love that you've read the entire Common Core. You make me laugh, you piss me off, you bring out a protective streak I didn't know I had in me." He picked her hand up again, lacing his fingers through hers. "I know you turned me down when I asked you out at the festival, but my feelings haven't changed. I want us to see if this can work. I want us to go back to the stage where we probably should have started."

"Explain."

"I want us to see what happens together. I want us to try to date each other for a while."

She smirked. "Are you saying you want to be my *boyfriend*?"

He started to laugh. "Yes, I admit it, I want to be your boyfriend."

"How would that work?"

"Never had a boyfriend before?"

"Stop being a wise ass. Seriously, what are you suggesting?"

He suddenly looked more serious, but hopeful. "I'd like us to start slowly. Maybe I could come back up tomorrow and make sure you're taking care of yourself and spend some time just hanging out with you. I'll bring food and we can eat together. Then, over the week, we talk at night; make plans for next Friday or Saturday night— we could get together here or at my house for dinner and some time together." He brushed a curl back from one of her eyes, his fingers lingering on her face for a moment. "I'm not suggesting that we stay out of the public eye because I don't want people to know, I'm just saying I'd like us to have time alone for a while."

"Okay."

"After a while, we could start going out in public." He squeezed her hand. "Then, only then, get physically intimate again."

"Okay."

"Okay? You don't have any more to say than that?"

She looked up at him and he saw warmth fill her eyes. "I like your plan. And even with my cloudy brain, I still know I'd like to try that." She rubbed her temple. "I never didn't want to go out with you. It was just, I felt we shouldn't."

"I know."

She grinned unexpectedly. "Do we get to kiss?"

He leaned down so his lips were almost touching hers. "A little bit." He quickly pressed his lips to hers. "We need to take this slow." He kissed her again. "But I think a little kissing would be okay."

She laughed. "Okay."

Sunday night, Georgiana looked at Jack as he finished the dishes from dinner. "Thanks for keeping me company this weekend."

He walked over to her, and gently stroked the side of her face that wasn't bruised, smiling as she closed her eyes and leaned into his touch. "My pleasure. Lousy circumstances, but I'm really glad we're where we are now."

She could feel a blush sweep her cheeks. "Me too."

Chapter Twenty-One

Monday morning, Jack called Georgiana before he left for work. "Good morning."

"Morning."

"What time is your appointment?"

"Eleven."

"I'd take you, you know."

"I know. But Shroom will take me, and I'll call or text you as soon as I have news."

"Sounds good."

By noon, Jack was unable to focus at work, wondering how the appointment was going. By one, he'd given up trying to do anything meaningful, and found himself mindlessly reviewing paperwork. By two, he picked up his phone and texted. *"How did it go?"*

By three, when he still hadn't heard from either Georgiana or Shroom, he again picked up his phone, checking one more time to see if he'd missed a message. He texted. *"You okay? What happened? Getting worried."*

At four, he drove into her driveway, both frustrated and concerned. Shroom was coming out of the barn, and Jack demanded. "How is she? I haven't heard from her, and she hasn't responded to my texts." He knew his voice sounded harsh, so he tried to smile.

Shroom shook his head. "The princess is having a fit. She didn't contact you because she didn't like what the doctor had to tell her." His voice softened. "She would be rip-shit if she knew I was telling you this, but she went, got bad news, came home, and had a meltdown. Tears, swearing, yelling. Then she shut down, not responding to anything I said. Basically, she's non-verbal as she stews in her own little universe for a bit. She'll come back from there, but it sometimes takes a bit. I left her upstairs in the studio and told her I'd go back up and check on her after chores." He rubbed his forehead and Jack could see the worry on his face.

Jack felt his own frustration evaporate as worry blossomed. "What'd she find out?"

"The short version is that she's anemic, to the point that it's causing issues with her heart rhythm. Her head isn't healing as the doctor would like and they're faxing you a note later today saying she can't work until next Monday at the earliest. She has to go back to the doctor on Wednesday. If things have improved, she doesn't have to be seen again until the following Monday, but if her condition hasn't improved, she'll need to see specialists for both."

Jack felt Shroom's words slam into him like a tidal wave. *A heart issue? Her head wasn't healing?* "Jesus." Jack tried to keep the snarkiness out of his voice. "I wish you'd called me; I would have come earlier."

"I was going to, but I knew she needed time. You being here earlier would've just given you more frustration. I've seen her shut down like this before. She needed some time to be able to communicate with anyone, especially you."

Jack signed, knowing Shroom was probably right. The two men started across the road to the house. Shroom smiled at Jack. "So, seems to me that you kind of like her."

Jack suddenly felt like a teenager. "Yeah, I do. I was flipping out this afternoon waiting to hear from her. When she hadn't called me by two, I couldn't take it anymore and started texting her. By twenty minutes ago, I had to come out here."

"So go up and check on her." Shroom motioned toward his truck. "I'm gonna run home for a bit. I told her I'd make dinner tonight, want to join us?"

"Sounds good. See you in a bit."

Jack walked into the silent house and stood at the bottom of the stairs. "Georgiana? It's me. I'm coming in."

He walked up the stairs, listening for any indication that she'd heard him. At the studio door, he looked in to find her sitting in the armchair by the window, her feet up on an ottoman next to her knitting. His heart constricted seeing the absolute sadness on her face, her swollen eyes and red-streaked cheeks showing how much she had cried. He leaned against the doorframe. "Hi."

"Standing back because Shroom told you there was a good chance I would throw things?"

He grinned. "Yeah, I figure it's probably wise to have an escape route just in case."

She tried to smile, and he watched as her face crumpled. He hurried to her side and wrapped his arms around her. "It'll be okay." He kissed her hair. "It'll be okay. You'll see."

She was crying so hard she couldn't speak. He stood up and, picking her up in his arms, settled back into the armchair with her on his lap. He rocked her, murmuring soothingly until eventually she began to calm down. She looked at his shirt and he saw her eyes well up again. "I ruined another nice shirt."

He kissed her temple. "You didn't ruin my shirt." He hugged her close. "And even if you did, I don't care."

She snuggled closer. "I'm sorry I didn't call you or answer your texts. I wasn't trying to ignore you; I just didn't know what to do."

"You're forgiven." His arms tightened around her. "I wasn't mad you didn't call, just worried."

"You talked to Shroom?"

"Uh huh." He smoothed back her hair, careful not to touch the still-ugly bruise. "But I'd rather have you tell me about it."

She looked down at her hands. "It wasn't what I wanted to hear, and I know I'm being stupid and whiny, but it was just more than I could handle."

"So, tell me what she said."

"That I can't work for at least this week."

His voice showed his amusement. "What's your middle name?"

"What?"

"What's your middle name?"

"Grace."

His voice was stern. "Georgiana Grace Hewitt, I don't give a flying fuck about work right now. I care about how *you* are, that's it." He hugged her. "So now tell me what she said."

For a second, she let herself bask in his words. "She said my anemia has gotten worse since Wednesday and that I should be showing more improvement with the concussion than I am." Her voice got quieter. "And if I don't improve in the next few days, I have to go see specialists."

"Why are you anemic?"

Tell him! Her mind screamed and she shifted uncomfortably in his arms. "Because."

"Well, that was truly a middle school answer. Because *why?*"

"I don't know why I was anemic to begin with." In her mind, she could hear a voice saying, *Yes, you do. You were pregnant.* But she ignored that voice and spoke so softly he could barely hear her. "But I've gotten worse because I've been bleeding really hard since then."

Jackson pulled back to look down at her face, seeing that she was clearly avoiding his gaze, "Georgiana?"

"What?"

"Look at me." She slowly lifted her gaze, and he could see how uncomfortable she was. "Why did it bother you to tell me that?"

"I don't know."

He kissed her temple again. "I've seen every inch of your body, kissed and tasted most of it too, but you thought I'd be uncomfortable talking with you about this?"

She buried her face against his neck. "I know it sounds stupid; it just feels weird."

"Okay. But now that you've said it, let's keep going. Due to bleeding you're more anemic than you were a few days ago."

"Yes."

"And she checked you carefully to make sure this is just a passing thing? You're okay otherwise?"

"Yes."

"Okay. Explain to me about the heart thing."

"I noticed last night that my heart was racing a lot, but I just figured it was too much of doing nothing. When she checked me today, my heart was beating irregularly. She said that it's caused by the anemia. She said short-term it's not a problem, but it can't go on like that. I need to get my iron level back up."

Jack tried to push down the concern that filled him, knowing she needed him to be the confident one right now. "So, we'll work on that." He hugged her. "Just means that you're stuck with me nagging you to eat."

She truly smiled for the first time since he had come into the room. "Okay."

"Tell me about your head."

She tried to recall the entire conversation. "She said that my eyes are responding better to light than they were, but otherwise I'm not making the progress she would like to see. That's it. She said I need to be more careful for the next couple days and hope to see some improvement, or she's sending me to the medical center to a neurologist."

"We'll make sure you do exactly as you're supposed to and hopefully it'll all improve. If not, then we'll go see specialists."

Georgiana looked up at him. "You don't have to do anything, Jack. I'm okay, really, I am. I know I don't look like it right now, but you don't have to take care of me."

"Jesus, you truly are the most stubborn, infuriating woman I've ever met." His smile took the sting out of his words. "I thought we'd established over the weekend that there is an us here, so we'll face this as an *us*."

Her look was pensive, and she paused. Jack waited, knowing she needed to process what he said in her own time. "Okay." She touched his face. "I guess I'm still trying to wrap my brain around this, really I am."

He chuckled. "Don't try to wrap your brain around anything right now. Stick to simple."

"Okay." Suddenly her eyes filled with tears again. "I'm scared. What if it doesn't get better, Jack?"

He hugged her tightly, knowing she needed his comfort more than he needed to be careful of her rib. "It's going to get better, I promise. There's no need to be scared."

Her arms went up around his neck and she hugged him. "Thank you."

He kissed her hair, still holding her close. "For what?"

"I needed to hear that."

"Well, it's true." He looked her straight in the eyes, still seeing her fear and uncertainty. "I have an idea."

"Okay."

"I want to come up here to stay for the next few days." He saw her confusion. "Not as a romantic thing"— he rubbed her nose with his— "although you know how I feel. But as another set of eyes, nagging you to take care of yourself, and someone here in case you need something."

For a split second, he saw her struggle with the urge to assert her independence. But it was quickly replaced with a look of unmistakable relief in her eyes. Her smile was shy. "Really? You'd do that?"

Her response filled him with unexpected joy. "I'd love to. That way, you have company, I know you're okay, and you know if something goes weird, you have someone right here."

She leaned back against his shoulder. "I'd like that." Her voice was surer. "I'd like that a lot."

He rubbed her back. "Since Shroom already invited me to join you guys for dinner, how about I take a run home right now and grab some clothes? I can be back in under an hour?"

"That sounds good."

"Do you want to come with me for the ride?"

She shook her head. "No, I'd really like to, but movement makes me queasy right now."

"Then you stay here. I'll be back as soon as I can."

About an hour later, Georgiana was sitting in the kitchen watching Shroom prepare dinner when Jack returned. Dropping his bags in the hallway, he walked into the kitchen and leaned down to kiss her hair. "Hi."

She smiled. "Hi."

Jack glanced at Shroom, who was clearly amused. "Did she tell you I'm moving in for a few days to nag the shit out of her?"

Shroom grinned widely. "She did, and I think it's a great idea."

After dinner, Shroom kissed Georgiana goodnight. "Love you, little girl. Text me in the morning when you want company."

After he left, Jack smiled at Georgiana. "I'm not letting you look at a screen or text, so what do you want to do?"

She shrugged. "How about you watch the Red Sox and I'll just lie on the couch, close my eyes and listen?"

"Sounds like a plan." Jack led her by the hand to the couch and sat down. He pulled a throw pillow onto his lap. She joined him on the couch, lying on her healthy side and putting her head on the pillow. She smiled as he started to stroke her hair and she felt herself relax.

His voice was gentle. "You know, this is the longest period of time we've gone without a stand-off of some sort."

She smiled, her eyes still closed. "I know. Sorry it's been so dull."

"I'm still really sorry about how I screwed up about Abrams."

"I know. Let it go. It's done."

"And you've heard nothing from him since court?"

Her tone sharpened. "Jack, I would have told you. I would have told you even before we agreed to see where this can go, and now, we are together so much, I promise you would have known about it."

"Okay." He was quiet a moment, then said, "I'm also sorry about how I handled the Tim Mattison situation. I should have trusted your judgment."

"Thank you."

He thought for a moment. "Why didn't you talk to the CO about your concerns?"

"I had. I talked to Charlie, and a couple other admins did too. It never seemed to get enough traction. So, when you pushed it, I knew it was time to push back."

"You'd risk professional repercussions over this?"

"Hell, yes." She shifted. "I'm the only one who has the freedom to risk them."

"What are you talking about?"

She sat up, knowing this was going to be an awkward conversation. "I have the freedom, because at the end of the day, if I get mad enough, or get to the point where the boss is threatening to fire me, I'm financially secure without the job."

He tried to keep his voice light. "So, I'm dating a wealthy woman?"

"No. Yes." She paused. "Um…sort of."

"Well, that was a clear response."

She chuckled. "It's complicated. Leave it that I inherited well, did well in my divorce settlement, and make decent money here. I do a lot of consulting work and paid work for the UN, not just the volunteering at camps, but writing and editing for them, which adds up. My house is paid off, and I've paid off the solar panels and wind turbine so I'm off the grid. I paid cash for my car, and if push came to shove, I produce enough food for myself here. So, I have freedoms that most people don't."

He started to laugh. "Jesus, Georgiana. Just when I think I've figured you out, you throw me a curveball."

"Sorry about that."

"Okay, but how about this? Instead of you drawing a line in the sand where we get into a spitting contest, how about you use that sense of freedom to talk to me if there's an issue?"

She looked up at him and grinned like a child. "Where's the fun in that? Watching you get pissed off is amusing."

"Was it?"

"Yeah, it was."

He shook his head. "Could we find our fun somewhere else?"

"What do you have in mind?" He felt his body react as her eyes darkened with desire. "Suggestions?"

His kiss was gentle but lingering. "No suggestions right now. You're going to heal, one hundred percent."

Her voice was sulky. "Fine."

"Now that we've solved all the problems of the world, will you please lie down?"

She lay back down on the couch, her head resting on the pillow, and Jack smiled down at her. "Warm enough?"

"Yeah."

"Then close your eyes. I'm not turning on the game until your eyes are closed."

She closed her eyes, but her tone was cranky. "You're *so* bossy sometimes."

He stroked her cheek, seeing her smile. "Then how about I rephrase that? Could you please close your beautiful eyes for a bit to give your brain a rest?"

Her eyes remained closed, but he could hear the smile in her voice as she said, "Much better."

Jack turned on the television and slowly stroked her hair. As he watched the game, he thought about how the day had been full of such powerful emotions: anxiety as he waited to hear from her, frustration and worry when she didn't call him, fear when Shroom told him what the doctor had said, sadness while she'd cried in his arms, happiness when she'd so readily agreed to have him stay, and finally, absolute contentment in doing something as simple as listening to a ball game with her. He suddenly realized that in all of his dating, and his marriage, he'd never just sat for hours with a woman, just wanting to be near her. He looked down at the beautiful woman resting on his lap, careful to not let her know he was watching her. What the hell was he going to do with his feelings for her?

As the game ended, Georgiana stirred and he looked down at her. "Ready for bed?"

"I am." She sat up and he smiled, seeing how sleepy she clearly was.

"Where do you want to sleep?" He gestured toward the guest room. "I know you've been sleeping down here but it's up to you."

"I would love to sleep in my own bed." She looked shy. "You can sleep wherever you want."

He stood up and pulled her to her feet, putting a steadying hand on her hip when she swayed dizzily. "Where I *want* to sleep is right next to you. Where I'm *going* to sleep is down the hall from you."

"Okay." She smiled. "Since you put it that way, I don't feel rejected."

He looked at her intently and moved closer, his arms going around her to pull her close, then leaned down to kiss her deeply. Resting his forehead against hers, his voice was gentle. "Let's be clear, Ms. Muddled Brain. I want you. I want to be part of your life. I want to see if we can make this work. But between your head and everything we've done and gone through together, I want us to take this slow." He smiled at her. "However, just to be very clear, taking it slow is taking every single bit of my willpower."

"Hmm…" She reached up to wrap her arms around his neck, stretching up on her tiptoes to kiss him. "I like that."

Chapter Twenty-Two

The next morning, Georgiana awoke to the smell of coffee and rolled over to see that it was almost five-thirty, a half hour later than she would normally get up for work. Stretching, carefully she stood up, holding on to the headboard as her equilibrium recalibrated. A shower, she wanted a shower. A really hot shower. Stepping into her bathroom, she carefully reached into the stall and turned on the water, then gingerly sat down on the bench, undressing slowly. She pulled a towel over to the rack next to the stall and stepped into the warm spray. Slowly, she washed every inch of her body, as well as her hair, staying away from the still-tender lump on her temple. After washing her hair, she just stood under the spray, feeling the warmth cascade over her.

With a contented sigh, she shut off the shower and stepped out, snagging her towel to dry herself before she dressed. She took a second towel for her hair and stepped out of the bathroom, startling slightly when she realized Jack was sitting in her easy chair, a cup of coffee in his hand. "Hi."

"Hi." He gestured toward the bed. "I thought you might still be asleep, so I had a bit of a panic until I heard the shower running."

"Sorry." She looked sheepish. "When I woke up, I wanted a real shower." She smiled. "And it felt so, so good. I even washed my hair." She gestured toward the towel. "I couldn't dry it, but I could wash it."

He stood up. "Come sit down and I'll do it."

She sat on the ottoman. "Okay."

He crouched down beside her. "Good morning." He kissed her briefly. "Do me a favor, please?"

"Sure. What?"

"If you're doing something like taking a shower, would you tell me first? I just want to make sure you're okay."

"I will." She reached out put a hand on either side of his face, suddenly realizing how much he must have worried. "I didn't think, sorry."

He leaned forward and nibbled on her lower lip. "You're forgiven." He could see the raised flesh on her arms. "Cold?"

She nodded. "Freezing."

He snagged an afghan off the end of the bed and wrapped it around her. "Where are your socks?"

"Top left drawer." Jackson opened the drawer and had to smile seeing the perfectly organized rows of socks. He picked out thick woolly ones and knelt in front of her again, gently pulling them onto her feet.

"You didn't need to do that. I can put my own socks on."

"I know." His grin was wicked. "Undressing you is great, but I thought I'd try dressing you instead."

Georgiana was flustered. "Oh."

"C'mere. Let me do your hair." Standing up, he walked into the bathroom to retrieve a brush and before she knew it, he had gently dried, brushed, and braided her hair. "Done."

She looked at him in amazement. "How the hell do you know how to do that?"

He shrugged. "I have two sisters and three nieces. Last summer, two of my nieces came to stay with me for a month and I braided a lot of hair before soccer games."

She smiled. "So, I'm not the only one with hidden talents."

In the kitchen, the table was already set for two. He pulled out her chair. "Sit. Coffee?"

"Please."

Jack poured her coffee, and without asking added a splash of cream but didn't stir it in, then handed her the mug. She reached out to squeeze his arm. "Thank you."

"You're welcome." He leaned back against the counter. "What do you want?"

"An English muffin, please."

"With peanut butter?"

"Of course."

She tipped her head and looked at him seriously. "You know, for a controlling, stubborn, got-to-be-right pain in the ass, you can be very sweet."

"Thank you." Quickly and quietly, he fixed her English muffin and put it in front of her with a bowl of blueberries. She watched in amusement as he then brought over a large bowl of yogurt, granola, and fruit, along with a piece of toast. Before he sat down, he paused. "You all set?"

She smiled. "All good, thanks."

After breakfast, Georgiana went to lie down on the couch. Jack perched on the coffee table, taking her hand in his. "So, here's the plan. Once I leave, you take a nap. I'll be back by mid-day. Your phone is here, call or text me if you need anything, even if it's just that you're bored. I have nothing so important this morning that I can't be interrupted." He smiled. "And I'll stop by your school and make sure it's still standing, I promise."

"You know you're pretty bossy," she said in annoyance.

"I am." He leaned down. "Promise you'll behave?"

She grudgingly said, "I promise."

His kiss started lightly but deepened almost instantly as her arms came up around his neck. For a brief moment, Jack was swept up by desire, but caution quickly worked its way into his brain and he reluctantly pulled back. "I'm going to do the moral thing now and go to work."

"Okay." She straightened his tie. "By the way, you look good."

"Thanks. I was trying to impress you."

Georgiana smiled as she felt inordinately pleased by his answer. "It worked."

Three hours later, she was going mad with boredom. Out of desperation, she picked up her phone and dialed her assistant.

Dot's voice was subdued. "Hey boss, not supposed to talk to you."

"Why not?"

"The big boss sent all of us an email that we're not to contact you about work at all and that there will be absolute hell to pay if one of us breaks the rules."

Georgiana scoffed. "He's just blustering. Besides, all I want is for you to help me with something. You know me, I'm going nuts not being there."

Dot chuckled. "Fine. But if I get fired for this, the boys and I will have to move in with you."

"You won't get fired. Besides, if he catches us, he'll just be mad at me. You can just say I threatened you with my wrath."

"Yeah, yeah, you're scary as hell. What do you want?"

"Tap into my email and start reading them to me. I'll tell you how to reply."

"Okay, but he's here right now on recess duty, so if he comes in, I may hang up quickly."

"Deal."

Over the next ten minutes, Dot read emails aloud and Georgiana dictated responses. She was shocked when the phone buzzed in her hand. "Hey, Dot, hold on. I just got a text."

The text was short and to the point: *"You promised you'd behave. STOP EMAILING NOW!"*

With a sigh, she put the phone back to her ear. "Shit, busted. He must have had my account flagged. Log off and I'll talk to you later."

Chapter Twenty-Three

Twenty minutes later, Dot felt her stomach clench as Jack walked back into the front office, dropping the mesh bag of playground balls in the corner. He walked over to the counter, leaned on it and said conversationally, "So, you're more scared of her than of me?"

Dot quickly looked down at her desk, but not before he saw her smile. She pulled herself together. "Gee, Dr. Ryder. I have no idea what you're talking about."

He rubbed his forehead. "Does she have seltzer in the fridge?"

"She does." Dot got up, grabbed a cold can and handed it to him.

He pulled out the extra desk chair from the counter and sat down, crossing his long legs out in front of him. Taking a long swig, he smiled. "Knowing that you certainly read my memo about no school contact with Georgiana, and then seeing that emails were flying out of this building, I'm going to assume you have something to tell me."

"Dr. Ryder, let me explain."

"Jack."

"What?"

"I plan to be around for a while, and at least this week, you're going to be stuck with me a lot, so call me Jack."

"Jack." She shrugged. "She called and was in overload about not being here. She's bored out of her mind, so she asked that I read her messages to her.

I didn't read them all to her, I just scanned them to see what needed an admin response. Left the rest. She told me what to say. That's it."

"And you understand that you weren't supposed to do this, right?"

"I do."

"And your loyalty to her is so strong, you'd risk your own job to make her happy?"

Her smile was quick and broad. "I'd do anything for her, period."

Her answer was so sincere, Jack looked at Dot intently. She clearly wasn't prone to emotional outbursts. "Explain that to me."

"I did the email thing for her for two reasons. First, I know her well enough to know that keeping her from knowing what's going on here is increasing her stress level, making it less likely she'll get better. Second, sorry if it's not the answer you wanted, but yes, I'd do anything for George." She looked down at her hands for a moment, then back up at him. "Sir, what do you know about me?"

It struck Jack as an odd question at that moment. "I know that other than Priscilla, you're the best executive assistant in this district. I know you have two boys who go to school here, and that's about it. Why?"

"Seven years ago, my husband was killed in an accident on Route 2."

"I'm so sorry."

"Me too. Thank you." She looked at her hands again for a few moments, and sighed before she continued. "You need to understand; my marriage was a once-in-a-lifetime love. We met when we were sixteen and never loved anyone else. When Mike was killed, our boys were three and five."

His voice conveyed his empathy. "So young to lose their dad."

She continued. "I'd worked here for about seven years at that point and had been through three principals before George. She'd had been here about a year, having had a rough time of her own, what with the whole Tyler Abrams thing. And yet, when Mike was killed, she dropped everything and took care of me and my boys."

"What do you mean?"

"I mean, I fell apart *completely* when he died. And we don't have any extended family, so after the accident, I was on my own. The day it happened, I was given a sedative to calm me down, and I fell asleep. I woke up the Sunday morning after having been basically non-existent for my kids for like twelve hours. When I came downstairs, my boys were tucked in on the sofa bed, sound asleep. George was sleeping on top of the covers, with a boy holding onto a hand."

His voice was hushed with awe. "Wow." Dot's dedication to her boss was becoming so much more understandable.

"Yeah. She took care of my babies when I couldn't. Over the next month, I barely functioned. She cooked, cleaned, got them to school and daycare and back. When I forgot to register my oldest for second-session hockey, she took care of it. She made it so I could get through the day. As I started to get my head back on straight, I realized that I hadn't paid any bills. None. At all. For *three months*. Yet the lights were still on. We had fuel oil. Food. And the bank hadn't taken the house. George had taken care of it all. When I tried to pay her back, she just gave me a hug and told me to focus on the boys. To tell you the truth, there are a lot of people around here, both at the school and in town, who've had stuff like that happen. It's always an anonymous benefactor, but we all know it's George."

"Like what?"

"Like when Jane, the school cook, had her adult son move in with her unexpectedly after he came out of rehab. She didn't have a bed for him and couldn't afford one, so he was sleeping on the floor. Out of the blue a bed was delivered while Jane was at work. If people in town need medication and can't afford the copay, it mysteriously gets delivered, paid in full. When people have cars die and they can't get to work, suddenly the car is fixed and the bill is paid. Except for my case, no one can ever prove it's George. She denies it, but that's the way she is. So, at the end of the day, if she wants me to do something, and I think it's good for her, even if it's going to make you mad, I'll risk it."

Jack sat silently for a moment, then shook his head. With a smile of amusement, he said, "Okay," He started. "How about I modify the terms of my mandate? It's obvious that she is so involved with everyone and everything here, she cannot stay away without going bonkers." He smiled, considering his next words. "I guess it would be okay for her to call either you or Donna…not both of you…once a day, but not for more than twenty minutes. You can give her a daily update and keep her in the loop, but…I don't want you adding to her stress. Think you can do that?"

Dot nodded enthusiastically. "That would help her a lot. She'd feel back in control, and then would stop wondering about what's going on here so she can rest."

"And you'd promise me that if she tried any more than that, you'd let me know?"

"I promise."

"Good. I'll hold you to that."

A half-hour later, Jack pulled into Georgiana's driveway. Getting out of the car, he pulled the lunch bag from the passenger's seat. He opened the door and shouted, "Hey, get off email before I catch you."

On the couch, she smiled, hearing in his voice that he wasn't mad. "Sorry, too busy to eat, I'm writing supervision reports over here."

He laughed, dropping the bag on the kitchen table before walking into the living room. He sat on the coffee table and looked at her fondly. "You are a royal pain in the ass, you know that?"

She feigned indignation. "I am not!"

He leaned forward and gave her a quick kiss. "Yes, you are. You specifically promised me that you'd behave and then you dragged Dot into your scheme." He picked up her hand, tangling his fingers through hers. "When I realized you were emailing, I was about to send you a text that if you didn't knock it off, I was going to spank you, but thought that could be misconstrued."

She looked at him for just a moment, then burst out laughing. "That would've led to some interesting conversations."

"It would have."

"You know… I could be pitching a fit that you were monitoring my email."

"You could." He shook his head. "But the fact that you maneuvered around our agreement shows exactly why I needed Troy from the IT department to put a flag on your system to let me know if you were using it."

"Fine." She looked serious. "I wasn't reading anything; I was just listening."

He nodded. "I know. And after talking with Dot, I have a new plan."

"Is she in trouble?"

"No." He grinned wickedly. "It's not her fault her boss is a pain."

"Hey!"

He stood up and pulled her to her feet, smiling as she leaned forward to rest her head on his chest. He hugged her gently. "Come eat and I'll tell you the new plan."

At the table, he handed her a grilled chicken salad, then sat down and pulled a sandwich from the bag for himself. "Lunch."

She grinned. "You remembered!"

"You said you loved their chicken salads. I thought it might help you eat."

Georgiana nodded. "It looks really good, thank you!"

"Good." He took a bite of his sandwich, chewed, and swallowed. "Here's the deal: I get that not being at school is making you batty. And I have to tell you, it's running beautifully even without you there because you've built the foundation. But your loyal protector and partner-in-crime tells me that I'm inadvertently adding to your stress by keeping you under lockdown. She thinks that if you have some access, without looking at text, that you'll stop obsessing and get better quicker." He reached out to squeeze her hand. "It's pretty clear that I better not upset you because that woman would slit my throat in a second if she felt that I'd harmed you."

Georgiana shrugged. "Yeah, we're pretty loyal to each other."

"Is she right? Would it help if you had some access?"

Her relief was clear. "It would help a lot!"

"So, here's my offer." He raised an eyebrow. "And hear me clearly. You break your promise this time and I'm going to shut off all communication, period."

"Fine."

"You can call Dot or Donna each day for twenty minutes or so. Then at night I'll read you your emails."

She grinned. "What if they're from people saying what a pain you are?"

"All the better."

After she looked down at their hands, she raised her eyes, and they were glistening with unshed tears. "I'm sorry for breaking my promise this morning, I didn't really see it that way at the time." She bit her lip before whispering. "Thank you for taking such good care of me."

He raised her hand and kissed her knuckles. "My pleasure. Now eat." He grinned. "*One* of us has to go back to work."

At the end of the workday, Jack pulled into the driveway, smiling when he saw Georgiana sitting on the bench on the front porch. "Waiting for someone?"

Her smile was shy, as she realized how happy she was to see him. "Yeah. You."

"Did Shroom do the chores?"

"He did. He let me sit in the barn and keep him company."

"Good. Do you want to go for a walk?"

"I'd love to."

As the sun was setting, they walked back into the kitchen and Jack helped her slide out of her coat. "Sit down, you look tired."

"Okay." She sat and he realized that she was very pale.

"What's the matter?"

She tried to keep the panic out of her voice. "My heart is beating really, really fast, and strangely. It won't stop."

Without saying a word, Jack turned, opened the freezer and grabbed a big handful of ice cubes. A second later, he dropped them down her back, inside her sweatshirt, holding them in place as she screeched. When she twisted away from him, the ice fell on the floor and she looked at him in shock, holding her ribs. "What the hell was that?"

"How's your heart rate?" His voice was calm.

She stopped for a moment, then looked at him in wonder. "It's going back to normal."

He bent down to pick up the ice cubes and tossed them in the sink. He then grabbed a clean towel and motioned for her to turn around.

She turned and smiled as he pulled her shirt up, gently drying her back. She quipped. "Did you dump ice down my back just so you could pull my shirt up?"

He finished drying her, then leaned down to kiss her cheek. "If I wanted you out of your shirt, you would be out of it, I promise. I used the ice to give your heart a jolt."

"How'd you know to do that?"

"My little sister has SVT, a form of tachycardia. Her heart races at times and she can't always slow it. She had to learn a bunch of ways to get it back on track. One of them was to run out and jump in a snowbank." He shrugged. "I figured the ice might work."

She turned around and hugged him tightly. "Thank you. I was getting scared."

He kissed her hair trying to keep the frustration out of his voice. "Sunshine, if this was going on, why didn't you tell me?"

She leaned against him. "I was hoping it would just stop."

He pulled back so he could look at her. "Beyond getting you healthy right now, this relationship thing will work better if you talk to me about things."

"Fine," she said. She noticed her tone was rather cranky, so she tried to soften it a bit. "Thank you."

"You're welcome." He kissed her forehead. "Better now?"

"Yes."

"Then sit down and keep me company while I make us some dinner."

She sat down. "Will you tell me about school, please?"

While he made dinner, Jack told her all about his day, both at Deerlane and at the office. He noticed that as they talked shop, she became more engaged, and her color returned to normal.

After dinner, she stretched. "Could we watch the news, then you read me my emails?"

"Of course."

On the couch, he had to smile as she laid down with her head on the pillow on his lap. He stroked her hair gently as he watched, and she listened to the world news. When it was over, he turned off the television. "Where's your laptop?"

"On the desk in my office."

A minute later he came back, finding her sitting up waiting for him. "I know your username, what's the system password?"

"You didn't get IT to give it to you?"

He laughed. "I was going to but thought you might get irked."

She looked down and he realized she was blushing. "It's a really stupid password."

"Really? What is it?"

"Princess Gia, one word, all lowercase."

He grinned. "Princess Gia?"

"Shut up! It's what my grandfather calls me."

He started to laugh as he sat down on the couch. "I like it."

She gave his arm a shove. "Just read me the fucking messages." She flopped back and he noticed a greenish tinge cross her face.

He reached down to rub her bare feet. "You okay?"

She reached up to rub her forehead. "Not ready vertigo-wise for a dramatic flop."

He looked at her. "Lay back…gently…and shut your eyes or I'm closing the laptop." She complied as he opened her inbox, he watched scores of emails fill the screen. "How far back do you want me to go?"

She closed her eyes. "Wednesday night, please."

Over the next hour, he read the sender and subject line of each email. The ones she responded to, she had him put in her clearly organized system of virtual files. Eventually, he said, "That's the last one."

"Okay. Thank you for doing that." Even to her own ears, she sounded tired.

"No problem. Tomorrow night will be easier because you won't have a backlog." He stood up. "I'm putting the computer away. Do you want anything while I'm up?"

"Just a glass of water."

When he came back to the couch, she was very pale again. "Is it doing it again?"

"No." She opened her eyes. "No, it isn't. I'm just really tired and my head hurts a lot."

"Do you want to go to bed?"

"No. I just really want to stay here with you." As the words came out of her mouth, she realized how much she enjoyed being with him.

He sat back down, pulling the pillow onto his lap. "Then come here."

Chapter Twenty-Four

Georgiana woke up hours later and for a moment was completely disoriented until she realized she was in her own bed. How had she gotten there? She sat up slowly, and it dawned on her how thirsty she was. Gingerly, she put her feet on the floor and stood up, feeling the world tilt around her. When the spinning stopped, she started to walk toward the bathroom and was startled when she realized Jack was stretched out in the armchair, his feet on the footstool. He was watching her with amusement, the moonlight streaming in through the window. Her voice was husky with sleep. "Hi."

"Hey." He smiled. "Need something?"

She walked over to the chair and stroked his hair. "Water. You didn't need to sleep here."

He shrugged. "I didn't want you to wake up disoriented. You fell asleep downstairs and may not have realized that you were in bed. I was going to worry if I wasn't in here."

His dedication to her safety took her breath away. *He's been sleeping in a friggin' chair, so she'd be safe!* She leaned down and kissed him, unable to find the words to thank him.

Without realizing what he was doing, he pulled her onto his lap, pulling the blanket over her. She placed her arms tightly around his neck as she kissed him with all of the desire and emotion she felt. Minutes later, when they pulled apart breathless, he smoothed her hair. "What did I do to deserve that?"

"You're sleeping in a chair to make sure I'm okay." She leaned forward to rest her head against his. "Now I'll go get my water."

"I'll get it."

"No, I need to move around a little."

When she came back into the bedroom, she walked over to the chair. "You can sleep in a bed now. I know where I am."

He stood up. "I'll tuck you in first, my Princess Gia, then I'll go to bed."

The next morning, she awoke again smelling coffee. Getting out of bed, she went to the top of the stairs. "Taking a shower," she called out.

She walked him to the front door as he left for work. He put his hands on the sides of her face. "Look at me." Slowly she looked at him and he could see the fear in her eyes. "It's going to be okay; I promise. Worst case scenario? We go to the neurologist. If that happens, I'm going with you. Otherwise, best case scenario, you come home today and tell me that as of Monday, you can come back to work and irritate me again. Whatever happens, you'll be okay." He pulled her close to hug her. "I promise it's going to be okay."

He felt her arms go around him and she hugged him tightly. "I'm going to hold you to that."

"That's my princess."

"You're not going to let me live that down, are you?"

"Nah." His eyes were warm, sending sparks of awareness through her body. "I have to admit, I like the "Gia" part best. I love your name but none of the diminutives people use for you fit how I see you, except Gia. I may have to go that way." He grinned. "I mean, other than when I have to use your whole name, including your middle, to get you to listen to me." He kissed the tip of her nose. "Okay, I've gotta go. Call or text me when you're headed home regardless of what the doctor says, and I'll come back for lunch."

"You don't have to, you know."

His look grew very serious. "Are you saying that because you don't want me to or because you're trying to be a brave scout?"

She grinned. "Brave scout." She stroked the lapel of his blazer. "I like having you here." Standing on her tiptoes, she kissed him. "I *really* like having you here. A lot."

"Good." He picked up his bag. "I'll see you for lunch."

After he left, Georgiana took a short nap. A half hour later, she was surprised when her phone rang and it was Jack. "Hello?"

"Hey, it's me. I have a situation here at school and Dot says it's time to call you."

Georgiana started to laugh. "You need me to solve it?"

He could hear the humor in her voice. "You can give me grief about it later, but right now, help."

"Of course. What's going on?"

"You have a little buddy who seems to have hit the wall this morning about not having you around. He's locked himself in a bathroom stall. I can't get in because I'm too big and I'm not going to ask a staff member to slide on the floor in the boys' room to go under the door."

"Brighton?"

"Yup."

"Are you in the bathroom now?"

"Standing in the hall outside. Dot's in there right now."

"Okay, walk in and put me on speakerphone."

Georgiana could hear the bathroom door, then she heard Jackson's voice. "Brighton, I have someone on the phone who wants to talk to you."

The young voice sounded so upset that it made Georgiana's heart hurt. "Not coming out. I'm not coming out until she comes back. I'm gonna stay here until she's here. *Nobody* else here likes me. I'm going to stay right here until she comes back." Georgiana heard his voice break. "Wednesdays we play Uno if I've done my work. It's Wednesday and she's not here."

Georgiana spoke loudly. "B, can you hear me? It's me, Ms. H. I'm on the phone and I miss you so much, buddy, but I can't talk to you through the stall. If you come out, Dr. Ryder will let you hold his phone and we can talk, okay?"

"No. You're not here. You're always here on Wednesdays."

"Brighton, listen to me. I bumped my head really hard last week and I have to stay home a few days until I get better. But then I'll be back, I promise. As soon as I can, I'll be there, and we'll play Uno no matter what day it is. Right now, I want to talk to you, but I don't like yelling like this on speakerphone, so I need you to come out, okay? Can you come out and talk to me?"

Jack could see the little feet getting closer to the stall door. At that moment, Dot's phone buzzed, and as she looked at the screen, he could see she'd just gotten a text from Georgiana. *"Go get Chase. He's in study hall room 103 right now. Tell him I need a favor."*

As Dot headed out the door, Jack wondered how she knew exactly where a kid was at that very moment when her brain was so scrambled.

Georgiana spoke again. "Okay B, here's the thing. You know how I work. I'm going to hang up if we can't talk on the phone normally, so it's time to make the good choice."

There was a flurry of activity, and the little boy came flying out of the stall, his voice panicked. "Don't hang up!"

Jack handed the phone to him. He could still hear her as she spoke to the boy, and her voice was pleased. "Nice job, B. I'm proud of you. How are you, my friend? I miss you a lot."

"I miss you. I got a hundred on my spelling yesterday."

"You did? Dude, that's awesome. That was the list with the '-at' words, right?"

"Uh huh." He looked so sad that Jack just wanted to hug him. "When are you coming back?"

"I don't know. But when I know, I'll tell Dr. Ryder, and he'll tell you, okay?"

Brighton looked up at the tall man. "Okay. I don't know him, though."

"I know. And forgot to tell him that he's taking my place playing Uno with you today." Jack could hear the humor in her voice. "He's not as good as I am, but you'll teach him, right?"

Just then Dot reappeared with one of the boys Jackson recognized as a senior. Brighton said seriously, "Ms. Dot's back."

"Okay dude, then she's going to walk you back to class, then in a little bit, Dr. Ryder will come get you for cards, okay?"

"Okay."

Jack watched in fascination as Dot took the now-calm little boy by the hand to class, then said in wonder, "How'd you do that? We'd tried for almost a half hour."

"Magic." She paused. "Is Chase there?"

"He is." Jack handed Chase the phone. "Ms. H. wants to talk to you."

The boy clearly was thrilled. "DH, how are you? We heard you got hurt. Is the mushroom man doing chores or do you want us to come up and help?"

Georgiana's heart swelled with pride for this boy she'd watched struggle so hard to get where he now was. "All good here, Chase. I'll let you guys know if I need help up here, but I *definitely* need help down there."

His voice was serious, "What do you need?"

"The little guys. I think they may be falling apart. I need you guys to sit with them at breakfast until I come back, give them attention, make sure they know they can come find you if they need some TLC."

"You got it, DH. Do you want me to play Uno with Brighton today? I mean, it *is* Wednesday."

This boy knew about the Wednesday's Uno games. Jack was amazed again by the sense of community in the school. Georgiana's voice was sure, "No, Dr. Ryder's going to do that; good practice for him and it'll help Brighton to teach the game to someone. But since they're going to play pretty soon, could you go with Dr. Ryder to get him from class and walk him to my office? I think he'll trust him more that way."

"You got it."

"Thanks, Chase. I'll say it again, I think I'm going to fail you in the spring so I can keep you one more year."

"That works for me." He paused. "Offer still holds, DH. If you want, we'll come up and do whatever."

"Thanks, I promise I'll shout if I need you."

An hour later, after a rousing game of Uno with Brighton, Jack was headed back to the main office of Deerlane when his phone buzzed with a text: *"Can you call me?"*

He immediately walked into her office and shut the door for privacy before he dialed her back. "Hey. You okay?"

Her voice was tight. "I guess. I'm still at the doctor's, and I'm going to be here a while. I have to have an MRI my head, then they're doing a virtual consult with the neurologist."

"Why?"

"The good news is that my iron level has improved. Not great, but better. And I've gained a pound this week."

"How many had you lost?"

"Eleven."

"Okay, keep going..."

"So, all of that is good. She's not making me go to a specialist about the heart thing, at least not yet. She'll check that again on Friday. But for my head, she wants the neurosurgeon to see the scans and make sure they aren't missing something."

"Do you want me to come over to the hospital?"

"I'm okay. Shroom is here. And if it's okay with you, I'll keep calling or texting you between steps."

"Of course." His voice was sure. "It's going to be fine, babe, you'll see."

Chapter Twenty-Five

When his phone buzzed three hours later, he was surprised to see it was a message from Shroom. *"Headed home. She's going to sleep for quite a while. Will call when we get back."*

About a half hour later, his phone rang.

"Hey," said Shroom. "We're back at the house and she's down for the count."

"Why? What happened?"

"She did okay through multiple blood tests, a CAT scan, and an x-ray of her ribs. Then they got her ready for the MRI and told her after that she was having a lumbar puncture. They put her in the machine, and she had an anxiety attack. They had to take her out and sedate her so they could do the MRI and puncture while she was out." Jack could hear the exhaustion in the man's voice. "I don't know if they gave her a lot of the sedative or if it's because her system is so out of whack right now, but she's been asleep ever since. When we got home, I woke her enough to get her inside. Now she's completely gone on the couch."

Jack stood up to look out the window, trying to push down the frustration that she hadn't let him go with her. "What did they find?"

"We don't know yet. Her doctor was going to meet with the neurosurgeon without us since Georgie was so out of it, so I figured I might as well take her home and they'll call with results."

"So, what's the plan now?"

"Let her sleep it off."

"Can you stay for a bit until I can get there?"

"Of course. I figure she's going to sleep for at least a couple hours, but I don't want to leave her alone because she's likely to be pretty disoriented when she wakes up. I'm going get some lunch, then I have some work I can do here."

Jack looked at his schedule on the computer. "If you could stay for the next two hours or so, that would be great."

"Sounds good. When you get here, I'll do the chores. Do you want me to make dinner?"

Jack had to smile at how quickly this man had become part of his daily life. "I'll make it when I get there. What sounds good?"

When Jack walked into the house later that afternoon, he found Shroom working at a laptop at the kitchen table. "Hey."

"Hey." Shroom looked up and stretched. "Sleeping Beauty is still out like a light."

Jack smiled. "She definitely needed the rest, but when do we worry about how long she's slept?"

"Doc said if she wasn't awake by five or six, to try waking her."

"Okay."

"I'll go do the chores, then go home to deal with stuff there. I'll be back around six-thirty."

"Sounds good."

After Shroom left, Jack walked into the living room and sat down on the coffee table to watch Georgiana for a few moments. Curled up under the blankets, she looked so fragile, and he felt his heart constrict as he looked at her. "Damn, lady, how the hell have you gotten under my skin so fast?" He leaned forward to stroke her cheek, wanting nothing more than to pick her up and hold her. Never in his life had a woman inspired such urges in him.

Forcing himself to give up his vigil, Jack returned to the kitchen, and tossed a stew together. After putting it on the stove to simmer, he set the table, then grabbed his bag and went back into the living room to read reports. It was almost six o'clock when he heard a noise from the couch and looked up to see her eyes opening. "Welcome back."

"Thanks." She started to sit up and swayed. "What happened?"

He came over and sat down next to her to kiss her temple. "Move slowly, you probably still have a fair amount of sedative in you."

She looked at him in confusion. "The last thing I remember, I was being taken out of the MRI, then nothing."

"As I understand it, they sedated you to do the test, then did a lumbar puncture while you were out."

She rubbed her face. "And what did they find?"

"We don't know yet. Shroom said the doctor is going to call with results."

She leaned against him and closed her eyes again. "Jesus, I feel like I got run over by a truck."

He pulled her onto his lap. "I bet you do."

She snuggled into his warmth and just listened to his heartbeat, feeling the safety of his embrace. How she loved being in his arms! "So, you were right that I should've had you go with me."

He grinned. "Of course, I was right. When are you going to accept that I'm always right?"

She laughed. "Fine." She reached up to stroke his face. "I missed you today. I mean, the part of the day I can remember."

"I missed you too."

"When did you get here?"

"A little after three. Shroom stayed with you until then. He'll be back soon; he's going to have dinner with us."

"Good." She shook her head a bit. "Damn, my brain is even foggier than this morning."

"Don't worry about it. It'll pass."

Chapter Twenty-Six

Several days later, Georgiana stretched in the armchair, and set down her knitting as her cell phone rang. With a smile, she picked it up. "Hey, Mol!"

"Gigi! You answered!"

"I did."

"Your warden away for a bit?"

Georgiana laughed, "Yeah. He's run into town to get pizza, so I'm sitting here knitting."

"What the hell has been going on? Except for a couple texts, there's been radio silence for a week."

"I know. The short version of the story is that after they did a bunch of tests, they found that I had this infection of the spinal fluid."

"What?"

"Yeah, this really rare thing. I was sick as hell and had to have IV antibiotics for a couple days. But now the infection is passing, and I feel almost human."

"And Mr. Wonderful? Still as perfect?"

Georgiana sighed happily, "Better than I can express. He'd been staying here, taking care of me, keeping me company, but basically keeping hands off with the idea that once I was better, we'd start going out."

"Finally! So, you're over the stupid nonsense that you can't date him?"

"Yes! He's going back to his place in a couple days, but it's been amazing having him here."

"You really like this guy."

"I do." She paused. "I think I like him more than any guy I've ever been with…"

Chapter Twenty-Seven

A few days later, Dr. Liz looked at Georgiana happily. "I can honestly say that you're getting better. Still not out of the woods, but definitely better. Your iron has improved, your potassium is back up a bit, and your rib is going to be fine as long as you don't overdo it. Most importantly, you're finally showing improvement with the concussion."

Georgiana's smile showed her relief. "I thought so. My mind is beginning to feel a little sharper."

"Good to hear! Keep being super careful, continue to follow the recommendations, and you should heal up just fine."

Georgiana's tone was hopeful. "Work?"

"You can start back to work tomorrow…one hour. No more than that. Wednesday, two hours, Thursday and Friday, three hours. Then I want to see you on Friday afternoon. If all goes well, next week you can go back half-days. Half-days only. And yes, I'm sending the letter to Dr. Ryder outlining everything I just said." She grinned as Georgiana rolled her eyes. "You are *not* being given the all-clear just yet, so don't push it. And remember, still no driving for the rest of this week."

Georgiana sighed. "Doctor's orders?"

"Doctor's orders."

That night, Georgiana stood in the kitchen as Jack checked around for anything he might have left. He put his computer bag by the front door and came back to take her hands. "I know this is what we agreed but I still don't like it."

She took a step forward, then leaned against him as his arms wrapped around her. "I know. I know we said that as soon as I was cleared to start working a bit that you were leaving. While I'm really glad I'm getting better, I'm going to miss you."

"Me too." He kissed her hair. "But remember, it's not like we aren't going to be together. It's just that I'm not staying here."

"I know." She hugged him. "I know I was the one putting up the stupid roadblocks between us, but now that we've moved past that, I hate being away from you."

He put a finger under her chin to make her look at him. "Likewise, babe. But we'll be together whenever we can."

"Okay. That sounds better."

"Shroom is going to take you to work tomorrow and pick you up, but how about I bring dinner tomorrow night?"

She nodded. "I'd really like that."

An hour later, her phone buzzed with a text. *"Give me a call when you can."*

She dialed his number. "Hi."

"Hi."

"What's up?"

Jack paused. "I was going to wait until tomorrow to tell you, but there's an announcement in the agency's news blast coming out to principals tomorrow morning that I thought you'd find interesting."

"What is it?"

"Tyler Abrams has resigned, effective immediately. He's taken a superintendent position in Los Angeles and starts there next week."

The rush of relief surprised her. "What? Seriously?"

"Yeah. The blast says that his board here agreed to release him from contract, they're going to promote his assistant super for the remainder of this year while they do a full search." His voice radiated happiness. "I called someone I know up there, and he's already moved to California. It sounds like they kept the whole thing pretty quiet around here, but he actually moved last week."

"No shit!"

"He's gone, babe. Gone."

Georgiana couldn't stop smiling as she hung up the phone.

Chapter Twenty-Eight

Tuesday of the following week, Georgiana sat on the bench by the alpaca pen and looked at Shroom pensively. "So, we're going to go out to dinner on Saturday night. Like… a real date. In public. I mean, I know we've had dinner together almost every night since he went home, but we're going on a *real* date."

"I know, you told me." His voice was gentle but firm as he kept working. "Speaking of telling things," he turned to give her a look that spoke volumes. "You need to tell him, kiddo."

"Tell him what?" She tried to sound innocent but couldn't quite pull it off.

"You know what. You can't keep dating him with a secret like this between you."

"I know." She sighed, leaning her head back against the fence. "But what if he breaks up with me over it?"

"He won't, Georgie. That man is absolutely crazy about you. But if you don't tell him and he finds out some other way, it could get ugly."

She stared into space for a moment. "Do you think it would work if I wrote him a letter?"

"You mean instead of talking to him face to face?"

"Yeah. I would make more sense that way."

"I don't think the delivery method matters, just that you do it."

That night, she sat on the couch with her laptop trying to find the right words. In her heart, she knew she'd fallen in love with Jack, and wanted a future with him, but by not telling him the truth when it happened, she now had to figure out how to tell him everything. Never in her life had any piece of writing meant as much as this one. As she took a sip of water, her phone buzzed with a text. *"Hey, what're you doing?"*

Out loud, she said, "Writing you a letter that I hope you'll take the right way." She typed. *"Paperwork."*

"Tell your boss you shouldn't be working so late. And get away from glowing screens."

She put a smiley emoji in the next message.

Her phone buzzed again. *"Can I call or are you too busy?"*

"Of course, you can call!"

The phone rang almost immediately. She smiled as she answered. "What took you so long?"

He laughed and the sound of him caused sparks of anticipation to run down her spine. "I was playing hard to get. How'd I do?"

"Horrible job."

"How was your day? I didn't hear from you at all today, so I didn't know if that was a good sign, or a bad one."

"It was fine. Really busy. Still trying to find my stride."

"And you only worked a half-day, right?"

He couldn't see when she rolled her eyes, but he could practically hear it in her voice. "As promised; I'm behaving."

"Good." He said with a small chuckle. There was a pause. "Of course, that doesn't mean I will always want you to behave."

His words gave her a rush. *Damn, how she wanted him!* "How was *your* day?"

"It was good. I went to Montpelier first thing, then back here. This afternoon my brain was completely off-task trying to fight the urge to come check on you."

She wanted to enjoy the warmth that thought sent through her, but looking at the blank Word document in front of her caused her anxiety to bloom. "I missed you too."

"Am I going to see you tomorrow?"

She swallowed, knowing that she needed to deliver the letter to him at some point tomorrow and really hoped it could be without actually seeing him. "Probably not, it looks to be a really busy day."

"Okay. Maybe Thursday?"

"Maybe." Her voice grew softer. "I can't wait until Saturday." She paused, needing to tell him the truth about her feelings. "I really miss you. I'd gotten used to us being together all the time outside of work, and now it feels like I haven't seen you in forever."

"I miss you too." He chuckled. "I know it was my idea to take things slow, but damn, it's been too long."

In his living room, Jackson stretched. "I'll let you go finish your paperwork. Remember that I have the legislative breakfast tomorrow, so I'll be on the road early. You can always call if you need me."

"I will."

"Talk to you tomorrow night?"

"Talk to you then. Goodnight, Jackson."

"Night, Gia."

On her way to work the next morning, Georgiana drove to Jackson's house, knowing he'd already left for his meeting. With a nervous sigh, she tucked the plain white envelope into the small space next to the weather stripping on the door to the garage, knowing he would pass that way when he came home.

Chapter Twenty-Nine

That afternoon, as Jack was packing up for the day, Priscilla came into his office. Seeing her, he smiled, having gotten to be very fond of the seemingly ditzy secretary who he now knew to be absolutely dedicated and organized, with a generous and kind heart. While she made him crazy with her hovering at times, he had to say that his office had never run so smoothly. "Jack, I just need you to review these before you go so I can get them organized in the next few days."

"What are they?"

"The seniority list for administrators' letters of intent for next year. I just need to make sure I have all of the admins in the right categories, no plans of assistance, things like that. They need to get these by December 15th but, if possible, I'd like them to go out well before then."

He looked the list over carefully. He tried to hide a smile when he reached Georgiana's name. Maybe he'd take a chance and drop by her house after running his errands. He knew she'd said she'd be busy today, but he wanted to see her in person, even for just a few minutes.

Priscilla smiled. "I'm so glad Georgiana's feeling better."

"Me too."

"She's my favorite principal. She's the only one that treats office staff like equals."

That didn't surprise Jack, having seen how she treated everyone she met. "She is impressive."

Priscilla looked thoughtful for a moment. "I'd wondered earlier this fall if she was pregnant, but I knew that Boone hadn't been around for a long time."

Jackson stopped what he was doing. "What're you talking about?"

Priscilla didn't catch the intensity in his voice. "Georgiana. I was worried about her. I thought this fall when she lost all that weight and had the stomach issues, that she was pregnant. When my sister was expecting the second time, she was just like that. She got so fragile and had horrible nausea. If Boone had been around at any point since last winter, I would've really thought she was pregnant."

Jack felt the world begin to spin around him as he tried to keep his voice calm. "Wow, Priscilla. That was definitely two plus two equals five."

She chuckled. "It was. Sorry. Obviously, I was wrong. And I'm so glad she's finally getting over that concussion."

Jackson kept looking at the papers, trying to keep his breathing slow and even. He finished reading the last lines and handed them to her. "Thanks so much for getting these together for me. They look good." He put the pen away. "Okay, I'm going to head out for today."

"Sounds good. I'll see you in the morning."

Jack walked out to his car in a fog, his mind swirling with Priscilla's comments. *Was she right? Was Georgiana pregnant?* For a moment, a flash of pure joy filled him at the thought, but it quickly vanished as he remembered Georgiana telling him that she'd been bleeding soon after the accident. *Had she been pregnant? Is that why she'd been so sick?* Thinking back to her comments, he knew that by then, she hadn't been pregnant anymore, if she ever had been.

Jack got in the car, put on his sunglasses, and drove to Deerlane practically on auto-pilot. Sitting in the parking lot, his mind kept going over what Priscilla had said. Georgiana had gotten so frail back in the fall and the nausea was so severe. She'd mentioned that the Monday after being sick she'd gone to the doctor and that was when they'd noticed her low iron. He stopped, his heart racing. She had gone to the doctor on the Monday after being sick. *Had she gone to end the pregnancy? Had she ended it and not told me? Had I cared for her after she'd been injured while she was also recovering from an abortion?*

Jackson felt a tidal wave of rage wash over him. *How could she have not told me she was pregnant? How could she have ended it without even talking to me? How could she have done this?*

He angrily threw the car door open and strode to the front door of the school. Instead of using the call box as usual, he used his key fob to let himself in and strode down the hall to the main office. Dot looked up in surprise. "Jack, I didn't know you were stopping by."

He couldn't even try to make small talk. "Is she in?"

"She is."

"Is she alone?"

Dot looked down at the phone console. "She is. She was on the phone but is free now."

His voice was deadly calm and for a moment Dot feared whatever was coming for Georgiana. "We are not to be disturbed; do you understand? Absolutely no interruptions."

She looked at him questioningly, but still said, "I understand."

Jack walked past Dot to the closed door to Georgiana's office, opened it without knocking, and closed it behind him with such force that it was nearly a slam.

Georgiana looked up from her desk and for a moment, she felt absolute joy at seeing him. *Could he have already read the letter and was okay about everything?* She stood up. "Jack!"

"How could you? How fucking could you, Georgiana?"

"How could I what?"

"How could you have been pregnant and not told me?"

Georgiana swallowed hard. Clearly, he'd gotten her letter and hadn't taken it the way she'd hoped. "I was going to, but..."

His voice was sharper than she'd ever heard it. "When? When exactly were you going to tell me? When were you going to tell me that you were pregnant with my child?"

"I was going to tell you that day when I'd set up the meeting with you at my house. That was why I'd arranged it, Jack. It was."

His voice was cutting. "But after you had the abortion, you decided that I didn't need to know?"

Shock hit her and she felt her knees go weak. "I didn't have an abortion, Jack. I didn't. I wouldn't!" His look clearly said he didn't believe her. "I swear I was going to tell you I was pregnant, but then when I got injured it caused a miscarriage. Then I couldn't tell you. I'm so sorry, Jack. I'm so sorry. I still should've told you. I would *never* have had an abortion."

"You had a *miscarriage*. You want me to believe that? Pretty convenient, don't you think? You get confronted with the truth so you make up a cover story?"

"It's the truth." She tried to keep her voice calm, and tried to keep her mind focused on speaking, feeling herself shutting down under his attack. "When I found out I was pregnant, I was so excited. I would never have done anything to hurt our child." His face stayed stony, and Georgiana felt hopelessness fill her. "I would never have hurt our child. Never."

"Bullshit! You kept this a secret the whole time I took care of you. Was it a big joke?"

"Of course not!"

"How could you do this?"

"I was wrong to not tell you. I was. I am so, so sorry for that."

He stood there looking at her, his anger still so great that he could barely hear her. Finally, he said coldly, "I can't forgive you. You lied to me." He shook his head. "Goodbye, Georgiana."

Arriving home, Jackson walked into the house, still reeling from the shock and anger he felt. He tossed the envelope he had pulled off the garage door onto the counter next to his bag, and didn't give it another thought.

An hour after her exchange with Jack, Georgiana sat down on her own couch. The tears she'd been fighting to keep inside, ran unchecked down her cheeks. *How could Jack think I'd ever get an abortion? How could he have gotten that from my letter? How could it have all gone so badly? Why, oh God, why didn't I tell him the second I found out I was pregnant?*

The next day, Georgiana worked her half-day then went home again, thankful that she hadn't seen or heard from Jackson. While at work, outwardly she showed a calm but weary face. Aside from Dot, who had been filled in on everything, she avoided any sort of personal conversation.

On Friday, she came into school mid-day and worked for an hour before walking out to Dot's desk with her bag over her shoulder. "I'm headed home to change before the reception."

Dot's voice was full of concern. "You sure you should go?"

"What do you mean?"

"You haven't seen him since your fight. You sure you're up to seeing him?"

"I work here. I can't avoid contact with him. I might as well get it over with."

Standing outside the reception hall, Georgiana took a deep breath, then decided to stop in the ladies' room. Once there, she stood looking at herself in the mirror, pleased that no matter how nervous she was, she appeared put together and professional. She pulled the door open and strode purposefully to the doorway, smiling brightly at the principals already in the room.

Jack turned as she walked into the room, and advanced over to her, reminding himself not to notice how good she looked in the dark gray sweater dress and high-heeled black leather boots. He didn't bother with pleasantries. "What're you doing here? You're supposed to be working half-days."

"This *is* my half-day. I came in at noon so I could be here."

"You need to go home."

"I'm working my half-day." She looked him straight in the eyes, keeping her tone completely cool, refusing to cower in front of his anger. "Thank you for your concern but I'm fine."

"You're leaving." He put a hand under her elbow. "Now, Georgiana."

Her eyes narrowed, but she didn't change her tone or volume, so no one noticed the conversation. "Dr. Ryder, while I greatly appreciate your concern, I told you that I planned to attend as I've been on this board since I came to the district. I plan to stay just until the announcement of the scholarship, then I'll leave." She lowered her voice. "Take your hand off me, now."

"You're being foolish."

"My prerogative." She glanced down at his hand, still on her arm. "Now!"

Just then, the Secretary of Education came over, and Jack stepped back a tiny bit, dropping his hand. "Gigi! So glad you could make it after all. I asked Jack if you'd be joining us tonight and he said that you were under doctor's orders to not push yourself too hard." The silver-haired man smiled warmly at her. "I told him there was no way you'd stay away…"

Chapter Thirty

After the reception, Georgiana drove home in a funk. Two hours of staying away from any interaction with Jack had been totally exhausting. Clearly, it was going to be hell working for him. How long could he hold on to that level of anger? She needed to figure out what to do with her life…

In her kitchen, she listlessly ate a piece of toast with hummus, then opened her laptop. A new email in her work inbox caught her attention immediately.

Georgiana,

Please forgive what may seem like a random email but I'm wondering if you might ever be interested in taking a one-year position at UVM in the teachers' ed department (may be longer, not sure). If so, give me a call on Monday morning to talk.

Enjoy your weekend, Bob

Georgiana sat staring at the computer in shock. *Was this the answer she was looking for?*

After a weekend of moping around her house, Georgiana was relieved when Monday came around and she could head back to the distraction of work at noon after her doctor's appointment. When Dot was leaving at 4 p.m., she popped her head into her boss' office. "Hey, Georgie, time to go home now."

"I will soon, Dot. I am just going to make two more calls."

"George, you aren't supposed to be working so much. You know that."

"I know. I will leave as soon as I make those calls."

"Scout's honor?"

"Absolutely."

She gave an exhausted sigh as she finished up her work. When she looked at her cell phone, she noticed a text from her therapist. Therapist. Not just her therapist. Joe was her therapist, her psychiatrist, and was a noted brain researcher and neurosurgeon. She was lucky that he also had taken her on as a client years before soon after her divorce. She had called him that morning hoping to talk but had been unable to reach him. The text was short. *"George, free until 5:30. Call me."*

Thankful, she picked up her cell phone, moving to the window overlooking the back fields. She dialed Joe's number, smiling when he picked up on the third ring. "Georgie! How are you? You got my notes about the scans, right?"

"Hey, Joe. Been better but been worse too. And yes, I saw the notes, thanks." Over the next half hour, she told Joe everything: the miscarriage, her feelings for Jack, their fight, her health issues, and the job offer from UVM; all with him interjecting only a few questions along the way.

When she was done, he exhaled loudly. She could picture him sitting in his office chair, his feet up on the desk, and just the mental image made her feel safe. Her hand was tired from holding her phone, so she put it down on the windowsill, switching to the speakerphone.

"So, is this a therapeutic call where you want me to just make supportive sounds, or do you want advice?"

She laughed. "When have you ever made supportive sounds? You normally kick me in the ass and tell me to stop feeling sorry for myself."

"All true."

"I suppose I needed to tell someone who understands all of it, but I guess what I'm trying to figure out is my next step. So, oh guru of mine, guide me."

He chuckled. "You know my guidance. Get off your ass and get exercise as the doctor says you can. Definitely no running yet, too much bouncing on the brain. But you can walk or do yoga. Eat well and get as much sleep as you can. Then you need to decide if you can continue working for the man. I mean, it would be different if it was just a crush, but this sounds more complicated."

Georgiana leaned against the cold glass. "I know."

"So, what's the plan for the near future?"

"PJ, Boone, Diego, and Parker are coming next Sunday, staying through Thanksgiving."

"Good. It'll do you good to have them around. You can be fully yourself with them."

"I know. And I'm going to that stupid governor's ball with my grandparents on Saturday night."

"Going stag? Ouch, Georgie."

"Damn it, Joe, you're supposed to help, not make me feel like more of a loser."

"It's my job to be the voice of reason."

"*Fine*. Okay, keep going."

"Think about how the ball may trigger you. Going to an event with all those couples? Is this going to help, or hurt? I know it's important to your grandparents for you to go, but I'm concerned that it's going to make you feel even more alone. We both know how you've handled that in the past."

"I know. But I committed to it when I was with Jack, and I'll feel like more of a loser if I bag it."

"Then why don't you see if Boone will come up and go with you?"

"I can't ask him. We're in a good place. That would just complicate things again."

"Then you need to be diligent in taking care of yourself that night."

"I will."

"And as a side note, I want to see the new series of brain scans; the ones from this morning."

"Already done. I don't know if they're sending them electronically or not, but you should have them soon."

"Good. I'll look them over and get back to you. I'll say it again, Georgie, damn fine catch on the part of the neuro up there with that infection. Damn fine catch."

"I know." She paused. "Joe, any chance you'd have some time for me around Christmas? I can't go to Chad because I still can't fly, so I thought I could come to Virginia for a bit. Probably time for a 50,000 mile check-up in person."

"Of course, I'll have time. Let me know when you plan to be here, and we'll work it out. In the meantime, call me if you need me, day or night. If it's an emergency, call my pager." He paused, his voice deepening in concern. "Georgie, serious questions: should we put you back on medication, and are you safe?"

There was a silence as she reflected. "Yeah, Joe, I'm safe. And no, I don't need to go back on the meds. You know I'd tell you if I did."

"Fine, kiddo. Do you still have some Valium on hand if you can't break the cycle?"

"Of course. I have a full bottle. Haven't needed it at all in a year but I always make sure it's still good."

"Good. Beyond the emergency meds, if my little visiting snitches have concerns, we'll need to talk more about it. Did you eat today?"

She snorted. "I have to eat, no matter how much I don't want to. The doctor has me on a fucking eating plan, so yes, I'm eating."

"Are you feeling hunger?"

"Of course not, Joe."

"Are you understanding why?"

"That is a stupid question, and you know it! I'm not feeling hunger because I'm triggered. It's why I'm freezing all the time right now. I get it, Joe. I know why it's happening, but I'm not able to stop it yet."

"Okay, you can do this. You've gone through worse."

After hanging up the phone, Georgiana stood silently, her head resting on the cool window. How had her life gone so wrong so quickly? A sound behind her made her stand up sharply, whirling around in fear. Her fear subsided only slightly as she realized Jack was standing in her office doorway. Anger blossomed immediately at the idea that he might have heard the conversation. "What are you doing here?"

His voice was cold. "I could ask you the same thing. It's almost five-thirty. You're supposed to only be working a half-day and you're still here."

She started picking up, closing her laptop and putting it in her bag. *How long had he stood there? Had he heard her profess her love for him to Joe?* Clearly, he hadn't cared when she'd said she loved him in her letter, so did she look like more of a loser now that she'd still expressed it to her therapist? "I needed to make some calls before I left. I'm headed out now."

He walked into the room. "Who were you just talking to?"

"Good night, Dr. Ryder."

"Georgiana, who were you just talking to?"

"Why? Why does it matter?"

"Because it does. Who were you talking to?"

Her voice crackled with anger. "Not that it's any of your business, but I was talking to my therapist. I tried to call him this morning, but we didn't connect. He was free now." She rubbed her forehead. "I wouldn't normally talk to him from work."

"Who is he and why would he want to see the brain scans?"

Georgiana was too tired and sad to fight his questioning. "Because he's a neuropsychiatrist and years ago, I was part of a study he did. There are brain scans from back then. He's been looking at the scans over these last weeks for any changes."

"*Another* thing you neglected to tell me…"

That was more than she could take. "Jack, enough. You've already made your feelings clear, as did I. I'm so sorry for what I did. I can't express that enough. But I can't take another round of you beating the shit out of me for it. I can do that on my own just fine. So, yes, I called him today and I have no idea how long you were standing there but whatever you heard, you heard." She picked up her bag. "Goodbye, Jack."

As she started to walk by him, he grabbed her arm. "Why were you part of a study where they looked at your brain?"

Her eyes glittered dangerously. "Take your fucking hand off me."

He stood there, his hand still on her arm. "No, not until you answer me. Why were you part of a study?"

She wrenched her arm away from him. "Not that it's any of your concern now, unless it impacts my job performance, but before I came here, I was in treatment for PTSD. He's the neurosurgeon and psychiatrist who runs the program and even though I graduated, he's still sorta my therapist."

His shock was clear. "You have PTSD? And you didn't tell me?"

"Jesus, fucking Christ, Jackson. Yes, I have PTSD. Have for a long time, always will, although I've learned to live with it. And yes, I didn't tell you about it because frankly, it's not easy to tell someone, *anyone*, but especially someone you want to think highly of you, that you're broken and always will be." With that, she stormed out of the office.

Chapter Thirty-One

It was almost two in the morning when Georgiana finished her email to Jack.

Dear Dr. Ryder:

I am writing to you in order to formally request a one-year leave of absence for the next school year, pursuant to paragraph 6, section 13 of the administrators' contract. I have been offered a professional opportunity that I feel is in my best interest to pursue. Please let me know if you would like a signed letter of request for the board.

Respectfully,

Dr. Georgiana Hewitt

When she got out of bed at 5 a.m. to get ready for work, she opened her email with trepidation. His reply was brief, sent just five minutes before.

Georgiana,

Request denied.

JR

With a spurt of anger, she typed a response.

Dr. Ryder,

It is part of our contract. Why is my request being denied?

Georgiana

She had just stepped out of the shower when she heard her email ping.

Georgiana,

Until you have a clean bill of health from your doctor, it is my professional opinion that such a huge change not be considered and therefore, I am unwilling to present the request to the board. If/when you have such a report from the doctor in January, and you are still interested in pursuing this, we can discuss it then.

JR

Sitting at the kitchen table with her coffee and toast, she read the email again. Anger swamped her and she could feel tears prickling her eyes. What options did she have left? She couldn't stand the thought of continuing to work with him for more than a few more months. Was it time to use the nuclear option and resign? She could take the UVM job and hope it worked out…

Georgiana struggled to concentrate at work. At noon, she thankfully packed up, calling out to Dot. "I'm heading out."

Dot came to the doorway. "Sounds good. You look beat."

"I'm going to go take a nap. I'll be turning off my cell when I get home, so call the house if you need me."

"We won't need you, see you tomorrow."

Walking into the kitchen, Georgiana dropped her bags on the floor, turned her phone off, and got a glass of water. Should she take a nap or go outside for a bit? *A nap, then outside.* Minutes later, dressed in leggings and a hoodie, she climbed under the blanket on her bed and the sudden wave of grief hit her hard. She curled up into a ball and cried herself to sleep.

An hour later, she woke up and laid there, looking at the ceiling. How the hell was she going to fix her life? How could it have all gone so wrong? How could they have gone from a week before being sure they were headed into a future together to the anger now? How could she have been so stupid as to not listen to PJ, Boone, and Shroom when they had all told her that she needed to tell him when it happened? It had all been so amazing when they were a couple, how could she have ruined it this way? If only she'd agreed to go out with him at the festival, they would have been a couple when she found out she was pregnant, and then maybe it would have all been different.

With a sigh, she sat up, glad that her head was pounding less than it had when she had gotten home. Slowly, she walked into the kitchen and poured a small glass of juice.

Just then her house phone rang. It was her mother. "Hi, Mom."

"How are you, sweetie? I thought you might be home this afternoon since I know you're still just working half-days."

"Yeah, I'm okay."

"Just okay?"

Georgiana felt a flash of uncertainty. It was unlike her mother to catch such a subtle use of wording. "Just okay."

"Do you want to talk?"

Why was her mother acting like a *mother*? "No, Mom. It's okay. What's up?"

"Sweetie, there's going to be a change of plans." Georgiana detected a sudden note of nervousness in her mother's voice. "I was wondering if it would be okay with you if I came to the farm for Thanksgiving."

For a moment, she felt fear. Was something really wrong with her mother? They'd never spent a Thanksgiving together in Vermont in her memory. "Are you okay?"

Katherine laughed. "I'm fine. I just, well, I was thinking we could do the whole family holiday thing."

"Really?"

"Really. PJ told me he was going to Vermont and said Julia was coming up for some of it and I'd really like to meet her finally. I thought we could all be together for a few days."

Georgiana sat down on the couch, reeling from the suggestion. "Really?"

"Georgiana, you have the best vocabulary of anyone I know, and all you can say is 'really'?"

"I don't know what to say, Mom. This is so unexpected."

"I know. I just thought it would be nice." Georgiana heard her mother swallow. "I thought maybe you and I could do a spa thing one day while I was there. Maybe Julia could join us." Her voice got softer. "I know I didn't do those mother-daughter things with you, Georgiana, and I regret that now. I'd like to try."

Georgiana felt her throat tighten with emotion. "I'd like that, Mom. I'd like that very much."

"And I'd like to bring a friend with me to meet you guys."

She started to laugh. "Mom, do you have a boyfriend?"

Happiness rang in her mother's voice. "I do. One I like…a lot. I want you both to meet him. Is that okay?"

"Wow, of course it is." Georgiana tried to process the information. "I've never met someone you liked before; it would be a new experience."

The next ten minutes were filled with the two of them making plans. After hanging up, Georgiana flopped back on the couch. "Shit, *that* was unexpected."

The house phone rang again and from the caller ID, she could see it was her brother. "Hey."

"Why isn't your cell on?"

"I needed to unplug."

"What's wrong?"

Georgiana hadn't spoken with her brother since the night she'd written the letter because he'd been on a training mission. "I gave him my letter and he flipped out. Understandably, I know. But now he's convinced I had an abortion, and I couldn't get him to understand, so it's over."

"Shit. I'm so sorry." His voice was concerned. "How're you handling it?"

"You'd be proud. I kept in body enough to speak, then walked away while I could."

"Good for you. And since then?"

"A fight on Friday night when I went to a work reception."

He interjected. " You're supposed to be working half-days."

"Don't you start too. We'd planned on going together, not like a date, but just like a work thing. Then we broke up and I still wanted to go."

"To piss him off, or to show him you're in control?"

She pondered. "Mostly the latter. I mean, I've been on the state committee the whole time I've been here. But, yeah, deep down, I did it to make sure he knew I make my own decisions."

Her brother chuckled. "Baby sister, I know more about your control issues than most people, but don't push yourself too hard health wise just to prove your point."

"I know. Then I stayed too late at work last night and was on the phone with Joe. Turned out Jack came in and heard some of the conversation and we had another fight. So in the middle of the night, I sent him a request for a leave for next year, which he denied. I worked my half-day this morning, then came home. I just needed to unplug and figure out what to do with my life."

"Did you figure anything out?"

"Yeah, I figured out that I was an idiot right from the beginning. When he asked me out after Seattle, I should have said yes like I wanted to, but because I was too afraid, I said no. Then, just like all of you told me when I figured out I was pregnant, I should have told him immediately. *I own this*. But I don't know how to *fix* it. So, I was trying to figure that out this afternoon."

"Then Mom called with her plans…"

"Yeah, for a minute I thought she was dying."

He laughed. "Me too. Since when does our mother want to do the American holiday thing?"

"Since she's got a boyfriend."

"I know!"

Georgiana smiled. "Well, it actually sounds like fun."

"It does." There was a pause. "Gigi, I have a surprise and I was going to wait until Thanksgiving to tell you, but after Mom's call, I thought I'd tell you today."

"Okay."

"I'm not re-upping, neither is Boone. We started a security corporation and we're moving to Vermont in the spring. We just found out today that we got a huge contract with Eisman to work their corporate security. Jules is moving with me."

The news filled Georgiana with a wave of joy. "You're moving home? Like *home* home? Like my *next-door neighbor?*"

"Like your next-door neighbor, little sister. The whole fam-damily, as we used to say."

Georgiana started to cry. "That sounds so good, PJ. So very good."

Chapter Thirty-Two

Earlier that same afternoon, Jackson drove home to have lunch. His mood was too vile to stay in the office and make small talk. In the kitchen, he microwaved a dish of pasta and then walked down the driveway to get the paper. Coming back into the kitchen, he tossed the paper on the counter where it uncovered the envelope he'd found on the door Wednesday night.

Picking it up, he recognized Georgiana's handwriting. He hesitated. Should he read it or just recycle it? Would anything change if he read it? With an angry toss, he threw it into the recycling box unopened, then turned to get some lemonade out of the fridge.

He sat at the kitchen counter looking at the headlines on the paper, while his lunch was heating up. After retrieving it from the microwave and taking a small bite, he tried to read the article about proposed changes to the property tax system until he had to admit that all he could think about was the letter in the blue box. With a huff, he retrieved the envelope and sat back down. Carefully he opened it, pulling the folded paper out.

Jackson,

Forgive me for doing this in a letter. I know I should be brave enough to tell you this in person but I'm not. I hope that you can read this and understand.

I love you and I'm in love with you. I should've said that before now. I think I've loved you for a while now but definitely since the day you offered to stay overnight with me after I was hurt. I wish I'd been brave enough to tell you that I love you before now.

For months, I've had a secret that I should never have kept from you. When we were in Seattle, I got pregnant, but I didn't know until the beginning of October. The day I threw up at the meeting, I knew I didn't feel well but it wasn't until the next day, when I got sick again, that I realized I might be pregnant. I took a home test that night and all I could think about was how excited I was to be having your baby. It was funny, I had bought really fine yarn in Seattle, for no apparent reason, and when I bought it, I'd had the thought that the blue in the yarn was the exact color of your eyes. That night, after taking the pregnancy test, I started a blanket for our baby with that yarn. Yes, that night I told PJ, Shroom, and Boone that I was pregnant, and that was wrong of me—you should have been the first one to know.

The next Monday, I set up a doctor's appointment and made that appointment for you to come to my house so I could tell you in person. The doctor confirmed I was pregnant, told me I was anemic, and sent me home. I was so excited, so happy, so full of wonder. I sat on the couch that night, talking to our baby, knitting on the blanket, just needing to do something to show our child how much love I felt.

Then, Wednesday night, as I told you, there was a problem in the barn, and I went out to see what was going on. The ram hit me, giving me a concussion and breaking my rib. I didn't know until Thursday morning that it had caused a problem with the baby. By Friday morning, I knew I had probably miscarried, and the doctor told me I had to rest while my body tried to pass the fetus. You came over Friday afternoon. You were so kind, so protective, so caring, and I should have told you then, but I couldn't. My brain and emotions were so screwy, I couldn't tell you.

Then, well, <u>we</u> happened. Being with you, seeing what we could be as a couple, I couldn't work up the nerve to tell you the truth. I knew you'd be so hurt and angry that I didn't tell you that I'd been pregnant or that I'd miscarried, I just couldn't do it.

But the thing is, I love you. I can't tell you enough how much I wanted to have your baby, or how much it broke my heart when the pregnancy ended. I can't let go of my own guilt about my stubbornness harming our baby.

So now the ball is in your court. I can't say enough how sorry I am for not having told you all of this at the time, or at least since then. I love you.

Georgiana

Sitting at the counter, Jack read and reread the letter, then put his head in his hands. How could he have so misunderstood what had happened? How could he have treated her this way? How the hell did he make things right between them? Did she still love him? Did he love her? Oh, hell, yes, he loved her. *Can she forgive me for how I've treated her?*

Chapter Thirty-Three

After sitting outside for an hour, Georgiana heard a noise and knew that Shroom had arrived to do chores. She kept him company in the barn for a while, went back to the house to throw in a load of laundry, then sat down at the loom to try to clear her mind.

Finally, around five, she pulled a yogurt from the fridge and got a handful of cashews. With a sigh, she carried the food over to the table and opened her laptop as she powered on her cell phone.

As her email list populated, her phone began to buzz indicating she'd missed messages throughout the afternoon. The email list was pretty simple: a few purchase orders to approve, a letter from a parent with a suggestion about a field trip, then seven emails from Jackson. She counted them again. Seven.

She pushed her phone to the side, choosing to ignore it while she opened the other emails and debated whether or not to look at his messages. She listlessly took a spoonful of yogurt. From the subject line, she could see that four of his messages were to all the administrators, so she could open them without heartburn. None of them needed a response so she just read them and made notes on her calendar. Then there were three emails that were clearly meant for her alone. The first had the subject line, "?," the second, "please respond," and the third, "NOW!!!"

She picked up her seltzer and took a sip. "I don't think so." She put her feet up on one of the other chairs as she picked at her food, trying to ignore the phone on the table. When it buzzed for the third time in fifteen minutes, she shook her head and pulled it over to her. Throughout the afternoon she'd missed texts from Boone, PJ, and Dot, all just checking in. She took a deep breath and scrolled down, seeing that during the course of the day Jack had called five times, three of them in the last hour. He'd also texted her five times. Should she read them or just delete them? What good would come of reading them? She fought the tiny surge of hope that his messages meant he still cared but then shook her head. "Bullshit. After what he said, it's not going to work. Stop being an idiot." She put the phone down, disregarding his messages.

After eating, Georgiana walked back over to the couch. Her cell phone rang with the distinctive ring that meant her brother was calling. "Hey."

"Hey, Gi. How was the rest of your afternoon?"

"Okay. Yours?"

"Fine."

She could guess why he was calling. "He called you?"

"Three times. The first two, I was out running so I didn't answer. The third was just a few minutes ago. We were making dinner and Julia answered, trying to be helpful."

"What did he want?"

"George, I'm not saying what he accused you of is right, but the man is fucking flipping out. He says he's been trying to reach you all afternoon, by phone, text and email. With what's happened, he doesn't feel he can just go up to the house to see you." He sighed. "I told him you were turning off your phone and that you're okay, but he's worried."

Her voice was louder than she intended. "Why the fuck is he worried? He's the one who flipped out, not me. I just had the sense to walk away."

"Hey, don't yell at me. I'm just telling you that regardless of what happened, he's worried. In the five minutes we were on the phone, he alternated between flat-out freaking out worried and being rip-shit mad."

"What do you want me to do?"

"Nothing. Stop being pissy with me."

"Sorry."

"Anyway, I told him that I'd let you know."

"*Fine*, you did."

"Hey, I'm not the enemy here. I'm just giving you a heads up. I wouldn't be surprised if he shows up at the house, no matter how upset he thinks you are."

Remorse filled her at how she'd treated her brother. "Sorry, PJ. I just, shit, I'm sorry."

"It's okay. I understand. Anyway, I'm gonna go eat dinner, but I love you."

"Love you too."

With a sigh, she picked up her laptop and opened her school email account.

The first message from Jackson was short and to the point:

Georgiana, I realize we need to talk. Really talk. I can't seem to reach you by phone. Please call me, Jackson

The second email had the "please respond" subject line.

G. I realize you are probably very angry with me and hurt right now and I understand that, but please call me. I've tried to reach you repeatedly today. I'm worried and would really like to talk. J.

The third had the subject line "NOW!!"

Georgiana, I have tried to reach you by email, phone, text all afternoon today -- I understand you're upset but to not respond is childish -- call me now please. J.

"Gosh, that one makes me *really* likely to respond." She tapped open the text message inbox.

There were five texts from him. She scrolled to the earliest, deciding to read them in chronological order. "*G. we need to talk - please call me. I can come over if that would help.*" Then, "*Okay, I've emailed, called and texted -- could you please respond?*" The third, "*G --putting it simply, please call me!*"

For a moment, Georgiana let herself try to decipher whether he was angry or not. Then she read the next message. *"You seriously are going to walk away from what we have by not even responding to me?"* And the final text, *"Could you have the decency to at least answer me?"*

Georgiana rested her forehead on her hand, trying to calm her racing heart. Pulling back, she scrolled through the texts again. The first one made her feel slightly hopeful, the subsequent ones showed his growing frustration.

Just then, the house phone rang. Still looking at her messages, she leaned over and picked up the receiver distractedly. "Hello?"

His ire was clear. "You won't respond to cell calls, texts or emails but you'll answer your house phone?"

Instantly, her tone was bitingly sarcastic. "Why, hello, Jackson. If I'd known it was you, I wouldn't have answered *this* phone either. Clearly, I should've looked at the caller ID."

"Do *not* get snippy with me, Georgiana!"

"Or what? Are you going to *punish* me for my tone? I mean, how could you treat me any worse than you already have?" She looked at the clock. "Besides, I'd like to remind you, I'm only working half-days, so I have no obligation to respond to you outside my work hours."

"We aren't talking about your workday right now. We're talking about *us*." He tried to keep his temper in check. "Damn it, if you truly love me, fight with me, don't fucking shut me out!"

"What the hell are you talking about?"

"You said you love me. How the hell can you say you love me, then just walk away today and shut me out completely?"

She needed to make him understand. "I wasn't shutting you out today. You walked out of my life, remember? Not the other way around. I unplugged today because I had a screaming headache and needed time to clear my head."

"And you didn't think I might want to know that you were disconnecting? That I might want to know you're okay?"

"After our conversation last night and our email exchange early this morning, I wasn't getting the warm fuzzies from you. I took a half sick day today as mandated by my doctor, which was shared with you both in person and by Google calendar. *That* entitles me to being off the damn clock. I have no fucking obligation to answer my phone or emails during that time. I instructed Dot to call the house if she needed me. That's all I needed to do for the district, period. Beyond that, Jackson, you made damn sure I understood that there is no *us* anymore, so I have no obligation to share *anything* non-work related with you."

"There's still an *us* and you know it." She heard him take a deep breath. "Damn it, Gia. You scared the shit out of me today. I mean, truly *terrified* me. I started calling and emailing you at lunchtime and you didn't respond. I thought it was just because you were angry with how I had treated you, then I got worried after I heard that guy ask you last night if you were safe and I couldn't reach you. Why? What the hell is going on?"

Georgiana was flooded with overwhelming sadness. "Jack, I didn't mean to scare you." Her voice broke. "Actually, after our last discussion, I didn't think you cared enough to worry. I'm sorry. If I thought you would have cared about it, I would've let you know I was unplugging."

"How could you think I wouldn't care?"

"Our last conversation wasn't exactly a love sonnet." She rubbed her eyes tiredly. "Our emails were worse. If I was to understand something differently than I did, I apologize. But it's over. Let it go."

"*Let it go*? How can you say that?"

Georgiana closed her eyes. "I can't tell you enough how sorry I am that I didn't tell you in October. That was wrong of me. I know that. You have every reason to be furious with me for that, but it's time for us to admit there's too much water under the bridge and we need to just let it go before it gets even uglier." She gripped the phone with sudden anger. "After all, since you won't let me take a leave, we have to work together, so we damn well need to keep this from getting any worse."

The finality in her tone frightened him. "Listen to me. I just read your letter today. *Today*. I know you left it days ago, but it got shoved under things and I didn't see it again until today. I *just* read it. I get it now. And it's not over, *we are not over*. Please talk to me."

She began to shiver with cold. "I need you to understand that I would never, ever, have ended that pregnancy." Tears started to run down her face. She could see the fuzzy dots from anxiety beginning to close in on her visual field and instinctively, she began to rub the raised skin on the inside of her arm. Her voice trembled. "I'm so sorry, Jack. Please forgive me but I need to go. I can't talk right now." With that, she hung up.

She got up and almost ran to the bathroom, splashing cold water on her face in an attempt to bring her body and mind back to some semblance of calm. When she started to get dizzy from the anxiety, she crouched down, putting her cheek on the cold porcelain of the basin. Every ounce of her energy went into trying to slow her breathing.

Many minutes later, returning to the couch, she saw she had a new text from Jackson. *"Please call me. Or answer the phone if I call you. Please, Gia."*

Her hands trembled as she responded. *"I can't right now."*

"Why? Please."

How could she make him understand? *"I can't talk to you right now. This hurts too much."*

"So, you'd rather just give up?"

How could she explain it to him? *"It's not that I'm giving up. I'm overwhelmed. Having trouble even thinking, let alone speaking."*

"Would it help if I came there?"

She looked at the last text for several minutes, unsure how to answer. Finally, she whispered to herself. "Man up, George. If you love him, pick up the damn phone and call him."

Just then another text arrived. *"Why aren't you answering? Are you ignoring me or thinking about my offer?"*

Truth was the best way to respond. *"Because I'm sitting here trying to work up the nerve to pick up the phone and call you instead of doing this by text!"*

"Oh. Please call."

She picked up her phone and stared at the screen. She dialed one number at a time instead of the speed dial, needing time to compose herself.

He answered on the second ring. "Hi, thanks for calling."

Her voice was timid. "You're welcome."

Jackson sat on his couch, putting his feet up on the table. "Let's try this a different way. How are you?"

Her response was automatic. "Fine."

"Really?"

Georgiana's voice was serious. "No, I'm just barely okay."

"Let's pretend this is a normal conversation. What did you do this afternoon?"

"I took a nap. Sat outside and did some thinking. Tried to weave for a while and then decided to act like an adult and turn my laptop and phone back on."

"Okay."

"So how was your day?"

He took a sip of the beer in front of him, trying to keep his voice calm. "I came home at lunch, read your letter, then spent the afternoon trying to pretend I was doing my job while I was really calling, texting, and emailing you."

"I'm sorry, Jack. I didn't mean to worry you." She rubbed her forehead. "Truly, if I'd thought you would worry or want to talk— I'm sorry I worried you, that was never my intent. I just needed to step away."

His voice softened, hearing her distress. "It's okay. I know you didn't mean to worry me. If I take a step back, I can see that."

"Thank you."

He took a deep breath. "I need to say something."

"Okay."

"I love you."

"Oh."

His voice tightened. "*Oh*. That's all you have to say?"

"Lately you accused me of some pretty awful things, now you say you love me. It's a bit of a switch and I need time."

"Okay. I guess."

"But I love you too. That's never been in doubt."

"I'm so sorry, Gia. I had no right to accuse you the way I did. I read your letter today and realized how awful I was to you. I'm so sorry."

He could hear her swallow. "Can you hold on? I'm not trying to *not* respond but I'm freezing and need to get another shirt."

Worry filled him, knowing her so well, and his voice became stern. "So, you're stressed, and now you're freezing like you do when you're not taking care of yourself?"

Her temper flared. "Jack, stop! I'll be right back and then you can remind me of all of my faults."

A minute later she came back on the phone. "Okay, I'm back."

"I'm sorry for making the comment about you not taking care of yourself. I should've kept my mouth shut."

She considered smiling as she said, "True."

"So now that you're warmer, let me say again, I love you and I'm so sorry about how I treated you."

Guilt filled her. "You had every right to be livid over what I did. You *do* have every right to be mad. I just couldn't take what you accused me of in that conversation. You have to believe me. I would never, ever, have done anything to hurt our baby."

Her voice cracked. "Shit, I feel so bad that I went out to the barn that night. The doctor told me I could do whatever I would normally do, and that was normal. I never thought about it when I climbed into the pen and even when I got hit, I was sure that it was okay. I was just banged up a bit.

She started to cry in earnest. "I would've called Shroom to help me if I'd known. Then the next morning when I started to bleed, she told me it might still be okay. I went home and did everything she told me to do, and it still happened. I'm so, so sorry, Jack. I fucked up."

"Baby, you didn't fuck up, it was an accident. It happened." His voice cracked and she realized how emotional he was too.

"I should've told you. I should've told you the night I took the home test."

A sudden realization slammed into Jack, taking his breath away. "You told Boone that night because you were afraid I'd reject you. Reject both of you."

"I didn't realize that was why I was doing it at the time but"—her voice was so small he had to strain to hear her—"maybe." She paused. "I told him because he's one of my best friends and I feel safe with him. But probably deep down, I was afraid you weren't going to be supportive."

His voice showed his disbelief. "Jesus, how could you think I would *not* be supportive?"

"How could I think you *would*? We didn't talk about those things. I didn't know if you'd jump up and down with joy, tell me to get an abortion, or just walk away."

"And you needed to make sure your baby had a father no matter what…"

"Yes."

His voice was cold. "And did he agree?"

"This isn't about Boone right now. It wasn't really about him *then*. It was about me growing up without a dad, and no matter what, if I was having a child, that child was going to have a dad, preferably a biological one, but if not…"

"Answer the damn question: did he agree?"

Anger filled her at his insistence on this line of questioning. "Yes. He said if you didn't want us, he was going to come to Vermont and raise the baby as his own."

"Jesus Christ. And you were okay with this backup plan?"

"No, that wasn't what I wanted. As soon as I went to the doctor that Monday, I called to set up a time for us to talk so I could tell you. That was why I called you, remember, but we couldn't meet because you were going to D.C. I didn't want to tell you over the phone, I wanted to see your face. I didn't call Boone as a conscious back-up plan. I just called the people who make me feel safest. My intent all along was to tell you and I hoped you were going to be excited."

"When we couldn't meet that night, you were waiting almost a week to tell me!"

Her tone softened. "Again, I tried to have us talk earlier in the week. It wasn't that I wanted to wait to tell you, I wanted to be able to see your face when I told you. So, yeah, when you went to D.C., I did set up the meeting for the end of the week. In hindsight, I should have told you the night I took the test, even if it was just to tell you that I *thought* I was pregnant. I am so sorry I didn't."

"Then after you miscarried, you spent a lot of time with me, and you didn't tell me." His voice sounded confused, with underlying hurt, and Georgiana's heart ached hearing it. "Why?"

She tried to form an answer that would make sense to him. "I was so sad, so broken that I couldn't even think straight. Since the pregnancy was over, I didn't see that it would help anything to open it up. Once it was clear that something more was happening between us, I got so excited at the thought that we were together, I would've done anything to keep things going. Then I got so scared that if I told you, you'd walk away. I just kept saying I'd tell you when the time was right."

Sitting in his living room, he shook his head in frustration. "You let me hold you while you cried. You told me you were bleeding, you talked with me about medical issues, you slept in my arms, but you held that all inside. I even asked why you were bleeding and you told me you didn't know. It wasn't just that you didn't tell me, you consciously chose to lie to me."

His anger and pain sparred with his sense of unfathomable sadness at the whole situation. "Even when I step back from that, knowing how scrambled your brain was, it's still so *sad*. You were mourning the death of our child but doing it *alone* with me right there with you. I held you while you mourned but didn't know you were grieving. We could've been together in that pain."

"Jack, again, you can't imagine how sorry I am. Now, it all seems so clear to me but then I wasn't thinking straight. I didn't know if it would be shared grief or not and it hurt so much. I took the path of least resistance at the time."

There was a long silence. She had to wait to let him speak, even though the wait was killing her. Finally, he cleared his throat. "Are you going to sit there all night and wait for me to say something?"

"Yes."

"Knowing that patience is not one of your virtues, you must be ready to burst."

She wanted to smile, but simply said, "I am."

He sighed. "I love you. I'm not giving up on us. Right now, this sucks. I'm still hurt and mad and I need to wrap my mind around a lot of things."

"Uh huh."

"Things like, when I thought about you being pregnant, I was so excited I couldn't stand it. And now, I need to work out my own grief."

"I know."

His voice became slightly defensive. "You've had *weeks* to mourn, and I've had a couple of days."

"I know."

"When you walked away last night, I thought we were done. But I love you and I need us to try to figure this out."

"Really?"

He sighed, feeling the first flickers of the desire to smile. "Really."

"I'd like that."

"Me too. Any chance you'd let me come up there tonight to sit with you for a while?" he asked.

She tried to keep the astonishment out of her voice. "Do you think that's wise? Last night we were shouting at each other. Do you really think we're ready to see each other?"

His voice softened. "I don't know if it's wise or not, but I want to see you so badly I can't stand it." He paused. "If I promise not to yell or be a bossy ass?"

She let herself chuckle. "Not sure if you can hold to either of those."

She could hear the humor in his voice. "If I promise to try?"

"I'll leave the porch light on. Come on in when you get here."

Chapter Thirty-Four

Fifteen minutes later, she heard his car pull into the drive. She walked to the front door, unsure as to how to greet him. She finally opened the door and looked at him through the screen. "Hi."

"Hi."

She opened the door and he stepped into the house. He looked down at her and smiled nervously. "Am I allowed to hug you?"

Her eyes filled with tears, and she threw her arms around him. "Of course, you are."

His arms wrapped around her almost convulsively and he hugged her close. As she leaned into his strength, she felt the warmth and safety of his embrace.

Long moments passed before she finally pulled back reluctantly to look up at him. "I didn't think we'd ever do that again."

He rested his forehead on hers. "I didn't either."

He stepped back and tipped her chin up to look him straight in the eyes. "Georgiana Grace Hewitt, I love you."

"Jackson James Ryder, I love you too." Her eyes filled with tears again. "I'm so sorry. I never meant to hurt you."

He hugged her tightly. "I know you didn't. Forgive me for what I said. I was so out of line—"

"Forgiven."

"Can we sit and talk?"

"Of course." She gestured toward the living room. "Go sit on the couch. Would you like a glass of wine?"

"Yes, please." He rubbed her arm. "I know where it is. You sit and I'll get it."

She tried to joke. "Bossy, bossy."

He softened his tone. "How about I help you get it?"

She smiled, "Deal."

Sitting on the couch, he poured the wine and handed her a glass. "To us."

She tried to smile. "To us."

He took a sip. "Tell me why you look so sad."

She needed him to understand. "Jack, I'll say it again. There's an awful lot of water under the bridge. No matter how much I want this to work, I'm not sure that some of it isn't going to come back to bite us."

"Like what?"

"Like right now, you say you've forgiven me, but what about when we have a fight? Is it going to come up again? Last night you accused me of not telling you things just because you heard me talking to Joe."

He shifted uncomfortably. "I did."

"And I can't live in fear of the next time you're mad, thinking that we're going to rehash this again."

"We aren't."

"Are you sure?"

He put his glass down and pulled her onto his lap. He kissed her gently and then rested his hand on her stomach. "When Priscilla said she thought you'd been pregnant this fall—"

Georgiana interrupted. "What the hell does Priscilla have to do with this?"

"That's what I was trying to tell you earlier. I just got your letter *today*. The day you dropped it off, Priscilla made a comment, thinking you might have been pregnant. I went from disbelief, to excitement, to putting pieces together in the wrong way. I realized today that I'd found the envelope on Wednesday, but I'd thrown it on the counter and forgotten about it."

He looked down at his hand, still resting on her stomach. "For those couple of minutes when I thought you were pregnant, I was over the moon excited. My emotions were so out of control with joy and anticipation. Then when I figured it out that you weren't pregnant anymore, it just felt like a betrayal."

He kissed her hair. "Listen to me. You made the comment last night that you didn't need me to beat you up, that you were doing that yourself. I finally understood that today. I forgive you. I love you. I want us to go forward. I need you to forgive yourself." He chuckled and she felt the rumble under her cheek. "And I need you to promise that if I get you pregnant again, I'm the first person you tell."

Georgiana began to feel the first licks of hope in her brain. "Taking a lot for granted, aren't you?"

"You mean, I'm taking it for granted that we're going to make love again?"

"Yes."

"We are. I love you; you love me. I want you." He nuzzled her neck, seeing her body respond instantly. "You want me."

Georgiana pulled back to look at him, then without saying a word, she wrapped her arms around his neck and kissed him deeply. Pulling back, she smiled. "Yes, I love you and I want you. Of that, there is no doubt."

"Then we can work this out." His voice was serious. "You didn't promise yet."

"Huh?"

"You didn't promise yet that if, or *when*, you get pregnant again, I'm the first person you tell."

She looked deep into his eyes and solemnly said, "I promise."

Over the next half hour, they talked quietly, sipping their wine and staying away from deep topics. Finally she yawned, and he kissed her forehead. "Tired?"

She nodded. "Exhausted. It's been an emotional few days and I didn't get a lot of sleep last night."

His tone was dry. "Obviously, when you're emailing me at two in the morning."

Immediately she grew defensive. "I slept for a while before I sent that. It wasn't that I was awake that late."

He raised an eyebrow. "And then you emailed me again at five."

"Responding to *your* email."

"True." His voice softened. "I know you didn't like my answer. I fully admit part of it was me reacting emotionally and part of me was trying to protect you."

She tried to relax her posture. "I know."

He squeezed her hand. "Do you still want to talk about it?"

She nodded. "I do. But not right now. I have until the middle of December to decide."

He took a deep breath. "As much as the bossy, controlling part of me wants to get details and do this right now, could we say that no matter what happens with us, we would have a perfectly calm and reasonable professional discussion about this during the first week of December?"

She laughed outright. "You and I have a calm and reasonable professional conversation? I guess there's a first time for everything."

"Going back to where this conversation started, you're tired and need sleep." He stroked her cheek. "I don't suppose you'd let me stay tonight?"

"I can't. Not yet." She kissed him lightly, pulling back before he could respond. "I love you, and more than anything, I want this to work. Taking a page from your book, I need us to go slowly. I need to know we're all good before we sleep together."

Before he could argue, she smirked with a slow, sexy smile. "But I have a suggestion."

"Go ahead."

"I'm going to suggest that this week, we text, email, call at night, maybe a couple quick visits."

"And? So far your suggestion sucks. Basically what I'm hearing is that I barely get to see you."

"And…" She ran her hands slowly down his chest, feeling the taut muscles under the grey sweater. "And Saturday night you meet me in Burlington to go to the governor's ball like we originally planned. I'm asking you to be my date and maybe share a room with me that night."

His voice deepened. "Are you asking me on a *date*?"

"I am. A real, formal, *public* date where we have to get dressed up, show the world our relationship, then hopefully become lovers again."

He pulled her close and kissed the tip of her nose. "So, for a few days I have to basically stay away from you? At least until the ball, that is."

"It's not like we won't have contact—just not see each other a lot. Give you time to think and make sure you really are okay with what happened. Then go to the ball."

"Hmm…" His hand slid up her ribcage and he smiled slowly as her eyes darkened with desire.

"Stop it, you're not playing fair."

"Wasn't trying to." He grinned. "I like my idea of me staying here tonight better, but fair is fair. I asked you for time and this will give it to me. If this is what you want, this is what we'll do."

She shook her head. "No, it's not what I want. Truly, what I want is to kiss you for hours, then beg you to make love to me. But it's what I feel we *need* to do." She rubbed her thumb gently across his lower lip. "I love you. Thinking we were done hurt more than I can tell you. I don't have the strength to become your lover again and then have it fall apart. I need to know that you've had time to really think, not just have a hormonal rush today because we seemed to work it out."

He chuckled. "To be clear, every time I see you or hear your voice, even when I'm incredibly pissed at you, even when I thought we were through, I have both an emotional and hormonal rush."

She pulled him closer. "And I feel the same. So can we try this?"

Chapter Thirty-Five

A few hours later she texted him. *"Are you still awake? Can I call you?"*

"You're the one who's supposed to be asleep, but... Of course. Call me."

He answered on the first ring. "You okay?"

Georgiana's voice was timid. "I am, but I need you to do something."

"Of course."

"Don't you want to know what it is before you agree?"

"Gia, if you need me to do something, I'll do it. What is it?"

She paused. "I need you to talk to PJ and Boone and Shroom about some things." He heard her take a deep breath. "There are some things in my past that I can't talk to you about, but I need you to know them. They can tell you."

Jack felt jealousy swamp him at the thought of Boone knowing things that he didn't. He tried to push that down. "Okay."

She immediately heard the catch in his voice. "Jack, listen carefully. I'm not suggesting you talk to Boone because he was my lover. He's PJ's best friend and when I had a hard time long ago, he and some of PJ's other friends were my support network."

"This isn't meant to be a confrontational question, but *you* can't tell me these things?"

She could feel how cold she was getting and knew that soon it was going to get hard to speak. Her voice shook and she rubbed the raised design on her arm. "I can't. I am able to talk about bits and pieces of it sometimes, but other times…" She took a deep breath. "I've never wanted anyone to know it all before. But I want *you* to know. I want you to know it all."

"And this is why you were in treatment with that guy, Joe?"

"Yes. I was a patient in his trauma clinic a long time ago."

"And you're still in treatment? You referred to him as your therapist last night."

"No, not really. I refer to our sessions as my 50,000 mile check-ups. Sometimes if something triggers me, I need to talk to him to get back on track."

Jack took a deep breath. "Nothing they could tell me will change how I feel about you, but if this is something you need, I'll do it."

"Thanks." She cleared her throat. "PJ will call you tomorrow."

"Sounds good. Go to sleep now. I love you."

"I will. I love you too."

After hanging up, she texted Shroom. *"Breakfast at my house tomorrow?"*

"I'll be there."

At five the next morning, Georgiana awoke and checked her phone, smiling when she saw a text from Jack. *"Good morning, Princess Gia. I love you. Talk to you later."*

"Good morning, love you too. Talk later."

An hour later, she put bagels and cream cheese on the table and handed Shroom a cup of coffee. They ate in companionable silence for a while before he looked at her seriously. "Okay kiddo, what's on your mind?"

"What do you mean?"

"You're clearly trying to figure out how to say something and for the life of me, considering all the things we talk about, I can't figure out what you'd hesitate to tell me."

Georgiana put down her bagel and looked at the older man, her heart constricting with her love for him. "Okay, I need to say this all in one piece."

"Okay." As always, when she needed his attention, he turned his gaze on her with his full intensity, his eyes never leaving hers.

She reached out to take his hand. "I love you. I can't imagine my life without you. You've been my helper, protector, sounding board, mentor, one of my best friends, and ultimately, my *father* for my entire life. Other than PJ, I listen to you more than anyone else and I may listen to you more because you rarely piss me off. I can't tell you how much I love you or how thankful I am to have you. But it makes me sad to know that you were in love with Uncle Jason, and you *never* told me that. And I know you're in love with Mark and he's in love with you, but you keep it a secret. Jesus, Shroom, I love Mark. He's amazing, and I love being around him, and you, and the two of you together. You've been a couple for years, but you've never told me that, I had to figure it out on my own. I don't want you to do that anymore. I love you and I want you to be happy without having to feel like you have to hide."

Shroom sat in stunned silence, staring at her with his mouth open. Finally, he reached out to take both her hands in his, tears filling his eyes. "How'd you know?"

"About Uncle Jason?"

"About everything."

She squeezed his hand, seeing the tears begin to fall. "In one of my earliest memories, I saw you crying as you sat under Uncle Jason's tree. I was maybe three or four years old. I came in and asked Grandma about it and she told me that your heart was broken because Uncle Jason had died and that you'd never love anyone like that again. Over the years, I've known how hard it was for you around his birthday or the anniversary of his death. I just figured maybe one day you'd tell me yourself. As for Mark, anyone who's around the two of you together would know. I know that's why you're so careful to not see each other in public, but Shroom, you love the man. Stop hiding."

He brushed away the tears. "I loved, *love* your Uncle Jason more than I can express, Georgie. A once-in-a-lifetime love. When he got drafted, I enlisted because I couldn't stand the thought of him going there alone. Our plan was to tell your grandparents after the war, and hope for their support, then live our lives together. When he died, part of me died too."

"I know."

"And all I could do was try to help your grandparents, and you and PJ. I've tried to take care of you like he would've done." His eyes were full of love. "The two of you would've been peas in-a-pod. Your spunk and fearlessness, your ability to love. He would've loved you more than I can imagine." He took a sip of his coffee. "And after he died, it took me almost a decade before I was ready to even think of going out again. Then years later I met Mark."

"And you love him?"

"And I love him."

"And does he love you?"

He smiled. "He does."

"Then, dammit, Shroom, go public. Bring him to a family event as the man you love, let us get to know him. I mean, I know him from when he helps with chores, but I want to actually get to know him with him *knowing* that I know, instead of pretending I don't."

"What about your grandparents? I don't want to hurt them."

"Shroom, they know. They've always known but I think they're waiting for you to tell them yourself. So instead of us all pretending, how about we open it all up?" She laughed. "Hell, the whole town talks about all of us anyway."

He was silent for a moment. "Okay." He let out a sigh as he leaned back in his chair. He pondered the ceiling, then said, "I suppose you are right. No, you are right." Another heavy sigh. "Okay, I'll talk to Mark, since, obviously, this impacts him too." He nodded. "But I think you are right. It's time."

She grinned from ear to ear. "Mom's coming home for Thanksgiving with a guy. PJ told me yesterday that he's moving home with Julia, and Boone is moving here too." She paused. "And I'm in love, and..." she hesitated, "and I'm going to have you guys tell Jack everything."

"Seriously? Katherine is coming home for Thanksgiving? PJ's moving home? And you want Jack to know everything. *Everything*?"

"Yes, yes, yes, and...yes. Everything."

"Holy shit, Georgie. Holy shit!"

Later that morning, after the day got rolling, Dot came into Georgiana's office with two cups of herbal tea, handing one to her boss. "Okay, spill! You left here yesterday looking like death warmed over and then you came back with a bounce in your step. What happened?"

With a giggle, Georgiana told her friend everything, thankful for their relationship. When she was done, she leaned back in her chair. "So, there you go."

"Wow!" Dot was grinning from ear to ear, thrilled for her boss and dear friend. "Good for you, George."

George giggled. "Yes. Yes, it is good for me…"

Chapter Thirty-Six

Georgiana was completely exhausted by the time she drove home, surprised by how quickly she still tired. While eating her meal of a bowl of brown rice, tuna, and kimchi, she sat in front of her laptop trying to decide about rooms at the Hilton for the night of the governor's ball. *Two rooms or one?* Was booking one being presumptuous about where they'd be this weekend? Was two safer? Did it seem sexy, or desperate to book just one room?

Just then her phone buzzed with a message. *"Are you taking a rest?"*

"No. In the midst of playing flag football here, call later."

"You are the most irreverent person I've ever met."

"Thank you—call me!"

The phone rang and he sounded amused. "You know, you can call me too."

"I know. But I thought you had meetings today."

"I do, but you can still call, or text and I'll get back to you as soon as I can."

"Hmm, then maybe we need to talk about our schedules a bit more, so we'd know when to call."

"Let's. So now that we're talking, how was your morning and what are you doing now?"

"Good, long. I still get tired so quickly. And…"

"And…?"

"I'm sitting here overthinking."

"Overthinking what?"

"Whether we want one room or two for Saturday night. I need to book now and can't figure out what to do. I feel stupid for asking." The last words came out in a rush.

There was a pause, then his voice deepened, and she felt a jolt of arousal. "One room. One. So, help me God, I won't make it through another week without making love to you. Going slow was wise. I get it, and I appreciate your idea that I needed to make sure my head was on straight, but Saturday night I'm taking you back to *our* room."

He lowered his voice and spoke softly. "I'm undressing you. I'm going to start by kissing every inch of you, including that very sensitive spot behind your right knee." Her soft whimper let him know his words were working, "Then, and only then, we are going to make love. And no, I'm past the point of us wanting to do the proper thing with two rooms. I love you, you love me, and we're not going to have separate rooms." He paused. "This sounds stupid, but I want our toothbrushes on the same counter."

"Wow." She swallowed, fighting the urge to beg him to come over to her house right then. "One room it is."

He tried controlling his rising desire. "Do you want me to book it? Here, let me give you my credit card…"

"I can take care of it…"

"Fine." He cleared his throat. "So, I'm meeting Shroom tonight and we're going to call PJ and Boone from his house. Is it okay if I stop by first?"

"Please."

Just after four-thirty, Jack pulled into her driveway and had to smile seeing her already waiting at the door. He cradled her face in his hands and gave her a deep and lingering kiss. "Hi."

"Hi," she whispered. "Come in for a few minutes." She took him by the hand.

Just then another car pulled in. She looked at the car in confusion for just a moment, then muttered. "Holy shit!!!! No way!!!"

The driver's door opened, and Jackson watched with interest as a man he recognized from photos emerged.

PJ's smile went from ear to ear as he saw his sister. "Heya, Gigi."

In the months he'd known her, Jackson had never seen such a look of joy on Georgiana's face. With a screech, she catapulted down the steps into her brother's arms and the two of them hugged. As the twins were busy, another man, clearly military, got out and came around the car for Georgiana to hug him tightly too. He pulled back to look at her intently. Jackson immediately knew this was Boone and his stomach clenched with jealousy.

Striding up the steps, PJ held out his hand. "Jackson, great to finally meet you in person. Thanks for taking such good care of her."

"My pleasure."

Boone bounded up the steps and put out his hand. Jack looked at him as he returned the greeting and, much to his surprise, his jealousy evaporated instantly.

Georgiana took Jack's hand and looked to her brother. "What the hell are you doing here?"

PJ shrugged. "Well, we were coming Saturday anyway. We had leave time and figured we'd come talk to Jack face to face, then help you get ready for Thanksgiving."

She looked at them fondly. "Fucking Joe called you, didn't he? And now that I asked you to talk to Jack, you're both all puffed up in protective mode."

Boone laughed. "Get off your high horse, Georgie. Yes, Joe called and he's worried. So, when you said you wanted us to talk to Jack, we thought it was a good time to be here."

She rolled her eyes. "Whatever."

PJ smiled at Jack. "We're headed over to my house. Shroom will be there in about ten minutes. Come over when you're ready."

Still slightly stunned by their arrival, all Jack could think to say was, "Sure."

The two got back in the car, and Jack and Georgiana watched them drive off in complete silence.

When they were out of sight, Georgiana turned, wrapping her arms around Jack. Leaning against him, she breathed in his scent. "I love you, Jack. Now and forever. Forgive me for sending you next door to talk to them. I wish I could tell you, but I'm not ready to say the words. I need them to do it for me." She stretched up on her tiptoes. "Know that no matter what, I love you."

He gazed down at her, seeing the fear in her eyes. "Gia, you are the love of my life. Nothing they tell me will change that, and you need to know that, and to believe it." He kissed her forehead. "I will see you later, I promise."

Jack walked up to PJ's front door with his stomach in knots. As he raised his hand to knock, PJ opened the door. "Hey, come on in."

In the kitchen, Boone and Shroom were already seated at the table. PJ gestured to an empty chair. "Have a seat."

Jack sat warily.

PJ still stood. "Jack, coffee, beer?"

All three men had beers in front of them. "A beer would be great."

PJ handed it to him after twisting off the top and sat down. "Jack, the three of us, and my grandparents, are the only five people on earth who know this entire story, other than Gigi, but her brain has blocked some parts out. Even our mom doesn't know all of it."

"Okay."

PJ's tone was painfully serious. "Do you love her?"

Jack's answer was immediate. "More than I can say."

PJ nodded. "Good. The fact that she asked you to come talk to us about this is the greatest gesture of love and trust she can give." He rolled the bottle back and forth in his hands. "She married Rick, and he never knew anything about the first part of this."

That statement hit Jack hard. How could she have kept such a secret, whatever it was, for all that time? Jack had to ask, "Why can't *she* tell me this?"

Boone answered. "Because she *can't*, literally. It's a trauma thing. We'll explain that, we promise."

"Okay." Jack took a deep breath. "Okay."

PJ took a swallow, then put the bottle down. "So, the three of us, we've never told anyone all of this, so I'm going to do my best to explain it in reasonably chronological order. They're gonna break in as needed."

"Okay." Jack felt stupid, unable to say anything else.

PJ started slowly. "Gigi said you asked about the scarring on her arm when you were in Seattle, and about her tattoo."

"I did."

PJ continued. "The marks on her arm are actually termed ritual scarification."

Jack wondered what this had to do with anything. "Okay."

"You know that we lived in Ethiopia for a while?"

"Yes. Gia mentioned it to me."

"Mom moved us there when we were twelve. It was our second tour there. That's where Gigi and I originally met Deng who you met at the refugee festival. Several of the Lost Boys were there in that camp with us. Anyway, Mom was working around the clock, even more than usual. So, George and I did what we always did when we moved to a new camp, we tried to get to know kids our age." He smiled. "I met a couple of boys and, even in that hell hole, we had fun. We played soccer day after day. But I have to admit that I was ignoring George." He looked down at his hands. "I'm not justifying it, but I'd spent every second of my life with my sister, my twin. We had always done everything together. And then, suddenly I had male friends, males my own age. But, George was left on her own. I didn't notice that she'd started hanging around with a certain group from the camp, and certainly Mom would never have noticed." He shook his head. "George met a guy named Abdirahim Abdi."

He looked up and Jack could see the anger burning in his eyes. "Abdi was twenty-six at the time and George was thirteen. She didn't act thirteen. Frankly, she was a little adult. Anyway, Abdi was living in the camp as a supposed refugee, but what we know now is that he was running a black-market organization. He started paying attention to George. I'm not sure if it was that he cared about her at all, or if it was just a power thing. He knew there were suspicions about him, but if he was connected with Mom's daughter, no one would bother him."

He took a sip of beer. "So he started, for lack of better wording, *grooming* her." Jack could feel the cold tendrils of horror starting to swirl in his gut. "First it was a few wildflowers, then it was a piece of fruit. Then it became a small piece of tribal jewelry or something to wear. If any of them had been larger items, we probably would've noticed, but it was a slow progression. As for George, I think she was so lonely that *any* attention was welcomed."

Shroom reached over and put his hand on PJ's shoulder. "Let it go. It wasn't your job to watch her."

His self-loathing erupted. "It was! God knows Mom wasn't going to. I was all she had, and I abandoned her for *soccer*."

Jack needed to know what had happened. "Keep going."

PJ blew out a deep breath and looked at Jack, noting the intensity in his eyes. "So, Abdi kept the process going. It evolved into the two of them spending lots of time together. At first, with others around, then just the two of them." He held the bottle so tightly; Jack could see the man's knuckles whiten. "I don't know exactly when it became physical. I think I have a pretty good idea because she became especially secretive. It was during that time he had her start undergoing the ritual scarification on her arm."

"What does it mean?"

"It meant that she belonged to him. Like *property*. Not all that different than our branding of cattle here in the United States."

Jack tried to think of a response but had none as he wallowed in the horror of what he was hearing. PJ continued. "It's the precursor to marriage vows. If it had gone on longer, the scars would've continued all the way around her arm like a cuff and eventually she would also have had a band around her hips, just below her waist, which would've signified that she was ready to bear children."

"Jesus. She let someone do that to her?"

PJ nodded. "From talking to other women who have been scarred, they say it's akin to being tortured. The pain is mind-boggling, and it hurts as it heals. She did this to make him happy. And we didn't know because she was able to keep it covered."

"And he was *how* old? No one thought this was wrong?"

"Twenty-six. No, we're talking a society of multiple wives and much older men with young girls. Culturally, it wasn't an issue there."

Jackson shook his head, trying to form coherent thoughts. "Go on."

Boone held out a hand. "PJ, hold up." He looked at Jack, seeing the shock on his face. "Jack, you okay?"

"No, I'm not okay. Jesus Christ, how, how—"

PJ spoke. "How the fuck could our mom put us in a place like that?"

Jack nodded. "Yes!"

Shroom spoke. "She thought she was helping the world and that it would be good for them. In some ways, she was right. And believe me, this has eaten at her too."

PJ shook his head angrily. "So you say, Shroom. Not that we've ever seen it."

Jack leaned back in his chair; his arms crossed in front of him. "Keep going."

"So, somewhere in this time, he started sexually abusing her."

Just hearing the last three words made Jackson nauseous. "God almighty."

PJ snorted. "I don't think God was involved in any way. It's a safe bet *God* didn't give a shit what was happening to her." He looked down at his hands. "I don't know how often, or how long it went on really. She was so secretive at that point; I really didn't know much of anything. Then," his voice broke. "Then…"

Boone reached out and squeezed PJ's forearm. For a moment, Jack had to marvel at the incredibly deep bond between the three men and their profound devotion to Georgiana. Boone's voice was quiet. "PJ, do you want me to go on?"

PJ shook his head forcefully. "No, I can do it." He looked at Jackson. "Then she got pregnant."

Jack shook his head; unsure he had heard PJ correctly. *Pregnant*? Leaning forward, he said, "What?"

"Yeah. *Pregnant*. With child. All those wonderful sayings, that all came down to she'd been sexually abused, and now was carrying the abuser's child. She had just turned *fourteen*. I don't really know how long she knew before she told us. Mom found out and immediately realized we had to get the hell out of Ethiopia before Abdi knew what was going on. Under tribal law, she would have immediately been expected to become part of his family and removed from us to be his de facto wife."

"At *fourteen*?"

"At fourteen. Instead of doing the sane thing, and bringing us home to Vermont, Mom immediately transferred to a camp on the Iraqi border, so we could leave Ethiopia immediately. Then, once the transfer was approved, she took us to London. She said it was the way we needed to travel to get to Iraq, but we left Ethiopia in the middle of the night."

"Jesus..." Jack wanted to beg them to stop, every additional word hurt more to hear.

"In London, Mom had Georgiana see a doctor and..." Jack realized tears were beginning to roll down PJ's cheeks. "And Mom and the doctor tried to convince her to get an abortion. She refused, and refused, and refused." He glanced at Jack and gave a bit of a chuckle. "You think she's stubborn *now*? You should have known her then." He sniffed, "So, Mom invoked some parental law and took her to the doctor, telling her she needed a vaccination for the pregnancy. Really the shot was a sedative that knocked her out. While she was out, they terminated the pregnancy."

Bile filled Jack's mouth. He swallowed hard as he understood what PJ was saying. "She had an abortion by *force*?"

"Yes." PJ swiped away a tear angrily. "She woke up confused and was told it was done."

"And I accused her of having an abortion." The words came out softly, but Jack felt panicked. He stood up so quickly he almost tipped the chair over. "I didn't know. Shit, I didn't know!!!"

Boone stood up and walked around the table to put his hand on Jack's shoulder. "Jack, there was no way you could know. There was no way you could've known."

Boone continued, "As for what you said then? Yeah, it was harsh, but she was wrong to not tell you she'd been pregnant and miscarried. We *all* told her that repeatedly. The fact that she wants you to know all of this now, means that not only has she forgiven you, but she wants you to know it all." He pulled out the chair. "Sit down and hear the rest." He paused. "Please, Jack. Gigi loves you. You need to hear the rest to fully understand."

Jack sat down, his now miserable heart still racing. PJ offered him a weak smile. "So, when she realized what had happened, she flipped. I mean *flipped*." He looked down at the table. "She became suicidal."

Jack interrupted. "That's why Joe asked her if she was safe."

"She wondered if you'd heard that part of the conversation that night." PJ nodded. "That was the only time that we know of that she *wasn't* safe, the only time she had the potential to consciously hurt herself. Yeah, we all check on her occasionally now to make sure she's doing okay. But then? It was *bad*. She was a fourteen-year-old who had been sexually abused, gotten pregnant, and undergone a forced abortion while sedated. And she lost it and wanted to die. Not only did she want to die, but at this point, she was also actively *trying* to die. So, they sedated her again, by force, and kept her medicated for a week. Then Mom, in another one of her best parenting moments, announced that she needed to get to Iraq. She said we were going to stay with friends in London for another week and then join her. She just left us there."

He paused, taking a swig of his beer. "Now let me be clear. I do think the abortion was the best option, but the way it happened, it was *so* cruel. Georgiana was stripped of the right to control her own body. She wanted this baby, misguided as that was, and she thought Abdi loved her. She was ripped from him, violated again by the abortion, then medicated to keep her calm. So, I did the only thing I could think of. I called Shroom and told him *everything*. He told our grandparents, and the three of them got on a plane that night. Then, via some really nasty phone calls, they got Mom to give my grandparents custody of us, and we moved to Vermont."

Shroom cleared his throat. "Georgiana went into a shell, locked inside herself emotionally. She did well academically, was well-liked, and every teacher said she was well-adjusted. Truly, though, she was just so broken. However, she covered it well. She basically got through the day at school so she could come home to the animals. Her sheep, goats, and alpacas all kept her going. As long as she could come home to them, to the land and the gardens, she could survive. She never even dated."

A realization hit Jack. "She never dated?"

"Well, she had a boyfriend in high school, but he was—is—gay. Guaranteed not to touch her. It was the perfect relationship at the time. Gradually, great therapy, good food, fresh air, a real bed, constant love, vegetable gardens, and the animals, and she began to come around. She even got to a point where she could forgive her mom for what she'd done and started going to visit her again."

PJ resumed the story. "Then she went to college at seventeen and met Rick. My understanding is that she went on a couple dates with other guys when she first got to college, seemingly to prove she was like everyone else. Then she started seeing Rick, and she never thought of dating anyone else. She wanted a normal relationship like she thought people should have. She didn't realize that while I think he loved her, he was never *in* love with her. If anything, I think he was more attracted to her connection to Mom. He was always *in* love with Molly, who was George's roommate all through college. Gi never thought it was weird that he always invited Molly to do things with them. But George and Rick got married, did okay, then she came home early from a trip, wanting to surprise Rick with a romantic weekend, and she found him in bed with Molly. So, she filed for divorce, finished the last couple months of the school year, resigned from that job, and went to Grand Manan to think, to write, and do research."

Boone grimaced. "And we"—he gestured to the three of them—"blew it. We assumed that she was doing okay until PJ and I decided to go up to surprise her with a weekend visit. We got there and found that in the six months she'd been there, she'd lost thirty pounds and had completely shut down." He looked at Jack sadly. "She'd basically fallen apart, and we didn't know."

"What did you do?"

Boone shrugged. "We kidnapped her."

Jack thought he'd heard wrong, "What?"

Boone's voice was sure. "We *kidnapped* her. We tried convincing her to come back to Virginia with us, but she refused and told us to leave. She shut us out completely, so we" —he looked uncomfortable—"we told her we were just going to Maine shopping, then we would bring her right back to the island. We convinced her that we would just go to the Walmart there and get her groceries and a few essentials. She finally agreed, thinking it was our version of a peace offering. Once we crossed the border, we just kept going until we got to Virginia. Not right, not pretty, but we felt it was the only way we could help her."

PJ spoke. "Once we got south of Maine, she knew we weren't backing down, so she didn't fight us anymore. In fact, once we got about an hour south of the border, she stopped speaking to us and didn't talk to us again for almost a week. *Nothing*."

Jack shook his head. "Nothing? She didn't say anything?"

Boone answered. "Nope. No yelling, no crying, no questions. She just sat. Didn't look at us, didn't speak. She dissociated."

"What did you do?"

"Well, we'd gotten back to our base in Virginia, and for Boone and the rest of our unit, it became a community effort to save her. We got her into a fabulous clinic with Joe, got her on meds for a while, made her eat, got her working out, and even taught her martial arts as a way for her to vent her rage. If I had to be away, the others would watch her. For months, she had company 24 hours a day. She was never left alone."

"As she got stronger, as she continued therapy and began to come back from the shadow she'd become. She finally recognized that her falling apart wasn't due to Rick, it was due to her own rage at having been, as she put it, 'a fucking idiot victim *again*.' She had to 'walk through the valley of death' to face the reality of the pregnancy and the abortion, then had to face what had happened in her marriage. She had to learn to make peace with what she saw as her stupidity about Abdi and Rick. And that was the easy part. The hard part was what came next; dealing with PTSD, learning how to read herself when something triggered her and how to handle it. And she did."

"And that's why she's so close to you guys…"

Boone grinned. "You mean, that's why she's so close to me that she told me she was pregnant before you?"

Jack gave a somewhat sheepish smile at the blunt question. "Yeah, that's what I mean."

PJ nodded. "Yeah. It was a group effort. The guys in our were—*are*—amazing with her. All of them. To this day, they all are deeply connected to Gigi. There were times when she needed to be away from me, and they stepped in. It was Diego who first started running with her. She'd run occasionally before, but with him, she started really training. Then Boone and I had her come to hand-to-hand combat training with us. It was all of us working together to help her find herself."

"And she obviously *did* come back."

"She did. Then Charlie offered her the job here. Once she settled in, she hit her stride again. Not saying she doesn't trigger anymore, but it's pretty rare."

"But she won't talk about it?"

"Nope. It isn't that she won't talk about it; it's more that she *can't* talk about it. She still talks to Joe once in a while, but he doesn't know if she'll ever be able to really talk conversationally about Abdi, the pregnancy, or the abortion. She can, however, talk about Rick now and, for whatever reason, she's forgiven him."

Boone looked down at his hands and muttered. "Asshole. Still would like to kill him."

PJ grinned. "Me, too. She keeps telling me to let it go."

Jack ignored them. "And Abdi?"

Boone answered by turning over the iPad in front of him, hitting the power button and handing it to Jack, who looked at the screen with interest. "On *Time Magazine* last month. Biggest fucking war lord and arms dealer in Ethiopia and Yemen."

Jack looked at the picture, hatred filling him as he looked at the picture of the man who had violated Georgiana. Suddenly he remembered something. "That came in the mail, I mean the print copy, it came last month when she had the concussion. She saw that cover." He thought back. "I remember thinking it was odd. She picked it up and put it in recycling. When I asked her about it, she made a joke, saying she wasn't supposed to look at texts. But she was really quiet all that night." He put the iPad down with a sigh. "Jesus Christ."

PJ knew it all was a lot to take in, but he knew that there was more Jack needed to understand. "She said you asked about her tattoo."

"Yeah. The star on her shoulder. In August she had one star. I saw it last week when she pulled off her sweatshirt, now she has two. When I asked her about it, she changed the subject."

Shroom pulled a necklace from under his shirt, showing a pendant of a tree with a star above it, and Jack immediately recognized the star from her tattoo. "This was Jason's necklace. I gave it to him when he turned eighteen." His voice broke and PJ reached over to squeeze his hand. "When he was killed, the necklace came home and Ruth and James…George and PJ's grandparents… gave it back to me. Ruth got a tattoo of the star to show her grief. She said it was because she'd talk to the stars to talk to Jason." He rubbed his hands together as if cold. "On Georgiana's eighteenth birthday, she went to Burlington and got the same star tattoo as Ruth, for *her* baby."

The realization hit Jackson so hard it took his breath away. "And she just got the second star for *our* baby."

PJ nodded. "I would assume so. She didn't tell any of us that she did it, but it makes sense."

Boone looked at Jack. "She wanted that baby so very badly, Jack. She was beyond excited. She really hoped you were going to be excited too. Then when she lost the baby, besides that loss triggering her, she also had the broken rib and the concussion, both of which jumbled her thinking. We tried to convince her then and kept telling her, that she needed to tell you about the baby, but she couldn't seem to do it. In hindsight, I think we" —he gestured at PJ and Shroom—"missed how fucking terrified she was by the combination of the miscarriage and the concussion."

"She was dealing with the loss of another baby, feeling it was her fault...*again*, and was also afraid of going stupid. Then when you guys got together, she was terrified that you'd leave her. She just reached a point where she couldn't do anything." Boone looked at Jack and smiled before he continued. "But she loves you so much that she had us tell you all of this. There's no single gesture of trust bigger than this for her."

"I would never betray that trust."

Boone continued. "Now you have to decide whether what you now know changes how you feel about her."

Jack's face gave the answer, but then he spoke. "I already didn't get how she could possibly be so put together after the way she was raised. But this? This all makes me even more astounded that she can function at all, let alone be the amazing person that she is. Does it change how I feel about her? If anything, I love her even more now than when I walked the door here today."

Over the next hour, the three men told Jack the details of Georgiana's therapy process. Finally, Shroom leaned back to study him. "Now that you know this, you need to act one way or the other. She's probably about to lose her shit, worrying about how you are reacting to all of this."

"What do I do?"

"What you have to." Boone's voice became even more serious. "Jack, you have to let her know that you know, and how you feel, but it can't be a discussion."

"What do you mean?"

PJ shrugged. "You need to *show* her how you feel. Words don't work when she's triggered."

Shroom explained. "Like when I know she's triggered, I go sit in the little grove of trees and wait for her. She knows that means I understand."

"Grove of trees?"

"When Jason died, we planted a maple tree for him. After the abortion, we planted another tree for that life." He looked uncomfortable. "She and I planted a tree for your baby in October."

Jack tried hard to push down the flash of pain that they had done this without him. He sat, staring ahead for a long time thinking, then suddenly smiled. "I know what to do." He looked at Shroom. "Any chance you'd like to help me with something? We'd need to run into town first."

Shroom grinned. "Absolutely."

Jack looked at the other two men. "Could you guys get her out of here for an hour or two?"

Boone nodded. "Of course. We'll take her to look at the Eisman plant."

Jack was confused. "What?"

PJ clarified. "We told Gigi that we were moving back here in the spring, starting a security firm, and our first client the Eisman Company, which makes goggles for the military. We'll tell her we want her to go look at it with us."

"That makes sense." Jack nodded. "Okay, that'll work. We need an hour, two tops."

All four stood up and Jack looked at the others seriously. "I can't tell you how much I appreciate this. I want you to know that I love her just as much."

Boone looked at PJ, then grinned at Jack as they pulled him into a group bear hug. "We know. If we'd had any doubt about it, we wouldn't have told you. Welcome to the family."

In Jack's car, Shroom asked, "So where are we going?"

"To Walmart."

At the store, Jack walked quickly toward the holiday decorations, Shroom hurrying to keep up with him. Jack obviously knew what he was looking for as he pulled three boxes off the shelves. He held them out to Shroom. "Look, the lights are stars, just like the stars in her tattoo. Let's put lights on the three trees in the grove."

Jack was shocked as Shroom's eyes filled with tears. Without warning, he hugged Jack hard, then said in a breaking voice, "I've always wanted to put lights on Jason's tree but didn't know if that was okay."

Jack shrugged. "Well, I don't know if it's okay either, but I do know that I need to try. Help me find the outdoor extension cords."

Back at the grove, the two men worked quickly and in silence as they decorated the trees. At one point, Jack said quietly, "I'm so sorry about Jason, Shroom."

"Thanks." He paused. "It was a once in a lifetime love."

"Georgiana's so happy that you're bringing Mark to Thanksgiving."

"Me too." Shroom looked at Jack. "Are you coming?"

"I wouldn't miss it."

When they were done, they plugged in the lights and stood back to admire their work. Jack looked over and saw that Shroom was standing there in silence, tears running down his face. He moved closer and put his arm around his shoulder, never saying a word. A few minutes later, Shroom said, "I've wanted to do this for decades but never had the balls to do it. Thank you."

"You're welcome. Thanks for helping me." Jack looked down at the newest tree, a symbol of his child's very brief life. "If they don't kill us for doing it, what do you say we do this each year? Together."

Wiping his tears, Shroom replied. "I say it sounds like a plan to me."

As they walked back, Shroom looked at the dark windows of the house. "She's clearly not back yet. Want to help do chores?" He smiled at Jack. "I assume you plan to stick around to see her today."

His voice was certain. "Today, tomorrow, and every day for the rest of my life."

Georgiana sat in silence as they pulled into the driveway, feeling her stomach clenching with nerves. Had she done the right thing? Should she have tried to tell Jack herself? Could she have said the words? Should she have let him know at all? Jack's car was in the driveway but the lights in the house were off. Maybe he was still with Shroom.

PJ stopped the car. "You want us to come in?"

She looked at her brother and the rush of love took her breath away. "No, this part I have to do alone." She reached out to squeeze his hand. "I love you, you know." She looked over her shoulder at Boone. "And I love you, too."

PJ smiled. "We know and we love you too. And *he* loves you."

Georgiana tried to return his smile, praying he was right...

Coming into the house, she turned on the lights, then went to add wood to the stove. Jack had to be planning on coming back to see her if his car was still here. He wouldn't still be around if he planned to walk away, would he? Going into the kitchen, she decided that she'd start dinner, hoping it would be dinner for two. Standing at the sink, she looked out the window, and her heart skipped a beat as she saw the lighted grove. She dropped everything as she went running out the French doors and down the path.

At the barn, Shroom pulled the door shut behind them. He looked at the house. "Looks like she's back. Lights are on." He turned to Jack. "This is where I leave you, my friend. This is between the two of you now."

Jack stood there, looking at the older man. "Shroom, thank you. Thank you for being there right from the beginning for us."

"My pleasure." Shroom gave him a hug. "I told that girl the first day I met you that you were meant to be."

Jack opened the front door. "Georgiana?" There was no answer, but food was out on the kitchen counter. "Gia?"

Jack suddenly realized where she was and quickly crossed the room, opening the French doors, then headed out to the trees.

She was sitting on the small bench in the grove. When Jack came around to the front of the bench, he could see tears streaming down her face and for a moment his heart sank. He sat down carefully. "Hi."

She looked at him and flashed the most blinding smile he'd ever seen. "Hi." She gestured toward the trees. "How'd—?"

"I wanted to show you how much I love you and—" He wiped away some of her tears. "I saw you crying, and I was afraid I'd upset you."

"Oh my God, no, Jack. I always wanted to do this, but I was afraid it would upset Shroom."

Jack started to laugh. "He wanted to do it too but was afraid it would upset you and Ruth." He suddenly realized she was shivering, just wearing a thin sweater. "Baby, you're freezing. Come on, let's go inside."

"No. I want to sit and look at them."

He sat up, unzipping his jacket. "Then come here. Sit with me and let me keep you warm."

Georgiana moved to sit on his lap, and he pulled her close, wrapping his jacket around her. With a contented sigh, she leaned against him. "Thank you. It's so beautiful."

"You're welcome." He kissed her temple. "I love you. I wanted to show you how much I love you, no matter what." His voice cracked. "And I wanted to show you that won't change."

"I was so scared this afternoon. I wasn't sure that you'd still be here when I got back."

He hugged her. "You're stuck with me. I'm not going anywhere."

Georgiana looked at the smallest tree. "I'm sorry I didn't tell you about the tree."

"It's okay. Now I know and it really helped. Putting the lights on it gave me a sense of peace." Even wrapped in his arms, he could feel her shivering with cold. "I'm happy to sit here all night if you want, but if we are, I'm going to go get your coat or something."

"No, I'm ready to go in now."

Chapter Thirty-Seven

The next night, Thursday, Georgiana rolled her head back and forth as she stretched her back. She had decided to work in the afternoon and then not go home before the basketball game, and it was taking its toll on her. She wandered out to the front office fridge, hoping there was a yogurt, or something left for her dinner; she knew she didn't have time for anything more. Just then she heard the door lock beep, meaning someone with a key fob had just entered the building, nothing unusual. She crouched down, shuffling through stuff in the fridge and searching in vain for a makeshift dinner.

A deep voice rumbled behind her. "My God. Dr. Hewitt, looking for food. What *is* the world coming to?"

Georgiana jumped up; joy clear on her face. "Jack, what are you doing here?"

He held up a bag. "Well, since someone brilliant gave me access to her calendar, I could see that you were planning on working late and I know you well enough to know that you forgot to bring food." His eyes darkened. "Besides, I couldn't take it anymore. I needed to see you, even if only for a few minutes."

She walked toward him slowly, savoring the sight of him. Under his winter coat, she could see he was wearing a dark blue dress shirt with a gray patterned tie. She felt the visceral, primal sexual pull and all she could think of was how very good that particular shirt looked on him. He always looked gorgeous, but the times she had seen him in that shirt, her brain had been unable to think of anything other than unbuttoning it.

Stepping close, she stretched up on her tiptoes to put her arms around his neck and kissed him. With a growl, he pulled her close, wrapping his arms around her, pulling her close so her body was in full contact with his.

Reluctantly, she pulled back, painfully aware of where they were, and how easily someone could walk in on them. "You said you have food."

They walked down the hall to her office and once there, sat at the table. Jack pulled a wrap out of the bag with a bottle of seltzer and chips and handed it to her with a smile. "Turkey with cheddar, hummus, spinach, extra hot peppers, onions, sprouts, peppers, and cucumbers."

His attention to detail made her breath catch, "You remembered!"

"I remembered. And plain chips and plain seltzer." He pulled a second sandwich out of the bag. "And roast beef with horseradish for me."

She snagged napkins out of her desk. "Thank you." Sitting down, she reached out to squeeze his hand. "I'm really glad to see you." She blushed. "I missed you today."

"I missed you too."

The two ate their sandwiches, chatting about the day and the upcoming basketball game. When the food was gone, Jack leaned back in his chair and smiled with satisfaction. "I think that's the most I've ever seen you eat at one sitting."

"It's one of my favorites and I was hungry." She looked down. "I had coffee and part of a granola bar this morning but then got so busy that I didn't think about it again."

He shook a finger at her. "You need to eat more, you know that."

She wanted to make him understand. "It's not that I don't want to eat. Most of the time, it's that I forget to eat." She smiled at him. "Sometimes it's just that eating alone is dull, so I don't do it."

"Then maybe we should have more meals together."

"Maybe we should."

Voices in the hallway told them that the players were beginning to arrive. Georgiana stood up, took care of their trash, then walked into the bathroom to brush her teeth. When she came back, Jack was still sitting relaxed at the table. She wrapped her arms around him from behind, resting her chin on top of his head. "You staying or going?"

Before she knew what was happening, he'd pulled her onto his lap. "That's up to you. I'm happy to stay but I'm not willing to pretend we're not together anymore. If you aren't ready for the public spectacle, I understand, and I'll go home."

She leaned forward and rested her forehead against his. She didn't say anything for a long time, and he finally reached up and stroked her cheek. "I love you and I know this is hard. I'm going home because I can see in your eyes that you're struggling."

Her eyes suddenly filled with tears. "I'm sorry, Jack. I just need a little more time."

"Time before being with me, or being public?"

Her voice was clear. "Time before being public at my job. At *my job* only."

"Ahhh." He kissed her again. "That makes sense."

"Thank you." She stroked his cheek. "I'm just not ready to spend my entire day tomorrow with students giving me the third-degree about you."

"Fair enough." His hands slid up from her hips and as they approached her ribcage, he felt her take in a deep breath. "So, you're ready to be with me? How ready?"

She jumped off his lap and said in a mock stern tone. "Okay, get the hell outta my office and let me run this game."

He stood up, his smile wide and confident. "How ready, Gia?"

She stood up on tiptoes, her lips almost touching his. "So ready, I blush just thinking about it."

"Good answer." He kissed her briefly. "Go. Have fun. Call me when you get home."

"I will." As he was just about out her door, Georgiana called, "Hey, Dr. Ryder?"

"Yes, Dr. Hewitt?"

"I love the hell outta you."

"Likewise."

Later that night, Georgiana thankfully locked the school door behind her. As she drove out of the parking lot, she called Jack. "Hey."

"Hey. How was the game?" He grumbled, "You know you should have gone home a while ago. By no stretch of the imagination is this working a *half-day*."

She ignored the last part of his statement. "The game was good. What did you do?"

"I went grocery shopping, then came home and put stuff away."

"Can I stop by?"

"What do you think?"

Five minutes later, Georgiana pulled into his driveway. She smiled as she saw him open the front door and step outside right away. "Waiting for someone?"

His grin was slow and sexy. "I am. My *girlfriend* is stopping by."

"Really? What's she like?"

He held out his hand and she slipped hers into his as he pulled her toward him. "She's brilliant, gorgeous, stubborn, passionate, and infuriating…and I am absolutely crazy in love with her." He opened the door. "C'mon in, it's cold out here."

In the foyer, she looked up at him. "Nice description of your girlfriend."

"She's pretty awesome." He held out his hands. "Here, take off your coat."

"No, I can't stay, I just needed to stop by and say something."

He immediately became concerned. "What's the matter?"

Georgiana smiled, seeing that he was still wearing the dark blue shirt, although the tie was gone and the shirt was now untucked, the top button undone. "Stop worrying. Not everything I tell you is something bad." She stepped forward, put her hands on his chest, and tugged gently on his shirt, pulling him close to her. "What I was here to say is that you are never, *ever* again to wear this shirt to my job. Never, ever."

He smiled, seeing the look in her eyes. "And why is that?"

She reached up and undid the second button. "Because ever since we met, this shirt has made me stupid. This is my favorite and every time you've worn it, even when we're doing the keep away game, all I can think about is how good you look in it, and how badly I want to get you out of it. So, no more wearing it if I can't take it *off* you."

His hands settled on her lower back and then started sliding up, slipping under her sweater. "Are you trying to tell me that you find me attractive?"

"You know I do. But this shirt on you?" She tugged the fabric. "It makes me crazy."

"Good to know." He leaned down, smiling as she stretched up to kiss him. "So how about I wear it when you *can* take it off me?"

"Perfect."

"You can stay and take it off me now."

She laughed and pushed him away playfully. "Nice try."

He sighed. "I know, I know, patience is a fucking virtue."

As she opened the door, she looked back at him. "I'll see you in the morning?"

"I'll pick you up at 9:00." He closed the door behind them, standing on the porch looking down at her. "Thank you for letting me go with you."

"You're welcome. And I get it. You need to be able to ask questions." She stood on her tiptoes and kissed him gently. "I love you."

Chapter Thirty-Eight

The next morning, Jack sat nervously in the waiting room at the doctor's office. Finally, a nurse popped her head out. "Jack? They're ready for you."

He followed her down the hallway to a small office, smiling when he saw Dr. Liz standing in the doorway. "Jack, good to see you. Come in."

Georgiana was already seated by the desk, and she smiled upon seeing him.

Liz sat down behind her desk. "Okay. George has signed a release for you, but she'd already signed one for the district about her concussion, with you as the only person to whom I could disclose anything. However, this is different. She's granting you permission to ask and know anything, as long as she's in the room to hear it too. To be clear, you can't call and ask me anything, but with her around, all is fair game."

"I understand." He looked at Georgiana with pure love. "Thank you."

"You're welcome."

Liz opened the file. "So, here's the summary from today's appointment. George has already heard all of this but asked that I tell you as well. She's gained two more pounds. I want her to gain at least ten more over the next couple of months. Her iron level is better; still not where it should be but is steadily improving. I'll check it again in two weeks. If it's not improved by then, she knows I'll be putting her on a supplement for a while. Her potassium level still sucks so she's going on a short-term supplement now. With both, eating is the key. She needs to eat, and she knows it. The rib is completely healed, although I'd suggest she refrain from heavy lifting or wrestling with the big animals for at least another couple of weeks just to be on the safe side. Last but certainly not least, the post-concussive symptoms are showing huge improvement."

She looked at Georgiana, pointing her finger for effect. "And I know you're going to be unhappy, but I'm still insisting on only half days Monday and Tuesday next week, then you're on break. After Thanksgiving, you can go to six-hour days for a week, then one more scan. If that's good, you can go back to work full time. Dr. Fatay is pretty sure it's gone already just by the improvement you've shown, but at the end of the first full week of January, you'll have to do the puncture again, so we can be certain. You'll need to take at least one day off when you have the puncture. I'd prefer you take two or have it on a Friday so you have the weekend to rest."

Liz looked at both of them fondly. "As far as for other matters, her uterus has healed fully and looks normal. Knowing the two of you are going away this weekend, have all the fun you want."

Jack cleared his throat. "And birth control?"

Liz nodded. "I don't know how much you've talked about this lately. I gave George a monthly birth control shot four weeks ago, trying to knock her hormone levels back into line. Technically, George"—she smiled at her—"it should be at full clinical strength now, and you're getting the next dose before you leave. However, I'd really prefer if you also used a secondary method, like a condom, for the next week, just to be sure. By *next* Saturday night, the shot will be enough. You just need to make sure you don't miss a dose."

Jack nodded. "Of course. And if she got pregnant by accident in the next few months?"

"You mean health ramifications?"

"Yes."

She thought for a moment. "I'd be concerned, at least until the tests in January. If it happens, I wouldn't panic or recommend termination, but I'd prefer to get the all-clear on the infection and have the iron and potassium levels up, as well as have her weight up just for strength and endurance." She smiled. "But after that, Jack, since I am guessing this is what you really want to know, after that, there is absolutely no reason that George can't get pregnant and have a healthy baby." She pulled a paper from the file. "Georgie, I got this report last night from the neurologist. I wanted to wait until Jack was in the room to share this with you."

He could see the sudden worry on her face and slid closer so he could put his arm around her. Liz continued. "Dr. Fatay says that there is a fairly high likelihood that the blow in the barn did cause the miscarriage, but he feels that even if you hadn't gotten hurt, the pregnancy might not have been viable due to the infection. There is research showing that when animals have this infection, their bodies most often self-abort due to the infection making the venal system weaker. I can't say it would have definitely happened, but I can say it was very likely." Her smile was gentle. "So, forgive yourself, my friend. Get healthy. Let's make sure that blasted infection is fully gone, then go make healthy babies."

Ten minutes later, Jack and Georgiana walked hand in hand to the car. Sunglasses covering her eyes, Georgiana sat completely silent. Jack started the car and instead of heading toward her school as they had originally planned, he headed toward his house.

Georgiana didn't say a word until he'd pulled in the driveway and turned off the ignition. "I'm pretty certain this isn't my school."

"Come inside."

"Jack, I need to go to work."

"Bullshit. Right now, I want a few minutes of your time without an audience."

She followed him into the house, still silent. In the kitchen, he slipped her jacket off, then pulled her into his arms. He felt her hesitate before she melted against him and within seconds, he could feel the tears that he'd known were threatening wet his shirt. He held her tightly, waiting until she stopped shaking with sobs, then he whispered, "I cannot express how much I love you."

She hugged him. "Likewise." She stroked his chest, still not looking at him. "What the hell is it with me crying all over you all the time?"

He smiled, then kissed her hair. "It's okay." His voice was gentle. "You understood what she was telling you, right?"

Georgiana shook her head. "I'm having a hard time with it."

Jack reached down to take her hand, leading her over to one of the kitchen stools. "Sit down."

She sat and finally looked at him.

His tone was gentle but firm. "Gia, you've carried the blame for what happened when you were fourteen for all these years, even though, if one of your students got pregnant at that age, you'd assert to the ends of the earth that someone that young can't make a sound decision regarding the situation. As for the abortion, I think your mom probably did what was best, she just didn't go about it in the best way. You were a baby. That man abused you and you have borne the weight of that for all these years, when you shouldn't have. Now here, Liz just said that even without you getting hurt, you most likely would have miscarried anyway." He reached out to stroke her cheek. "Let it go, my love. Let go of that guilt you've carried alone for so long. Grieve for the lives lost, but drop the guilt here and now."

She reached up to cover his hand with hers. "It wasn't my fault this fall, was it?"

"No."

Tears started to roll down her cheeks again. "I'm so tired of feeling guilty."

"I know."

"I'm so tired, period."

"I know." He looked concerned. "Any chance you'd just take the afternoon to rest without me having to order you to do so?"

She smiled and Jack could see the sparkle coming back into her eyes. "Nope." She gestured toward the fridge. "But you can feed me then take me back to school, and pick me up at 3:30." She suddenly became shy. "Would you come have dinner with me?"

"Of course. What do you want for dinner? I'll cook."

She shook her head vigorously. "No, I want to cook. Please."

"Okay. What can I bring?"

"A really good bottle of wine."

After lunch, he drove her back to school. In the parking lot, she turned to smile at him. "Thanks for going this morning."

He paused. "I know it was a lot for me to ask but I needed to hear it from Dr. Liz directly."

"I know." She leaned over to kiss him and for a moment, she felt herself get lost in her desire for him. "Damn, I love you."

"And I love you." He kissed her just as there was a knock on the window and both of them looked into Chase's shocked face.

Georgiana started to laugh, and Jack opened the window, laughing. "Hey, Chase."

The student was clearly mortified. "Hi, Dr. Ryder, DH. Crap, I didn't mean to interrupt."

Georgiana kissed Jack quickly on the cheek. "You didn't interrupt. Hey, come grab my bag for me, will you?"

As the embarrassed senior came around to get her bag, she leaned back into the car. "Love you, see you later."

Jack grinned from ear to ear, knowing that she was publically making her statement. "Love you too."

As Georgiana and Chase walked toward the school, she elbowed the boy. "So, there you go. You're the first student to know."

"Thanks, I guess. I really didn't mean to interrupt."

"I know."

Suddenly the boy grinned. "I really like him, DH. He's a good guy."

"Yeah, he is."

Chapter Thirty-Nine

Late Saturday morning, Georgiana called Jack. "So, we're all set?"

He smiled, hearing her nervousness. She always seemed so confident socially, it still surprised him how unsure she was about the upcoming event. "We are all set. You're driving your grandparents to Burlington, I'm going to my meeting in Montpelier, then I'll meet you at the hotel. If I get delayed, you go to the ballroom, and I'll meet you as soon as I can."

She paused, wishing deep down that they could just drive together, but knowing that he needed to attend the legislative school budget meeting. "There will be a key at the front desk for you if I've already gone with my grandparents."

"I'll find you; I promise. Breathe, Gia. We're going to have an amazing night."

Later that evening, Georgiana walked into the ballroom with her grandparents, praying that Jack would get there soon. His last text message fifteen minutes earlier had said he was about to get off the interstate, just needed to change, then he'd meet her there.

Within seconds of their arrival, the governor came over, kissed Ruth, shook hands with James, then turned to Georgiana, his eyes twinkling. "So glad you could finally join us!"

He held out his arms and she hugged him. "Glad to be here, sir."

Minutes later, her grandparents were swept away as the elite of Vermont's Democratic Party vied for their attention. Looking across the room, she felt joy as she saw her old friend Phil standing by the bar, clearly ordering drinks. Walking quickly across the room, she sidled up to him, her voice sultry. "Hey sailor, buy a girl a drink?"

Phil turned in shock, happiness filling his face as he recognized her. "George! What the hell are you doing here?"

She kissed his cheek, smiling as he hugged her. "Each year I get invited and I always turn them down, so this year I figured I'd make my grandparents happy."

The bartender came over and Phil turned to her. "What can I get you?"

"I was just kidding about the drink."

"Shut up, Georgie, what do you want?"

"White wine, please, and thank you."

"You got it." A few minutes later, as the two laughed together, Phil nudged her. "Hey, I have to go suck up to donors. Will you go keep Steve company for a few?"

"Of course."

Georgiana walked over to the tall blond man standing by the window, making small talk with several people. When he saw her, he grinned and smiled sweetly at the others. "Please excuse me for a moment, I need to talk to Dr. Hewitt about an upcoming interview."

He turned, opened his arms, and hugged her tightly. "Gorgeous. Fucking gorgeous as always."

"Thanks, Steve, you too."

The two stood to the side of the room, his arm firmly around her, sipping on their drinks as they chatted. "Okay, George, how the hell does a woman who looks like you not have a date tonight?"

"How do you know I don't have one?"

"Because you're hanging out with me. Now, you *could* be off making the rounds. God knows most people in this room see you as a member of the royal fucking family of the party. But instead, you're with me?"

"Because I love you." She grinned. "And Phil said to come save you."

The two of them turned and looked out over Lake Champlain, the lights from the buildings on the shore beginning to reflect off the water. Steve took a sip. "Hey, remember when we went out on the ice that January night and tried to walk across to New York?"

"Of course, I do. Except we had to go to the bathroom so badly that we turned around."

Just then a warm hand settled low on her back and a deep voice said, "There you are."

She turned, and Jack felt like a sledgehammer hit him in the chest as he looked at her. She was dressed in a scintillatingly low cut, dark blue gown, a long necklace drawing his eyes down to her spectacular cleavage, her feet in painfully sexy stilettos. She smiled happily. "Jack!" She stretched up to kiss him.

He smiled, tamping down his reaction to seeing another man touching her. "Hi, babe. Sorry I'm late."

"No worries, you're here now." She turned, "Jack, this is my friend, Steve. Steve, this is my date, Jack."

The two men shook hands and Steve looked at Georgiana fondly. "I stand corrected."

Jack looked confused. "Corrected about what?"

Georgiana slid her arm around him. "He thought I was here without a date."

His arm moved up around her shoulder and he pulled her closer. "Oh no, she has a date."

Steve smiled. "Good. Jack, great to meet you. Georgie, lunch soon?"

As he walked away, Georgiana turned toward Jack, her hand coming up to rest on his cheek. She looked at him seriously. "Hi."

He took a deep breath, trying to center himself. "Hi." He leaned down to kiss her lingeringly. "You look amazing. Damn, you're breathtaking."

She looked so pleased, he felt himself begin to relax. "Thank you." She stroked the lapel of his suit coat. "So are you."

"Thank you. Sorry for being late."

"It's okay. I finally listened to you and just breathed." She could still see the tension in his face. "What's going on?"

"What do you mean?"

She moved closer. "My sexy boyfriend is being overshadowed by the cranky guy who I only see occasionally, and usually only professionally. Something tweaked you and it's coming off you in waves." She slid her hand under his suit coat, resting her palm over his heart. "Talk to me."

He tried to relax, seeing her distress. "I came into the ballroom, couldn't find you, then saw you with an attractive guy who clearly knows you well, with his hands on you." He stroked her cheek. "The jealous control freak in me just reared up in a major way."

She stepped closer, pulling him to her, and she stretched up to kiss him. "Jackson Ryder, you don't *ever* have a reason to be jealous. I love you, period. Even if you hadn't gotten here tonight, you still are the man I'm with. No one else."

He smiled, his arms going around her tightly. "Thank you. I love you too."

"Now come with me for a minute."

Before he knew what was happening, she pulled him over toward the back of the room and suddenly they were standing next to Steve and another exceedingly well-dressed man. She grinned. "Phil, c'mere."

The second man looked at her fondly. "Hey again, Georgie."

Steve and Phil turned toward the couple. Georgiana looked at Jackson. "You just met Steve, who you may or may not have recognized is the anchor of Channel 5 news. This is Phil. Phil Watson, our Attorney General, and more importantly in this conversation, Steve's *husband*. Phil and I went to high school together."

Jack shook hands with Phil, then looked at Georgiana with a raised eyebrow, smiling outright as she giggled. Phil looked at the two of them with interest. "What's so funny?"

Jack chuckled. "I just gave George a hard time about something and she's schooling me."

Steve was interested. "What about?"

Jack looked uncomfortable for a second. "I thought you might be hitting on her."

The two men looked at each other and burst into laughter. Phil pulled out his phone and Georgiana looked at him in horror. "No, Phil. No way."

"Way, Gi." He opened the photos and swiped through, then turned the screen toward Jackson. "Georgiana and I went out in high school; even went to our junior prom together. I hadn't come out publicly yet, but she knew, and we were the best of friends. I keep this photo on my phone to make sure she doesn't get too full of herself."

Jack looked at the picture of a very young Georgiana and Phil, all dressed up for the prom. Even then, she'd been so beautiful, in spite of the hideous pink dress with the long, full taffeta skirt.

The next two hours were great. Jack and George visited with a lot of people and were seated for dinner with her grandparents. When the band began to play, Jack looked at her intently. "Will you dance with me?"

"I thought you'd never ask."

On the dance floor, he pulled her close, wrapping his arms around her. "Have I told you how much I love you?"

"Not recently enough."

"I love you." He kissed her hair. "Have I told you how gorgeous you look tonight?"

"Yes, but you can always tell me again."

They danced in silence for almost an hour. When the band took a break, Jack took her hand and kissed her knuckles. "Okay, any chance I can convince you that it's time to go and let me take you out for a drink, just the two of us?"

She looked at him with wide eyes. "I'd love that."

They said their goodbyes and left. In the hallway, he looked down at her. "Where to?"

"There's a hotel bar downstairs."

"Lead the way."

They sat at a back corner booth, and after ordering drinks, Jack leaned back and looked at her, his eyes burning with love. "Remember the first time we had drinks together?"

"You mean after you kissed me in the Seattle airport?"

"That's the one." He stroked her hand. "You were wearing that rose-colored mandarin blouse."

"I was."

"For future reference, that blouse affects me the same way my blue shirt does you. I remember sitting there, trying to remember that we were there to go to a professional conference and all I could think about was how much I wanted to start unbuttoning that blouse."

"I'll keep that in mind."

While they sat there talking quietly, both of them felt the pull toward each other. When a group of guys came into the room loudly arguing about the UVM basketball game, Jack smiled at her. "Déjà vu. Ready to go upstairs?"

"So ready."

As he unlocked the door to their room, and stepped aside so she could enter first, Georgiana could see a bouquet of red roses on the dresser, and a bottle of champagne in an ice bucket between two armchairs looking out at the lake. She walked over to the flowers and smelled them before she noticed the envelope tucked among them. Opening it carefully, she pulled the card out. The note was simple. *"There are not enough words in the English language to tell you how much I love you, now and forever."*

Her eyes filled with tears as she stood holding the note. Jack came up behind her, his hands sliding down her arms to wrap around her. She leaned back against him, and he kissed her temple softly. "Do you believe me?"

She nodded. He tightened his arms around her. "Then why are you crying?"

She turned in his arms, her arms going up and around his neck. "Because I love you and I can't believe we've gotten to this point."

"We have." He motioned toward the window. "Come sit with me, drink some champagne." He grinned wickedly. "Then I am going to finally get you out of that absolutely amazing dress."

Sitting by the windows, Jack looked at her pensively. "I have an idea."

"Which is?"

"Would it be okay with you if I called my parents tomorrow and convinced them to change their Thanksgiving plans from Pennsylvania to here so they can meet your family?"

Her voice was full of wonder. "Really?"

"Really."

"I'd love that!"

"Then that's the plan." He took a deep breath. "Then, I have a second idea."

"Okay..."

"I want us to live together."

She jumped up. "Really?"

"Really."

She started jumping up and down. "Oh, my God, Jack, yes. Yes, yes, yes."

He stood up and she wrapped her arms around his neck and kissed him. The kiss was one of love, devotion, and understanding. Within seconds, desire blossomed, and he pulled her close, picking her up in his arms and taking her back to his chair. "I want us to live at the farm. That's where we really got together. Bully likes his pasture, and the trees are there. We can't leave the trees."

She looked up at him, needing to make sure he meant it. "Do you mean it, or are you just saying it because you think that's what I want?"

He smiled. "It's what *I* want."

"I'd move to your house if you wanted."

"I know you would. But I love it at your place."

"Then let's make a home together at the farm."

His voice was hopeful. "Tomorrow?"

"Tomorrow."

Jack wove his fingers through hers. "It's been quite a week, hasn't it?"

She nodded. "Considering that last weekend we weren't speaking to each other and now we're moving in together? I'd say so." She reached out and lightly stroked her fingertip over his bottom lip. "I know I was the one who wouldn't let you stay over these last few nights, but…can I beg you to take me to bed now?"

"No begging needed." In one graceful movement, he stood with her still cradled in his arms and carried her toward the bedroom before setting her on her feet. "Again, you look amazing in that dress. Now… I believe it's time to get your out of it." He kissed her. "Turn around."

She turned and felt the zipper slide down her back. Slowly, he slid the straps down her arms. As they reached her elbows, the dress dropped the rest of the way down her body, leaving her in just her necklace and a tiny silk thong. His intake of breath was sharp. "Jesus, Gia. I knew you weren't wearing a bra but if I'd known what you *were* wearing under that dress, I would've tossed you over my shoulder and brought you up here hours ago."

She turned around and reached up to loosen his tie, a smile on her face. "If we had gotten ready together, as we had originally planned you *would* have known."

He muttered. "Damn budget meeting." He couldn't take his eyes off her.

She removed his tie, then started unbuttoning his shirt, pulling it free of his pants before she tugged on his belt. "Are you going to help me here?"

"No." His eyes were dark. "I like you undressing me while you're dressed like you are. It almost makes waiting to make love to you seem worth it."

She unzipped his pants, then started to push them down. He took her hands. "Not yet." He reached out, lifted the necklace off her and placed it on the bureau, then slid the panties down her legs. "Lie down."

Georgiana laid down on the bed, reveling in the feeling of the cool sheets against her flushed skin. Looking at Jack, still standing, she ached to run her hands down his chest, to feel all of him. Her voice was pleading. "Now, Jack."

He grinned. "Not yet. I told you. I plan to kiss every inch of you first. When you're as crazy with desire as I am, only then." He leaned down and kissed just above her navel.

"Jack, please."

He ignored her and took first one hand then the other, kissing her palms, her fingertips, slowly working up her arms to her shoulders, nibbling on her neck, then starting a slow descent down over and around her breasts. As he reached her waist, he suddenly stopped, moving down to kiss her knees before moving back up. As he reached her upper thighs, she was beginning to move, restless for the release she knew was coming. Suddenly he stopped. "Turn over."

"Jack..."

"Turn over, Gia. I told you what I was going to do."

As she turned over, he dropped his pants and boxers to the floor and for just a moment she could see how very aroused he was. He started the tortuous process all over, kissing every inch of her back. As he reached the back of her knee, he blew gently on her skin, and she almost came undone. "Now, Jack?"

He kissed the back of her leg, and she turned over, seeing him roll on a condom. He moved onto the bed, bracing himself on his forearms as he looked down at her. "*Now*, Gia." With those words, he slid into her warmth, hearing her soft sound of pleasure as their bodies connected.

Slowly he slid in and out of her, feeling her body strain toward his. He tried to hold back, wanting to savor every moment but as she reached out to pull him closer, he thrusted into her again and again. Her body tightened around him as she reached her release and called out his name just as he poured into her.

Later, they lay naked in each others arms as their heart rates slowly returned to normal. He slowly stroked her hip, loving the feel of her skin under his fingertips. His fingers moved up her side, caressing her, and without thinking, they brushed against the scars. He quickly pulled his hand back.

Georgiana reached out, took his hand, and put it on the scars. "It's okay to touch it. That doesn't bother me." She took a deep breath. "You can ask about it." She shrugged. "I can't promise that I can answer but I'll try."

He slowly slid his fingers over her arm, feeling the raised pattern, feeling the sharp difference where the scarring stopped. "Does it hurt?"

"No, it hasn't hurt for years."

"*Did* it hurt?"

She nodded. "It hurt a lot."

"What does it feel like?"

"You mean now, or then?"

"Now."

"It doesn't really feel any different than any other part of my body. Sometimes, in certain clothes, I guess you could say that it's more sensitive than normal."

"Are you okay with me touching it or would you prefer I don't?"

"I like you touching me *everywhere*. Maybe, I don't know, if I was having a hard time and was triggered, I might feel differently, but otherwise, you can touch it whenever you want, however you want." She paused. "It's okay, you can ask more about it."

He looked at her intently, needing to know. "Did you love him?"

She reached out to stroke his lips. "Did I love him? Maybe. I don't know. I was a child; I know that now. More than anything, I wanted someone who thought I was the center of the universe. I thought he felt that way."

His voice was low. "I feel that way."

"I know you do." She moved closer to him. "And that's probably how I can have you know everything."

He reached out to smooth her hair. "So, switching topics, tell me about the job offer."

Her eyes widened and she pulled back. "Seriously, right now? We're in bed, naked, and you want to talk about it now? What about the waiting until the first week of December?"

"I was just trying to buy time to convince you not to take it, but that's not fair or honest. So, tell me about it and let's make a decision as a couple. Then I'll worry about it from a work standpoint."

She continued to stroke his chest. "UVM has offered me a one-year job in the teachers' ed department with the possibility of it being long-term if all goes well."

"And you want to take it?"

He could see her brow furrow. "I think I do."

"When did they ask?"

"I got an email about a week ago. When I first read it, we weren't together, so I thought about it as a possibility. I wasn't sure I could keep working with you if you didn't love me." She smiled. "Then we worked things out and I was going to turn it down just because I *want* to work with you, but…"

"Tell me more about it."

"I'd be the head of their teachers' ed field placement. I'd teach one section of seminar for each elementary and secondary placement, then do field observations and meetings. They're thinking it's a three-day-a-week position, for one year, until they find out if the current person comes back after being abroad."

He tried to stay focused on the conversation while her touch was making it harder and harder to concentrate. "You told me in Seattle that was your long-term goal."

"I did."

"Why does it appeal to you?"

"I'm ready for a change. It's always been one of my goals and—" She looked down and Jack could see she was uncomfortable about something.

"And?"

"And now that we're together, I have to admit that working less, having the summer off, not having games every night, especially now that you'll have fewer board meetings since the district is now fully consolidated, well, it sounds good."

He growled. "Oh, low blow. Go for the jugular, telling me that I get more time with you if I agree to this…"

She laughed. "It's true. It hit me the other night when I had you go home instead of staying for the game, and I worked two more hours. I know that we'll always have times when one of us has a night meeting, but right now, between your schedule and mine, I'd bet we're talking at least four nights a week one of us has something, and yes, I know you could go to my school events, but…"

He stopped her hand by picking it up and kissing her palm. "Here are my thoughts, as the man who loves you." He wove his fingers through hers. "I think you'd be fabulous at it, and I think it's a great career move. However, I'd have some conditions." He grinned, his eyes sparkling. "Not employer conditions. We'd have to make sure there was a safe, consistent place for you to stay in the winter in Burlington if the weather got bad. I can't take the thought of you making that drive in crappy weather. Then, if it's possible, I'd ask that the days be grouped."

"What do you mean?"

"Monday through Wednesday, Tuesday through Thursday, Wednesday through Friday, like that, with some flexibility. What I want is that if I'm traveling for work, you could come with me if you wanted."

"I love that idea!" She nestled closer to him. "After all, we did have fun when we went to that conference together…"

"We sure as hell did." He squeezed her hand. "And what's your suggestion for your school?"

"How do you know I have one?"

He laughed. "Because I know you."

"Make Donna Simms, the current assistant principal the interim principal. Next year is probably her last anyway, give her the income boost in her last year. Make Angus, currently the Dean of Students, the assistant principal; he's got licensure, he'd be great."

He reached out to stroke her face. "Okay, Dr. Hewitt, your request is approved. I'll take it to the board two weeks from now."

The next afternoon as they drove back home, Jack reached out to take her hand as he drove. "So, you ready for me to move in today?"

"I am."

"Then how about we stop at my place and get some clothes and things for the next few days? Then over the break, we can figure out the details for really making it official."

"Sounds good."

At his house, Jack unlocked the door, and hung up her coat. "Go wander, start figuring out what, if any, furniture you want us to move while I get organized." He hung up his coat. "Other than my desk and the rocking chair in the living room, I'm not attached to much."

She smiled. "We can figure it out."

Jack was in his home office, making sure he had his laptop, phone chargers, and everything he would need for work the next day. He realized that he hadn't heard Georgiana in several minutes. Putting the last file in his briefcase, he carried it out to the kitchen. Before he could go look for her, he heard Georgiana call out. "Jack, can you come help me for a minute? I'm upstairs."

"Be right there."

Focusing on what he needed for clothes and toiletries, he headed to the staircase, stopping in astonishment as he realized that Georgiana's leggings were on the floor at the top of the stairs. With a smile, he headed down the hallway, finding her sweater on the doorknob of his bedroom. With the sun streaming through the sheers, he felt his heart catch as he found her sitting on the bed in just her camisole and the lacy panties he'd so admired that morning as she'd dressed. "I figured that if I was looking at furniture, it was probably a good idea for us to try your bed to see which we prefer. I mean, we've already *slept* in mine…"

He walked toward the bed slowly, desire flooding his veins. "Really?"

She moved to kneel on the bed, reaching out to start unbuttoning his shirt. "You know, from a research standpoint."

By the time she was done speaking, her hands had finished with the shirt, and had moved to unbutton his jeans. Her breathing changing as he reached out to stroke her breasts through the thin fabric of her camisole. He shrugged out of the shirt, then with one fluid motion, dropped his jeans and boxers. For a moment, she felt almost light-headed with desire as she looked at him in the sunlight.

He smiled as he gently pushed her back on the bed. He then hooked his fingers under the wisp of silk on her hips, pulling the panties down to join his clothes on the floor. "I *like* research." He leaned down and placed a kiss just above the lower blondish curls and was rewarded by her sigh of pleasure. He moved onto the bed resting on one elbow, and, with the other hand, began to slowly stroke her inner thighs. She started to pull on his shoulder, wanting him on top of her, but he resisted. "Tell me what you want."

Her voice showed her frustration as she pulled on his arm again. "Now."

He gently pinched one nipple, seeing it harden. "Not yet." He leaned forward to nuzzle her neck. "Tell me what you want."

Georgiana started to blush, but her gaze remained steady. Her voice dropped so low that he almost couldn't hear her. "I want you to make love to me…right *now*."

He felt he would burst at her declaration. He rolled on a condom, then slowly slid into her, his hands holding onto her hips possessively. He plunged in and out of her, hearing her breathing change as she got closer to her release. her hips. She reached out to pull his head down, kissing him. "I love you so much."

"Jesus, Gia, I love you."

She crushed herself against him, wanting their bodies to be as close as possible. Her breathing started to hitch as she pleaded, "Harder, Jack! Faster!"

He changed the tempo, and all he could think about was the feel of their bodies together. As he felt her body tightening around him, it drove him to his own release.

A long time later, as they laid entwined, he started dropping light kisses down the side of her face, her neck, and her shoulder. She purred. "I like your bed more than mine. It's going with us."

Chapter Forty

Jackson awoke Monday morning with Georgiana in his arms, moving slowly against him. At first, he thought she was still sleep, but it soon became obvious she was not.

His voice was husky. "You know, you keep rubbing against me that way, and there is no way we are getting out of bed when the alarm goes off."

She chuckled. "Yes, there is. It's not even light out."

He slid his hand up to cradle her breast. "Aren't you supposed to still be trying to get extra rest?"

"Who wants rest when I can have you?" She reached down to stroke him, smiling at his sharp intake of breath. "Tonight, we will have houseguests, and I don't know how squeamish you might be about making love when my mom is staying here. So *carpe diem*."

He reached over her and grabbed a condom. "We just became lovers, so I don't think there is any way I can go for days without making love to you, regardless of who is in the house, but just in case..."

Two hours later, Jack opened the school door, holding it for Georgiana. As they walked into the school office together, Dot, Angus and Donna all looked up at them expectantly. Georgiana rolled her eyes. "Seriously, you guys. Yes, it's official, and we moved in together yesterday."

While Angus and Donna rushed forward to congratulate them, Georgiana's eyes narrowed as she noticed the grimace on Dot's face. "Dot, tell me you all didn't."

Jack looked at Georgiana in confusion. "Didn't what?"

Hands on her hips, Georgiana looked at each colleague in turn. "Tell me you didn't."

Dot started to laugh before standing up to give Georgiana a hug. "Of course, we did."

"Damn it! Who won?"

Jack raised his voice. "Didn't what?!?"

Shaking her head, Georgiana rolled her eyes. "They bet on when we'd start living together, or when we'd officially be together, or something like that."

Jack looked at each of them in turn. "You did?"

Dot nodded. "Uh huh."

"And who won?"

"Charlie. He said you'd be living together by Thanksgiving."

Late that afternoon, Jack had just finished the chores and was standing in the barn watching the alpacas contentedly munch their grain when he heard a noise behind him. Turning, he was surprised to find Boone walking in, carrying a couple of beers. Jack looked at the animals, then back at Boone. "I think they're more of a wine crowd."

Boone smiled and twisted the cap off one bottle and handed it to Jack. He then opened the second for himself, leaning on the fence to look at the animals. "Figured you and I probably needed to talk without the family audience."

Jack said, "Thanks," as he lifted his beer in salute.

"Are we okay?"

Jack smiled. "You mean, am I okay with the fact that the last lover my woman had is here for the holidays and is moving to town, or am I okay with the fact that you knew she was pregnant before I did, and you offered to raise the baby if I didn't step up?"

Boone tried to contain his laughter, with little success. "I meant, were you okay with me leaving my Harley in the barn until I get a place. I figured you were good with the other two things."

"That bike? It's *fine*. Frankly, it can stay here for good." Jack leaned on the fence and looked at Boone. "You know, the night I was first here after she got hurt, you texted her a couple times. In one of them you told her you loved her. I would have slit your throat if I could have. Then, everything happened, and I was still so pissed at you. When you got out of the car the other night, I truly hated you." He took a swallow. "I've never felt jealousy like that in my life. Ever." He smiled, shaking his head in wonder. "But when you looked at her, there was something in that look. The jealousy just disappeared. So, yeah, we're okay."

"She loves you, man. In all the years I've known her, this is the most at peace she's ever been. When she was with Rick, there was always an edge, but with you, she's free."

That meant a lot to Jack, knowing Boone wouldn't blow smoke at him. "Thanks." He gestured back toward the house. "You coming to dinner tonight?"

"Nah. Both Georgie and PJ invited me, but this whole thing of their mom bringing a guy, that's so different from what they've known, it should just be you guys."

Jack was just coming back from the kitchen where he'd checked on dinner, when Georgiana shouted, "They're here! PJ, they're here!"

PJ grumbled. "I heard the damn car, Gi, I know they're here. Calm down."

A few short minutes later, Katherine Hewitt came through the front door and hugged Georgiana tightly before turning to hug PJ. While that was going on, a tall, blond man walked in behind her, looking slightly uncomfortable. Jack, Shroom, and Julia looked at each other in confusion, seeing the uncanny resemblance at once.

Katherine pulled back from PJ, still holding one of his hands while her other hand took Georgiana's. "Georgie, PJ, I want to introduce you to someone." They both looked at the man with piqued interest, but clearly weren't seeing what the others could see. "This is George Payton James III, my fiancé and..." She paused for a moment, then continued. "...your father."

Jack watched with concern as the shock hit both PJ and Georgiana like a physical blow. They both dropped their mother's hands, stepped back, and immediately clasped each other's hands tightly, something he figured had been a source of comfort to the twins their entire lives. Long moments passed before Georgiana swallowed, then, took a deep breath, stepped forward. "I'm Georgiana. Welcome to our home. It's nice to meet you."

PJ's tone was dry. "Yes, it's nice to meet you...*finally.*"

They both shook George's hand as he smiled nervously. "It's really nice to meet you too."

The conversation stayed light as they all learned that George was a military officer as well as a doctor. They also found out that he and Katherine had connected by accident almost ten years before. They'd started contacting each other, and in the last year, had started visiting each other. George proposed thirty-six years to the day from their first date. Jack noticed that while PJ seemed to be getting increasingly engaged in the conversation, about halfway through dinner Georgiana was becoming more and more quiet.

After dinner, Jack and Georgiana offered to clean up the kitchen while everyone else took a tour of the house, and Shroom headed home. No matter how hard Jack tried to engage Georgiana in conversation, she responded with one-word answers. After the last dish had been put away, he walked up and wrapped his arms around her tightly. There was a moment's hesitation before she settled back against him, and he leaned down to kiss her neck. "I love you."

"I know and I love you too." Her voice was trembling. "Right now, it's all that's keeping me sane."

"Talk to me."

She shook her head. "I can't yet. My brain is racing too fast. I just need to get through the next couple hours, curl up with you, then maybe I can breathe."

She turned in his arms. "Just know that I love you and this has nothing to do with us."

He paused as he tried to understand "Fair enough."

Just then the group came back down the stairs and PJ shouted to his sister. "Gigi, want to grab some cookies and bring them out to the living room?"

Her tone was cutting. "Of course, my lord."

PJ came into the kitchen, his look showing his confusion. "What the fuck was that about?"

"Nothing." She turned toward the pantry. "I'll go grab them."

PJ followed her into the pantry. "What's going on?"

"Nothing."

PJ blocked the doorway. "Nothing, my ass."

"Move!"

"No! What's the matter with you?" When she didn't respond, his voice became full of concern. "Talk to me, Gi. You're acting weird."

"I'm not acting weird." She grabbed the cookie jar. "Here are the cookies."

PJ took the canister. "Why the hell are you pissed right now?"

Her voice rose. "I'm not *pissed!*"

"Bullshit. Are you mad at me?"

"Of course not, you idiot."

"Then what's going on? Why are you mad?"

"I'm not mad. I just don't get how you can be so calm and accepting about all of this."

"About what? I don't get it."

She looked at him in disbelief. "Don't you care that our mother has told you for years that you're an embarrassment for joining the military, and that I was for getting married. Now we're supposed to be dancing in the street that she's marrying a military man. Seriously, this doesn't piss you off?"

PJ looked at Georgiana in fascination. "*That's what's* pushing your buttons?"

"Yes— no! I mean…" she snorted in exasperation, "…we've spent years being told we were shit for our choices and then she makes the *same* choices. That doesn't grind your gears?"

PJ leaned against the shelves behind him and started to laugh, much to Georgiana's chagrin. "For our entire lives, I've been the one angry at Mom. You tried to make it all right year after year and somehow *now* you've finally gotten pissed off?"

Just then, Katherine walked by Jack in the kitchen muttering. "I can't believe they're taking this long." She stepped into the pantry doorway. "What are you two doing? We have guests, you know."

That was the final straw for Georgiana. "Seriously, Mom? You're going to lecture us about manners? You show up here, announce you're getting married, to our *father*, no less; a man we've never met and whom we didn't even know you were seeing…after years of giving us crap for getting married *and* being in the military. And now…NOW…you're going to lecture us?!! You're too much. Too fucking much." She gestured to the cookie jar. "There are your cookies. I'm going for a walk."

Her mother stood up straight and glared at her. "Georgiana Grace Hewitt, you'll do no such thing. You'll come out and join us for dessert. And you'll be pleasant and join the conversation."

Jack watched as PJ stepped forward, his free arm going around his sister in a protective gesture, his face stony. "Mom let's be clear. We are no longer children you can boss around. For whatever reason, I'm doing better with all of this than Georgie, but I understand her reaction. Especially after how hard she's tried for decades to make you happy. If she wants to go for a walk, she's going, and you won't give her a hard time about it."

For a moment, three very similar faces stood glaring at each other. Katherine shook her head then gave her children a rueful smile. With a voice full of regret, she said, "You're absolutely right." She reached out and stroked a wayward curl back from her daughter's face. "I owe you both an apology." She paused, as tears formed in her eyes. "A *lot* of apologies. I should never have made you feel that I wasn't proud of you, that I didn't support your life choices." Reaching out her hands to her children, "I am so sorry, for so much. No matter what I've done wrong in life, you two are amazing."

PJ looked at Georgie for a moment, then back at his mother. With his arm still around his sister, PJ's voice was low. "Thanks, Mom."

Georgiana looked up at PJ for an equally long moment, then back at her mother. "Thank you."

"Take your walk, Georgie. Take as long as you need. I love you."

Coming out of the pantry, Katherine stopped dead in her tracks as she looked out the kitchen window. "What the hell?" Without saying anything else, she grabbed a barn coat off a hook and ran out the back door, headed toward the grove of trees. Georgiana took off right behind her.

With a shrug, PJ looked at Jack. "Guess we're going for a walk now."

At the grove, they found the two women holding hands. Katherine was crying as they looked at the lit trees. Just as they walked up, they heard Georgiana say, "We miscarried in October, Mom."

Katherine looked at Georgiana in horror, pain clear on her face. "Oh, sweetie. I'm so sorry. Why didn't you tell me?"

She shrugged. "It's a really complicated story." She sounded unsure. "Maybe we could talk about it while you're here?"

"I'd love that." Katherine looked up at Jack, who had come to stand behind Georgiana, draping a coat over her shoulders. "And will you try again?"

Jack answered before Georgiana could. "Definitely."

The group stood and talked for a few minutes before Katherine took PJ's hand and started back to the house, leaving Georgiana and Jack standing in the grove. His arms were wrapped around her as she leaned back into his warmth. After the others were out of earshot, Georgiana asked, "Definitely?"

He kissed her temple, leaning down to nuzzle her cheek, then her neck. "Definitely."

She turned around to look up at him, her arms going around his neck, her voice incredulous. "Moving in together, having my brother and company move home, Shroom coming out publicly with Mark, me finding out who my father is, not to mention my mother *marrying* him, and us deciding that I'm changing jobs… all of this doesn't put enough on our plates? You want to throw in us trying to have a child too?"

He leaned his forehead against hers, his eyes glowing with love. "I didn't say we were starting to try tonight, babe. That's why I asked Liz all those questions. I want us to have a child together. But I also want you to be healthy because I can't live without you. I'll do anything to protect you. So, yes, definitely, we are going to try to have a child together. When the time is right. Of course, that's if it's what you want too."

She reached out to rest her hand over his heart as she had done so many times before, and even through his sweater, she could feel the steady beat of his heart. "I'd really like that." She looked up at him, her eyes filling with astonishment. "You really *want* to have a baby with me?"

"I do." He cradled her face in his hands and kissed her tenderly.

The next morning, Georgiana came out of the bathroom and leaned down to kiss Jack. "What do you want for breakfast?"

"I'll make breakfast when I come down, just let me take my shower."

"I'm cooking." She grinned, "Scrambled eggs it is, then."

He swung his legs out of bed. "Sounds good."

Georgiana was startled when she walked downstairs and realized that the kitchen light was already on, and she could smell coffee. George was sitting at the table, clearly waiting for the coffee to finish brewing. Her voice was tentative. "Good morning, George."

"Good morning." He gestured toward the coffee maker. "I hope you don't mind, I got it started."

"That's quite alright. Did you have any trouble sleeping?"

"A little, actually. I'm still on Rome time, so my internal clock is messed up. Katherine seems to be able to self-adjust anywhere, but I can't do that."

"Me either." Georgiana pulled three mugs out, adding sugar to Jack's, then turned toward George. "What do you put in your coffee?"

"Just cream. You don't need to stir it in."

Her look was amused. "Well, I guess genetics are strong. You, PJ and I are the only three people I know of who take our coffee just like that."

He took his coffee, "Thanks." After the first sip, he looked at her seriously, "You okay with all of this? I know it's a lot to take in all at once."

Georgiana turned from the stove, where she'd been warming a pan for the eggs. "George, in the last couple months, my life has been turned so inside out and upside down. It's hard to explain how much has happened. So yeah, I have to admit that I was a little shell-shocked last night." She looked at the man who was her father and smiled. "But somehow, this morning, it seems like it's going to be all right."

Tuesday evening, Jack sat in the bedroom armchair and watched in amusement as Georgiana stood in front of the bedroom mirror, fussing with the scarf around her neck. "You look amazing. What are you doing?"

Her voice sounded so young, "I want to make a good impression on your parents."

Her vulnerability touched him, "Gia, come here."

She walked toward him, and he pulled her hands so that she sat on his lap. As he kissed her cheek, he said. "Love, no one *ever* has not been impressed when they met you. Not even me, and I really wanted to be able to ignore you."

"But what if they don't like me?"

"They will love you, just like I do." He looked at his watch. "Are you almost ready?"

"Go downstairs. I'll be down in five minutes."

Jack complied, finding PJ and George sitting at the kitchen table. PJ looked at Jack, "She's nervous. This is how she acts when she's nervous."

"She's changed her clothes like fifteen times."

George stood up without saying a word, then called out from the bottom of the stairs. "Georgiana?"

Her voice was muffled, "Yes, George?"

"Can you come to the top of the stairs, please?"

Less than ten seconds later, all three men could see her at the landing, "Yes?"

His voice was calm, and almost stern. "Georgiana, yesterday I flew across the Atlantic, landed in Vermont, drove here, and met my son and daughter for the first time in my life. I didn't have a chance to shower or change first, just came here. I was more nervous than I've ever been in my life, but I got through it. All that matters is that this man is still going to love you with all his heart, no matter what. So, get dressed and go meet them, now." He started to turn away, then added. "And wear red. You look fabulous in it, just like your mother. Besides, it'll make you feel more confident." He looked down at his watch, "You have two minutes. Move."

Her smile was blinding, "Yes, sir!"

After she disappeared from sight, George looked at the other men and winked. "Sometimes you just have to give an order."

Since the rent was paid up on the house Jack used to be in, it only made sense for his family to stay in it over the holiday. As he pulled in behind his father's car, they could see the welcoming glow of the lights inside. He reached over and squeezed Georgiana's hand. "Ready?"

She nodded. "As ready as I'll ever be."

Three hours later, Jack was sitting up in bed, as Georgiana came out of the bathroom. As always, he smiled seeing her wearing one of his t-shirts, thinking it was the sexiest outfit she could wear.

She slid into bed. "It was a great night."

He chuckled. "I told you so."

She shoved him. "Stop gloating."

His tone softened. "Gia, you are the love of my life, my family knows that. Now they can't wait to spend more time with you too."

The next night, the old farmhouse was filled with noise and laughter as Jack's mother, father, two sisters, their spouses, and all of his nieces and nephews came to have pizza with all of Georgiana's family, including her grandparents, Shroom and Mark, and Boone. After dinner, the group splintered into smaller conversational groupings, the kids playing board games, everyone getting to know each other.

Hours later, after Jack's family had headed back to his old house, Georgiana stretched, "I think I'll call it a night."

She missed the look that passed between Katherine and Jack. Katherine shifted in her chair, "Georgie, before you go to bed, can you explain that knitting pattern to me one more time? I am still so wide awake; I think I'll knit for a while tonight."

Internally, Georgiana groaned, wanting to head upstairs, but gave her mother a tired smile, and said, "Sure, Mom."

"Let me get my glasses, sweetie."

Jack stood, "Then I'll go brush my teeth. See you in a few."

"As soon as I can."

After half an hour, Georgiana was ready to scream. Her mother seemed to have lost her ability to read a knitting pattern. Finally, Katherine smiled. "Oh, now I get it, sweetie. Oh, okay, now I'm all set."

Tiredly, Georgiana climbed the stairs. Their bedroom door was closed, which surprised her. Opening it, she found the room aglow with candles, the fireplace had flames dancing as well. Her steps were cautious as she walked into the room, seeing Jack sitting in "their" armchair, a smile on his face. "Hi."

She gestured toward the candles, "What's this?"

"Shut the door." He softened his tone, "Please."

She did as he asked but was perplexed. "Jack, what are you doing?" Her tone became suspicious. "Did you have my mom delay me downstairs? Was she asking about knitting so you could get this ready?"

"Guilty as charged." He stood up slowly, then led her to the love seat in front of the fire. On a small table was an ice bucket with a bottle of champagne, and a red rose. Once they were seated, he took both of her hands in his. "Gia, I love you more than I can say. You make me a better person. I can't imagine my life without you." He kissed her gently. "Would you please marry me?"

The look of surprise on her face changed quickly to indescribable joy. "Really?"

"Really." His voice was sincere. "I know we just moved in together, I get that some people will say that we are jumping into this, but I know what I want. I've been ready to propose to you for almost a month. I've wanted to find just the right moment. I had all these visions of grand romantic scenes, but the truth is, love of my life, I just plain want to marry you. These last couple days, with all the craziness of all our relatives being here, just made me realize anew that this is what I want for the rest of my life, to love you now and forever. Please marry me." He reached behind his back, pulling out a small velvet box. "I've been carrying this around for weeks." He opened the box and Georgiana felt lightheaded with elation as she looked at the stunning diamond solitaire sparkling in the candlelight. "Gia, my princess Gia, would you please marry me? Be my wife, my best friend, my partner in everything, the mother of my children?"

Georgiana looked up at Jack, her eyes glowing. "Yes, Jack. I'll marry you."

With trembling hands, he removed the ring from the box and slipped it on her finger. "I love you more than I can say, forever."

"Forever."

Epilogue

Georgiana held the phone to her ear and forced herself to speak calmly. "Of course, I get it. I'll see you when you get home."

"You sure, love? I know I said I'd originally be home by five, but it should be no later than six-thirty now."

"Jack, stay and finish up the meeting, it's okay." She took a steadying breath. "Just let me know when you are leaving there, I'll pop dinner in the oven then, so it'll be ready soon after you get here."

"Sounds good. Love you."

"Love you, too."

After hanging up, Georgiana looked out at the deck, seeing the table she'd carefully set looking at the pond. An extra hour or two was okay, it wasn't a crisis. She just needed to be patient…

Jack opened the front door, dropping his bag on the bench next to it. "Gia, I'm home!"

She stepped out of the kitchen. "Hi."

He gazed at her appreciatively. "Wow, being on break agrees with you, babe. You look amazing. Is that a new dress?"

She smiled shyly. "It is."

Jack came forward and leaned down to kiss her. "I like it." He stroked her cheek. "Missed you today."

"I missed you, too." She bit down on her lip. "Do you want a shower before dinner?"

"Nah." He grinned devilishly. "I thought I might convince my gorgeous wife to take a swim with me after dinner."

"I think that might work." Georgiana took his hand. "Come on, I set the table on the deck."

"Nice. Need me to bring anything out?"

She couldn't stand it anymore. "No, just you. But…" her voice grew lower, "could you close your eyes? I have a surprise for you out there."

"You do?"

"I do. Close your eyes."

Georgiana held tightly onto his hand as she led him through the kitchen out onto the deck. Carefully, she guided him to his chair. "You can sit now."

Jack sat, not saying a word. Georgiana took one final look at the table, then whispered. "You can open your eyes."

His eyes flew open. With interest, he gazed at the table, set with crystal and silver, a bouquet of fresh flowers in the middle in a vase they'd received as a wedding gift. A smallish box, wrapped with bright wrapping paper, sat in the middle of his dinner plate. "For me?"

"For you."

His look was curious. "What's the occasion?"

"Just open it." Georgiana realized that sounded like an order. "Please." She shifted with excitement. "I've been waiting all day to give it to you."

"Oh, shit, Gia, and I was late coming home. I'm sorry."

Georgiana couldn't stand it anymore. "Jack! Open the damn present!"

With a grin, Jack pulled the box over to him. "Nice bow." He carefully removed it, putting it on the table. "What a great job wrapping." He was taking his sweet time unwrapping the gift, enjoying every second of watching Georgiana squirm. "I should really try to save this paper."

"Jackson, I swear to God, if you don't open that present *now*, I will not be responsible for my actions."

Finally, he pulled the top off the box, seeing the tissue paper inside. With devilish twinkle in his eyes, he turned toward his wife. "You sure you don't want to eat before I open this?"

She wailed, "Jack!!!!"

Jack pulled back the tissue paper and saw the porcelain mug inside. In bold rainbow letters, it read, *"DADDY."* Shocked speechless, Jack's hands trembled as he took it from the box, then gently placed it on the table. His eyes filled with tears as he turned to Georgiana. "Yes?!?!"

She nodded. "Yes. I took the test this morning, then got in to see Dr. Liz right away to confirm it." With joyful tears streaming down her cheeks, she moved to sit on his lap, cradling his face in her hands. "Jackson Ryder, you are going to be a daddy. We are having a baby."

Jack kissed her tenderly, then hugged her close. "Jesus, Gia. This is the second-best gift I've ever been given." He stroked her cheek. "You, are my greatest gift, and now…" he rested his hand on her abdomen, "…now, we have created a gift together."

Acknowledgements:

Thanks to Sutton, Cyn, and Penny for their amazing work as editors. Thanks to Between the Lines Publishing for being such a fabulous publishing house, and to Cherie for her amazing artwork.

Thanks to Ben, Ryan, Kayla, Linnea, Shane, Amie, Jen, Rowan, Shay, and Sora, for being my cheerleaders in this writing journey.

Kris Francoeur, writer and educator, lives in Vermont with her family and a menagerie of interesting creatures. Kris also is a grieving mother, who has found joy and light again through the practices of conscious and deliberate gratitude, unconditional acceptance, and connection with nature. Kris is an accomplished author of contemporary novels, and a successful ghostwriter of both fiction and non-fiction. Kris loves to spend time with her family (including sons, daughter, and grandchildren), spending time in the garden, and spinning the alpaca fiber for yarn for knitting.